I Love the Sound of Breaking Glass

Also by Paul Charles

Last Boat to Camden Town

I Love the Sound of Breaking Glass

Paul Charles

 St. Martin's Minotaur ⁂ New York

I LOVE THE SOUND OF BREAKING GLASS. Copyright © 1997 by Paul Charles.
All rights reserved. Printed in the United States of America. No part of
this book may be used or reproduced in any manner whatsoever without
written permission except in the case of brief quotations embodied in critical articles or reviews. For information, address St. Martin's Press, 175
Fifth Avenue, New York, N.Y. 10010.

www.minotaurbooks.com

Library of Congress Cataloging-in-Publication Data

Charles, Paul.
    I love the sound of breaking glass / Paul Charles.—1st St. Martin's
Minotaur ed.
        p. cm.
    ISBN 0-312-31902-9
    EAN 978-0312-31902-1
    1. Kennedy, Christy (Fictitious character)—Fiction. 2. Police—
England—London—Fiction. 3. Camden (London, England)—Fiction.
4. Sound recording industry—Fiction. 5. London (England)—Fiction.
6. Music trade—Fiction. 7. Musicians—Fiction. I. Title.

PR6053.H372145I2 2004
823'.914—dc22   2004050927

First published in Great Britain by The Do-Not Press

First St. Martin's Minotaur Edition: November 2004

10 9 8 7 6 5 4 3 2 1

Thanks are due and offered to Nick Lowe, the Bard of Brentford, for the use of the title of his truly Fab song; Linda McFall and all the St. Martin's Press gang for support and energy; Andy and Cora for all things parental; Stephen McCusker for words on the force, and to Catherine for everything else.

Prologue

He could see, but he could not speak. Was that a good or bad thing?

His hands and legs were bound individually, by gaffer-tape, to the legs of the red plastic chair which bore his weight.

The walls which contained and restrained him were windowless. The light by which he had judged the passing of two days spilled into the room in rich sharp beams through corrugated perspex roof sheeting.

The smells in his room of isolation were a mixture of freshly baked pitta bread and moussaka, the stink rising from the stains in his trousers and the lingering whiff of sweat and talcum powder of his absent captor.

His frustration was due, not to his detention, but to the fact that he could hear people continuing their daily lives around him, through the walls that held him.

He passed the time by simultaneously counting numbers and trying to figure out why he was bound by tape to a cheap, uncomfortable chair, and why this chair was positioned on a platform two-feet-six-inches above the concrete floor.

He also wondered who would miss him. Not who would notice he was absent from his normal daily routine, but who would miss him because he was absent from their lives.

He could not think of a single person.

This realisation threw him into a moroseness which, although brought on by a depressing appreciation of the facts, was an emotion he found pleasant to wallow in.

This shield of loneliness somehow made his capture almost acceptable, for it didn't seem to matter whether he was outside going about his chosen business, or restrained there in the large, windowless room.

Either way, he was alone.

Perhaps his jailer had even done him a favour by removing him from the chore of twelve-hours-a-day of decision-making. A chore he had hitherto been unsuccessful in escaping.

Chapter One

The coat she wore still lies upon the bed
                                    – Gerry Rafferty

a nn rea's vintage Ford Popular chugged down the road. She left Christy Kennedy staring fondly after her as she carefully negotiated the corner of Rothwell Street and Regent's Park Road and disappeared from sight.

Kennedy felt empty and listless. He had a million things to do around the house; a million things he knew he should but would not do. Would not because the million things – more realistically, nine or ten things – would never be able to fill the void left by her departure.

So he wouldn't even try.

Noticing that the dry patch where her red-and-blue car had been parked, was slowly disappearing in the autumn mizzle, he closed the strong, varnished wood door of 16 Rothwell Street, London NW1, and wandered up the stairs, feeling warm about the weekend they had just spent together. He tried to tidy his bedroom, but stopped when he felt the bed sheets: still warm from the heat of their recent passion. He could still smell her freshness and scrubbed cleanness.

Their relationship had gently nudged the eighth month, and he was still not sure of her feelings toward him. Kennedy returned to his basement kitchen, and switched on the CD player. He felt like listening to some music – perhaps to act as a soundtrack for his thoughts. The selection was easy: the Don Williams album, 'One Good Well', but he could easily have selected any of Williams' albums, they all shared a quality of transforming sadness into near-enjoyable melancholy.

Kennedy heard a quiet, siren-like keyboard sound in the song, 'We're All The Way'. He'd never noticed it before, but there was no mistaking it. Now that he had become aware of the tone, it seemed to get louder and out of harmony with the rest of the song. Kennedy felt that the siren effect did not really fit in. But whenever he mentioned any such observations to ann rea, she would taunt him with her, 'Everyone's a critic,' line.

Then he realised that the sound was not coming from the speakers, but from outside the house. As the noise became even louder, eventually drowning out Don's dulcet tones entirely, it dawned on Kennedy that it was a fire engine – or fire appliance as they are now called. The volume increased to a St Paul's like-pitch, before gradually quietening. Kennedy calculated that the appliance had turned the tricky corner of Regent's Park Road and had continued up Primrose Hill Road.

'Not too far away from the sound of it,' he confided in Don, who seemed totally unperturbed by the commotion outside, as a second and then a third engine raced up the golden-leafed hill. Curiosity, boredom and a sense of adventure – not necessarily in that order – got the better of him and he grabbed his green jacket and cap, leaving Don Williams to entertain the ghosts in his empty house with a flawless performance of 'Flowers Won't Grow in a Garden of Stone'.

The fire engines were peaking Primrose Hill Road by the time Kennedy reached Regent's Park Road and they were showing no sign of slowing down. He guessed that the magnet drawing these red monsters must either be in Highgate or Hampstead. By the time he turned right on to England's Lane he was out of breath. Pausing, he noticed vibrant flames stabbing violently through clouds of black and grey smoke shooting furiously through the drizzle into the slate-coloured sky above the rooftops.

His breath recharged with large gulps of oxygen, Kennedy followed the buzz of activity down a small turning marked 'Private', which veered off to the right on England's Lane before it reached Haverstock Hill. This cul-de-sac, whose privacy was being universally ignored by Kennedy's fellow thrill-seekers, opened out after thirty yards into a large courtyard. The well-trimmed green hedge continued along two sides of the yard, the remainder of the perimeter edged with five large dwellings, all variations on the popular theme of English school houses. Any school that had ever existed on that site would have sent its last pupils off into the world many years, and probably a few million pounds, BY (Before Yuppie).

It was the loudness of the crackling fire that surprised Kennedy the most. It reminded him of the sound hailstones make bouncing off a tin roof; magnified through hi-fi speakers, turned up so loud you could actually hear them ripping apart. The air smelt hot and unhealthy, but somehow intoxicating.

Two of the fire engines had made their way precariously down the narrow lane, leaving scrapings of their red paint on the hedge, and the crews were efficiently engaged in a vain battle to save the biggest of the five houses. It looked like they'd been in time to protect the remaining four, the smell would most likely stink the occupants out of their homes for weeks. But, unlike the owner of the main house, at least they would still have a house to be stank out from.

'I didn't know CID were on call for domestic fires, sir.'

Detective Inspector Christy Kennedy turned to see WPC Anne Coles standing behind him, but before he had a chance to answer, the ever-efficient WPC clocked his casual dress and realised he was off-duty.

'Sorry, sir, I forgot – you live near here, don't you?' she offered with a smile, which lit up the delicate features on her misleadingly innocent face. Anne Coles was a thoroughly professional and experienced police officer.

Kennedy returned her smile as he zipped up his jacket. 'We all love a little excitement in our neighbourhood, don't we?' Feeling a twinge of guilt at the flippancy of his remark in what was after all a potential life-threatening situation, he added, in a more business-like tone, nodding toward the flames, which had just broken through the grey slate roof of the lean-to section of the house, 'Any idea if anyone was in there?'

He was thinking of his own house, of his books, records, furniture and the other treasures he had accumulated over his twenty-three years in London. He was thinking of the grief he had suffered, first collecting, then moving them all around from bedsit to bedsit, bedsit to flat, flat to flat, flat to house, house to house to their current place, his eleventh address in the capital. He was thinking how pointless all that moving and collecting would have been, were it all to go up in smoke.

'No, sir. As far as we can tell from the neighbours, the owner of the house hasn't been seen all weekend. But that's nothing unusual sir. He runs a record company.' She checked her notes. 'A Peter O'Browne of Camden Town Records. He frequently travels around various parts of the world with some of the pop stars he works with.'

'Hang on – Camden Town Records; isn't that the blue building opposite the nick?'

'Yes, sir. Seems he's your neighbour at work as well as at home.'

'Yes well, I'd hate to return to find my home like this,' Kennedy replied, his attention drawn again to the sight, smell and sound of the fire: home-comforter turned home-destroyer.

'Well, sir, I'd better get on with crowd control and keep all these gawpers out of the firemen's way.' She straightened her hat in order to reclaim a few wisps of fine blonde hair from the steady mizzle.

'Firefighters.'

'Sorry, sir?'

'Firefighters. They like to be known as firefighters these days.'

'They've been watching too much TV, if you ask me, sir. They'll always be firemen to me. Much more sexy than all that handlebar moustache, Village People firefighter stuff. Yes well, I'll be getting on with it.'

'Yes, yes, of course', Kennedy smiled. 'I must be getting home, myself.' There was no reason for him to be there, especially as he didn't want to be cast in the role of gawper. Despite the drizzle, Kennedy's journey down Primrose Hill Road was undertaken at a more leisurely pace than the journey up it.

Chapter Two

For the sound of a busy place
Is fine for a pretty face
Who knows what a face is for
— Nick Drake

'I know you feel that there is something macabre about this one,' began DI Kennedy the following day, as he wandered around the deceased Marianne MacIntyre's living room.

Mind you, Detective Sergeant James Irvine could be forgiven for making such an assumption. He was Scottish, and the Scots, like the Irish, have a tendency to dig deeper (and more successfully) to find the darker side of life. And the room which had become the final resting place of this poor unfortunate middle-aged woman was dark – as in very dark.

Her ground floor flat was defended from the light by a precariously high hedge, about two feet away from the window – just enough space to create a wind trap for rubbish and, at this time of the year, dead leaves from the street.

The future former owner had not helped matters with her obvious lack of taste in interior design. She had painted her hallway a very deep brown, the room dark green, and the windows were covered with chocolate-brown curtains. The two inch strip of glass showing at the bottom testified to a better fit elsewhere.

This was a functional room, not a room for comfort or recreation. The bed, on which she lay sprawled like a scarecrow, looked as if it folded back towards the wall into a sofa – a black sofa. The sheets were ruffled about the corpse, covering the bottom part of one of the legs, but leaving the rest of the body exposed. A red towelling dressing gown had either been pulled open or had fallen open in the struggle. A black baby-doll curly wig had been partially shaken, or fallen, off, exposing short natural blonde hair.

'Why is everything so dark?' questioned Kennedy.

'Well, sir, as my mother would say, it disnae show the dirt,' answered DS Irvine impishly.

The carpet and curtains stank of a mixture of cigarette smoke and stale beer, a combination that reminded Kennedy of mornings after college parties. He noted the absence of a television set and of books. A few days' worth of *Daily Mirror*s were scattered under a small coffee table stained with multiple cup rings, that stood in the centre of the room.

There was one easy-chair (dark and light brown striped pattern) and three hard chairs. Kennedy tried to view the room through the mirror that hung on the wall just above the fireplace – the original hearth had been replaced with a two-bar electric fire – as he found this a surreal but effective way of examining the crime scene.

On the mantelpiece below the mirror were two photographs in cheap brass frames. One showed the deceased with a young boy who looked about five or six years old. It could have been ten years since the photograph was taken. The other picture was more recent. This time the victim was with a man who looked to be in his mid-forties. They both seemed to be laughing, for each other's, rather than for the camera's benefit.

There were no other visual distractions, nor apparent clues. Kennedy, happy to have an excuse to escape the glaring eyes of the corpse, went off to investigate the rest of the flat.

It was the type estate agents would oversell as a 'two-roomed apartment with bathroom and garden'. Kennedy thought the Monty Python team might have more accurately described it as 'large shoe box with slop bucket (one owner).'

The second room in this Dickensian dwelling was a kitchen with black-painted walls. A formica table, comforted by two canework chairs, bore a quarter-full bottle of HP Sauce, a nearly empty bottle of vinegar and a wooden pepperpot. Wedged between the vinegar bottle (Crosse and Blackwell) and the pepperpot were a few envelopes, carelessly ripped open.

Kennedy removed these from their lazy vice and found that they all contained bills. London Electricity (£59.84), British Gas (£48.29), Thames Water (£12.83) and Camden Council (£124.89 for council tax), all final demands issued in the previous three-to-five weeks. All were in the name of Marianne MacIntyre. Kennedy had already recognised in the woman's body more than a passing resemblance to her namesake, Marianne Faithfull. Both shared blonde hair and faces obviously once beautiful but now – shall we say? – better described as 'distinguished-looking'. Both had 'been there', but only one had come back.

As Kennedy wandered around the kitchen, his fingers twitching as he thought of Marianne Faithfull and her early recordings, he was reminded of Camden Town Records and its owner. Kennedy wondered how he had taken the news of the destruction of his home.

The small flat was starting to fill up with various scene-of-crime (SoC) personnel and Kennedy was anxious to leave before someone started swinging a cat. But first he had to conclude his examination of the flat. The sink was half-full of unwashed dishes – in pairs. Marianne MacIntyre had obviously not been alone when she had enjoyed her final meal.

The window-sill above the sink (funny, Kennedy thought, how most architects seemed to have decided that people like to look out of the window as they wash their dishes) was very busy. It supported Fairy Liquid, Daz, plastic roses (several, various colours) in a vase (dirty cream earthenware with a v-chip on the brim), clock (small, round, yellow metal case and showing near enough the correct time), clothes-pegs (plastic, blue, red and green, packed in a cylindrical container which had once stored Paterson's Oatcakes – top missing), a beer bottle (Guinness, dirty with three of last summer's wasps dead drunk on the bottom) and a wine glass (tulip, with a hint of white wine residue).

To the right of the window-sill, the metal draining-board gave way to a gas cooker in the corner and then a wall cupboard squeezed so tightly against the cooker that opening the oven door and the lower cupboard door simultaneously must have been a difficult, if not impossible, operation. In the cupboard nestled various tins of soup and other canned stuff you would only use if you had no money for proper food – or if your money was disappearing down your throat in another form. Occupying the other corner was a fridge, empty but clean.

Kennedy turned round slowly, taking care not to disturb anything, to look at the room from a different angle. This position afforded him a view under the table, where he spotted five empty Guinness bottles. The kitchen smelt of stale dishwater. A towel, once damp, was now dried to stiffness on the radiator behind the door.

He squeezed past one of the SoC officers and both had to turn sideways to accommodate this manoeuvre. Thankfully, they both resisted the 'We'll have to stop meeting like this,' line. Kennedy made his way to the bathroom, which was painted in lime green, which must have been very encouraging after two-and-a-half pints of Guinness.

DS James Irvine joined him in the bathroom, which was quite a feat.

'You could sit on the toilet, scrub your partner's back in the bath with one hand and wash your own face in the sink with your free hand without too much of a strain,' Kennedy said with a smile.

'Very hygienic I'm sure, but you'd want to make sure you didn't mix up the actions,' the DS replied in his best Sean Connery accent, which was in fact his only accent.

'Time to check out the neighbours, Jimmy,' Kennedy announced as he led the way back out to the front door and rang the bell marked, *Flat Two: Hurst*.

As they waited, Kennedy inquired, 'Do you know anything about…' he checked the name on the doorbell again, '…this Hurst?'

The Detective Sergeant noticed that Kennedy was flexing the fingers of his right hand, which delayed his reply for a second or two.

'Yes, sir, Brian Hurst. He's the one who rang us. Apparently a friend, female, came round this morning to see Marianne and when she couldn't raise her, she buzzed Mr Hurst, who…'

'HURST!' the rough electronic voice pronounced from the tiny door speaker, cutting DS Irvine short.

'It's Detective Inspector Kennedy and DS Irvine. We'd like to talk to you about...'

'Okay, I'll buzz you in. Come on up,' instructed Mr Brian Hurst, cutting short a member of Camden Town CID for the second time in a minute.

Chapter Three

Who do you talk to.
When a body's in trouble?
        – Mary Margaret O'Hara

Capital Gold, London's most popular radio station was airing the Beach Boys' classic 'Good Vibrations' as Kennedy and the DS entered the second-floor flat. The DS grabbed the volume button and inconsiderately faded the flawless song during the ouija board (synthesizer) bit.

Brian Hurst's flat was a total contrast to his neighbour's: bright, airy, clean and packed to the ceiling with books, records, CDs, prints and photographs. It was obviously a flat furnished and decorated to be lived in and enjoyed. Mr Hurst was dressed in keeping with his habitat; a man comfortable – cocky, even – about who and what he was. Even in the privacy of his flat he was dressed as though he were at a dinner party: brown leather slip-on shoes, fawn slacks, red button-up cardigan (the lower buttons under some strain), white shirt top button undone to reveal a yellow cravat. He had well-groomed but thinning hair and was the kind of chap who always had trouble impressing his girlfriend's mother.

He greeted DI Kennedy (straight to the senior officer) with a formality and lack of warmth that immediately set the tone of business. Business which had to be done, and the sooner the better.

Kennedy had other ideas. He liked to be in control of the pace of such proceedings. He asked if it would be possible to have a cup of tea. The immediate implication was that this was not going to be a quick couple of questions. Brian Hurst, surprised at the request, agreed. He was not to know that the DI was something of a connoisseur as far as tea was concerned; in fact its preparation and consumption was one of his principal interests.

Kennedy followed Hurst into the long kitchen. He had long since discovered two very important facts: one, that most people don't wait until the water is properly boiled before applying it to the tea; and, two, that people find it harder to lie while part of their mind is engaged on another function. There just might be a tell-tale pause at a vital stage in the conversation. On the other hand, there just might not.

'These kitchens really are, er, tiny…' Kennedy didn't know how to complete the sentence, and wished he'd never started it.

'Oh, I suppose it all depends on your needs, sergeant. It quite suits me. Milk and sugar?'

'Fifteen-love,' Kennedy thought wryly, smiling at his sudden demotion. 'Yes, milk and two sugars for myself and the Detective Sergeant here takes it black.' Perhaps not fifteen-all, but definitely a net ball.

He noticed three empty Pouilly Fume '94 bottles neatly lined up along the back of the bleached wood drying board beside the sink. They appeared to be guarding a solitary Guinness bottle.

'Now, how can I help you, gentlemen?' began the unwilling host.

'Well, you could start by telling us if you heard anything suspicious last...' DS Irvine attempted a start.

'Suspicious? Suspicious? Only if you'd call the start of World War bloody Three suspicious.'

'How's that?' Kennedy's voice and eyebrows quizzed.

'Well, they were at it again last night, weren't they?' Hurst replied, as he led the officers through to the living room. 'She'd obviously got some money from somewhere, and she and her friend – bloody noisy boyfriend – came back from the off-licence and fought.

'They were always either fighting or bonking, either way it was a major racket. Last night it was a fight.

'I banged on my floor a few times, but to no effect. After some time it went quiet and then it got noisy again, worse than before. Then she must have thrown him out because I heard the door bang. Nearly pulled it off the hinges, they did. The entire building shook.' Brian Hurst kept eye contact only with DS Irvine.

'What time would this have been?' Kennedy quizzed as he sipped his unexciting cup of tea.

'About 11.45. Yes, 11.45 – that silly Richard Littlejohn TV show was just finishing. I mean to say... now I ask you, how does someone like that get on TV for a spot, let alone their own TV show? Prat. I was glad to see the end of him and I was waiting for the midnight movie to start.

'Maybe it could have been a bit later. I'm not exactly sure, to be perfectly honest with you. I was so annoyed at them.' Hurst nodded in the direction of his floor – Marianne Bloody MacIntyre's ceiling.

'Do you know the name of her boyfriend?' the DS inquired, he too putting to one side his insipid tea.

'Yes. Yes, I do actually. He's called Ray Morris.'

'Perhaps you'd be kind enough to give the Detective Sergeant here a description, Sir?' said Kennedy. He tried another sip of tea before giving up it up as a lost cause. 'I'm going back to North Bridge House,' he told Irvine. 'Can you make sure everything downstairs is taken care of, and get someone on to finding this Ray Morris.'

He smiled at Brian Hurst as he let himself out. 'Thanks for your time and your tea, sir.'

Chapter Four

You've broken the speed of the sound of loneliness
You're out there running
Just to be on the run

– John Prine

WPC Coles was walking up the steps of North Bridge House, former monastery and current home of Camden Town CID, as Kennedy arrived.

'How did your man take the news that his house had burned out?' he inquired, overtaking and beating her to the large wood and glass doors, before holding the left one open for her. A gentle mizzle refreshed the streets of Camden.

'He hasn't found out yet,' she replied, smiling her thanks and accepting his courtesy. In the ongoing war of equality, Anne Coles felt good manners were still good manners and even if she didn't expect it from men in the police force, she respected it. 'I've been across to his office this morning and they've promised to contact me the moment he returns.'

The burly Timothy Flynn, desk sergeant at North Bridge House for Kennedy's eight years there and probably a lot more besides, greeted the WPC and Kennedy with a warm smile. 'DS Irvine rang for you, sir. He left a number – it's here somewhere.' He rummaged through the organised chaos of his desk. 'Ah! Here it is.'

Kennedy settled into his comfortable office in North Bridge House, the oldest building in Camden. He had spent the first couple of years in Camden making his office a comfortable home from home, all at his own expense. He couldn't abide the traditional police office, which was practically a bomb site on wheels: furniture as comfortable as sitting on stones, case files and reports gushing out of every cupboard and drawer and threatening to drown the inhabitants. The DI honestly didn't know how men and women were expected to work, let alone think, in such surroundings. So he visited the Camden antique and second-hand furniture stores and, like a bird lining his nest, kept returning with bits and pieces. Now he had a room he was happy to spend hours in.

It is an established fact that the majority of victims know their murderers, and Kennedy had already put the death of Marianne MacIntyre down as a domestic. But on checking the files, he discovered that there had been no reports of assaults on Marianne, nor on anyone else at that address, for that matter.

He dialled the number Irvine had left with the desk sergeant. The phone rang several times before it was answered with a gruff, indignant 'Yes?'

'DI Christy Kennedy here. Could I speak to DS Irvine, please?'

Kennedy could hear, through the telephonic static, 'It's for you.'

'Sir?'

'Yes, Jimmy.'

'The weirdest thing, sir. Ray Morris – you know, the boyfriend?'

'Yes?'

'He turned up here at Marianne's flat about half an hour ago, looking a bit the worst for wear. Totally bedraggled, but no visible bruises or obvious marks on his body. They're bringing him down to North Bridge House now, sir.'

'Good. I'll be waiting for him, but I might let him sit it out for a bit till I receive the initial report from Dr Taylor. How did he react?'

Kennedy conveyed down the telephone line.

'Well, perhaps it would be best if I see you when I return to the station, sir.'

'What?' Kennedy pictured the DS at the other end of the line wearing a tweed suit hopping from foot to foot in his well-polished brogues and playing his cards so close to his chest that he was in danger of wiping the spots off them. 'Oh, is our good friend Brian Hurst nearby?'

The electronic signal in his earpiece translated into, 'Yes, exactly. Well, I'll see you shortly, sir.'

The line went dead. Well, not completely dead. It sounded like the Irish Sea, just after the pubs close.

Kennedy, if he were a betting man, which he wasn't, would have put his money on Ray Morris not showing up for some time.

Kennedy guessed that both Ray and Marianne liked to suck on a Guinness bottle, and after a few bottles, could have turned to fighting. Perhaps with a recurring theme, such as one accusing the other of drinking too much or (a popular one with drunks) the Northern Ireland Troubles; maybe even a new subject like how useful the fin on a Porsche really is. Perhaps even the stupidity of drinking.

In her stupor, perhaps Marianne egged him on, and on, perhaps a scene they had enacted several times before. Only this time, when he took his hands from her throat, she did not move; they did not mix alcoholic vapours with a kiss, and make up and make out.

Marianne MacIntyre had not regained consciousness.

Ray Morris, Kennedy supposed, had scurried off, full of remorse. The same remorse which had forced him to return to the scene of the crime.

In a considerable number of cases such unfortunates are happy to be caught; in fact they need to be caught to gain redemption. Such culprits are novices, amateurs in crime, and it is always only a matter of time before they are arrested by the (supposedly) professionals: the police. Even so, things were never quite this clear-cut for Kennedy and his colleagues at Camden Town CID, who spent many a long hour (not to mention a few pounds) on their investigations and still failed to find the culprit 60per cent of the time.

How could they devote all this time and money to their work and still get it wrong? Not only do they get it wrong. When they finish, another set of professionals, the legal system, would sometimes convict and punish the wrong person, thereby creating a second set of victims for one crime.

Such notions and other thoughts, such as more pleasant musings about ann rea, filled Kennedy's mind as he busied himself on his paperwork. It certainly looked as if he was going to move this case into his out-tray in double-swift time, thus freeing his manpower, not to mention brain power, for the five other cases currently battling for attention on his desk.

Chapter Five

But it's easy come and it's easy go
All this talking it's only bravado
– Paul Buchanan

'So listen now, Morris, and listen good. We know there were mitigating circumstances and in these liberal days, judges and juries seem to be taking that into account. But – and it's a big but – for that little scenario to work, we have to say in our report that you were co-operative. At the moment I would need to say that you were being anything but co-operative.'

Raymond Morris just stared at his interrogators. The senior didn't look much older than the junior, who was Scottish and dressed rather too smartly, and he looked rather too proud to be a policeman. The boss, too, was well-dressed in fresh blue shirt, black tie with green stripes and the trousers and waistcoat from a dark blue suit. He had green bands on his arms to keep his shirt cuffs from getting grubby or frayed. They were both staring at him willing him to make their work easier.

'Sure, it's simple Detective Inspector, I didn't do it. I didn't kill Marianne.'

'But you were heard arguing with her last night, laddie, and this morning she's dead,' the Detective Sergeant cut in, gently pushing the pressure up a notch.

'I did not kill Marianne!'

'Look, maybe, and I mean maybe, it was an accident; maybe you both had too much to drink and things got out of control and you didn't mean to kill her,' reasoned the Detective Inspector.

'Why would I have gone back to the flat for you lot to find me? Why wouldn't I just have kept on running?'

Morris definitely looked the worse for wear. Three-day beard (ginger), dirty jeans (blue Levi's), even dirtier T-shirt (blue and white Van Morrison '88 Tour). Though his breath smelt of alcohol, his wits were keen.

'Look, yes we argued,' he went on. 'Sure, we argued. I was, well, to tell you the truth, I was trying to leave her.

'She was dragging me down, she had no self-respect. She just didn't care about anything, anymore. And every time I tried to get us both out of the drink, she'd pay no heed. She'd just laugh.

'And I wanted to… I want to… stop drinking, Inspector, I really do. I want a life again. I need a life. I've looked over the edge, and it's ugly, fucking ugly, as ugly as growing old. I've got to give myself a chance.'

Morris paused and Kennedy nodded to DS Irvine to let the silence hang.

Outside the room they could hear people walking up and down the corridor, doors shutting, echoing laughter, darts of conversation. From the street, sounds of busy traffic in Parkway were muffled by the double-glazing of one of the twenty-one windows fronting North Bridge House.

When it became apparent that Ray Morris was not going to break the stilted silence within the room, Kennedy spoke. His voice was soft and almost soothing. 'Well, Ray, I can accept that. I can. And I can see how it would have happened. You wanted to get sober. You were trying and Marianne was taunting you and laughing at you, and pretty soon all you could hear was her laughter. You weren't mad at her, you were mad at yourself, because you saw that your life was less than useless and that you were unable to do anything about it.

'And you tried to talk some sense into her but she wouldn't listen, all she could do was laugh at you.' Kennedy could see the scene so clearly; he continued describing it in a slow sympathetic tone. 'You grabbed her by the throat to try and either shake some sense into her or to stop that hideous laughter, or even both. And the more she laughed, the more you squeezed and squeezed and squeezed. And it felt good, it felt great. If only she had stopped laughing you could have stopped. But now the squeezing is not enough, so you start to shake her head at the same time, and then slowly she stops laughing and struggling and she goes limp and you let her go.

'After she's been lying there for a few minutes, motionless, you try to bring her round but she's totally unresponsive. You think she's passed out from the drink, like she has done hundreds of times before, so you leave her to sleep it off. Then you come back this morning, expecting her to have sobered up, and that's when and why you bumped into my men.'

Again silence filled the room, relieved only by the slightest of hums from the tape-recorder waiting to absorb the well-prompted inevitable confession.

'Look, sir, I don't know how, but I've got to find a way of making you, making both of you, believe that I didn't kill her – not by accident, not on purpose, not on anything. I just didn't kill her.'

Detective Inspector Christy Kennedy and Detective Sergeant James Irvine participated in the age-old Metropolitan Police sport (not as yet a fixture of the Olympics) of synchronised sighing.

This was going to take longer than Kennedy had imagined. He was just going to have to find another way of opening the door. He was totally confident of what awaited him on the other side. He sat back in his chair, a signal to Irvine that he wanted to back off and let the DS take the lead for a while.

'Ray,' Irvine began in his soft but firm Scottish accent. 'We've seen from the photograph in your wallet that Marianne was a beautiful woman a few years back.'

There was no response from Morris.

'She was a stunner,' persisted Irvine. In his accent the word 'stunner' was very sensual. 'What happened to her? Why the...' He searched for a word which would not be offensive. 'Why the... er, fall?'

'When I first met her, you wouldn't believe how beautiful she was. She looked so innocent.' said Morris dreamily.

'How long have you known her?'

Morris gave him an odd look. 'You should have said had, not have.' The horrible truth was starting to sink in. He returned his attention to the question, not without difficulty. 'It's coming up to twelve years now, so she would have been twenty-five when we first met.'

'What, you mean she's only – sorry, was only – thirty-seven?' interrupted Irvine in disbelief, before he could stop himself. It was not a question which should have been asked at that point, just when Morris seemed ready to go into a ramble – a ramble which may have offered a few clues. The narrator so caught up in his own recollection that he fails to take time to hide some of the hints of truth.

Irvine cursed himself. But the simple fact of the matter was that he was so utterly shocked. He'd have sworn that the body he had seen not forty minutes before had been that of a female in her early to mid fifties.

But Morris surprised both Kennedy and Irvine by simply smiling and continuing his story. 'I know, man, but you know it's as though she died ages ago. She'd just given up. She didn't give a shit.

'I couldn't believe that she was interested in me. It was a bit like, "What, me?" But she was fun loving and game for a laugh. If only I'd noticed that she had already checked out, or was in the process of checking out, even in those days, perhaps I could have done something to help her.

'But I was so up on being in her company – I was real proud, you know? I'd never been out with anyone so beautiful, or even dreamed that I would. She was five years older than me.'

This time Irvine kept his disbelief in check and allowed Morris, now happily lost in his memories, to carry on uninterrupted. 'The first night we met she asked me to move in with her. I knew that she was drunk, but she asked me again the following morning. Here I am, I've just met the most beautiful woman I've ever seen in my life and the first night I get, well, I get to share her bed. And then I get asked to move in with her.

'Yeah, I can see you thinking: it must have been a great first night. It wasn't actually. That was the most surprising thing in a way. I was stunned that this sex creature... well, she wasn't really interested in sex. It was always like another, not unpleasant, chore she had to do. Don't get me wrong, we did it a lot in the early days but even when it was great it was more about what's in your mind – as in that beautiful body – than what was actually happening. It was like she was loaning you her body for thirty minutes or so for you to take your own pleasure.

'To start with, I put it down to the fact that she was drunk most of the time. Then I realised, as the years passed, that Marianne didn't really care whether we made love or not. In the end, about two years ago we just stopped doing it altogether.

'She told me it was nothing to worry about, that it wasn't my fault.' Morris looked like he was about to drift off into his thoughts, he seemed content to regret what could have been but, in reality never would have been. 'She said that it had been the same with all her boyfriends, and girlfriends, and that she'd never really got off on the sex end of it. She liked the companionship and the warmth of a body in bed beside her.

'When I realised that she was using sex to pay for companionship I kind of went off it.' Morris paused again, thinking of Marianne. Kennedy thought of ann rea and DS Irvine thought of Staff Nurse Rose Butler. Irvine imagined saying to Rose, 'Could I borrow your body for 30 minutes?' She would probably reply, 'What do you want to do with it, have sex fifteen times?'

Dispelling these collective thoughts of lost love, fun love and trying to make love work, Ray Morris cleared his throat and continued. 'I'd decided to try and put my life in order. I, well, we'd tried so hard to get our lives together. She'd be fine for a day or two, sometimes even for as long as a week, but then I'd come back to the flat and she'd be plastered.

'It was so pathetic I couldn't even bear to be with her. So I'd try to crash at a friend's flat. She'd find out where I was, come round and make a scene. I was running out of places to stay.' Morris sighed and scratched the itchy growth on his chin.

Kennedy sat, barely moving – his eyes had scarcely left Morris' face. He still felt that at any point Morris was quite likely to say something like, 'and I just couldn't take it any longer so I killed her.' If only he could find the key to unlock the whole affair. Now that Morris was verbally uninhibited, the right nudge, the correct prod, could set him off on a full confession. But Kennedy hadn't yet found the right key, so instead he continued to sit in silence, his blue suit jacket measuring the angle of tilt of the back of his chair.

'I wanted to leave,' Morris went on. 'I knew that it was my last chance to make the change and if I didn't leave then, I never would. I'd end up just like Marianne. A lush. A total fucking lush. No matter how much I pitied her, I knew that I had to leave, and I hoped that if I left – when I left, actually – she'd bottom out and ask for help. They say nothing can be done for drunks until we reach out and ask someone – anyone – for help, don't they? Marianne had me so mad at her last night, I forgot pitying her and I forgot how pathetic she was. I just started to think of myself in a selfish way.'

Come on now, you're ready to tell us, thought Kennedy. Get it off your chest, tell us what you did. All the time, the angle of his chair was becoming more precarious.

'She'd been sitting on the sofa, sipping her bottles of Guinness and smoking, and she just dozed off. Just dozed off, leaving the ciggy alight. It burnt her fingers and she didn't wake up. I suppose she'd burnt them so many times before that she couldn't feel the pain any more.

'I was in the kitchen – you know, trying to clean it up a bit – and I went in and smelt the burning skin. I knocked her over to wake her up and I started having a go at her and we started yelling and screaming at each other.' Morris's breathing was growing heavier now.

'Yes!' said Kennedy under his breath, nearly sending the chair all the way backwards. 'Here it comes!'

'So I yelled at her, something like, "Do you know what would have happened to you if I hadn't been here? The whole fucking place would have gone up in smoke. Burnt to the ground with you in it." And she replied, "Better fucking job. Better for me if it had. It's only a matter of time till you go, asshole!" And so on – I'm sure you get the picture.

'She quietened down for a time while I tended to the burns on her fingers. Then, instead of feeling sorry for her, I just felt this compelling need to get out while I still could. I had this overwhelming thought that if I didn't get out at that moment then I never would.

'I told her I was going. Another screaming match started and I left her to it. When I left she was still screaming at me. I'm sure the Peeping Tom upstairs heard her slam the door after me. In fact I'm sure the whole fucking street heard her. She nearly took it off the hinges.

'But she was alive when I left her. That is, if you could call what she had for a life being alive. I wandered around all night and I could feel that I had broken away; that the hold was gone. But I thought, if only for the sake of decency and the years we had been together, I should go and see her one last time and try to convince her that she needed help.

'When I got there you people were there and Marianne was dead. And you know what, I couldn't feel sad. It's kinda like that was the release she was after.'

'But it wasn't a release, was it?' DS Irvine interrupted. 'Marianne MacIntyre was murdered and you were the last person to see her alive.' Irvine felt as if he'd sat through a movie, only to be cheated by the ending.

'That means nothing. Nothing at all! She was alive when I left her. She was alive!' Morris seemed to be trying to convince himself as much as the two detectives.

Chapter Six

Do you like what you're doing?
Would you do it some more?
– Nick Drake

'Why do you think someone would fall so low?' Kennedy
quizzed ann rea.

It was later the same evening and they were sitting in The
Queens pub on the corner of Regent's Park Road and Primrose Hill
Road, having a quiet drink (he a white wine and she a shandy).

'Oh, come on, Kennedy,' ann rea began, wanting to avoid a doom
and gloom evening. 'You know several of the answers to that question, all of them equally valid.'

'And they are?'

'Her father abused her.'

'Her only true love left her.'

'She left her only true love.'

'She figured out early on the reason for life: there isn't one. It
doesn't mater how much money you make, how brilliant a genius you
are, how important a job you have, how powerful a person you are;
one day you are going to die and your body will return to dust and all
this shit we have been through will all have been in vain.

'She loved the oblivion of the bottle! Take your pick.'

'Oh, come on, ann rea,' Kennedy offered, trying to put the brakes
on the direction the conversation was taking.

'I'm not saying that I think like that. I'm giving you reasons why
she let go of herself. She was an alcoholic.' ann rea smiled as she
realised she had picked that exact moment to drain the remainder of
her shandy.

'Do you think she was an alcoholic because of one of those reasons,
or that another possible reason is that she was simply an alcoholic?'

'Oh Kennedy, I don't know, I really don't. Can we just go to your
place, close the door, leave all this shit behind us and have some fun?
Get a life, as the septics say?'

'Septics?'

'You know: septic tanks – yanks.'

Kennedy smiled at the cockney rhyming slang and thought about
ann rea and about how sometimes she seemed so far away from him,
and he was silently frustrated about not being able to get any closer
to her. He thought back to the first time they had met. Well, he wasn't
actually sure when they had first met.

Things, people, plots, incidents; they all seem to venture into view before you acknowledge and accept they are there. For instance, the case in point: his first sighting of ann rea. The location was Heathrow Airport, but, by the time Kennedy eventually talked to ann rea, he was unaware of having already seen her twice. Once in the bookstore in Departures. The vision of her short sharp black hair burned its way into his subconscious. The second time was in the coffee shop when he heard her quietish, soft, smiling but confident voice order a cappuccino. The length – or lack of length – of her black business-suit skirt and the friendliness of her voice registered somewhere in the depths of his mind.

So, by the time he found himself accidentally seated beside her (on the return Aer Lingus Dublin to London flight, the following morning) he didn't feel a stranger and a conversation started up naturally. Sitting up close he realised her head-turning looks were not created by expertly applied make-up, for ann rea wore no such camouflage. Her eyes were slightly almond-shaped, with eyelids blending straight into the side of her face. The shortness of her hair placed emphasis on her dark eyebrows and pale clean skin. Kennedy could not help but stare at her.

During their chat, he discovered ann rea was a journalist working on his very own local newspaper, the *Camden News Journal*. Kennedy had immediately recognised the name from her distinctive all lower case by-line, which was an idea ann rea explained she had nicked from kd lang (who in turn had borrowed from ee cummings) to receive attention as a writer. She had certainly grabbed Kennedy's attention and it was only a matter of time before they had bumped into each other a few more times around Camden Town and he was inviting her out – or, had it been ann rea who had invited Kennedy out? The entire adventure had been so natural, neither remembered nor cared who had first made the invitation.

The more he got to know her, the more convinced Kennedy was that she was 'the one'. He had never felt that sure before. ann rea buzzed him in every possible way. He never tired of her company.

They never made love with anything less than 100 per cent passion. Now he pictured them making love, silent apart from the occasional involuntary animal grunts, dripping in sweat from their endeavours to pleasure each other and their own bodies. He thought that making love could sometimes be somewhat industrial, and awkward, trying to fit all the body bits together at the precise time and in the correct location. Nothing was so annoying as when you were doing the business thinking how great it was and how great you were, only to find out your partner's moans were not moans of ecstasy, but groans of pain because she was getting cramp in her leg. But not so with ann rea. It worked, they worked well together.

'Yes, you're right,' he smiled. 'Let's leave all this shit behind.'

Two hours and twenty-three minutes later Kennedy left ann rea in bed with the promise to return from the kitchen with her dinner.

As he prepared the meal – a speciality of his: a bowl of Alpen covered with milk – he thought back to the time, eight months before, when he was still trying to get it together with ann rea and was frightened that he never would. He was certain at the time that failure would have been the biggest disappointment of his life. What would suffering the biggest disappointment of his life have done to him? Had Marianne MacIntyre suffered something similar?

Even now, now that he and ann rea had got it together, he felt it was something that he should protect. Perhaps letting this chance go could destroy him in the same way something had destroyed Marianne.

'I'd better not keep her waiting on her food,' he said aloud to the kitchen as he placed two brightly painted earthenware bowls on a Shaker wooden tray and returned to the warmth of the bedroom on the second floor.

'Kennedy, you're all heart,' she laughed, as he put the tray on the bed.

'I don't believe you, I really don't. You buy a girl a half-pint of shandy. You bring her back to your place and jump her bones. And jump her bones, and jump her bones. And then you feed her with a measly bowl of grain or corn or something.'

'Don't forget the sultanas – don't you think they're delicious?' Her host laughed, spooning a single dried fruit through her full red lips.

'You'd better get your act together before I move in,' ann rea said self-consciously.

This was something neither of them had spoken about. Kennedy did not speak of it because he did not want to rush her and risk scaring her off; ann rea because she had been there, and done that, been fucked-over and had promised herself that she'd never let it happen again.

As he munched on his Alpen, Kennedy was worried that if he didn't say something, ann rea may think he had no interest in such an eventuality. But if he revealed his true desire – to drive her over to her house this minute to help her pack her stuff – he might be pushing her too quickly.

'Well I'd better write off to Alpen for some new recipes, just in case I ever need them,' he said as nonchalantly as possible under the circumstances.

ann rea smiled at his reply. Kennedy smiled at her smile.

Chapter Seven

Yes if you come when it's late at night
And everyone is out of sight
We'll give you a performance you'll never forget
— Clifford T Ward

Kennedy was just about dozing off when he felt the weight of ann rea disappear from the bed. He heard her flick on the reading light on her side of the bed. It was now officially her side of the bed. Kennedy had felt some kind of commitment was being made when she started to leave some of her books and a wire-spined reporter's notebook on her side of the bed.

Sometimes, as they lay in bed, he imagined her reaching for her reporter's notebook and interrogating him on his most recent case for the *Camden News Journal*. He knew it was a stupid idea; a totally stupid idea. Nonetheless it was one he kept going back to.

It was eleven-forty and ann rea was dressing to leave him to go back to her apartment. Sometimes she would stay over and they would play house, but more often than not she would go home. As Kennedy watched her pull on her white pants and then her bra (it wasn't the bra but the contents which deserved the word wonder), he thought idly that, all ladies' underwear must be designed by men. Without exception they were uncomfortable, barely functional, but always a splendid sight for the male eye. Singular in this case since Kennedy risked opening only one (slightly) for fear of being caught spying and missing this unexpected late night-delight.

He felt guilty (a little) about watching her without her knowledge or approval but the excitement the vision created submerged and drowned the guilt in a sea of pure lust. ann rea wriggled temptingly to try to find the one comfortable position for the underwear and then sat on the side of the bed to put on her white ankle socks. She was so close he could have put his hand out to trace the sensual curves of her snow white skin, he loved the way the shape of her legs blended in tight curves and arcs and became her back, no human alive could have sculptured a form so simply exquisite.

He realised at once why Moore's ugly shapes were displayed in Hyde Park; should the passing motorists experience the magnificent form of ann rea in this position, the traffic jams would extend back up to the M1. She was beautiful; so fucking beautiful it took his breath away.

From the tip of the toe she had tucked in the sock to the exquisite Beatle-bob haircut, she was flawless in Kennedy's eyes, even though ann rea had her own list of her flaws and frequently reeled them off to Kennedy when a little wine was making him a pain.

As she stood up straight again, he nearly shouted out loud at the sight of her rear secured in white briefs; sweet as a strawberry milkshake. Her beautiful bum disappeared as she wriggled into a skintight pair of black jeans. The last of her body flesh evanesced under a loose jumper in racing green.

Finally ann rea put on her cute black pumps.

'That's it, Kennedy, I'm off. I hope you enjoyed the show,' she declared.

'What?' he exclaimed so surprised he forgot to even fake sleepiness. 'How did you know?'

'Well,' ann rea began eyeing the curve of the bedclothes. 'It's pretty obvious you enjoyed the show!'

She came and sat down on his side of the bed, looked deep into his eyes and ran her fingers through his copper hair. She continued the stroking for several long moments. They both just looked at each other. She found his centre parting and pushed his hair to either side. ann rea liked his hair not too long, not too short, just long enough to lose your fingers in. They both just looked at each other. Neither spoke. It was magic, pure magic. Neither was looking for anything from the other, other than what they had.

'Look, Kennedy,' she began, breaking the spell. 'I'd love to stay and lower the tent but I've got to go home. I've got an interview to do tomorrow morning at Camden Town Records.'

'Who at Camden Town Records?'

'The boss. A friend of mine works there, for him, in fact. She was meant to fix me up with an interview today but he didn't come in the whole day.'

She rose from the bed in search of her jacket. 'I wrote a profile of him a while back and it seems his house was badly damaged by a fire on Sunday evening. The Journal wants to do a piece on it. Apparently, they've got some great photos.'

'Yes, I saw the fire, actually. Isn't his name Peter O'Browne? I didn't know you had a friend at Camden Town Records. They're just opposite us, you know.'

Of course she knew. ann rea knew Camden Town better than most.

'Oh – Mary Jones, a friend – I suppose she is really, we get on well, mostly through business, and I do like her. I suppose it's just that in the music business someone is your friend if a) you know their telephone number and b) they take your call. So maybe I don't really consider us to be best buddies or anything like that'

'Oh I see,' Kennedy replied, not really sure that he did.

Chapter Eight

We have one life
But one life won't do
– Mary Margaret O'Hara

'Are you sure we should have let Ray Morris go, sir?' DS James Irvine inquired of DI Christy Kennedy the following morning at North Bridge House. Irvine's soft Scottish accent, when not making him sound like Sean Connery, tended to lend every statement the air of a question. Kennedy often ignored this inclination of interrogation and this was the justification he used for not answering the DS on this occasion.

Instead, he chose to read Dr Leonard Taylor's report, which was, as Taylor's reports usually were, informative, precise and never, ever, speculative.

Marianne MacIntyre had been drunk (as in very drunk – about four times the normal level permitted for a human in charge of feet). The severe bruising around the neck showed she had been strangled to death – or, as the good doctor was fond of telling Kennedy, 'death was due to lack of breath'. The lack of marks or bruising about the rest of her body, led the doctor to presume that Marianne had not put up too much of a struggle against her assailant.

Miss MacIntyre had died 'around midnight' and had had sexual intercourse just prior to death. Doctor Taylor finally surmised that the victim's liver was, 'in the worst state I have ever had the misfortune to view,' and observed that, 'without a transplant she certainly would have died in the next twelve months.'

'If someone hadn't helped her on the way, that is.' Kennedy muttered as he concluded reading the report.

'What, sir?' DS Irvine inquired.

'Doctor Taylor's report states that Marianne would have died during the next year due to liver failure.'

'Hardly surprising, is it, sir, after what Morris told us?' The DS was loitering around Kennedy's door, unsure as to whether he was needed or not.

'The good doctor also states that Marianne MacIntyre had sex just before she died. Our Mr Morris told us that they hadn't indulged for the last couple of years. Now, that's not something he's going to need to, or want to lie about, is it? I suppose in a way it lets him off the hook.'

'I'm not so sure about that, sir,' began the DS, mulling over the facts. 'He could have caught her having sex with someone else, or found out about a wayward bonk and topped her in a fit of rage.'

'It's a possibility, but I'm not sure; if what he told us yesterday was true – and I kind of feel that it was – then he would have been very very happy if Marianne had found another guy. It might have let him off the hook. Emotionally I mean, about leaving her.'

Kennedy picked up his phone and dialled a number.

'Ah, Detective Inspector, you've read my report,' Doctor Taylor responded in his characteristically theatrical tones, after having recognised Kennedy's words of greeting.

'Yes, yes thank you, Doctor. Just one thing. You say she had sex just prior to death?'

'Yes.'

'Was she raped?'

'I doubt it, Kennedy. There were no bruises on the vaginal wall, nor about her upper thighs, that would have been consistent with a struggle. But with the amount of alcohol inside her, she would probably have been the proverbial sack of potatoes, anyway. And as I said in the report, frankly old chap, her personal hygiene was practically non-existent. She was in a very sorry state, including an infestation of what are commonly known as crabs.'

'Thanks again, Doctor. See you soon for a cup of tea – my turn I think. Bye.' Kennedy replaced the phone on its cradle and stared at it for a few minutes.

'Did you notice whether our friend Raymond Morris was scratching himself?' Kennedy grasped his hands together under his chin.

'No I don't think so,' said Irvine. 'Funny you should mention that sir, because Brian Hurst was. Scratching himself, I mean. Quite a bit, in fact.'

'Let's bring in Mr Hurst, Jimmy. I think he may have a few more things to tell us,' Kennedy muttered as he set about answering the ringing telephone.

Chapter Nine

Saddle the horses
and we'll go

— Paul Buchanan

'Hello, DI Kennedy here.'

'I know it's Kennedy there, I just dialled your direct number.'

'Hi, ann rea. How did your interview go?' Kennedy's voice smiled.

'Well I'm there – or rather here – now. Peter, the boss, still hasn't shown up and Mary is beside herself with worry. He's never done this before. He always checks in with her at least twice a day when he's off somewhere.

'I know missing persons is not exactly your thing, Kennedy, but could you do me a favour and come over and have a chat with Mary? Try and put her mind at rest?' ann rea pleaded down the phone line.

'Okay, okay, I'll come right over.' Kennedy sighed, it might do Brian Hurst some good to be kept waiting for a while. 'But it's probably nothing. Your man's bound to be sorting out the mess the fire left.'

'Great, thanks, I owe you one.'

'It's already written down in The Book in big bold letters, believe me,' Kennedy laughed, before replacing the receiver, unhooking his jacket from the peg on the back of the door and racing down the single flight of stairs.

Chapter Ten

It's coming from so far away
It's hard to say for sure
                    – Jackson Browne

K ennedy had walked, driven and cycled past – in fact he'd probably even flown past – the Blue Design Building, home of Camden Town Records. But he had never ever set foot in the offices. It held no surprises: modern, open-plan, more plants than the Chelsea Flower Show, and the proverbial hive of activity. He followed the arrows marked 'Reception', which directed the visitor towards the far end of the building, near the stairs. ann rea was waiting for him in there.

'She's through here.' ann rea's gentle squeeze on Kennedy's arm was the only hint of intimacy between them. She nodded in the direction of a corridor behind the reception desk. Kennedy was slightly charged by the numerous conversations, some on the telephone, some not, going on all around him. There was a strong smell of ink from the newly printed posters, of cardboard from the many 12' x 12' x 6' boxes laying around and an aroma of freshly-percolated coffee. Kennedy immediately marked the place down as a coffee-conscious building, which meant that tea would be provided on request, but that the chance of a proper cup was remote.

As he followed ann rea along the five-foot-high partitions he checked out the posters, some quite pornographic, proclaiming new releases from Camden Town Records.

'Mary, this is Detective Inspector Christy Kennedy.'

The first thing Mary Jones noticed about Kennedy was his snazzy waistcoat and the second thing was that the fingers of his right hand were continuously flexing. She also noticed his friendly, smiling eyes and that he and the journalist were obviously more than the 'just good friends' ann rea had claimed a few minutes before, when she had suggested they ring her friend at Camden CID.

'Hello, sir.' Mary had a beautiful Welsh accent. She invited Kennedy and ann rea into her office, off the postered corridor to the left, which was small, busy and tidy. In the middle of her desk stood a computer terminal and monitor. The walls were filled with yet more posters, mostly of Camden Town Records acts and one of the Welsh rock band, Man, which showed a bearded bunch standing outside a train station. Pride of place was given to Bruce Springsteen (often referred to as Loose Windscreen by ann rea in the many Dylan-vs-Springsteen conversations she had had with Kennedy). Apart from the posters, Mary Jones' office, her desk, her dress were all basic: very tidy and very colourful.

Mary Jones had the most amazing head of black curly hair which tumbled all over and around her face as she moved. She wore only a little make-up around her eyes.

'ann rea tells me you love tea and the Beatles,' she smiled nervously.

'A suitable epithet for a headstone, don't you think?' Kennedy replied, amused at how ann rea had chosen to describe him to others.

'Well, I can help you with the tea.'

'That would be brilliant,' Kennedy said rubbing his hands together. 'Absolutely brilliant. White with two sugars, please.'

'Look,' announced ann rea. 'I'll, er, leave you two to it, if you want.'

'Don't go,' said Mary. She needed the informality of the journalist's presence to keep her worries in check.

'It'll be fine if you stay, ann rea,' Kennedy smiled at her, realising that ann rea was worried about infringing on his working space. Now it was his turn to gently touch her arm as he lead her to the sofa opposite Mary's desk. Mary spoke into an intercom on her desk to order tea (for Kennedy) and mineral water (for the two women) from an invisible but loud crackly voice.

'I believe you have already spoken with WPC Anne Coles?' Kennedy started.

'Yes, but that was about the fire at Peter's house on Sunday evening. But I still haven't heard from him. I don't know if he even knows about the fire. It's so out of character for him not to call.'

Kennedy tried to smile reassuringly. 'When did you last see him?'

'It was last Friday, in the evening. We were both here late and I was meant to see him later that night at a gig at the Forum in Kentish Town. One of our new bands, Roger's Theory, was playing support there to the Hothouse Flowers.

'I suppose I wasn't that surprised when he didn't show up. He'd had a really busy week and I figured he had probably just gone home and crashed out.'

'When you say that you were both here late,' said Kennedy as he added two sugars to the milky tea that had arrived, 'what time did you leave the building?'

'We both left at, um, let me see, about 8.20pm. No – sorry – that's not right. We were leaving at 8.20pm, but just as we were about to go, a call came through for Peter. He hesitated but eventually went back to his office to take it and told me to go ahead.' Mary took a sip of her mineral water.

'You said Peter had had a busy week. What was he doing?'

Mary reached for what Kennedy assumed must be an engagement diary. 'Let's see. Well, at the beginning of the week he'd just returned from New York and then on Tuesday,' she licked her finger to turn over the page, 'he had a marketing meeting which went on all day. On Wednesday a lot of the Europeans were in town for a meeting with our distributors, Repeat. So Peter took the chance to bring them all up here to discuss our autumn release schedule, particularly our three new signings, Roger's Theory, Zinc Damson and Paul Kavanagh, the best new singer-songwriter I have heard since...'

Kennedy followed her eyes to the Bruce poster and there was no need for her to finish her sentence, but she did anyway, giving him the feeling he was being treated to the company sales pitch. Mary took Kennedy, and ann rea, through the rest of Peter's busy schedule. 'Does Peter have a family? Girlfriend? Mother? Father? Life partner?' Kennedy added the last option in recognition of the fact he was talking about a showbiz type person.

'No, not really.'

'Not really?'

'Well, his parents have been dead for years and he broke up with his last girlfriend well over a year ago. Diane, that was her name. Peter's last girlfriend.'

'So he lived alone up on England's Lane?'

'Yes he did, he did indeed. He had a cleaner – a housekeeper, really, I suppose – a wonderful Yorkshire woman he always referred to as "Mrs". She would even ring up and say "It's Mrs here". Anyway, she "did" for him, as they say, four days a week: Monday, Tuesday, Thursday and Friday.'

'And has he never done this before – just disappeared? Never fallen in love, sagged off, done a bunk, a Basil Bond for a few days?' ann rea, sitting about two feet away from him, hadn't noticed him taking out the small leather-bound notebook in which he was now jotting down notes.

'No, never,' came the emphatic reply, with just a hint of heavier Welsh in the voice. 'He always rings me at least twice each and every day, just to check up on things. Usually first thing in the morning, to see if there are any overnight faxes or mail that needs his attention. And then again towards the end of the day to see if anything has cropped up and to give me instructions on matters he wants me to attend to in his absence.' Mary's voice seemed to show more concern as she confirmed the seriousness of the situation to herself.

'So,' Kennedy continued, deciding to move the conversation on to a less worrying topic. 'Who else is he close to do you think?'

'There's his lawyer, Leslie Russell. He likes him a lot. He's one of the old school, very straight and that's why Peter likes him so much I think. No matter how much crap was going down with his dealing with Grabaphone Records he could always have a direct conversation with Leslie.

'Sometimes he spends weekends with Leslie at his parent's place in Steyning.' Then she added, as if reading Kennedy's mind, 'I've already checked and Leslie hasn't spoken to Peter since last Thursday.' Finally her voice faltered: 'God I do hope he's okay. What can you do, Inspector?'

'Well, we can now officially list Peter as a Missing Person, as he's been gone for over twenty-four hours. That means every bobby on the beat in the UK will be furnished with his details and will be on the lookout for him. We can also try to build up a picture of the hours leading up to the last time he was seen. Let's see…' Kennedy checked his notes. 'You last saw him at 8.20pm on Friday evening, so I'll take it from there.'

'It's funny,' mused Mary. 'But when the Inspector was going through his stuff just now it reminded me of us working with an artist or a group.'

'How do you mean?' asked ann rea.

'Well they come in here and sit down where you are sitting, and they ask us what we are going to do for them to make their record a success. And we give them the list, you know: we're going to get it to the radio stations and we're going to get it to the papers and we're going to try and get them TV and we're going to try and get them on a tour and we're going to do a photo shoot and a video. And we'll help get them a manager, if they don't already have one, and an agent, and so on and so on.

'And all the time you're going through this you can tell from the eyes of the more astute ones that they are thinking, "Yes, but is it going to work? Will you make me successful? Do you have the secret of success?" Of course, the honest answer is that we don't. We don't know the secret of success – unless it's in the music – and if, and it's a big if, you are lucky, then you might have a chance. But naturally, we never say that. We just try and reassure them, just like you're trying to reassure me now.' All this was leading up to the question Mary Jones was dreading asking. The question that had been scurrying around her mind like the sour smell of milk in an unwashed fridge, ever since that first visit from WPC Anne Coles on Monday morning:

'Has his disappearance anything to do with the fire in his house on Sunday night?'

'All I can tell you is that there were definitely no remains found in the debris of the fire. The fire officer said that he thought the fire was probably caused by a faulty plug, although his final report is due in this afternoon.' Kennedy's reply was confident: it was better that Mary did not dwell on such dark thoughts.

'I would have to say that it would seem to be a strange coincidence that both the fire and his disappearance happened on the same weekend.'

With that Kennedy excused himself and returned to North Bridge House, leaving ann rea to give further comfort and solace to the troubled Mary Jones.

Chapter Eleven

There's one thing you've gotta do
To make me still want you
You've got to stop sobbing

– Ray Davies

Glancing at his railwayman's watch, fixed to a chain and housed as always in the right-hand side of his waistcoat, Kennedy noted that it was 12.35pm as he reentered North Bridge House. The build-up in traffic at the top of Parkway confirmed that lunch time was approaching.

Kennedy tried to find WPC Coles but she was out on a call. Somewhere on Camden High Street a man and his common-law wife, both somewhat the worse for wear, were having a go at each other. By all accounts the man was losing the scrap and would probably be very grateful to the WPC for a timely intervention.

Kennedy left a message for WPC Coles to report to him upon her return. He was anxious for any additional news on the fire in Peter O'Browne's house. In the meantime, he advised DS Irvine that he wished to conduct a formal interview with Mr Brian Hurst, who was by now cooling his heels in the bowels of North Bridge House.

A few years earlier Kennedy would have been happy wandering around the room asking his questions, viewing and circling the suspect the way an animal stalks its prey, ensuring that, before the final lethal leap, the quarry was completely in his grasp. Kennedy liked to sit on the floor, or on the table, or to stand behind his suspect so close that he could be smelt, his breathing heard. He would do anything (anything legit) to distract them from planning their lies. If you were busy protecting yourself you had little time for lies, or so ran Kennedy's logic.

But now, under the alert ear of a bloody tape recorder he, and all his colleagues, had been instructed to sit at the table facing suspects, so that conversations could be captured clearly. Kennedy felt inhibited by this, but the rules were there to be followed.

Brian Hurst was already in the interview room and obviously DS Irvine had already conducted the preamble for the sake of the tape, because Kennedy was greeted with a formal: 'Detective Inspector Christy Kennedy enters the interview room at 12.48pm.'

Brian Hurst was first off the starting block. The prey was on the run.

'Okay, what the hell is this all about? Come on! I extended hospitality to you and to your men, and then you return it by coming to my house and taking me away like a common thief in a marked police car.

'Look, what's this all about?' he repeated, fidgeting with the left lapel of his grey herringbone jacket. 'Why couldn't you have asked your questions in my house?'

Kennedy smiled, first to himself and then at Mr Brian Hurst. Sometimes the first one out of the blocks is the first one to run out of steam. To finish first you first have to finish. Tactics, those are what win races and catch quarry. Tactics.

'Oh, I've no questions for you, Mr Hurst,' was Kennedy's opening gambit.

'What? What do you mean, no questions? What the fuck am I doing here, then?' Hurst's clean shaven face registered disbelief and he stopped worrying his jacket lapel and surreptitiously gave his crotch a quick scratch.

'Well,' began Kennedy in leisurely fashion as he stood up and removed his jacket, placing it carefully on the back of the chair before sitting down again. 'I thought I'd bring you down here and tell you exactly what happened at your place on Sunday evening.'

Brian Hurst's look of disbelief was matched by one from DS Irvine. One (Hurst) mouthed 'What?', the other (Irvine) had seen this movie before and remained motionless, noticing Hurst's unease and growing itch.

'Okay,' Kennedy began in a quiet voice. 'On Sunday night you were at home watching TV and enjoying your Pouilly Fume wine. As the evening wore on you enjoyed your wine a little more. Such a pleasant way to spend a Sunday evening. A bit of TV, a few glasses of chilled wine, but too lazy to do much after a big lunch.

'And then, around eleven o'clock, the racket downstairs created by Marianne MacIntyre and Ray Morris started to annoy you.

'Around eleven-forty you breathed a sigh of relief as you assumed, judging by the slamming of the door and the rocking of the house, that she had thrown Morris out.

'You were waiting for the midnight movie to start, still pleasantly merry at this stage, when you heard a knock on your door. You answered the door only to find Marianne MacIntyre standing there, probably ranting and raving about Ray Morris and sucking on her bottle of Guinness.

'She was scantily dressed. Her dressing gown was revealing more of her flimsy slip than you'd ever dreamed of. Although she had seen better days, she was still a magnificent woman – I'd say very appealing to a man who had just consumed the best part of a bottle of wine. So being the generous neighbour that we all know you are, you invited her in.'

Brian Hurst was about to say something (probably to protest that this was not true) but Kennedy raised a single finger to his lips to silence him before continuing: 'Marianne moaned to you about Ray leaving her. She was drunk, but, like all drunks, she wanted to cry on somebody's shoulder. And on Sunday night your shoulder was elected to support that blonde-haired head.

'The more she babbled on to you, the more you ogled her. She finished her bottle of Guinness and went off in search of more of the Liffey's finest. You had only wine in your flat so you helped her back down the stairs to her place, leaving behind the solitary empty Guinness bottle.'

'The empty Guinness bottle,' Hurst interrupted with a short, nervous laugh. 'I can explain that.'

'Later,' Kennedy cut back in firmly. 'There's more – as Jimmy Cricket might say.' DS Irvine smiled a smile that threatened to break into a laugh. He contained it, but was clearly enjoying himself; thoroughly enjoying himself.

'Where were we? Oh yes, you were helping Marianne down the stairs. This was most likely a very complicated manoeuvre, both of you being drunk and you having only one hand to help her, the other supporting a glass of wine. But you managed. You'd probably got yourself so worked up in anticipation of the delights in store that a little effort to negotiate the stairs seemed a small price to pay. When you reached her flat, she would probably have flopped on to the bed, exposing herself and her charms even further. She was probably so languid that she didn't even notice you were having sex with her.'

'Please stop this. I must protest,' Hurst flustered more for the benefit of the tape-recorder than for Kennedy or Irvine. 'This can't go on. It's all so stupid. I mean, the thought, the very thought of me and that, that slag together. Please!'

'Okay, patience, you'll have your chance shortly. So you had sex with her, and like all men, your feelings after sex were not as warm as they were before and so you got angry at her, angry at yourself, for having sex with this "slag". So you strangled her.' Somewhere along the line there was one almighty big step missing, but Kennedy had to carry on with the bluff.

'The following morning you went through the obvious motions of being concerned about your neighbour so you let her friend in, hung around, and rang the police. But, you forgot to remove your wine glass.'

'What? Is that what all this is about: a bottle of Guinness in my flat and a wine glass in hers?' jibed Hurst.

'Actually a Guinness bottle. It was empty,' DS Irvine corrected.

'Isn't that known as circumstantial evidence, gentlemen?' Hurst ignored Irvine, but began fidgeting with his lapel once more.

'No, it's known as the correct use of the English language, sir.' Kennedy was watching his prey, trapped, struggling every which way to escape. Getting madder because he was being played with.

'Not that, you prick, the fucking Guinness bottle and a wine glass don't prove a fucking thing. They are both circumstantial evidence, and would be laughed out of court.'

'Yes,' Kennedy admitted. Then waited in silence, feeling as well as hearing the red second-hand on the clock behind him, banging away in a never-ending cycle.

After exactly seventy three bangs Brian Hurst's fingers slowly extricated themselves from his lapel and made their way downwards, stopping briefly on the wooden table for three flicks of the second hand, before descending to scratch his crotch.

'But what you are now doing is not circumstantial evidence, it's proof of very live evidence,' announced Kennedy, his eyes burning through the table to where the busy fingers of Hurst's right hand sought to rid him of the itch. The hand had made the journey totally involuntarily: he had never known an itch which blazed so.

'What? What are you on about?' he spluttered self-consciously bringing his hand back on to the table, where it grabbed its partner, seeking comfort from guilt.

'Your itch, sir. I'm afraid Marianne MacIntyre had an infestation commonly known as the crabs. I'm sorry to say that, from your action, I would guess that you have caught them. Actually, I'm not sorry – in fact I'm glad, damned glad, if you really want to know. This is not circumstantial evidence. That is water around your feet, sir. Your ship is sinking.' Kennedy allowed himself a grin of triumph before continuing in a more serious tone.

'I'm afraid that I have to charge you with the wilful murder of Marianne MacIntyre. Anything you say can be taken down and given in evidence against you. Anything you choose not to say but later wish to use in court may be...' Kennedy finished his caution though the remainder was drowned out, as Hurst began to talk.

'It's her own fault you know. Yes, she was drunk, but she did act like she wanted me and then when we'd finished, she started to cry. She started crying for Morris. Can you believe that? She kept crying for him to please come back, on and on, "please come back". She just wouldn't stop babbling.

'I just tried to shut her up, but she kept on sobbing. I put one hand over her mouth to quieten her and then the other hand found its way on to her throat to stop her from thrashing about so much. The harder I pushed the hand on her mouth, the more she babbled.

'The harder I grabbed her throat the quieter she became.

'So I squeezed it tighter and tighter until she quietened down and then she just passed out. I slapped her face to bring her around but she was totally lifeless. Then I felt for a pulse and there was none, no vital signs whatsoever. So I just left. It was an accident – honestly, an accident. And then the bitch has to go and give me crabs.'

Detective Inspector Christy Kennedy could feel neither pleased nor annoyed at tying up the case. Once again a debris of victims had been left in the wake of a murder. The prey now caught, no longer occupied the mind of the hunter.

As they walked back to Kennedy's office, DS Irvine said, 'Ah, "That's water around your feet, sir, your ship is sinking". Where did that come from?'

'I don't know,' Kennedy laughed. 'It just came out. I couldn't believe I'd said it.'

'Well it was a good break, sir, anyway. If only they were all that easy.'

'If only we were always so lucky, Jimmy. Time for tea I think,' said Kennedy, as he added an inch to his step.

CHAPTER TWELVE

The Commander-in-Chief answers him
While chasing a fly

– Bob Dylan

Kennedy stood by the window in his wooden walled office, staring across at the blue building; the home of Camden Town Records. He tried to visualise the various scenarios which might have involved Peter O'Browne.

Perhaps he'd fallen head-over-heels in love, or maybe just done a Houdini.

Perhaps he'd been at home after all when thieves had arrived on Sunday. Perhaps when they didn't find anything of value they'd kidnapped him. Any minute now, Mary Jones would be on the phone saying that she'd been asked for a million-pound ransom.

Perhaps he'd been drunk and fallen into the Regent Canal. It was not exactly what Nash had designed it for, but the canal had become the final resting place for too many careless walkers over the years.

Detective Inspector Christy Kennedy removed the cards bearing the names, *Marianne MacIntyre*, *Ray Morris* and *Brian Hurst* and all the other relevant notes from his noticeboard. He wrote out the name *PETER O'BROWNE* in large letters on a card with a blue felt-tip pen and pinned it up in their place. The noticeboard was covered in green felt and proclaimed Guinness is Good For You. He had picked it up at Camden Market about five years earlier, during his attempts to 'personalise' his office. He had become quite attached to it.

There was a knock on the door and Superintendent Thomas Castle entered without waiting for an invitation.

'Oh, hello, sir.' Kennedy greeted him.

As ever, Castle was immaculately dressed. He was a crisp man, tiny – five foot three inches tall – but his outstanding success in the Met made up another nine inches. He was jacket-less in dark blue pin-striped trousers with matching waistcoat, starched white shirt and red tie.

Sometimes Kennedy wished he could dress as smart as the Super (only sometimes mind you). Even his well-worn brown shoes were as shiny ('spit and polish mate') as his mother's prized dinner service.

'New case, Kennedy?' the Super began reading Kennedy's noticeboard. 'Peter O'Browne... And how did he die? This one hasn't reached my desk yet.'

'Well, actually, I don't know, sir. That is, I'm not even sure he's dead.'

'What?'

'He disappeared towards the end of last week, sir.'

'Shouldn't someone else handle this? If you're without work, I've a lot you could take off my desk. Isn't this more a case for missing persons?'

'Yes, normally,' Kennedy started drawing the words out awkwardly like chewing gum you're trying to remove from your fingers. 'But he's been behaving totally out of character. And to complicate matters, on Sunday night his house, up off England's Lane, was badly damaged by fire.' As he spoke Kennedy wondered whether, had it not been for the involvement of ann rea, it would have been anything other than a missing persons case.

'Peter O'Browne. Don't I know that name?'

'Yes, sir, you probably do. He's our neighbour. The boss of Camden Town Records in the blue building across the way.'

'Yes. Yes, of course I remember him. He kindly supplied some of his pop memorabilia for a charity function the missus was involved in. That's it. He gave her a couple of gold discs. Tin Lizzie, yes that's it.'

'Ah, I think you mean Thin Lizzy.'

'What? Yes, that's what I said: Tin Lizzie. They fetched quite a bit of money. I remember it because the wife was extremely pleased and wrote him a thank-you note.

'Well, I hope he's okay and you are jumping the gun a bit. Keep me posted,' the Super announced, and then, in what appeared to be an afterthought but was in fact the reason for his visit, he added, 'Oh yes, and well done with that Faithfull-lookalike case. That's what we like: quick and efficient detective work.

'Nothing to beat it if you ask me. You can keep all your computers, just give me a good detective and a bit of legwork every time.'

Kennedy decided against claiming that it was all due to luck. He realised such a claim would have fallen on deaf ears and been as useful as a chocolate teapot. No, no use at all, because the Super was already halfway up the corridor, striding purposefully away in his shiny shoes, his very shiny shoes.

No sooner had the shiny shoes disappeared than WPC Anne Coles stuck her head around the door of Kennedy's office, the rest of her following shortly behind.

'I've just received the Fire Officer's report, sir.'

'Good, great. Come in. Have you had a chance to go through it yet?'

'No it's only just arrived.'

'Okay, no problem. Here's what we'll do. I'll get Jimmy over here, I'll make us all a cup of tea and you can read the report and share your findings with us over a brew. How does that sound?'

The WPC couldn't work out if he was warming his hands or just rubbing them in glee over the anticipation of a cup of tea.

'Sounds neat to me, sir.'

So Kennedy went about one of the joys of his life: preparing a pot of tea. In his case the ritual, although enjoyable, was not as rewarding as the drinking, which somewhat disproved the popular belief that anticipation was better than participation. He didn't give a hoot whether the milk went in first or last. Hot, medium strong, a little milk, two sugars, served in a china cup and saucer, rather than a mug, was all it took to satisfy Kennedy's inexpensive habit.

Chapter Thirteen

We're sailing in a strange boat
Heading for a strange shore
– Mike Scott

The trio gathered in Kennedy's office tore into the Walkers Chocolate Chip Shortbread (the perfect tea-dunker, Kennedy claimed), drank their tea and got down to business.

'So, WPC Coles; was the fire an accident?' Kennedy began.

'No, sir, not at all. According to the report the fire was started in the study, ground floor back room, adjacent to the dining room, by an incendiary device.'

'Hmmm,' Kennedy and Irvine sighed in harmony, Irvine taking the high note.

'Apparently, it was housed in a music cassette box…' The WPC waited to ensure that the Robson and Jerome of the police force were not up for a repeat performance, before continuing. 'Goes off of its own accord. Devices of this type are usually left in shops to ignite after closing, when no one is there, and they can cause the greatest amount of damage and create the maximum inconvenience.'

'Aye, nasty piece of work,' DS Irvine commented.

'So,' mused Kennedy. 'Did someone set out to destroy Peter O'Browne's house? Or, was he meant to be at home asleep when the device went off?'

'I doubt it, sir, I mean, I doubt they meant to get him as well. The fire started around 7.30pm. So if whoever planted the device wanted to kill or hurt Peter O'Browne, then surely they would have timed it to ignite later, in the sleeping hours?' WPC Coles deduced proudly.

'Unless it was just meant to be a threat, a warning, sir,' offered DS Irvine dunking his third piece of shortbread.

'Anything else in the report, WPC?' Kennedy inquired.

'Yes. The fire brigade don't think that whoever planted the device broke in. There were no forced locks or doors. And all the broken glass was on the outside, caused by the build up of heat. And that's about it, apart from…' The WPC located the precise part of the report, so that she could quote verbatim. "No human remains." But we knew that, anyway, sir. They told us that at the scene,' the WPC replied, her confidence growing all the time.

'Okay. Jimmy, let's get our forensic boys up there and see if they can find anything else. And then let's muster everyone we can to go over and question all the staff at Camden Town Records and see if we can pick up anything over there. Liaise with Mary Jones, Peter

O'Browne's PA. Try to find out who else was in the building on Friday night at 8.20pm. And let's try to find out who that last call was from.

'I'll chat to Mary again myself when you're all set up. I'm sure she'll know as much as many, if not more, on Peter O'Browne. She seemed genuinely upset at his disappearance. It's a whole new world for us and we're going to need as much help as we can get to find our way around it,' Kennedy added as he drank the final exquisite drops of tea.

WPC Coles and DS Irvine took this as a signal to get going and so they completed their cups of tea (Irvine in one gulp and Coles in three sips) and departed Kennedy's office just as the phone rang.

'Ah, Kennedy, it's yourself,' ann rea laughed in her execrable Irish-going-on-Scottish accent.

'I'm glad you rang. Listen, we've just received the fire report.' Kennedy told her about the findings.

'It gets more and more suspicious by the minute. Mary Jones has just called and told me that she has just noticed that a few things are missing from Peter's office.'

'Did she say what?'

'No, she wouldn't. She wants me to go over there to see her. Do you want to meet me there?'

'Fine. I was going to question her again anyway. We're going over with the troops to see if we can learn anything else from the staff. But do me a favour: don't mention the incendiary device. We'll want to keep that quiet for a while.'

'Okay. I'll see you there in four or five minutes. Oh and by the way, I've got something for you,' ann rea replied.

'Promises!'

'See you one-track.' The line went dead.

Chapter Fourteen

I just don't know where to begin
— Elvis Costello

The first thing that crossed Kennedy's mind as he walked into Peter O'Browne's office and saw the hundreds of music cassettes, was the incendiary device.

Without alerting anyone, he asked ann rea and Mary Jones to accompany him back to Mary's office, locking Peter's office door as they went. He then rang North Bridge House and put in a request for Bomb Squad officers to be sent for immediately.

Three hours later, after their search had turned up nothing more suspicious than an old Brendan Croker demonstration tape, Kennedy returned once more to the tranquillity of O'Browne's office. He was surprised that the workplace of such a leading light of the music industry should be so sober and tasteful. He had not really been sure what to expect, but whatever he had been expecting, this was definitely not it.

What the Inspector found was an office not unlike his own; comfortable to be in and probably even more comfortable to work in. The desk was American arts and crafts and owed a lot to the more functional elements than to any particularly aesthetic aspect. Three drawers to the direct right and left of the knee space. On the opposite side, away from the knee space, were three well-packed book shelves. The books were all about music, most of them reference books.

The ten editions of the *Guinness Book of British Hit Singles* by Gambo and Double Rice, and the six editions of the *Guinness Book of British Hit Albums* by the same authors, had pride of place on the top shelf. Other volumes included several leather-bound song catalogues, *The Guinness Encyclopedia of Popular Music*, volumes 1 to 4, edited by Colin Larkin, and George Martin's wonderful book, *The Summer of Love*, about the making of the classic 'Sergeant Pepper's Lonely Hearts Club Band' album. Kennedy knew it was wonderful because ann rea bought it for him as a present and he had found each and every one of the 168 pages to be an absolute joy.

A few more tomes on the Beatles included two exquisitely leather-bound editions by George Harrison, *I, Me, Mine*, and *Songs by George Harrison*. Kennedy was tempted to remove them from the shelf and have a browse, but he managed to resist the temptation, feeling it may not be appropriate.

Lost in his exploration of the book shelves, his concentration was abruptly broken by Mary Jones, who, by this time, had grown impatient to impart her news. 'Look,' she began, turning her head so quickly from ann rea to Kennedy that her hair spun out like a Flamenco dancer's skirts. 'I think you both should know this. I've only just found out.

'I was going through Peter's things and his desk, like, trying to find some hint, some clue to his whereabouts.' Both ann rea and Kennedy noticed that tears were building up in her eyes and beginning to roll down her snow white-skin.

ann rea went over, put her arm up round Mary's shoulders and led her to Peter's wooden (with leather inlay) swivel American arts and crafts chair. 'Whatever it is, Mary? You have to tell us. The sooner, the better.'

'Well, I think, I think. You see, I was going through his desk, wondering why he might…' Mary babbled on in her infuriating way of starting the sentences several different ways before she could finish it.

'Yes? And?' ann rea prompted.

'Well I found this, you see. Well like, I thought. Well, I think Peter was being blackmailed!'

Mary stood up and took two sheets of white paper out of the left hand pocket of her baggy blue skirt. She handed them to ann rea, who removed her arm from Mary's back. Mary comforted herself, wrapping her own arms around her sides and rocking back and forth.

ann rea gazed at the papers for a few seconds before passing them unopened and unread to Kennedy.

'Ah, at last!' Kennedy said in his mind's silent voice as he carefully unfolded them twice to reveal two full sheets of foolscap. Both pages had word processor style type in the centre of the page.

Kennedy read the first one aloud:

> 'On 16/10 NW14
> 38 2 43
> on 23/10 NW14
> 43 2 29
> ????????
> I KNOW!'

None the wiser, he turned his attention to the second sheet of paper:

> 'SO DO U!
> NO ONE ELSE WILL
> IF YOU DO AS I SAY'

ann rea leaned over for a better look. She was so close to Kennedy she could smell his honest non-perfumed smell, the smell which reminded her of their shared moments.

Four eyebrows in Peter O'Browne's office arched a question mark; the remaining two drew an almost straight line, beneath which teardrops fell.

Kennedy read the two notes again. He surmised that the contents were not exactly a code, but were probably some sort of shorthand which would hide their meaning from strange eyes.

'Do you know what any of this means?' he asked Mary in a businesslike manner which begged her to stop crying. Sometimes the official approach was not as encouraging to tears as a more personal tone.

'I think so,' Mary said, beginning to pull herself together. She reached behind Peter's desk and what had appeared to be a wall sprung out at the touch of her finger to reveal a large cup and saucer, some headache pills, a bottle of what seemed to be more headache pills, a first-aid kit, three fresh, neatly-folded blue shirts, half a dozen white shirts (apparently brand new and still in their boxes) and a box of Kleenex. Mary helped herself to a tissue or three and then closed the door.

The lines of the door were carefully camouflaged into the lines of the wooden panelling which completely covered the wall behind the desk. Kennedy wondered if there were any more hidden compartments in the wall, or anywhere else in the office for that matter.

'Okay.' Mary wiped her eyes and blew her nose. 'NW14 is the number, the serial number of our fourteenth single, and I think, though I have to check, that on 16th October it dropped from number 38 in the charts to 43 and then the following week it rose again to 29.'

Kennedy reread the first page and declared, 'Yes, that makes sense. That makes perfect sense to me. The question marks obviously mean, "How did this happen?" and the author, in the last line, claims he knows. Simple, I suppose, when you know what you are looking for.

'What, tell me, is so mysterious about a single going up and down the charts? I thought that's what happened all the time,' Kennedy inquired with his voice, eyes and hands.

ann rea had the impression from Mary's eyes that the Welsh girl was deciding how much she should tell Kennedy and, more importantly, how much she shouldn't.

Chapter Fifteen

Let X = X. You know it could be you
– Laurie Anderson

Kennedy came away from Camden Town Records with three things that afternoon.
1) Information about the life, near death and resurrection of NW14.

2) A cassette.

3) An envelope containing fifteen typed pages entitled, 'Peter O'Browne – A Profile'.

ann rea's cassette would prove to be valuable to Kennedy because it contained an interview she had conducted with Peter O'Browne about eight months previously for the *Camden News Journal*. Peter had obviously been in a talkative mood and ann rea had just let the tape keep rolling.

North Bridge House was packed to overflowing. Mary Jones had sent some of the Camden Town Records staff over to the station for their interviews, claiming it was the only way to get them off the telephones long enough to hold a conversation. Kennedy tried unsuccessfully three times to listen to the tape. He had decided to play it before reading the profile. He wanted to hear Peter O'Browne's voice to see if he could piece together anything about his character. But on each occasion he was interrupted. Once by ann rea ringing to ask him if he'd listened to the tape; once by DS Irvine checking whether any new info had surfaced on Peter O'Browne; and, finally by the Super wanting to know why there were so many people with serious haircut problems wandering around the station.

Kennedy was well aware that there were enough real cases to command his time, with real victims and real perpetrators, unlike the intangible scenario surrounding Peter O'Browne. But his curiosity had been awoken and his detective's nose sensed the unmistakable whiff of something decidedly off, even if he could not quite identify what it was.

In the end he decided to nip home and listen to the tape in peace. Normally he would walk the short distance to Rothwell Street, but well aware of the pressure of time, he hailed a cab on the corner of Prince Albert Road.

Kennedy leaned into the cab and gave his address through the half wound-down window. Thousands of disgruntled passengers (what the cabbies call 'fares') would be familiar with the balding driver's reply: 'Nah, mate, sorry. I'm going the opposite way.'

Kennedy, unlike those thousands of disgruntled fares, replied: 'I don't think so.'

Keeping one hand inside the window he reached inside his jacket, extracted, and flashed, the warrant card. 'I believe you're going my way, "mate".'

Getting a London black cab to take you where you want to go is about as easy as getting into a Marks and Sparks triangular sandwich packet. Kennedy hated using his police ID for such a privilege: if you could call insisting that someone does their job a privilege. He consoled himself with the thought that he was striking out for all the fares left stranded by the kerbside.

His house was quiet, as silent as a Canadian art movie; lots of static noise but nothing of substance. He felt like a trespasser, if not on the property itself then definitely on the time that had surely been marked down somewhere as house silent time.

The little room under the stairs which he used as his study/office/storeroom/den housed a midi music system which he fired up immediately, inserting the cassette ann rea had marked, 'P O'Browne Oct 10th, '94.'

ann rea's voice comfortable and casual said, 'I like to keep one running, it saves me making notes, and it saves me making mistakes.'

'Yeah sure, fine. No problem.' What was obviously Peter O'Browne's voice replied with a gentle Irish accent. 'Um, Mary assured me this was not going to be a critical piece, or a bitter, spiteful attack like the ones the music press love to do.'

'Oh no,' ann rea assured him. 'I like to make all the words I write sweet; just in case I have to eat them some time!'

Kennedy's speakers crackled with laughter. 'Fine, good one,' said Peter. 'Look, ann, I wouldn't mind a glass of wine. It's been a long day, a bit of a drag. Would you care for one?' Kennedy felt slightly uncomfortable. He couldn't tell if his discomfort was caused by eavesdropping on someone else's conversation or by the fear he was going to hear something he really didn't want to hear. Perhaps it was slightly spooky because he was hearing Peter's voice for the first time and even though Kennedy had been unaware of his existence before the fire, his name had been around a lot in the following forty-eight hours.

Kennedy was going to look a right fool if Peter O'Browne showed up. How would he explain away all the wasted people-power to the Super? As the Sony electronic speakers under Kennedy's stairs faithfully reproduced the sound of footsteps walking across a room, he came up with a bright idea. If Peter O'Browne did reappear then he would get ann rea to persuade Mary Jones to persuade Peter O'Browne to donate another of his many gold discs to Castle's wife's charity.

Kennedy heard a cork popping and footsteps coming back across the room to their original position. Was this O'Browne's office, or were they in his house? Just how well did ann rea know him, anyway. It must be the office, Kennedy decided, because the footsteps had moved from a wooden floor to a carpet, which muffled the sound. There had been a more informal area to one side of Peter's office, where he had a large wooden coffee table surrounded by two large comfy (dark blue) sofas on the long side and two easy-chairs (dark green) at the short ends, all standing on an island made by a vivid multi-coloured Native American carpet.

'So this is for a feature about Camden Town Records?' O'Browne continued, his voice betraying a slight hint of suspicion, as he poured two glasses of wine.

'Yes. And I'd love to know about you and how you started it all.' ann rea had discovered that there were two main things the majority of the people in the music biz loved. It wasn't doing drugs and having sex; it was making money and giving interviews.

'Well,' began Peter before taking a large gulp of the wine and exhaling a loud, 'Ah, now, let me see.'

Thirty-five minutes later, Kennedy nipped into the kitchen, made a cup of tea and returned to the study to read ann rea's profile of Peter O'Browne.

Chapter Sixteen

Every generation throws a hero up the pop charts
— Paul Simon

From a combination of ann rea's cassette and article, Kennedy discovered that in 1965, Peter O'Browne had dropped out of Trinity College, Dublin, where he had been studying English and American Literature. His plan had been to become a teacher for fourteen or fifteen years and then try to become a writer, but he got himself bitten by the Sixties music bug. Bands like The Spencer Davis Group, The Animals, Kinks, Stones and a group from the wee 'North' (of Ireland) called Them turned his life upside down. The highlight of his week was listening to the Top Twenty every Sunday night on Radio Luxembourg.

The charts fascinated him and he became a life long scholar: cutting them out of *New Musical Express* each week and gluing them into scrap books. He still had all the originals and continued to collect the charts weekly, more recently from *Music Week* and leather-bound journals had replaced the scrap books.

A friend and fellow Trinity College dropout, Martyn Farrelly formed an Irish R&B group called Blues by Five. Peter started to secure them some gigs (bookings) in clubs supporting the likes of The People, Granny's Intentions, Taste, The Interns and The Gentry (the last two from the North). In order to finance the club appearances they would act as 'relief group' to showbands in ballrooms.

Martyn Farrelly was a talented musician and began doing his own arrangements of Dylan songs. The audience reaction to these arrangements was sufficient to give Martyn the confidence to write a couple of his own songs. He left the R&B roots behind seeking a more 'poppy' soul sound.

Eventually Peter and Martyn decided (in 1967, when they were both aged 19) that if Blues by Five were to have a future, and it certainly looked as if they had, such a future would be rosier in London, the home of all the major record companies.

Due to the fabulous success of The Beatles, The Kinks and The Rolling Stones, Pye, EMI, Polydor, Decca and RCA were signing up everyone and anyone who looked scruffy, sounded fab and appeared to be 'with it'. They hadn't a clue about the music, having only recently grown accustomed to the 'Bachelor Boy' sound of Cliff Richard, Marty Wilde and Adam Faith.

Peter O'Browne had thoroughly enjoyed reminiscing with ann rea and had gone to great trouble to explain that he thought that the teenagers of the Sixties, the first teen generation to have some kind of financial independence, were, as with all new fads then and since, consuming everything thrown at them. So the record company 'suits', eager to nurture this demand, were churning out soon to be forgotten acts like The Bow Street Runners, Honeybus, Hedgehoppers Anonymous and Dowlands.

Much to the annoyance of their parents and Dublin girlfriends, Peter and Martyn packed their bags and headed off to London to seek their fame and fortune. They stayed with Peter's uncle in Camden Mews and while Martyn spent his days banging away on his electric guitar (unplugged), Peter would visit as many pubs and clubs as he could in and around London. The idea was to secure as many gigs as possible and bring over the remainder of Blues by Five.

It is worth remembering that this was before the general availability of cassette-recorders made recording a demonstration tape ('demo') simple, and so Peter was unable to play the club owners the music of the Blues by Five. He used his natural Irish 'blag', helped by rave reviews and write-ups from Irish music papers such as *New Spotlight*.

Luckily for Peter, Martyn, Blues by Five and trusted roadie, Touche, there was a strong Irish contingent living in Hammersmith, Kilburn and Camden. So the pubs and clubs in these areas were more than happy to stage 'the darlings of Dublin.' Up to that point, Them were the only Irish band working in England and they were certainly too big to play there.

Within a couple of weeks, Peter had set up a month's worth of work. To fund the trip Peter had persuaded Gentleman Jim Aiken to promote a farewell concert for the Blues by Five in The National Stadium, Dublin. Jim Aiken, a Northern Irishman, promoted all the English groups on their visits to Ireland and had in fact used the Blues by Five several times to support some of the English names. The National Stadium, a dingy run-down boxing hall on the South Circular Road had never before been used to stage a headline show by an Irish group: this in itself became a contributing factor to heavy ticket sales.

Peter O'Browne was so confident in the success of the show that he agreed to split the door takings equally with Aiken. An astonishing 1368 people turned up, each paying seven shillings and six pence and Gentleman Jim rounded-up the Blues by Five's share of the door receipts to £500, with brave talk of their returning for two nights over the Christmas period.

The group arrived in London on a high but the high disappeared as quickly as a bank managers smile when they saw the size of the stage at their first gig in London: the Dublin Castle in Parkway, Camden Town. Kennedy was amused that O'Browne's first venture in London nearly thirty years before should have been so close to the hub of his current empire. 'Dublin Castle my foot, more like Dublin Cassy,' Peter laughed on the tape reporting the Blues by Five's drummer's first impression of their début London venue.

About mid-way through the month of gigs, Peter started to bring record company A&R people down to see 'my boys'; thanks to Eppy (Brian Epstein) all managers were then referring to their charges in this manner.

Decca Records passed (but then they passed on the Beatles), EMI (who signed the Beatles) passed, RCA passed (walked out of the Greyhound, Fulham Palace Road after only three songs) but Pye Records (who had The Kinks) liked the group and offered them a deal.

Peter's 'boys' received an advance of £5,000 against a 3 per cent royalty on 90 per cent of the wholesale price of each record.

What that meant in reality was that they received 2.7 per cent of the price their records were sold to (not from) the shops. The record company legal speak was just a way of making it appear that they were getting more than they were. The reality being that it really didn't matter anyway, as very few groups ever received anything over their advance.

Martyn, as the group's main songwriter, was encouraged – obliged, really – to sign a publishing deal with an associate company, BPE Music. This way the Company was looking after the Company all down the line. This part of the deal would later return to haunt Peter, as all of Martyn's early songs were locked into a terrible 55/45 per cent deal, with there being no doubt as to who was receiving the smaller share.

For now all was well and the group tore into the advance like advertisers into the break in 'Coronation Street', buying new equipment and paying a deposit on a large flat where all five members of the band and Touche would stay. Peter continued lodging with his uncle, preferring to avoid the late night cannabis aroma when possible.

The Blues by Five made their first record which was greeted with a multitude of indifference and sold 3,873 copies, 890 of them in Ireland. They slogged around for the next four years, releasing three more albums and selling a total of 16,587 copies across the four titles. Peter O'Browne laboured around with them building up a healthy reputation and an incredible network of contacts. They weren't a bad band really, neither were they great and Martyn Farrelly's priority was music and songwriting and not show-business.

Kennedy picked his way through O'Browne's career up to the time of ann rea's article, which was a couple of years old, and the main point of the article. Following Blues by Five, Peter had, with a partner named Paddy George, opened a record shop, Camden Records.

The shop became very successful, and from it Peter had formed his own record label.

The interesting thing, was the fact that Peter O'Browne, whereabouts currently unknown, had sold 51 per cent of his independent record company, Camden Town Records, to Grabaphone, one of the major companies, for a staggering six million pounds.

Chapter Seventeen

You had been saying that
Smoking was my only vice
– ABBA (Andersson and Ulvaeus)

'Six million bleeding quid,' Kennedy announced with great restraint the following morning in his office. Peter O'Browne certainly had made the most of a relatively short life, thought Kennedy. Like all great entrepreneurs he had stumbled on an opportunity, grabbed it and milked it.

Although nippy, the sun was shining and the ice blue sky was peppered with small fluffy clouds – the kind of day Kennedy preferred to be outside. He had given the DS and WPC Coles copies of ann rea's article and cassette. In theory everyone was up to speed.

'We've also learned from Mary Jones that there is a chance that Peter O'Browne was being blackmailed.' This raised a couple of Scottish eyebrows whose owner had still been treating this case as a missing persons job and had been wondering why the boss was spending so much time on it.

'The blackmail apparently has to do with something known as hyping,' Kennedy continued, right hand twitching. 'Mary explained it to me yesterday. Here are copies of the two letters she passed on to us.' Kennedy was now conscious that he was someone on an 'and here's one we prepared earlier 'demonstration. 'I'm still not sure about all of this. Perhaps our Mr. O'Browne is shacked up with one of his pop stars somewhere, but with the fire and these notes and his assistant's concern we'd best see what we can dig up.' He gave them a couple of minutes to read and re-read the two notes.

'The shorthand in the letter – we think – means:

'On 16th of October 1993, a single "O Vulgar Abbeys," serial number NW14, by a group called The Babtirs, dropped in the singles chart from 38 to 43. The following week, 23rd of October, the same single rose from 43 to 29.'

'Obviously the implication is that this was strange, and in the final line the author is claiming that he knows how it happened.'

'What's the big deal about a single rising and falling in the charts? Surely that's not a reason for blackmail?' a genuinely surprised Anne Coles inquired.

'Well, apparently the Top 40 is the yardstick by which the whole music business works. But if you have a hit single – that is, an entry in the Top 40 – it doesn't necessarily mean you'll make any money from the release itself,' Kennedy offered, repeating Mary's information.

'Why release a single at all if you'll not make any money out of it,' muttered DS Irvine.

'Well, each single will be on an album, and album sales do make large sums of money for the record companies. But the record companies seem to have lost the knack of promoting albums. Now they rely on the hit single, sometimes several from the one album, to sell the album. Apparently when you enter the Top 40 all the main record shop chains will automatically stock your record: shops like Boots, WH Smith, Our Price, HMV and Virgin.

'If these major stores don't stock your single until it gets in the Top 40, then how on earth does your single get into the charts in the first place?' asked WPC Coles.

'I asked the same question and basically you have to do it through all the independent stores. It's also worth noting that all the major record companies like WEA, EMI, BMG–'

'And the FBI, CIA, CID,' Irvine wisecracked.

'Not at this time, but with the drug connections, it's something they may wish to look at taking up in the future.' Kennedy gave him a stern look for interrupting.

'As I was saying, the major record companies can usually force the record shop chains to take their priority releases, usually big acts and new important acts, from week one. Once you get your single in the Top 40, as well as getting stocked in the chains, you are also racked in all the stores' Top 40 boxes, mentioned in the weekly Top 40 radio shows and in a position to take advantage of all the weekly radio/TV/press promotional activities.

'If and when you enter the Top 30, you become eligible for inclusion on *Top of The Pops*, the tired TV show for kids run by grandads.

'The Babtirs were off to a good start with "O Vulgar Abbeys". I have been advised that the single entered the charts on October 2nd at No. 54. Then, as you have seen, it moved up to 38 on the 9th and dropped to 43 on the 16th,' Kennedy said consulting his notebook.

'The significance of this is that in the British chart, unlike the German and American equivalents, once a single drops that's it. It's history. Maybe one in a thousand will move back up again, but that is very, very rare. It usually just happens in the Top 20 around Christmas time.

'Camden Town Records were faced with the prospect of losing a very important first single from an important album by an important group, and, as was explained to me, at a very important time for the company. The only solution was to hype the single back up the charts.

'Chart hyping goes back a long long way. I believe it is even alleged that Brian Epstein's family-owned shops, NEMS, had more than a few thousand spare copies of 'his boys' first single, 'Love Me Do'. Certainly the practice was very common in the Seventies, when some groups had what were called 'granny squads' who went around the chart return shops buying up particular records.

'Chart return shops are supposedly a cross-section of shops up and down the country used by the chart compilers as a sample to calculate what is selling and what is not. It's all done by computer now, which is supposed to make it impossible to buy your way into the charts, but there are people you can go to who have teams of people in the field, willing to spend the week crisscrossing the country, buying up singles in the important chart return shops.

'The number of singles you would need to sell to take you, for instance, from 43 in the charts to 29 might be as little as 5,000 copies. So, including paying the "marketing teams", as the hypers are euphemistically known, the whole exercise might only cost £8,000 to £12,500: peanuts when you consider the money you can turn over with a hit album.'

Kennedy again consulted his notes before continuing. 'It's not difficult to work out. An album which sells 300,000 copies grosses over £3,000,000. An album which sells 300,000 is called a platinum album. If you can sell 300,000 copies, you can with a little effort, and even less money, sell 600,000, and if you can sell 600,000 you can sell 900,000, triple platinum. The gross on 900,000 is just over ten million quid. So you can see that £12,500 is a small price to pay.'

'So you think that the week, "O Vulgar Abbeys" rose from 43 to 29 in the charts, Camden Town Records would have had these teams out buying the single,' the WPC asked.

'Yes. Mind you, the teams have to be clever because the computer will throw up irregular sales and if the chart compilers smell anything untoward, they check and recheck and report all suspicious releases to the industry watchdog, the BPI. The BPI will penalise a single if they are convinced something funny is going on. They can either remove the offending record from the chart altogether or freeze it for a week.

'What will happen to the record company?' asked Irvine, his notion of the Top Twenty Popular Music Chart spoilt forever.

'Well, what we have to realise is that the BPI's members are exclusively record company seniors.'

'So they are hardly going to give themselves a hard time,' supplied DS Irvine.

'Quite. ann rea said it reminded her of another high powered organisation, not a million miles from home, who do the same thing. The BPI might impose a token fine if a hype has had some publicity, but generally it's just, "Now, we mustn't do this again, must we, chaps?" and that will be the end of it.

'They'll issue a statement saying that the irregularity was caused by a "well orchestrated fan club" or that they've found "a slight discrepancy in the sales pattern", but nothing that could linked to the record company.

'I believe that our Fraud Squad people have looked at it a few times, but nothing has ever come of it. It just makes it all so much harder for real music and for the smaller record companies to compete, companies who can't afford to spend the extra £12,500 on a single.'

Chapter Eighteen

*Eventually they came for me
And there was no one left to speak.*
– Christy Moore

Kennedy took the break as an excuse for a cup of tea. The WPC and DS Irvine eager to enjoy the treat, helped with cups, saucers, sugar, milk and spoons.

'You know the other important thing here was the timing of the whole affair. All this hyping affair was going down with the Grabaphone negotiations as a backdrop. Perhaps Peter O'Browne might normally have told the blackmailer to eff off. He could have argued, successfully, that all he was doing was following standard record company practice. But at that point, he could not afford an investigation. Without a major to protect Camden Town Records, the BPI might have made an example of them. The adverse publicity could have cost him dearly, if not the entire deal.'

'That surprises me. From what you have said, I would have thought Peter's aggressive action would have endeared him to the majors,' WPC Coles offered as she took Kennedy's empty cup and started to refill.

Irvine and Coles took the interruption of a phone call from ann rea to leave Kennedy and go about their other business.

'This is funny, you know. Here we are, not even sure yet that a crime has actually been committed, but I'm already thinking up a list of suspects. You know, who would have most to gain from the disappearance, temporary or otherwise, of Peter O'Browne.' Kennedy was responding to ann rea's, 'Any news on Peter?

'Okay, who is on your list for the crime that, as yet, doesn't exist?' she inquired.

'Let's see now,' Kennedy began putting pen to paper. 'One, Martyn Farrelly. They were close in the early days.' Kennedy jotted the name down top of his list. 'Two,' he continued, 'Tom Best. I see from your article he was involved in both the shop and the record company. Three, Paddy George, O'Browne's partner in the record shop. Four, Jason Carter-Cash.'

'Actually his name is Jason Carter-Houston,' ann rea corrected.

'Yes, sorry, Jason Carter-Houston. What was the name of the group he managed?' Kennedy checked his notebook. 'Yes, Radio Cars. I supposed he could feel aggrieved at the way Peter handled his group. It would seem that they disappeared into obscurity after their initial success with Camden Town Records.

'Five, the blackmailer, if none of the above. Whoever he or she may be, we can't rule them out until we know more about them. Six, the Chart Hypers. Another set of mystery people we need to check out. Well,' Kennedy surmised, 'for a case that is not yet really a case, we have a healthy list of suspects. That's before we look at the aspect of Peter's life that, statistically speaking, is most likely to end in foul play.'

'His private life?' ann rea prodded.

'Specifically, his love life. Either a jealous lover or a lover's jealous husband. Are there any jealous husbands, any shunned "exes" who wish they weren't "ex"?'

Kennedy let this question hang for a few moments to see if ann rea could offer any information. He knew she hated gossip, but if there were any rumours out there, she might well be aware of them.

'Oh I see,' ann rea began smiling down the phone. 'You're asking me if I know of any skeletons, huh?'

'Well, it would help,' Kennedy pleaded, not sure how much he was pushing his luck.

'I know this may surprise you, but I don't know a lot about his love life. Okay, so a short time after our first interview he did ring me to invite me out to dinner and I felt that there was more than dinner involved, so I declined. Now, I don't know if you're relieved or disappointed,' ann rea teased.

'Oh, it was probably just a dinner kinda thing,' answered a relieved Kennedy, now trying to be cool about it.

'Kennedy, you're such an innocent. You'll never know the lengths that men – well, most men – will go to just to get intimate with a woman. They'll say anything, they'll promise anything. The sad thing is, most of them don't even realise themselves how much of a line they are giving. But you should see how quickly some of them change their tune once, once–'

'Once the tune has been played,' Kennedy added, offering an easy way out.

'Yeah.' ann rea, outwardly smiling, inwardly fighting back a pain, distracted herself by asking another question. 'So are you disappointed? You know, disappointed that I didn't date him, thereby closing down one avenue of information for you? Or, are you relieved that I didn't, shall we say, for more personal reasons?'

'Well, maybe we could discuss that later. Perhaps in the dark?' laughed Kennedy, happy they were sailing out of troubled waters. 'In the meantime,' he continued, returning to the matter in hand, 'how do we go about finding out more information on the people behind the chart hyping? I'm assuming Mary Jones can put us in touch with everyone else on the list if necessary?' Kennedy asked, rising from his chair and walking around his office, extending the cable on his handset to its limit. He wished ann rea were there in the room with him, so that he could touch her, even briefly, but gently, on the cheek.

'Let me make a few calls when I get you off my line and I'll see what I can dig up for you. If I'm finished with my police work for now, I'm off. See you later?'

'Brilliant, yes. But let's do something, let's go somewhere,' Kennedy suggested. He was happy to dine out or dine in and just hang out with her, but he desperately wanted ann rea not to be bored and he was always searching for things for them to do together.

'Kennedy,' was all ann rea would allow herself to say; but in her mind she kissed him ran and her fingers through his hair. 'Bye.'

Chapter Nineteen

You come home late
And you come home early
Sometimes you don't come home at all
— John Prine

Kennedy sat at his desk, lost in his thoughts. The morning sunshine had turned to rain and he watched the drops flow down his window picking up smaller droplets along the way. He spent some time wondering whether any of the classic singles of his youth had been 'helped' into the charts. ann rea had said that nowadays a record could reach the top of the charts with a total sale of 100,000 copies. In the good old days, a chart single would have sold such numbers in one morning.

The Beatles, for instance, had a pre-sale in excess of a staggering one million copies for their fourth single, 'I Want to Hold Your Hand' when it was released on 17th October, 1963. That was another ann rea statistic, but Kennedy himself remembered being one of the million people who visited their local record stores to place an order (paying a 50 per cent deposit: three shillings and four pence) to avoid release-day disappointment.

According to ann rea, the first single was recorded in 1895, featuring Emil Berliner, inventor of the microphone, reciting 'Twinkle Twinkle Little Star' on to a zinc disc. 1948 saw RCA Victor in America release the first vinyl single, a red one, with a series of popular classical pieces. It was not until 1953 that the UK saw its first collection of releases, which included Alma Cogan singing, 'I Went To Your Wedding'.

The biggest-selling single ever was Bing Crosby's 'White Christmas', with over 100 million copies (Kennedy knew that one); the biggest-selling UK single was the aforementioned 'I Want to Hold your Hand' by the Beatles, which had reached around 14 million. The Beatles also shared the record with Elvis for the most UK number ones: seventeen.

'A bit of good news, sir,' DS Irvine beamed through the door, dragging Kennedy back from his Beatles memories and ann rea facts.

'Yes?'

'We've checked out O'Browne's credit card company – actually he has several – but one card, his Access, has been used twice recently.'

'Yes?'

'Apparently, he took a train on Saturday from Waterloo to Wareham. If it was him using the ticket, that is.'

'Devon?'

'No, sir. Hardy country, Dorset,' Irvine replied, checking the information on the fax message he was clutching.

'Hmmm.'

'He bought a first-class single for £42.40. The ticket was purchased at 9.14am on Saturday morning, which probably means he caught the 09.30 train, via Chichester. This would have arrived in Wareham at 11.35am,' Irvine continued as he passed the credit card faxes on to Kennedy.

'You'll also see that he had lunch at the Morton House Hotel, Corfe Castle, which is about eight miles from Wareham on the way to the coast. He spent £28.30 on lunch – poached salmon and half a bottle of the house white – and tipped generously, £5.00.'

'Well, Jimmy, progress, I think. Well done,' Kennedy announced, his rich, green eyes smiling.

'Perhaps he just wanted to get away from it all for a few days. You know, head off to the country and lose himself. I hear it's quite splendid in that area.' DS Irvine slouched into a chair his shirt straining on his belt.

'I don't know, Jimmy.' Kennedy only used Irvine's first name when no one else was present. 'Mary Jones is convinced that no matter what Peter was doing, no matter where he was, he would at the very least make a couple of quick calls to her, just to check in. But, assuming that it was O'Browne, why Corfe Castle?' he said rising from his chair and going over to his large wall map of Great Britain. He easily found Wareham but the location of Corfe Castle took a little while longer. Instinctively he stuck a pin (red) in the map at the location. 'Swanage seems to be the nearest coastal port.'

'Or Poole,' chipped in Irvine, who had managed to ease the tension on his belt and was standing behind Kennedy, looking over his shoulder.

'No, that would be back-tracking through Wareham in the opposite direction,' Kennedy replied, scratching his chin and staring at the map to see if a clue might jump up from it and offer itself up in sacrifice.

'Could you get on to the locals and see if we can find out any additional information about the diner's identity? A description would help. And check whether any ferries sail from Swanage, and if so, to where.'

'Do you think he might have done a Stephen Fry and exchanged his baseball cap for a French beret?'

'Corfe Castle,' was Kennedy's only reply. 'What's Corfe Castle got to do with this? Perhaps Mary Jones can shed some light on it. Do we have a photo of O'Browne, by the way?'

'Yes, sir,' answered James Irvine, like a schoolchild eager to score points with teacher (saves wasting all those apples). 'Mary Jones gave us quite a recent one. I've already faxed it through to Wareham.'

'Good. I'll see you later,' Kennedy replied, doing up the top button of his shirt, tightening his tie and putting on his jacket, before leaving his office and North Bridge House.

The Camden Town Records building was quite strange, now Kennedy actually stopped to consider it. The shape was illogical, and the entire building looked like it might collapse if hit by a solid gust of wind. The outside shell was a third glass, the rest blue-painted partitions – Williams Racing Blue. Above the double door was a pink neon sign spelling out the company name to all on upper Parkway.

Camden Town Records seemed to have adapted the policy of business as usual in Peter O'Browne's absence. This made a lot of sense; Grabaphone who owned 51 per cent of the firm were obviously not going to see their investment go down the drain just because the softly spoken Irishman had done a bunk.

Mary Jones was accompanied by a sophisticated looking man in his mid-forties. 'Oh, hi, Detective Inspector. This is Peter's lawyer, Leslie Russell,' she said. 'Leslie, this is Detective Inspector Christy Kennedy from over the road.'

'Actually if the truth be known, I'm quite happy with solicitor,' smiled Russell. 'Though some of my music business colleagues, keen to emulate our American counterparts are eager to claim Lawyer as a new title and class. I'm pleased to meet you.' He grasped Kennedy's hand firmly.

Leslie Russell was one of those chaps who are instantly likable. He had such a warm welcoming smile. Yes, he did have the London solicitor's uniform of suit (beige today, and heavy; linen or cotton in the summer), red braces over blue shirt, red socks and matching red bow tie. His hair was untidily well kept, *à la* Michael Heseltine and showing the first tinges of grey through the copper brown.

His permanently clean shaven face added the final touch to a man who looked and was, very approachable and obviously had a manner to him which ensured his clients were comfortable in his company. The single most prominent feature of his appearance was his piercing sky blue eyes. Someday he would make a good judge, because eyes like that would make most men (and all women) feel very guilty should they be strangers to the truth.

Mary reassured by Russell's presence, was slightly less distressed on this occasion. She even managed a smile. 'You'll join us and have some tea, won't you? Detective Inspector Kennedy likes the Beatles and tea,' she told Russell before buzzing through an order on the intercom, without waiting for Kennedy's reply.

Kennedy nodded yes after the fact. He was thinking about ann rea spilling the beans on some of his secrets – not all, he hoped.

Kennedy took photocopies of the faxes from his inside jacket pocket. 'We believe we know where Peter O'Browne spent Saturday.'

'Good gracious,' Leslie Russell exclaimed leaning forward in his chair and rubbing his large manicured hands together in anticipation. Mary Jones was speechless, raising her hand to cover her open mouth. 'Did one of your chaps see him, then?' Leslie Russell asked, pronouncing each of the words fully and pausing after each one.

'No, no direct sightings yet, but his credit card was used to purchase a rail ticket from Waterloo to Wareham and at an hotel in Corfe Castle.'

'How extraordinary,' returned Russell. 'And here I was thinking the worst. Blackmail, drugs, murder and what-not.' He sat silent a moment, deep in thought as Mary tried in vain to hold back the large Welsh teardrops of relief that were rolling down her face. 'Now, now, Mary, you simply mustn't.' Russell went over to Mary and dried her eyes with his handkerchief.

'I should tell you both that at this point we only have proof that the credit card was used. We still have to confirm that it was used by its owner. We've sent a copy of Peter's photo to the local police and they'll check at Wareham Station, at the taxi rank outside the station and the hotel, the Morton House Hotel, where the card was used for lunch. The hotel should be the best bet.'

Mary Jones asked Russell the question Kennedy had intended asking her, 'Leslie, who on earth does he know in Dorset?'

'For the life of me I can't think. I've been wracking my brain since the Detective Inspector mentioned the location. Let me see now, isn't that near that village Moredon where that awfully strange chap Lawrence of Arabia killed himself on his motorcycle? Now there was the makings of a pop star if ever there was one: lived dangerously, died young – I wonder if he could sing? Perhaps Peter set off to see if he had any relatives with a chip off the old charisma block, eh?'

Kennedy couldn't be sure if Leslie Russell was considering the singing potential of TE Lawrence and his offspring or whether Peter O'Browne might know anyone in Dorset.

'No, sorry,' Russell announced. 'I can't say that I'm aware of Peter having any connections down there. Who else would know, Mary?'

Chapter Twenty

A policeman shines a light on my shoulder
– Mark Knopfler

Perhaps Mrs Hannah Castle was going to be presented with another fund-raising gold disc after all. Kennedy just hoped her husband (his boss) would be as happy as the owner of the social conscience.

But why Corfe Castle? he asked himself for the umpteenth time. And why disappear in the first place? There were so many unanswered questions, but until he knew for certain that it was anything other than a missing persons case, he felt unable or unwilling to move into a more functional gear.

He checked his map again. Poole, about a fifteen-minute taxi ride away from Corfe Castle, was the nearest ferry port. From there Peter O'Browne could have easily hopped a ferry to Jersey, without needing a passport, or caught a train back to London. Or anywhere else in the United Kingdom of Great Britain and Northern Ireland (ferry connection necessary), for that matter.

Such grand words, *United* Kingdom and *Great* Britain. ann rea had often declared that if Britain was allowed to call itself *Great* then perhaps Ireland should be *Excellent* Ireland and Scotland *Canny* Scotland. Wales could be *Rugged* Wales and on and on. Kennedy cut himself off in mid-thought. He didn't have the time for going off on tangents.

He took some pieces of paper from a drawer and wrote down the several avenues he felt he should be exploring, and pinned them all to his noticeboard.

Martyn Farrelly
Tom Best
Paddy George
Jason Carter-Houston
Chart Hypers
Love Life?

He also pinned up a piece of paper with Leslie Russell's name on it. Not that he was a suspect (not that he wasn't, mind you), but Kennedy believed he could supply a lot of background information required to move the investigation forward. An investigation still, Kennedy feared, in a state of warming up.

The phone rang. 'DI Kennedy,' he proclaimed to whoever had chosen to make a connection with him. You just never knew who was going to be at the other end of the phone. You never knew if they were going to bring you good news, bad news, new leads, or kill old leads.

'DS Hardy here, Dorset CID,' announced the voice, its owner confident and crisp.

Kennedy smiled at the obvious. He wondered if this was a wind-up. 'Hello, how are you doing?' He tried to hide his amusement.

'Good. Very good, in fact. DS Irvine advised me I should report to you when I completed the interviews at Morton House Hotel regarding the disappearance of a Mr Peter Browne.'

'Yes. He's actually O'Browne, Sergeant, Peter O'Browne.'

'Sorry.'

'No problem. It is quite an unusual name. To be honest with you, I've never heard it before.' Kennedy relaxed into his chair. 'Well, what have you found out down there for us, Sergeant?'

'It's a nice hotel, sir, friendly staff. A Mr and Mrs kind of place,' replied Dorset's less famous Hardy. 'The receptionist, a Miss Melanie Gibson, remembers your man. She remembered him more from the tip he left than she did from the photo. She said the photo must be out of date. She remembers him as being politely short, if you know what I mean. Didn't offer much of a conversation, but he wasn't rude. And, apparently he was sweating quite a bit.'

'Well, it was quite hot on Saturday,' Kennedy recalled. 'And he had travelled all the way from London.'

'Yes, true, I'm just telling you everything she said. She thinks he may have caught a bus following his lunch.'

'Why?' quizzed Kennedy.

'Well, it seems he didn't have a car. He arrived by taxi and didn't order one when he left.'

'A right little Miss Marple, your Miss Gibson. Let's hope her friends last longer than the original's did.' Judging by the confused silence, DS Hardy was not an Agatha Christie fan.

'It's just that in the Miss Marple TV show, one of her friends dies every week,' Kennedy tried.

'Nothing wrong with being observant, sir,' replied the DS haughtily. 'It helps us, you know.'

'Yes, yes of course.' Obviously it wasn't Kennedy's day. 'Look, any idea where he may have caught a bus to?'

'Well, the 142 stops just outside the hotel. The bus on the hotel side takes you into Swanage, six miles down the road. From the opposite side of the street he would have travelled in the direction of Wareham, about eight miles. Another nine miles would take him into Poole,' explained the ever helpful DS Hardy. 'As requested by DS Irvine, I got the hotel to make a photocopy of the Access credit card slip and that will be faxed to you shortly. If there's anything else we can do for you, sir, please get in touch,' he concluded.

'Thanks a million, DS Hardy. You've been very helpful, very helpful.' Kennedy smiled as he returned the phone to its cradle.

So DS Hardy of Dorset CID had a confirmed(-ish) sighting of Peter O'Browne and a signature proving that O'Browne had been in Dorset about thirty hours before his London home was burnt out with an incendiary device. What was the connection? Indeed was there a connection?

A (Very) Short Scene

From the dew soaked Hedge
Creeps a crawly caterpillar
Well the dawn begins to crack
— Ray Davies

Kennedy received a call at 9.05am the following morning. He was in his office and the call was from Mary Jones, who was in a highly excited state.

'Mr Kennedy, ah shit, Detective Kennedy, he's rung. Peter's rung and he's alive.'

'Peter O'Browne telephoned you?'

'Yes. He called about 8.40 this morning and left a message saying that he was okay. He said he would get in touch later and not to worry, for me not to worry.

'It's so great sir, isn't it?'

'Yes. Brilliant news.' Kennedy was about to ask Mary Jones if she could dig out one of Peter's Gold Discs but he decided to leave it.

But only until later.

Chapter Twenty-One

One little Hitler does the other one's will
— Elvis Costello

The murder of a 62-year-old grandmother next occupied Kennedy's attention. This case troubled Kennedy, but not because it was particularly complicated – he expected the two youths seen running from the scene to be caught within twenty-four hours. No, it occupied his thoughts because this kind of crime was part of a growing trend in drug-related robberies on elderly people in Camden Town. The generation who had carried the country through lean times now found their meagre pensions, savings, TVs, videos (if they were lucky) pillaged to fund the purchase of whichever drugs were giving a buzz that particular week. The buzz was what had become important; what induced it, irrelevant.

Invariably the pensioners (six this year already) would be shoved out of the way, maybe to hit their heads on a sideboard or the floor. Perhaps they'd even be knocked over the head with a bat or bottle or, as was the case with Mrs Mavis McCarthy, strangled until all life had left their limbs.

Kennedy did not care to enter the debate about evil versus 'deprived' or 'abused' childhoods. It fell to him to deal with the aftermath of these horrific events, whatever their cause. A never-ending stream of experts was busy debating the issue on TV and radio talk shows, offering up their advice. 'Give them five years national service,' or, 'Sixty of the best lashes will mend their ways;' 'Let's find a way to bring these people back into society,' or, 'Give them back their sense of responsibility.' Not to mention: 'After what Thatcher did to the country, what do you expect?'

No, Kennedy had to help Alfie, Mavis McCarthy's husband of forty-three years. What do you say to a man whose wife's life – and effectively his own, too – suddenly and violently ends just because two shits need to score and decide that the easiest way is to attack a poor defenceless woman who had spent her entire life loving her husband and bringing up a family. How did you explain all this to the remaining half of a couple who had seen each other through the troubled years and who had been looking forward to a well-earned rest?

What words would make Alfie understand? What was there to understand, anyway? All he really had to do was accept that in this world the rule, 'Life's a bitch and then you die' applied.

Not content with strangling Mrs Mavis McCarthy, a former ticket seller at Camden Town underground station, the two funsters had totally wrecked the house. Destroyed everything, every piece of furniture; and, to add insult to injury, had spread their own shit on the walls and carpets. What kind of people do this? Do they do it because they know they can get away with it?

Kennedy had lost his temper in the squad room that morning, angry not at the police but at the injustice of the situation. There had been a briefing on the case and no conclusions had been offered, no suggestions made. It wasn't a 'sexy' (the new corporate word) enough case for that.

'Look, I want every one of you – every single one of you – to get out there on the streets. I want you to sit on every fucking druggy you know. I want you to talk, and I want you to look, and I want you to do everything you have to do to get these two bastards. The caretaker has given us a credible description of both of them and I want them in here by the end of the day. I don't care what you have to do to get them, either. Please,' Detective Inspector Christy Kennedy seethed with liquid anger, 'go out and find them!'

Off they scurried, shocked but not surprised at his fury.

'Aye, of course we'll get them. We'll get them, put them into the legal system and some do-gooder will put them back on the street again,' DS Irvine whispered to WPC Anne Coles as they left the briefing room.

'I know,' she replied in a return whisper. 'But at least he, all of us, will feel that we're doing our bit.'

Later that evening Kennedy was still fuming. When he had first started to see ann rea (and the relationship had had a shaky start), he had made a mental note of all the dos-and-don'ts which, if adhered to, would (hopefully) help it work. And Kennedy wanted it to work. The probable number one on Kennedy's list was, 'Don't bring your working troubles home.' Now there he was, breaking rule number one.

Luckily, ann rea understood. Sometimes she had to cover pensioner muggings for the *Camden News Journal*. And anyway, she was anxious that Kennedy should talk about his anger rather than bottle it up and hurt himself.

Kennedy allowed himself to be calmed by ann rea. She was an extraordinary woman. He never had to pretend with her and she seemed happy with him as he was. He wondered who had helped or taught her how to deal with her own pain. And then, on top of all of her consideration and understanding, she had the most beautiful body he had ever seen in his life. Kennedy knew this was a sexist thought, but shit, wasn't it true? There were times when he literally could not keep his hands off her. He couldn't believe that they had found each other, but he was happy that they had.

Particularly on a night like that. After a drink in The Queens they walked up to the top of Primrose Hill to gaze at one of the most amazing views in London and to have a good old fashioned snog, but not necessarily in that order.

*

Suitably recharged, he entered his office the following morning to find that the two suspects in the Mrs Mavis McCarthy murder had been picked up. The two herberts were still so high they had readily admitted to the murder; indeed they seemed quite proud of it. 'Yeah, like, the old bag, like, we had to do her in, didn't we mate, she got in our faces, know what I mean?' one of them had sniffed.

Kennedy was relieved that he didn't have to interview them or suffer any contact.

On his desk was a note saying that Mary Jones had rung him late the previous evening. He called her back, fully expecting to be told that Peter O'Browne had returned to the office, that all was well and everyone was going to live happily ever after.

This seldom, if ever, is the case.

Mary was distraught again. 'You know Inspector, I've been thinking. Peter knows I never arrive in the office before 9.00am, ever. He just wouldn't ring me here before that. He would have called me at home. I've checked with the receptionist. She's new and she couldn't remember anything about the call apart from the fact it was brief. If someone wanted to pretend to be Peter, then early morning would be the best time, before I got in. Do you see what I mean?' she pleaded into the electric void.

'Yes, I see where you're going,' Kennedy replied, wondering how many more Miss Marples would turn up on the case. 'But equally we would have to accept that whoever is ghosting for Peter knows both his and your usual movements.'

'This has been driving me mad. After I got over the feeling of euphoria of thinking he was in contact again, I started to wonder why he was behaving so weirdly. Then I started to get a bad feeling about it all and it won't go away. I didn't know what to do apart from to ring you,' blurted Mary.

'Okay, look here's the thing,' Kennedy soothed. 'By about eleven this morning, I'll have the results of the handwriting tests on the credit card receipts from Waterloo and Corfe Castle. Let me ring after eleven and we'll talk some more.'

Chapter Twenty-Two

Oh the water,
Let it flow all over me
– Van Morrison

As it happened, Detective Inspector Christy Kennedy was too preoccupied to get back to Mary Jones quite as quickly as he'd promised. 'A little hush, please,' he announced to the packed briefing room. In five seconds, he had a lot of hush.

'Okay, we are now treating the Peter O'Browne case not as a missing person but as a murder,' he advised his captive audience. The hush evaporated in an instant.

The body of Peter O'Browne had been found in a building in Mayfair Mews, a tiny cul-de-sac impassable to cars, between number 75 and the florists, Fitzroy's, at number 77 Regents Park Road, Primrose Hill Village.

The scene there was still as vivid in Kennedy's mind as the wagging jaws that faced him. Peter O'Browne had been lying lifeless on the cold concrete floor of a building he had hoped to convert into a recording studio. The corpse looked as if it had been laid out by an undertaker. The heels, tight together, faced the door of the building, the arms were crossed, outstretched hands resting on opposite shoulders. Someone had placed a penny – an old penny – on each eyelid.

There were no visible clues. The floor was clean, though perhaps only to the naked eye, Kennedy had thought. O'Browne looked so peaceful, and there were no outward signs of violence. His clothes – brown cords, bottle green long sleeved pullover (not designer) – were unruffled; even his hair appeared to have been recently combed. But that would have been too bizarre, wouldn't it?

Trusty Dr Leonard Taylor and his new stunning assistant Bella Forsythe had carried out their examination in Kennedy's presence. Kennedy was still queasy about being around or touching a corpse but Dr Taylor, chubby, affable, theatrical, moved effortlessly about the dead body as he worked.

'Ah!' he had exclaimed, proud of a find. 'Rope burns around the neck.' He continued his search respectfully, but not apologetically. 'More of them on the wrists,' he added as he moved instinctively to the feet. 'Yes, and more on the ankles.'

'The burns are darker around the neck. Perhaps the rope carried his weight.'

Kennedy refrained from commenting, or questioning, knowing he would only provoke the 'Too early to tell' retort.

'See how the skin is lighter around the mouth?' Dr Taylor continued, happy in his solo performance on the stage. 'He had tape stuck over it.'

Kennedy left Dr Taylor to finish his examination, his fingers unconsciously flexing as he paced the room. It was a large room, about forty- by-twenty-foot, built of white painted breeze blocks. The roof was of corrugated zinc resting on A frames. Every eighth roof sheet was perspex which allowed some natural light. To the left, as you entered the main room from the mews, was a door which took you back on yourself to a little kitchen area through to a larger sitting room, serviced by a small bathroom. A badly painted staircase led to another floor which had what was perhaps a bedroom, though it was a bit on the small side, and a full bathroom with a bath and sink. The annex was covered with a cheap grey carpet throughout.

There was no through route from the upstairs of the annex to the double-height area where Peter O'Browne's body had been found.

Kennedy returned to the main room and made his way past the corpse to the wall opposite the mews door. This wall, about eight feet high, was mostly glass, (double panes about ten feet apart) with double sliding glass doors, obviously a sound-proofing device. The first door was stiff. One of the scene-of-crime officers came to Kennedy's assistance. The doors led into a lower-ceilinged room with no natural light, whose walls were covered with a bulky fawn canvas-like material.

All the areas, with the exception of the main room, were littered with rubbish: cardboard boxes, broken chairs, tables with three legs, old newspapers, parts of an (obviously defunct) air-conditioning system, disconnected electric flex and a very sad-looking broken acoustic guitar with a single string, which had apparently played its last note a long time ago.

Perhaps someone had made the effort to tidy up the main room by distributing its rubbish to the remaining rooms, so crowded were they. The only furniture left behind was what looked like two mobile platforms, both eight-foot square with one inch solid tops and skeleton sides. 'They look like drum-risers, sir,' one of the SoC officers suggested. 'I've seen them at concerts where the drummer will set up his entire kit on one of these.'

Kennedy wandered, fingers furiously flexing, back towards Dr Taylor. DS Irvine was carefully removing the two pennies from Peter O'Browne's eyelids. 'I haven't seen that in a long long time,' he commented. 'Not since I was a lad at a wake in Stirling.' He cautiously placed the pennies in individual plastic evidence bags which he duly sealed and marked up.

'Yes,' Doctor Taylor explained. 'Sometimes the eyes of a corpse won't close and this tends to bother people: the piercing eyes of death.

So coins – usually 10p coins these days – are placed on the eyelids. Hides the glare from the other side.'

'But why use old pennies?' DS Irvine said, his eyes still on the corpse.

'Look at the body. Look at the hands, at the feet. This body has been "laid out". As if someone is emphasising the death. "There, it's done: you're dead." Death marked a finality of some sort, apart from the obvious finality of death itself. This is a statement, a resolution. The murderer has taken the trouble to show off his corpse.'

Kennedy walked around the body, studying it, looking for something, anything, to give him a hint of the killer's intention.

Something was troubling him about the smell in the atmosphere. Yes, there was a smell of death and a smell of mustiness from the rubbish, and the smell from a large damp patch on the floor about six feet away from the body. But there was another smell too, something he remembered from his youth. He couldn't quite put his finger, or even his nose, on it.

How unlike the corpse of Marianne MacIntyre and the scene of her murder. There, clues had littered the place, vying with each other for attention. Together they had revealed the most obvious aspect of her death: that although Marianne had been killed unlawfully, her murder had not been premeditated. To some degree Brian Hurst had been a victim of circumstance (certainly of his own circumstances), and things, to use a well-known cliché, had just got out of hand.

But as the three of them knelt around the body of Peter O'Browne, Kennedy couldn't help feeling that this time the perpetrator had been proud of his (or her, as in 15 per cent of cases) work and had probably spent many a long hour planning it.

Such people scared Kennedy. People who could wake up one day and over breakfast plan the end of another's life, offering them as much compassion as they did their eggs. This was something with which Kennedy would never come to terms. These were people with whom he would never come to terms.

On that cold morning Kennedy felt that the calm, so different from the usual murder scene, was deceptive.

'I would say,' offered Dr Taylor, 'that our friend here has been dead for at least twelve hours.'

'I would say,' came the reply from Kennedy, 'that you had better wait until you carry out the autopsy and come up with a more accurate time for me.'

The Doctor bowed one of his 'touché' bows.

Chapter Twenty-Three

If songs were lines
In a conversation
The situation
Would be fine

— Nick Drake

Kennedy stopped off at ann rea's on his way back from Mayfair Mews. This was a very rare occurrence, so rare in fact that it had only one precedent, an occasion when he had picked her up for a dinner date. Kennedy broke the news of how Peter O'Browne's body had been found early that morning by a British Telecom engineer who had arrived to reconnect one of the studio phone lines – a line that was now being used by Kennedy's colleagues as a SoC site phone.

The BT engineer had picked the keys up from Camden Town Records the previous afternoon. Mary Jones had seen no reason to refuse him the keys. Despite her misgivings, she was hopeful that Peter would soon return, and anyway she didn't want to risk waiting another three months for the BT chaps to fit in another visit.

'I'll have to go and tell Mary Jones the bad news and I wondered whether you'd like to come with me. She'll need a shoulder to cry on.'

'Sure, sure.'

Kennedy was in ann rea's souped-up maroon Ford Popular. As they drove up Delancey Street, she asked him, 'So what was all that business about Corfe Castle and the phone calls?'

'Oh, stalling, some kind of delaying tactic, I would imagine. Maybe the killer was trying to prevent us from looking for the body. The good doctor reckons he died around nine-thirty yesterday evening.'

'So what was he doing from Friday last through to Wednesday evening? ann rea questioned as she crossed the lights where Delancey Street runs into Parkway. They turned right into Gloucester Crescent, where ann rea parked her prize possession.

'For some reason someone was stalling us, diverting our attention,' Kennedy repeated as he ascended the steps of Camden Town Records.

The extremely hip receptionist, a follower of 'stares-at-shoes' type of bands, took ann rea and Kennedy straight through to Mary Jones' office. When Mary saw the solemn look upon both their faces, the colour drained from her cheeks and she sank into her chair.

'He's dead, isn't he? You've found him, and he's dead. He's dead.' Mary spoke like someone using a Walkman and headphones, unaware of the volume of her voice.

'Yes. I'm sorry, yes. Peter O'Browne was found about two hours ago, and he is dead. We have reason to believe…' Kennedy was just getting into official-speak when she cut him off.

'But why?' Tears gathered in her eyes and started to roll down her cheeks. She hadn't heard a word Kennedy had said after 'dead'.

ann rea crossed the room to comfort the Welsh woman, holding her close as she sobbed uncontrollably.

Kennedy left them alone for a few minutes to order up some tea with extra sugar for Mary. When he returned he inquired, 'Is there anyone we can ring?'

'No. No, I'll be okay.' Mary coughed through the sobs. She blew her nose and tried to dry her face, as best she could with a tear-stained handkerchief. 'No, it's okay, really. I've been dreading this moment since Monday lunchtime and I…' ann rea gently patted her on the back with one hand as the other hand gently soothed her luxurious black curls.

'I just kept telling myself that I wanted to know. It's not knowing, that's the worst. But now I'm not so sure. At least then there was always some kind of chance that Peter would turn up, but now… You know, he really was very, very, good to me. I've been with him eight-and-a-half-years.' Mary tried a watery smile. 'And he was always, always great to me. No funny business, if you know what I mean. And not a lot of girls in this industry can say that.

'He was hard work some of the time, but… but…' she subsided into ann rea's arms, her face creased with grief.

Kennedy admired the silent strength of ann rea. 'Perhaps we should ring Leslie Russell,' ann rea offered.

'Yes,' agreed Mary as Kennedy lifted the phone.

'Three, eight, seven…' Mary recited as Kennedy punched the digits thoughtfully on her phone. 'I told you it wasn't Peter who rang me yesterday morning, she said. 'I think that's when I really started to panic. I knew that he wouldn't ring me here, so early. Oh my God.' She had caught sight of her reflection in the mirror just behind Kennedy's left shoulder as he sat at her desk on the telephone. 'I'm a mess, a complete mess. I'm going to be no use to anybody like this.' She excused herself and made for the lavatory.

'I thought she would take it a lot worse,' ann rea offered as soon as Mary had left the room.

'Yes, perhaps. But there is always a delayed reaction, which hits even harder once the reality has sunk in,' Kennedy replied. He raised his right hand to signify that he had Leslie Russell on the phone.

After the telephone conversation, he advised ann rea, 'Leslie Russell is on the way over. He'll be here in a few minutes.'

A thought occurred to ann rea. Startled, she shared it with Kennedy before it had even properly formed. 'Do you think Mary is in any danger? You know, being Peter's secretary and all, that perhaps she knows something of why Peter was killed.'

Kennedy had no time to reply before Mary Jones reentered the room, followed very closely by Leslie Russell who took her in his arms and gave her a huge, warm hug which, in an instant, destroyed all of Mary's repairs she'd just effected in front of the mirror in the lavatory.

Chapter Twenty-Four

And don't speak too soon
For the wheel's still in spin
And there's no tellin' who
That it's namin'

– Bob Dylan

Twenty minutes later, Detective Inspector Christy Kennedy was back in North Bridge House in the briefing room, hushing his team again.

'As far as Dr Taylor can tell us, Mr Peter O'Browne was murdered, probably by hanging, at approximately 9.30, yesterday evening.

'So, what we have so far is this: On the evening of Friday October 3rd at around 8.20pm, Peter O'Browne and his assistant, Miss Mary Jones, were leaving the offices of Camden Town Records when Peter stopped to take a telephone call. That was the last time he was seen alive. He failed to keep an appointment with Mary later that evening at the Forum in Kentish Town.

'The next day someone, probably not Peter, used his Access card to purchase a rail ticket from Waterloo to Wareham. The card was used again to pay for lunch at Corfe Castle, Dorset the same day, and – so our handwriting expert tells us – it was the same person. Although the signature is similar to Peter O'Browne's they feel it is a forgery, a good forgery, but a forgery, nonetheless.

'Early yesterday morning at approximately 8.45, someone claiming to be Peter O'Browne rang Camden Town Records and asked to speak to Mary Jones. On being told that she had not yet arrived, he asked the receptionist to tell Mary he'd called. Mary maintained that this couldn't have been Peter, as he would know that she was never in the office before 9am.

'Now, we have to assume that the phone call which interrupted his departure from the office last Friday had something to do with his disappearance. As I'm sure you will agree, Gaul!'

Kennedy had noticed that PC Gaul was not only not paying attention but was also competing with him for the attention of WPC Anne Coles. After a pause, Kennedy said conversationally, 'Tell you what, Gaul, do something useful for a change, will you? Go and fetch half a dozen teas and half a dozen coffees.' PC Gaul was obliged to acquiesce to the humiliating order and left the room rather sheepishly.

'Now,' Kennedy continued, assured of everyone's undivided attention. 'Someone must have seen Mr O'Browne between Friday and yesterday evening.'

'Perhaps the call was from someone asking Peter O'Browne to meet them at Mayfair Mews Studio, sir?' offered Anne Coles, happy to be rid of the pest, Gaul. 'And whoever it was kept him there by force until they murdered him last night.'

'Why not murder him right away, then?' countered DS James Irvine. 'Why all this fuss over the telephone calls and the trip to Dorset?'

'Why, indeed?' said Kennedy. 'Let's make some kind of start on this, anyway. Allaway, West, Franklin and our good friend Gaul, when he returns from tea duty, you all start with door-to-door from here up to and including Mayfair Mews on Regents Park Road. Take copies of the photograph with you and see what you can dig up.'

Kennedy then nodded in the direction of his Detective Sergeant. 'DS Irvine, get on to the media: *Evening Standard, Camden News Journal*, GLR, local TV news, radio. Send them the photo.'

'You'll have trouble getting a response on GLR, sir,' Irvine smiled. From him, in his soft Scottish accent, the reply had sounded funny rather than smart ass.

Kennedy smiled and continued, 'Yes, well, let's get the story out as soon as poss. And appeal for any information. Someone must have seen Mr. Peter O'Browne during his missing five days.'

The tea and coffee arrived at that point in the capable hands of PC Gaul, short-haired and red-faced. Each officer in turn took his or her tea or coffee and added, as personal taste dictated, milk and sugar. A packet of McVities Hobnobs appeared from somewhere and some severe dunking took place.

'Now we have to address the issues we were investigating, but which didn't seem to be getting us anywhere, when Mr O'Browne was merely a missing person, namely, chart hyping, and possible blackmailing over the hyping.

'Apparently our friends over at the Fraud Squad have investigated chart hyping a couple of times, so let's contact them, WPC Coles, and see if they can give us any leads worth following.

'DS Irvine, you and WPC Coles go and visit Tom Best, he was involved with O'Browne at the record shop and in the record company until he sold a share to Grabaphone; and Paddy George, his partner in the record store Camden Records. I'll speak to Martyn Farrelly, the first artist he ever signed. Let's talk to all of them as soon as possible; I want to hear what they say unprepared. There's going to be an almighty splash in the papers when we go with this. I can see the headline now: *Camden Pop Mogul Murdered!*

'Forensic are currently working on the Mayfair Mews studio. Dr Taylor has promised us the results of the autopsy late this afternoon. So let's see how much info we can pick up before we all meet back here for an update.'

Just as they were all about to leave, Kennedy added, 'And don't forget...' Everybody expected the classic *Hill St Blues* opener, "Let's be careful out there." Instead Kennedy counselled, 'Let's be sure to thank PC Gaul for the tea.'

Chapter Twenty-Five

It's only knock and know all
– Peter Gabriel

Although WPC Anne Coles and DS James Irvine had known each other and worked together for quite some time, they had never been officially partnered before.

'You can be Watson and I'll be Holmes,' laughed Irvine, filling the deafening silence caused by the absence of a radio-cassette player in the police car.

'No, I think not,' retorted Anne. 'You should be Lewis.' She pulled in on the left of Kentish Town Road, just up from Camden Town Tube Station. As she neutralised the gears and pulled on the handbrake she added, 'We could have walked, you know. Particularly with the traffic like this. It will take us a lot longer to get back.'

'Aye, you're right. I didn't realise it was this end of Kentish Town Road. Ah well, now we're here we might as well get on and see what this Tom Best has to say for himself.'

Tom Best ran his business above a record shop, as he and O'Browne had done in the early days of Camden Town Records. The shop, crowded with people and cramped with records was unusual for the nineties in that it was what it claimed to be: a record shop, with not a CD or cassette in sight.

The posters cramming every square inch of the wall clearly indicated that the shop's clientele preferred the music of Elvis Costello, The Clash, The Stranglers, The Sex Pistols, The Beatles, The Stones and The Kinks to the likes of '90s Bratpop. All racked releases, however, seemed to be on sale at prices way in excess of the original list price. The only time Take That would be mentioned in this store was when a happy customer used the words, 'I'll take that' to secure a mint copy of Elvis Costello's 'My Aim is True'. Such a purchase could set you back £50.

Neither Coles nor Irvine were into records, as in the vinyl variety, although both could boast of owning a few CDs. WPC Coles was happy to leave behind the musty smell of the shop as they made their way up the staircase they'd been directed to by the shop assistant who, by the look of him, was a train-spotter who still lived with his mum in Clapham Junction.

The posters continued up the stairwell, at the head of which they found Tom Best waiting for them. He greeted them (not warmly) and directed them through to his office which effectively occupied the entire first floor. All internal walls had been knocked through to create an open plan L-shaped room, complete with wooden beams (fake wooden facade with steel RSJ hidden centre) marking the lines along the ceiling, where a wall had once been.

The floors and window frames were exposed pine and well worn rather than shined. The walls had been exposed back to the original red brick, helping to create an overall olde worlde Americana feel. DS Irvine was entirely happy with this atmosphere, but WPC Coles couldn't help thinking that the room would benefit from a coat of white paint and a few carpets – red or blue, perhaps – to warm it up a bit.

DS Irvine noted that, apart from three gold discs, the walls here were not crowded. Careful examination revealed that the discs were 'presented to Tom Best from Camden Town Records for sales (UK) in excess of 100,000 units.' The artists achieving these sales were Wire Crates, Radio Cars and Half Moon Bay Express. Scattered around other spaces were various gravity games like the five silver balls suspended in a silver frame, and the blue water creating waves in a perspex container balancing precariously on a wooden fulcrum.

Tom Best sat down on a sofa used to give business meetings an informal tone, and invited the WPC and DS to join him in a couple of facing easy-chairs. There was no offer of refreshment.

'So, what can I do for you?' their host began. Anne Coles noticed that he formed the first word of his sentence with his lips a split second before his mouth produced the sound. Best had a wiry frame, the 'before' body in the Charles Atlas adverts. He wore a starched white shirt and a thin black leather tie, knotted slightly lopsided. He had black linen Japanese slip-ons, white socks and black jeans.

'Well,' WPC Coles began, since the DS was clearly waiting for her to speak. 'I'm afraid that a former colleague of yours was murdered last night.'

Both Coles and Irvine noticed that beneath the thick red hair spilling over Best's forehead, there was a slight widening of the eyelids behind the Lennon-style granny glasses. Apart from that little flicker there was no other acknowledgement of her news.

'Peter O'Browne, with whom we believe you worked for several years, was killed last evening at about 9.30,' the WPC continued, taking a note book from her top pocket, 'and we have a few questions we'd like to ask you.'

Tom Best was coming to the end of a hand-rolled cigarette. He performed the pot smoker's ritual of sticking three skins (Rizla papers) together (two long sides together and placing the third long side along the two short ends of the first two). However, now that he was in the presence of the constabulary, he left out the most important ingredient and settled for just tobacco. He lit the new ciggy with the old one, which he then stubbed in an ashtray as packed as the Rolling Stones gig at Brixton Academy in '95. The ashtray stood on a fifteen-inch cube box (stripped wood containing magazines and records) which also served as a small coffee table.

Best mouthed the word, 'Well,' before speaking: 'Well, well,' he smiled. 'So some bastard had the guts to pay him back.'

Holmes and Lewis were both shocked at the reply but only DS Irvine showed it.

'Look,' again a delay while he first formed the word. 'You're going to find all this out anyway, so you'd better hear it from me.' Best paused as he used the thumb and third finger, of his ciggy hand to remove a piece of tobacco from between his teeth.

'I was with him in the very beginning when his so-called record company was a complete and horrible mess. He brought me in – we'd been mates at Trinity College Dublin – to organise his company.

'Don't get me wrong. Peter O'Browne had his qualities. He was great at spotting artists, he was great at planning campaigns, he was great at schmoozing the artists and their managers, but he was crap, absolute crap, when it came to the follow-through; all the organisation, all the meat and potato stuff. Quite frankly it bored him. Bored him to the degree where he'd ignore it completely.' His Northern Ireland accent was kind of slow, something like Alex Higgins on Valium. Every sentence sounded either like a question or an apology.

'So, to cut a very, very long story short, I covered all of those areas for him and I'll admit he did pay me very well for it in the early days. But he'd always avoid my requests for a formal partnership. He'd just wedge me up a bit more. I wanted, and felt entitled to, a piece of the company but he always put me off with, "Don't worry I'll take care of you". He never did. We just worked harder and harder.

'I mean don't get me wrong, there was fun in the middle of all the hard work, a lot of fun, and we were going to change the music business. We were going to be the first record company to look after our artists.'

'What do you mean, "look after your artists?" Isn't that what record companies generally do?' interrupted DS Irvine trying unsuccessfully to find a comfortable position in the inappropriately named easy-chair.

Best's delicate face smiled an 'oh-you-think-so?' kind of smile. His mouth formed an 'A' and he continued, 'Ah, you think so?

'Not so! Look, go to an artist, any artist, and I guarantee you that 99 out of a hundred will have a gripe with their record company.'

'You mean like George Michael?' asked WPC Coles.

'Well, that's just a well-publicised fall out. But that could be just greed. I mean, you have him and Prince going on about being slaves. That's a laugh. Both of them make more money in a second than any genuine slave would make in a lifetime.

'But down the scale from that, artists feel that their record companies make too much money and don't promote them properly. The artists hate their artwork, hate the final sound of their CDs compared to the sound they spent hundreds of thousands of pounds of their own money creating in the studio. The artists hate interference from the knowledge-less record company executives, hate the fact that the record companies waste millions of pounds – usually millions of pounds the artists made for the record company in the first place – on talent less new artists.

'These new artists in turn hate the fact that the record companies spend millions of pounds promoting the old over-the-hill farts at their expense. Together the old and the new artists hate the fact that they spend their own money recording and then the record companies deduct packaging costs, tour support, video costs, and so on and so on and so on, from the artist's share .

'At the end of it all, who will own the masters of these works? Yes you've got it: the record companies. *That's* immoral.'

'But surely the record companies have to make some money too?' DS Irvine offered, not really sure why he was defending them.

'Oh they do. Believe me, they do.

'What we were trying to do at Camden Town Records was to change all that, in our own small way. Try to make it more of a partnership thing between the artist and the record company.' Tom Best paused in order to commence the cigarette rolling-up performance once again.

'How were you planning to do this?' WPC Anne Coles inquired. She couldn't see for the life of her what all this might have to do with the death of Peter O'Browne but the more they found out, the greater was the chance of a motive rearing its ugly head above the water.

'Well, we wanted to dump packaging deductions, which we did. It's really just another way for record companies to claw back money from the artist's royalties. We worked out a system whereby if an artist was in credit at the end of their contract, then two years later we would give them back their masters.'

'Why is it so important for the artists to own their masters?' asked DS Irvine.

'It's their work, their birthright. Okay, at the early stage of a record company's investment it is only fair that it should be allowed to seek a return on its investment. Although the artist's money is used to record the album, it's the record company who put the money up front.'

Best lit ciggy number three with ciggy number two. 'However. after that money has been repaid, and a bit more besides, the lion's share should belong to the artist. And when artists move from record company to record company they should be allowed to move with their entire catalogue, so that they can use it as a negotiating plus at the shallow end of their careers.

'The big record companies are fighting this, like they are trying to avoid the atomic inevitability of a third world war. But the reality is that the balance of power is not going to switch much. Because yes, the record company will lose his catalogue when Joe Bloggs leaves it but, equally it will gain the catalogue of Jane Bloggs when she joins it.'

'Okay so what else were you going to do?' pressed the WPC.

'Oh,' was a much easier word and took a lot less time for Best to form. 'Oh, involve them a lot more in their careers, really, just try to do everything necessary to show them that the record company does not need to be the enemy, but should in fact be the partner.

'We also agreed that we would never ever sign an artist in whom we, as a company, did not believe; no matter how strong we felt the commercial potential might be.'

'All sounds great to me,' smiled DS Irvine. 'So what went wrong?'

Best sighed, 'All our principles seem only to be our principles in theory. When we became successful Peter started playing by the rules of the big boys. We were in danger of becoming what we had supposedly hated, or at least what I had hated.

'It transpired that Peter had other goals in mind. He wanted to become a major player. Bit by bit, he changed our deals to fit in with the big boys. All the time he had been planing to sell out.

'I couldn't believe it: all the people he was prepared to shaft just so that he could pocket six million quid. I just couldn't believe it. He negotiated a salary of two hundred and fifty Gs for himself. He had just taken six million and he was worried about his salary. It must have been the status which appealed to him. You know, being the highest paid MD in London at that time.

'He was pissed off that I wouldn't go with him for ninety Gs a year. He wouldn't even talk about it. I took him out to get him pissed, like in the old days, and to remind him about our dreams as an artist-friendly record company. But all he kept on saying was, "Things have changed Tom, things have changed." Fucking sure things had changed.

'I suppose it's like Dylan said, "Money doesn't talk, it swears".'

It seemed to WPC Coles that Tom Best mouthed the whole of his next sentence before he voiced it.

'He'd become a fucking asshole,' Best spat. He took a deep drag on his cigarette and squinted as the smoke passed his eyes.

'So I figured, okay, that's the way he wants to go, that's his choice, but it's not mine. So I told him I was going to leave and start up again and asked for my share of the buy-out. He hit the roof.' Ciggy number three became four. 'He went berserk. Said it was his company and he would do what he wanted with it. It had nothing whatsoever to do with me.

'I reminded him that we both had built up Camden Town Records and he gave me some shit about there being lots of great foot soldiers but only a few generals. I told him that just because he was bald didn't make him Napoleon, which didn't go down too well.

'I genuinely thought that he'd beat me down to two of the six million pounds; hell maybe even a million. But O'Browne didn't want to give me a penny. It was only after a bit of wrangling that Russell, his solicitor, persuaded him to give me a hundred grand.' Best himself now was moving about in the sofa to find a comfortable position in his tight black jeans.

'When did you last see Peter O'Browne?' WPC Coles asked, wafting some of Best's cigarette smoke away from her face and wondering if she could sue the force if she contracted cancer. The smell of this hand-rolling stuff made her glad she'd given up smoking.

'I've seen him around gigs from time to time and around Camden Town now and then. But I've had no direct dealings with him since that final chat. All contact has been through his solicitor. And I've seen some of his staff from time to time.'

'Is there anyone you know who might have wanted to kill Peter O'Browne?' WPC Coles asked, ticking off another question from the ever-shortening list in her mind's eye.

'God, take your pick. Any of the long list of people that he crossed. It's not for me to say, but there are a lot of people out there who were unhappy with Peter O'Browne,' Best replied.

'Including yourself, sir?' posed DS Irvine, with a hint of a smile to make his question seem less threatening.

Best appeared to be practising his first word before he uttered, 'Listen, I can't tell you I loved the guy: that's why I've told you all this shit. But murder? No, not my style. No, sorry, not me.' After a few seconds thought, he puffed on his roll-up and continued, 'I'd take more satisfaction from making my company...' Best gestured around the tidy room, dropping fag ash in an arc as he did, '...Artists Co-op Records, more successful than Camden Town Records, and proving that our original ideals can work.'

As cigarette five made its way to his mouth he said, 'I only chain smoke because I can't afford the matches.' Coming from someone who smoked less, this remark might have been faintly funny, but from Tom Best, it did little to excuse the stale smell of smoke he would carry round with him. Anne Coles, with the self-righteousness of a recently quit smoker, pitied whoever shared his bed.

'What were you doing yesterday evening between the hours of eight o'clock and midnight, sir?' she asked.

The officialese hit Best like the ball you half-expect to hit you on the back of the head but which shocks you more because the precise moment of impact can never be predicted.

'Well, that's easy. We had a small dinner party at my house last night. The first Wednesday of every month six of us get together for dinner and a chat. Last night it was our turn, Mavis – my partner – and I.'

'What time did you all meet?' the WPC continued.

'Let's see. Brian and Sally were there by seven-thirty. I know because we all watched *Coronation Street* together, and Ted and John arrived just before eight,' Tom Best responded precisely.

'And what time did they leave?'

'Now, let's see,' Best began as DS Irvine tried unsuccessfully to guess from the shape of Best's lips what his first word would be. 'Brian and Sally left just after 11.30. They had promised the baby-sitter that they would be home by midnight at the latest. And as for Ted and John, I'm afraid we usually have to tip the house on its end to get them out. I think it was probably around 1.20 to 1.30am. They finally took the hint when Mavis made her excuses and went to bed.'

'Thank you. That would seem to be all for now, sir,' the DS announced as he and WPC Coles rose to leave. Best extinguished his roll-up and stood up too. For the first time since the meeting began, he was without a cigarette.

'Oh, just one more thing...' DS Irvine was trying his Columbo trick. 'What time did you get home from the office?'

'Mavis picked me up at about 6.30pm.'

'We may have some more questions, sir,' warned Irvine. 'If we do, someone will get back to you.'

WPC Anne Coles was not impressed with Tom Best and said so as they left the record shop.

DS Irvine agreed with her. 'Aye. He's the kind of guy who farts just as he's about to leave a full lift.'

Chapter Twenty-Six

The love you don't give words to
Is a love you give away
— Mary Margaret O'Hara

Kennedy and PC Gaul parked – that is, PC Gaul parked and Kennedy sat in the passenger seat – on Duke's Avenue in the heart of Muswell Hill. Martyn Farrelly resided among humble houses, but his own was quite grand. It was made up of two mews houses converted into one at the northern end of Dukes Mews.

The sound of the bell summoned an oblique figure to the thick glass door within seconds. The shadow metamorphosed into the owner of the house, Mr Martyn Farrelly, an important figure in the Peter O'Browne story. If only Detective Inspector Christy Kennedy knew at that point how important he was going to be.

'Hello,' began Farrelly as his eyes took in the details of the couple on his doorstep. One in police uniform, the other not. 'Can I help?' The musician was dressed only for indoor pursuits. He wore a blue crinkly tracksuit, matching top and bottom with a broad white stripe down both arms and legs. His hair was long but as the red scalp was partially visible, he would have looked better with a trim. His movements were tentative, lacking a confidence his bushy moustache failed to deliver.

'I'm Detective Inspector Christy Kennedy.' The owner of the twitching fingers rummaged in an inside jacket pocket for his ID. 'And this is PC Gaul.'

'Yes?' The voice was obviously originally from Ulster but had been so tempered by years of living in London and watching too many movies and US TV shows that it now hinted at an American twang.

'It would be easier if we could come in, sir, at least off the doorstep.' Kennedy wanted to observe, in the potentially more revealing context of his home, Martyn Farrelly's reaction to the news that Peter O'Browne, his ex-manager and former best friend, was dead.

'God – yes, yes, I'm sorry. Of course, come in,' Farrelly replied, opening the door fully and ushering them in.

'Thank you. Where shall we go?' asked Kennedy. The hallway smelled the way Kennedy believed a home should smell: homely. A rich blend of the aromas of gorgeous furniture polish, the flowers on the hat stand, disinfectant from the toilet, and the mouth-watering smell of freshly-baked bread wafting out into the hall from somewhere in the basement.

'I'm afraid we have some bad news,' Kennedy continued as he awaited Farrelly's directions.

Farrelly was now clearly distressed. He was openly having trouble deciding where to take Kennedy and Gaul. If they were to be the bearers of bad news, he did not want to take them to the heart of his home, the source of the fresh bread aroma.

'Who is it, Martyn?' an apparently Scottish voice called from the basement.

'It's the police – two policemen. I'm going to take them through to the music room.' His wife's words seemed to have shaken him from his spell of indecision.

'Oh Martyn, where are your manners?' the faceless voice replied. They could hear footsteps climbing the stairs and as the owner of the basement voice came into view, busily-wiping her flour-covered hands in her Guinness apron. A striking woman with dark eyebrows and long flowing blonde hair, she was probably slightly older than Farrelly's early-forties. 'Tea, Martyn. See if they want any tea.' She then turned directly to Kennedy, and, nudging Farrelly playfully in the ribs, said, 'Hello. I'm Colette, his wife.'

And strength, Kennedy thought to himself.

'Would you like a cup of tea?' she asked again.

Kennedy thought, 'Does a bear shit in the woods?' but in fact said, 'Yes that would be absolutely brilliant, I'd... we'd love a cup of tea, wouldn't we, PC Gaul?' taking immediately to this fine, warm, family woman.

'Youse go through to the music room with Martyn and I'll be through shortly,' Colette smiled as she vanished down the stairs.

Before they sat down, in the music room, Kennedy began: 'We believe you know a Mr Peter O'Browne?'

'Yes?' said Farrelly urgently, restricting his reply to a single word to speed up the procedure and get the bad news over and done with. He brushed his fingers through his shoulder length hair, as if by tidying his hair he was better preparing himself. He would not have made a good poker player.

'Well, I'm afraid we have to tell you that he's dead. He was murdered yesterday evening,' Kennedy said softly.

'What?' Farrelly groaned as he fell into one of the sofas in his music room. The room so named because it was where Farrelly carried out his work, or his art, if there can be said to be a difference. Right at that moment though, it was merely an empty white room moving on a stormy sea for Martyn Farrelly. Having difficulty finding his land-legs, he surrendered to the comfort and safety of the sofa.

'What?' he repeated in a high-pitched squeak. 'When? How? What happened? Was it an accident?'

'No sir, it was not an accident, he was murdered,' Kennedy repeated carefully.

'Woohagh! God! I just can't believe this. Peter dead? Murdered?

Are you sure that you are talking about the right man?'

'Positive, I'm afraid.' replied Kennedy noticing that the last of the blood had drained from Farrelly's face.

'What can I do? How can I help?' Farrelly inquired.

'We're trying to find out all we can about him to discover why anyone would want to kill such a decent fellow. Maybe then we can find out who did kill such a decent fellow.' Kennedy was struggling to keep his question going. He felt that in posing a question you needed to give your interviewee enough to bite on to reduce the chance of a straight yes or no answer. The longer his answer, the greater the chance that they will give something away.

At that moment Colette Farrelly tapped gently on the door to alert them to her presence and let herself in turning the door knob with one hand while the other precariously balanced a tray. PC Gaul, showing that he had a few uses, rushed up to help. Kennedy noticed that there were four cups upon the tray, indicating that Colette intended to join them. Farrelly would probably talk more comfortably and freely in the company of his wife.

In a way Kennedy was already moderately envious of this couple. Sometimes, but rarely these days, you find a married couple: a married couple the sum of whose combination was greater than the total of the parts. This was one such couple.

'Okay, Martyn you be mother,' Colette began. She had removed the apron and tidied her hair, freshened-up her make-up. She hadn't needed to, she had a physical power beyond beauty. This woman probably looked incredible the moment she woke up, she would look equally incredible under a mechanic's grease. She had a presence shared with ann rea. But her physical and mental power did little or nothing to connect with her husband at that moment.

He stared at her and said, 'Peter's dead, Colette. Someone has murdered him.'

The role of mother was played by Detective Inspector Christy Kennedy. He coaxed Colette, 'Milk and sugar?'

'Yes, fine, yes. Sorry. It's such a shock.' Her pallor now matched her husband's. 'We haven't seen Peter for some time, of course, but it's still a shock. Martyn and he were very close at one stage, early on in their careers.'

Kennedy suspended a full teaspoon of sugar over the virgin tea.

'That's how we met, you know, Martyn and I,' she offered. 'I was working for Martyn's music publisher, BPE Music. Martyn was in this group, Blues by Five. BPE published their songs – Martyn's songs – and Peter was the manager. 'God we've all come a long way since then.' Colette smiled and noticed Kennedy's hand poised to sweeten her tea. 'No. Sorry, no I wasn't thinking straight. Not for me, thank you, just milk. And two sugars and milk for Martyn, please.'

'Are you okay dear?' she almost whispered to her husband.

'Yes, yes thanks,' Farrelly touched the back of her hand gently and appeared to draw strength from her brown no-nonsense eyes.

Kennedy felt he should say something soothing. 'I didn't know Mr O'Browne of course, but a friend of mine did. She met with him a couple of times to interview him for an article she was working on. She liked him instantly, thought he was a nice fellow.'

'We were very close at one point, very close,' explained Farrelly. 'We shared a room together in his uncle's house in Camden when we first came over with Blues by Five.

'That was my first group. We were quite big in Ireland, you know. Peter and I decided to come to London and see if we could make it over here. We could have played around Ireland for twenty years and got nowhere.'

'So how well did the Blues by Five do in England?' prompted Kennedy, hoping it might nudge Martyn Farrelly into some free-falling thoughts.

'Good, very good. Yeah we did very well, but we thought we were going to do even better. It was fantastic to start with but what we didn't realise was that a lot of the audience, who were mostly, if not entirely, Irish, were coming to see us because they were homesick. They didn't want to go and see Big Tom and his like up in Kilburn, and we were the acceptable alternative for the younger audience. But I realised when we were making the second album that we really didn't have what it took to make the big time. We didn't really have a band commitment, a band vibe. Then other people had hits with our songs...'

'Your songs,' his wife corrected.

'Yes, well,' he smiled. 'It took another two years and two more albums for the band to accept what Peter and I had already admitted to each other. Peter had started to put his energies into other things, like the shop, Camden Records.

'And I had started to concentrate more on my songs. The publishers persuaded some of the other artists they shared with Pye to record a few of my songs. One of them "Why do Girls do This?" was a small hit but then a group from Basingstoke called, The Road, recorded "I Think I've lost You" and that reached number twenty-two in the charts and that prompted other artists to look for my songs.

'To be perfectly honest, I was a lot more comfortable writing songs in my new flat in West Hampstead, than sharing a transit van with four other musicians, two roadies and a load of equipment. The publishers put Colette in charge of my career and we became quite close and well...' Farrelly left them to guess the obvious before continuing. 'So by the time we decided to end Blues by Five, Peter and I already had some wind in our next sail.

'He was great at that time. He gave me an unconditional release from all my contracts. He had no need to do that, you know. I was already generating some money from the songwriting, quite a bit actually...' Again he smiled at Colette. 'And he would have been entitled to 20 per cent of that. Most people would have held on to it, just to see what happened. But Peter didn't. He said he had done nothing to help with the songs or the covers, so he wouldn't take a piece of it. If the Blues by Five records had showed any post-group life, then it would have been a different matter. He also felt that I would have an easier job getting a new management deal if there were no skeletons in the cupboard.

'I must admit it was only a lot later that I realised this. Actually, Colette kept pointing it out to me, but I refused to see it because I thought that he had made me sign a crap publishing deal. I always felt that I should have been making a lot more money out of my song writing.'

'Had you fallen out at that time? When did you become disgruntled about the publishing situation?' Kennedy inquired.

'We didn't really fall out in terms of a big fight or anything like that, but we weren't talking. In fact we didn't talk for ages and ages. Then Colette got angry with me and said that I disregarded friends, and that I'd regret it when I got older. She made me see, in no uncertain terms, that we were lucky, very lucky, to secure a recording deal and publishing deal with anyone in the first place.'

'I'm sure I've been told before what exactly the difference is between a recording deal and a publishing deal, and how a manager fits into all this,' said Kennedy. 'But could you remind me how it works?'

It was not Farrelly but Colette who answered him. 'You're going to need to know the overall picture if you're going be looking into Peter's death.' She took a sip of her tea before she began. 'Take an artist, a solo artist, male or female, or a group. To operate in the commercial music world he or she or they will need a team of people. The team is usually put together by the manager. Some managers consult their artists more than others on the selection of the team.

'The agent is sometimes the first person in place, even before the manager. The artists need gigs to show themselves off to managers and the agents are responsible for securing bookings – gigs, concerts, live appearances or whatever – for the artists. The agent will liaise with the promoter, whose job it is to promote the individual concerts – book the halls, sell the tickets, look after the smooth running of the show on the day.'

Colette ticked off the personnel as she dealt with them. 'Then there's the record company. It is their job to fund the recording of the records and manufacture and distribute them throughout the world.

'The publisher will protect the copyright of the songs. In the old days it was easier to define this as you had two types of artist, one who wrote songs and one who performed them on record and on stage. But since the Beatles, the writer is, nine times out of ten, likely to be the performer, too. So now most publishing houses are more or less banks who advance money to the artists and charge them for the privilege. 'Now and again, though very rarely, a publisher will fulfil the old-fashioned function of going out and finding artists to record the songs of one of their writers.

'Contracts between the manager, agent, publisher and record company are a legal minefield. For obvious reasons the artists' solicitor should not be acting for the manager, although this is sometimes the case. And if the manager puts together the perfect team of agent, promoter, publisher and record company, the artist will need an accountant to look after all the money, he, she or they are going to make.

'On top of that team there is also a secondary team – tour managers, road crews, musicians, stylists, hairdressers, record producers, studio engineers, concerts engineers, personal assistants, bus drivers, truck drivers and so on and so on. The bigger you are, the more you have.' Colette paused for a mouthful of tea.

'Let's say our artist has put together his team with the help of the manager and is about to make the first record. If it's a single it will consist of two songs. If it's an album, nowadays a CD, obviously there will be ten to twelve songs, usually written by the artist. Bob Dylan, for example, always records his own compositions, but Cliff Richard records songs written by other people. The writer's royalties are collected via a publishing company that protects the copyright of the songs. If the record company sell the CD for say, ten pounds, out of that they will pay the publisher of the song, say for argument's sake, one pound. They will pay another pound to the performing artist; more if you are Paul McCartney, less if you are a new group starting out…'

'Like the Blues by Five,' Kennedy offered.

'Yes, indeed,' smiled Colette, happy to have at least half of her audience still with her – PC Gaul's attention was more on how her free flowing dark blue dress was falling into the curves of her body. 'The balance of the ten pounds will go towards VAT, manufacturing costs, distribution costs, promotion costs, packaging costs and, of course, profit!

'From their pound per record, the publishing company will give the writer as little as fifty pence or as much as ninety-five pence, and will keep the rest. So, in effect, the record company looks after the performer of the song and the publishing company takes care of the writer of the song,' Colette concluded.

'So you see,' added Martyn Farrelly, 'Colette pointed out to me that if it had not been for Peter, then firstly, I wouldn't have had a record deal, secondly, I wouldn't have had a publishing deal, and thirdly, and most importantly, I wouldn't have met her. While my artistic integrity let me disregard the first two points, meeting Colette was down to Peter, so I contacted him again and we made our peace.

'And now... Oh God! I just can't believe he's dead.'

Chapter Twenty-Seven

We don't give out our ages,
And we don't give our phone numbers
— The Roches

As Kennedy was gratefully accepting a second cup of tea from Colette Farrelly, WPC Anne Coles was in North Bridge House, dialling the number of the Fraud Squad at New Scotland Yard.

She introduced herself to DS Sandy Johnson, advising him of the case she was working on and explaining that Camden CID had reason to believe their victim had been blackmailed by chart hypers.

'The whole chart hyping thing has been explained to us, but somewhere along the line it was mentioned that the Fraud Squad had been carrying out its own investigation. My DI wanted me to check with you to see if you have any additional background or anything new that might be of use to us in this O'Browne murder.' She occupied her free hand by rolling a pen around in her fingers in an effort to distract herself from missing the smoking habit she had painfully managed to kick.

'Ah. How long do you have? A couple of weeks by any chance?' laughed the boisterous voice at the other end of the phone.

'I'll take the short route. Let's leave out the tourist attractions, please,' the WPC requested into the handset, which took but a millisecond to relay Anne Cole's voice (slightly distorted) to the ear of DS Sandy Johnson.

'Okay.' Johnston primed himself as though he were Colin Jackson about to depart the starting blocks at forty miles per hour. 'Basically we found that the pop charts were being distorted – no, not by the noise – in two ways. First, the record company sales reps seek "ticks", which are sales marks from the shops they visit. Obviously in somewhere like the Outer Hebrides, where the rep and the sales assistant are mates, this is easier than in the cities.' DS Sandy Johnson went off into a verbal sketch between a rep and a sales assistant in a shop on the Hebrides, all the time keeping up two Scottish accents. He had DS Coles laughing out loud. She thought that this DS, Sandy Johnson from the Fraud Squad at New Scotland Yard, could be someone she would be interested in getting to know better.

But at the end of his sketch all she said was, 'And the second system?'

'The second system: ah well, that really is a continuation and a refinement of the granny squad.'

'The granny squad?' the WPC chuckled, anticipating another one-act play.

'Yes,' DS Johnson said with more than a little mischief. 'And never ever put your granny on the stove.'

'What? Why on earth not?'

'She's too old to be riding the range.'

'Oh please!' The WPC tried not to laugh. 'Can we be serious, I'm not sure my DI wants his after-dinner patter improved.'

'Sorry. Seriously, the granny squads started off in the Seventies. They were literally a group of grannies and bored housewives who went out in their hundreds to buy up records. They were usually organised by band members, fan clubs, managers and record companies, or a combination of all four. It was much easier then because there were fewer chart return shops.'

'I know a little about the chart return shop system,' Coles offered, avoiding an explanation.

'Well, nowadays the system is refined to the point where there are about two thousand chart return shops across the country on computer and a reading is taken from a varied five to six-hundred of them, so hyping has become harder and nowadays it's a lot more expensive, because you have to cover a lot more shops – perhaps as many as two thousand. But then again, the rewards tend to be a lot higher. And for £15,000 to £20,000 you can buy yourself some additional "marketing". It's very slick and professional compared to the old days of the granny squads.

'The record companies approach these new legit "marketers" to "work" the relevant single, passing on details, such as when TV appearances, radio plays, concerts, press are planned to happen. This way the surge in record sales can be explained by promotional activity. The marketers will invoice the record companies, who will pay a "marketing bill" and thus keep their hands clean.

'Marketers have, I believe, about three regional teams which, Monday to Saturday, travel the country – or at least their respective parts of the country – buying up the single in an attempt to create as natural a sales pattern as possible. Don't forget that every individual sale shows up on the computer, so if one person buys six copies of the single in one purchase, suspicions will be raised.' DS Johnson paused and WPC Coles could hear him lighting up a cigarette.

'What happens to all the records these people buy?' the WPC inquired, cutting into the telephonic pause.

'It seems that the records and all the receipts proving purchase find their way back to the marketers. The receipts would be made available to someone at the record company to show that they were getting their money's worth.

'The records – actually, the majority are CDs these days – are, we believe, in some cases being shipped to Holland to be exchanged for drugs. One such shipment we seized contained albums, which led us to believe that some of the record companies are using CDs and albums, to pay the marketers. Obviously £15,000 worth of CDs is easier to find than £15,000 in cash.'

'But surely it would take a hell of a lot of records, CDs, whatever, to buy enough drugs to make the exercise worthwhile?' reasoned the WPC.

'The shipment I'm talking about had a shop value of over half a million pounds. We worked out that it would raise about £100,000, which would buy enough drugs to realise a street value of a couple of million pounds,' the DS replied, between drags on his cigarette.

'But why bother? Why not just buy the drugs for £100,000? These drug dealers are not short of money.'

'Think about it. They are both getting something for nothing. The suppliers are getting £500,000 worth of legit merchandise for £100,000, and the dealers are getting over a million pounds worth, maybe even two, of drugs for free and as a by-product of another job. And it gives both parties a front, the appearance of participating in legitimate business.'

'I suppose that makes some kind of sense, but I still can't figure out how our blackmailer fits into all this.' The WPC jotted down some of the sums volunteered by DS Sandy Johnson.

'You've got to assume that it's not the marketer. He's got too much to lose. Perhaps it could be someone the marketer has fallen out with, maybe a member of one of his teams, or maybe, and more likely, the leader of one of his teams. People making their money illegally tend to become greedy very quickly and, well, there is always some kind of angle, isn't there?' the DS surmised.

'So how do we find out who it is? Do you know these teams? Do you know who the marketer is? Have you ever prosecuted?' Coles reeled off her list of questions.

'Hang on, hang on, one at a time, please. We've never prosecuted because hyping is very difficult to prove. There is nothing illegal in someone going into a shop once, or several times, and purchasing however many copies of a record they like. We've never been able to make a direct connection between the marketers – hypers – and the record companies. Either they pay the money direct to legit marketers through the books or they pay with CDs. So they stay clean.

'Any time a record moves up the charts on fresh air, it's put down to fans trying to help, or the band's and/or manager's family being overly enthusiastic. The record companies regulate themselves through the BPI and as they are nearly all at it, it's very rare for any action to be taken. When it does, it's always used as a PR exercise: look how straight we are, punishing our own.'

'We believe that there are about three marketers in London at the moment and we believe they may share team members. Look, tell you what, leave it with me for a time and I'll see if I can dig you up any names, okay?' Sandy Johnson offered.

'Brilliant, yes. I'll hear from you, then. That's great – thanks for all the info. Bye.' Anne Coles reflected that some days, maybe even today, promised lots. She could not help trying to imagine, from the vocal clues, what this DS Sandy Johnson looked like.

Her mother had often told Anne how, in her own schooldays, she used to day-dream about what her future husband (Anne's father) would look like. She had been way out.

The WPC wondered some more about Sandy and then thought, Shit, I've got work to do.

Chapter Twenty-Eight

You're tired of dreamin someone else's dreams
When they really don't include you any longer
          – Paul Brady

While WPC Coles was considering her dad from her mum's point of view, Colette Farrelly had proved two important points for Detective Inspector Christy Kennedy, which were that she made a dammed fine cup of tea, and that she was an excellent hostess; she kept his tea fresh.

Colette offered Kennedy and PC Gaul a helping of the oven-fresh bread which had been the source of the excellent smell as they had entered the house. Regretfully he felt he had to decline her kind offer, as he and ann rea were meeting Leslie Russell for dinner that evening. Kennedy was not a fitness freak, although he was not unhealthy or overweight. But he felt that unless he watched himself, he could easily be stretching the belt.

Kennedy continued the conversation, thinking that maybe one slice of bread wouldn't hurt. But no, back to the job in hand. It was Kennedy who asked all the questions. PC Gaul was diligently carrying out his instructions: 'Just keep quiet, note everything down and watch everything like a hawk.'

'When you and Peter reacquainted yourselves, did he act at all strange? You know, perhaps still a little upset at being cut off?'

'No, not at all. He isn't – wasn't – really like that,' Martyn Farrelly replied, unconsciously adjusting to the fact that someone he knew had recently died. It was a weird feeling, even for people who did not spend a lot of time together. When someone dies, the survivor has to deal with a permanent absence, regretting things he hasn't done or said.

'Peter was instantly friendly again. It was like we'd seen each other just the previous week and not several years before,' Farrelly affirmed. He leant forward in his chair, raising his left hand slightly with tip of forefinger and thumb touching and moving his hand a little to emphasise his point before continuing. 'He was working on his new shop and he wasn't a person to dwell on regrets. I really envied him for that quality. He always had this ability to just, to just move on.

'I remember I had a new bunch of songs and I played them for him. On the cassette player,' Farrelly added in case the policemen thought him vain enough to play the songs to his friend on a guitar in the room. 'He liked them and he was very supportive and enthusiastic. They were some of the songs I'd written for my first solo record. I was happy to have a chance to play them for someone whose ear I trusted. Having a group of musicians and a manager around can be a great sounding board. You may not even take any notice of what they have to say, but you take some comfort that they do not laugh at what you play them.

'I mean Colette knows a good song when she hears one. BPE, the publishers, were really annoyed when she left. But it's different.' Farrelly was obviously now picking his words carefully, not wishing to offend his wife.

'I think what my husband is trying to say, not too successfully, Detective Inspector,' Colette smiled graciously, 'is that I love him, and that therefore I am not going to be the best critical gauge of his work.'

'Exactly, exactly.' Farrelly enthusiastically took up the line, once again leaning forward in his seat, rocking gently. 'I couldn't have put it better myself, dear,' he smiled at his no-nonsense wife.

'Anyway, Peter also was on a high at that point. He had discovered that excellent band from America, Half Moon Bay Express, and he was thinking of starting a small label to help them in the UK. They were doing okay in America, but Peter told me that the English record companies were, surprise surprise, dragging their heels. Dragging their heels when they should have been encouraging new musical trends. That's one of the things I always loved about Peter: if he liked something, he didn't care what the rest of the biz thought.

'When it comes to spotting new talent the English record companies are about as effective as a glass hammer. Not Peter. If he liked someone, he would just get on with it and spend 150 per cent of his energy helping them find their audience.

'As that evening wore on, we were both attacking the wine and I think we were both relieved that we'd made up. Anyway, I offered him £500 to help him start up a record label, Camden Town Records. He accepted it and both of us went off happier men that night.' Farrelly smiled at the memory, rather than at the other people in the room.

'And you remained friends?' Kennedy asked.

'Yes. Well, probably not as tight as we were in the early days, but I suppose that was to be expected. We were both busy with our careers and I have a family. Obviously your priorities change. But we did keep in touch. For instance, he helped me with the final song selection for my first two albums and generally he would give me career advice when we occasionally spoke on the phone.

'And of course I gave advice on some of his projects. I'm not sure how much attention he paid to my input, but he did ask me about various mixes and songs on the first Wire Crates album. He was working so hard on trying to get that album perfect.'

'Did you ever make any albums for Camden Town Records?' Kennedy asked.

'No. I had my deal in place before Camden Town Records started. And you know, even if I hadn't, I would have needed a record company already up to speed. As it turned out, I picked the wrong one anyway, but at that time I needed a functioning company rather than one just starting up. But I would have liked to have worked with Peter again, in some way. After all, we had started out together,' Farrelly said regretfully.

'Surely you did, though?' prodded Kennedy, looking down from the Blues by Five poster behind Colette's left shoulder.

'What?' Farrelly sounded surprised.

'Well, you were part of Camden Town Records, weren't you? It was started with your money,' Kennedy qualified his earlier question.

'Oh, no. No, not at all. That was just a loan; more of a gift, really. I didn't have shares or anything.'

'Oh I see,' said Kennedy, scratching his left eyebrow. He was silent for a moment. 'When did you last see Peter O'Browne?' he asked eventually.

'Hmmm, let me think… we had a drink at the Edinboro, a pub near his office…' Farrelly began.

'I know it,' offered Kennedy. In fact he knew it well, not because he was a great pub person but because its proximity to North Bridge House made it a regular watering-hole for the majority of Camden CID. 'When would this have been?'

'About two weeks ago, I think. Can you remember, Colette?' Farrelly inquired leaning back fully into his seat for the first time since the interview had begun.

'It will be two weeks ago tomorrow. Don't you remember, I met you there and we went into the West End to see that Kevin Costner film?' Colette prompted.

Kennedy could not resist it. 'Did you enjoy it?'

'Yes, actually we did. We didn't know what to expect with all the fuss, and it's rare that we agree on a movie, but we both thought it was brilliant,' Colette replied on behalf of both of them.

Farrelly nodded in agreement at her opinion of the movie and to confirm the last day he'd seen Peter.

'How did he seem?'

'Well, he'd had a few you know. He was reflective. I think the problems he had to deal with on his new level were getting him down. He said he never found time to work direct with artists any more, and that depressed him a lot. He claimed he'd become a glorified salesman, albeit a highly-paid one, and he told me that the people who now owned the majority of his company did not give a shit what he sold. They were only interested in how many copies they shipped out. He said that there was no interest in developing an artist if the artist wasn't a success immediately. If he or she did not show a profit from record number one, they were on Peter's back to drop him or her immediately.

'Actually, we talked a lot about the days when major labels like Warner Brothers signed acts like Ry Cooder, Bonnie Rait, Randy Newman and Van Morrison. They would know right from the start that it was going to take several albums before they made money or broke even. But the executives in those days had a vision, and they stuck with the artists and eventually, made the money they needed. But Peter felt – and I agreed with him – that nowadays if your first album doesn't do over a million it's all over and you are dropped, and it's "next please". Music does not matter any more.

'He was very annoyed that he had become part of this machine that just wants to be continuously fed. That's why the CD revolution happened. The product had nearly dried up, the majors were losing out to the independents who were signing all the new worthwhile acts, as was the case with Camden Town Records.

'The majors decided to find a way to sell more of the existing product by developing a new format, the compact disc. They effectively killed off vinyl just so that they could keep the hungry machine fed.'

Farrelly rose from his chair and went off to his shelves, where he found his CD copy and his vinyl copy of "Abbey Road".

'Have a look at this. No comparison, is there? Look at the sleeve,' he pleaded passionately. 'It's a classic with the vinyl and it's merely product identification with the CD.'

Kennedy was not sure that he agreed with Martyn Farrelly's over romanticised view of this subject. He did prefer the old vinyl sleeves, but with the advent of the compact disc the dust and hair crackles disappeared; the needle scratching vanished.

The sadness of finding out that someone, maybe even yourself, had scratched your valuable copy of "Astral Weeks" was now a thing of the past. In fact the example that Farrelly had picked, the Beatles classic, "Abbey Road", could have been chosen to push the case for CDs. The CD version was, to Kennedy's ears, the best sounding recorded music he had ever heard. Just listen to the warmth of the acoustic guitars on "Here Comes the Sun". But Kennedy kept his opinion to himself. He was not there to debate the pros and cons of the CD.

'Do you think he was more than depressed, or was the nostalgia alcohol-induced?'

'Hard to know now, with what's happened I mean. I'll probably look back on that meeting for the rest of my life, wondering whether he was in danger. Did he know he was in danger? Could I have helped him? But I think he was just trying to come to terms with the fact that he had sold his soul for six million quid. And now he just had to live with it.

'He quoted Dylan to me, you know. "And don't go mistaking paradise for that place across the road". He said that he had, it wasn't and he shouldn't have.'

'But he didn't say anything which made you suspicious?' Kennedy pressed.

'No, no not at all. I felt he was depressed and that was it. I felt great when Colette joined us. I suppose it was a bit smug of me, looking at both our lives, he with all his money and sadness; me with my family and songs and happiness.' Colette briefly touched the nape of his neck.

'Do you have any idea of who might want Peter O'Browne dead?' It was another official-sounding question.

Martyn Farrelly thought carefully for a few moments aware that all attention was focused on him. Even as he opened his mouth to speak, he was unsure of what he was going to say.

'No... No... Not murder him. Sure, he pissed off a few people along the way, but not so much that he would get murdered. No I can't think of anyone.'

'Who did he piss off along the way?'

'Well you know,' Farrelly muttered nervously. 'I'm sure there are other people who would know the answer to that question better than me. I didn't deal with him as much on a day-to-day basis the way some did. Tom Best, say. Peter told me that they had a serious falling out. Basically it seems that Tom thought he was a partner and Peter thought he was an employee.

'Peter also fell out big time with the manager of Radio Cars. Peter was really mad at the manager, and at the band as well, come to that, for not being more loyal to him.

'But I don't know. I feel I'm drawing too much attention to these people by mentioning names. The incidents mentioned were probably more skirmishes than a full scale war, or even a battle for that matter. I can't see any of them actually killing him. It's a terribly big thing to kill somebody.' Farrelly sighed.

'How was he killed by the way?' he asked quietly.

Colette gave him an Oh-Martyn-how-could-you? look.

'We're not releasing that information just yet,' Kennedy replied and paused for effect before moving once again into official police-speak. 'What were you doing yesterday evening between 6pm and midnight?'

'God, you can't think that Marty had anything to do with Peter's death can you, Detective Inspector?' Colette spluttered, panic evident in both her face and her movements.

'What I have to do, madam, is eliminate as many people as possible from our inquiries. The easiest way to do this is to find out what people were doing around the time of the murder. If this information, the alibi, checks out, we can then move on to someone else.' Kennedy's reply was polite but firm.

'I was up here, in this room, working on my music. I'm working on a song I have promised to another artist for inclusion on her album. She, Amy Sels, is due in the studio next week to record it and I've been reworking some of the lyrics. They need to work from the female point of view.'

'What time did you start working?'

'I came straight up after tea at about 6.30, and finished at about 1am. As I said, I needed to finish the song.'

Kennedy turned to Colette, 'Did you come up here during that time?'

Colette hesitated for a second. 'No. No, I didn't. Martyn does not like to be disturbed when he's working.'

PC Gaul wondered whether Colette, in that moment of uncertainty, had considered giving her husband an alibi.

'When you record your albums, sir, have you ever used a studio in Primrose Hill called–'Kennedy checked his notes '–Mayfair Mews Studios?'

'No, I always use a studio called Konk. It's owned by Ray Davies of the Kinks. It's only two streets away and I always hope I'm going to be influenced by England's finest living songwriter when I go there. But I've never even come close to "Waterloo Sunset".'

As Kennedy drove away from the Farrellys' home, he found himself overcome by an overwhelming urge to listen to the Kinks' classic Farrelly had mentioned.

Chapter Twenty-Nine

Dirty old River, must you keep rolling
Flowing into the night
                                    – Ray Davies

The melody was engulfing Kennedy's brain. The cheeky guitar line from Dave, the other Davies brother, hooked its way into his mind as effectively as the times-tables had at school. Dave Davies proved to be a perfect foil for his older brother's cynical but endearing outlook on English suburban life. His guitar solo on 'Waterloo Sunset' was as sweet as any strawberry milkshake.

Kennedy had PC Gaul drop him off at the Salt and Pepper Cafe in Parkway. He was to meet ann rea there and she was already at their favourite corner table. Kennedy immediately ordered tea (naturally) and brought ann rea up to date with his interview with the Farrellys, 'Waterloo Sunset' and all.

ann rea interrupted his commentary on London's most elegant folk song.

'I worry, you know,' she began.

'What?' A startled Kennedy departed the melody.

'And then you tell me about people like the Farrellys and their life and I feel okay about things.'

'You don't mean "things", do you? You mean relationships don't you?' Kennedy cut across her words and her thoughts.

'Yes. I just feel that I want to try, but I like what we have now and I don't want to blow it. But then when you see a couple who have made it work, like Martyn and Colette Farrelly, that's how I imagine it to be, and how I want it to be – God, I don't even like talking about this. I'm so damned uptight about it, I feel that in a way, even by discussing it, you can ruin everything.'

When ann rea failed to find the words, Kennedy filled the space for her.

'Look,' Kennedy began in a quiet voice. 'It's okay. It really is. Yes I'd love us to live together but I can see that although part of you longs for that to happen as well, the other part of you is screaming and running for cover.'

Kennedy knew exactly why ann rea felt like running for cover. On the one occasion she had given her heart and her life to a man, she had found not only was he married, but despite all the words and gestures, he had little other interest in her apart from bedding her. This had all happened five years before she had met Kennedy and she still hadn't recovered from it, barely even talked about it. It seemed to him that the better they got on, the more worried ann rea became about their relationship.

'But ann, it's simple. When, and if, the time is right for us to live together, we'll live together.' And then he added,'Or not!' for fear she would think he was vain enough to be thinking, all he had to do was wait and she'd come running. 'It's not an issue and we shouldn't be making it an issue. For me it's simple. I love you. It's like I've been waiting all my life to meet you and be with you, and now that I've met you and you're here I want to be with you.'

'But how can you be so sure? Why are you so convinced it's me you want to be with? Why not your last girlfriend? Or your next girlfriend? That's what I can't work out. We've discussed this before and I told you then that I felt that my last boyfriend was the one and that we were going to live happily ever after. But then he turned out to be a shit. And he fucked me over. I keep wondering how I could have ever been so wrong. Why shouldn't my feelings for you blow back in my face as well? I just don't want to mess up, Kennedy.

'I don't want to find you staying out later and later. I don't want to one day realise that we haven't made love for six weeks and I don't want to.' ann rea hissed air through her teeth as Kennedy's tea arrived at their table. She smiled, not at Kennedy but at the table. But for his benefit. 'Look, Kennedy, I know you're a randy sod, and if you hadn't made love to me for six weeks you'd be off looking for it with somebody else.' Clearly ann rea felt it might be time to try to lighten up the conversation.

She was annoyed with herself for having got into this now. For heaven's sake, he was working on a case and he was seeking her help on it – the first time he had done so officially. It was just that the way Kennedy had described the Farrellys' home and their life together, in a way, he sounded envious. ann rea had wanted all her life to be like them – well, maybe not exactly like them.

The way Kennedy had described it, Colette Farrelly was slightly subservient to her husband. ann rea on the other hand, believed it was possible to have a complete relationship when both partners had a fulfilling career.

Her theory, in fact, went deeper than that. ann rea believed that such a relationship could be the perfect one – providing, of course, that love was present. But at the same time, love alone was never enough. It took more than love to take you through the novelty of lust, to still be buzzed by your partner every time he or she said something.

ann rea felt that she could have such a relationship with Kennedy. She loved him, but she worried that now that she had found someone she loved, and who evidently loved her, she didn't have what it took to take the relationship to the next level. She admired his ability to accept things and move with them ('or not', as he often told her).

Perhaps at this stage he was the one most prepared to risk all the hurt and shit that had to be gone through when you tried to go for something you wanted, and wanted desperately. Kennedy, ann rea felt, could accept failure; she was not sure that she could, not again.

'Listen to you, would you?' Kennedy laughed, responding to ann rea's need to lighten the atmosphere. 'If you hadn't practiced the fiddler's elbow for six weeks when you wished to have your evil way with me, I'm not sure I'd live to tell the tale of our banking.'

'Don't you mean bonking, Kennedy?' ann rea responded teasingly.

'No banking, I meant banking.' Kennedy smiled.

ann rea's raised eyebrows said, 'What on earth are you on about?'

'You know,' Kennedy said dropping his voice to a conspiratorial whisper. 'Banking. Where I make a deposit!'

'Kennedy!' she shouted, prompting all the other patrons of the Salt and Pepper Cafe to turn round and stare. They both turned bright red. 'Please,' ann rea dropped her voice a few decibels. 'Pl-ea-se. We're on a case.'

'Yes, of course,' he replied slyly as he finished off his tea. 'Let's go for a spin in your car and see if we can't find "Waterloo Sunset" on the radio. You never know, Martyn Farrelly may have been dropping a clue.'

Chapter Thirty

Time wounds all heels

– Nick Lowe

Needless to say, ann rea and Kennedy were not successful in their search for a play of 'Waterloo Sunset'. And even if they had been, they would not easily have found a clue to the death of Peter O'Browne.

By the time ann rea dropped Kennedy at North Bridge House, the rain had started to fall. It fell so hard it bounced three inches off the pavement and Kennedy decided against running across to the newsagent's at the top of Parkway to pick up an *Evening Standard* and *Camden News Journal*. Meanwhile WPC Anne Coles and DS James Irvine were pushing the brass button which activated the electronic chimes at a four-storey house at 25 Ellington Street, Islington.

The entire third floor – two main front rooms, two smaller, darker back-rooms, a tiny bathroom, (sink and WC), an even smaller kitchen (sink, small fridge and microwave oven) – of this house in a tree-shaded street was the headquarters (in fact the only quarters) of The Compact Management Company.

The Compact Management Company listed as its Managing (and only) Director a Mr Jason Carter-Houston, former manager of the Radio Cars, one of Peter O'Browne's early, and successful, discoveries. Jason Carter-Houston's private and personal, secretary, Miss Doreen Stephens, also acted as the company's receptionist. It was Doreen's high-pitched voice which greeted Coles and Irvine and advised them to push the door when instructed.

'Now?' the WPC inquired from the cream-ribbed intercom unit.

'No, not till I tell you!' came the terse reply from Doreen, who further instructed them to make their way up to the third floor. Having completed her orders, she told the WPC, 'Now, push the door'.

Confirmation that they had successfully carried out their instructions came by means of the sound of the same high-pitched voice, only louder, greeting them,

'I have advised Mr Carter-Houston that you are here and he will see you presently. Please make yourself comfortable,' Doreen said, ushering WPC Coles and DS Irvine in the direction of two very uncomfortable chairs. WPC Coles was convinced that Doreen would have loved to have inserted the actual word 'hyphen' between 'Carter' and 'Houston'.

She wondered about the parents responsible for such a name. Perhaps a Mr Carter, a modern man, had married an even more modern woman, Miss Houston and they'd adopted both surnames. Or, perhaps a Miss Carter had married a wimpy Mr Houston. Maybe, more boringly, a Miss Smith had married a Mr Carter-Houston. Or perhaps Jason himself had added his wife's name to his own. The WPC's mind mixings were interrupted by the arrival of an unassuming person whom the WPC and the DS – as was revealed in a later conversation– both took to be the tea- boy. Well, tea-young man would have been more accurate, though the WPC did not wonder if a Mr Tea had married a Miss Young Man.

As the young man drew closer, he looked less and less young, and introduced himself. 'Hi, I'm Jason Carter,' he said, adding, a beat later, 'Houston,' which answered WPC Coles unasked question. 'Why don't you both come through to my office.' No hint of an offer of tea.

Jason Carter-Houston wore a pair of black trousers with an elasticated waist. This in itself was not a problem. His black (plain and of a different shade) T-shirt ran out of material about an inch above his trousers and the gap exposed a bare belly which was fighting the waist of his trousers. His hair was also black, probably dyed, definitely dead. He had obviously seen some rock god similarly dressed, but in emulating his hero, Jason neglected to take account of the fact that he did not have the basic equipment to carry off the image.

WPC Coles was wondering how Miss Houston could have gone out with such a specimen, let alone hyphened-up their names. DS Irvine thought Jason's obvious hyperness was probably due to a heavy intake of either bad food, chocolate bars or beer, or a combination of all of them. Whatever the reason, Jason had all the rock 'n' roll clichés off pat.

'Okay, dudes how can I be of service?' Coming from a cool Texan, this would have been perfectly natural. From an Islington wimp it was pitiful, as was his, 'You know, man, time is money, and all that jazz.'

'We would like to ask you some questions about Mr Peter O'Browne,' said Anne Coles briskly.

'That shit. What an uncool cat. Hey man, don't expect me to lift a finger to help him.'

'I'm afraid it's a bit late for you to help him, sir.' The DS interrupted refusing to allow Jason Carter-Houston to make a complete prat of himself. 'He was murdered yesterday evening.'

'Dead? Murdered? Man, that's heavy. Mind you, it was only a matter of…' Carter-Houston seemed to think better of whatever it was he'd intended to say and left the sentence unfinished.

To WPC Anne Coles this whole aspect of police procedure was more than slightly suspect – telling someone, suspect or not, about a murder and then standing back and trying to gauge something from their every move and utterance. She was not even sure how effective it was. There was so much scope for bluffs and double bluffs.

For instance, the case in point. Was Carter-Houston behaving with bravado because he had figured a murderer would not be expected to react like this? Or was this merely the way that what passed for his brain dictated he behave? If he was innocent, he knew it, and perhaps feared no consequence from what he did or didn't say.

'Yeah, man. Look, I mean, what can I do to help?' Carter Houston said, appearing to pull himself together.

'Well, as I said, we'd like to ask you a few questions about Mr O'Browne,' WPC Coles began and DS Irvine continued, so that you couldn't notice the join. 'We believe you worked with him quite closely early on in both your careers? A group called Radio Stars?'

'No. I mean, yes. I did work with him. but, the group were called Radio Cars, not Radio Stars. Yeah man it was a long time ago. My first management gig, man, and he fucked them up. Major bad vibes, man. Total fuck-up.

'Yes, a long time ago, man. I remember in those days I thought it would be frightfully exciting to manage one of those pop groups.' Carter-Houston effected a plum in the mouth accent. 'I soon lost the accent and the greenness.'

'Did you get the group a recording contract with Peter O'Browne?' WPC Coles quizzed.

'Recording contract? Now there is a joke, man.' Jason afforded himself a little titter. 'Actually they had already made their first record direct with Peter. They were taking off, doing well. Shifting units, as we say in the biz. The leader of the group, Johnny Heart, brought me in to look after things. It was all happening so quickly they needed someone to take charge,' Jason answered proudly.

'How did you meet?' asked WPC Coles.

'Who, Peter?'

'No, Radio Cars.'

'Oh, Johnny Heart's lawyer worked with my dad, and my dad had asked him to look out for something for me to do. I dropped out at this point, man. My old man, a real suit-man, I think he thought I was on the path of ruin and destruction. I know the kids today have their E and all that shit, man, but I can tell you, we were pretty wild in the Seventies.'

Wild maybe; pretty, never. Not to mention fucking blind if you think someone as stunning as Anne Coles is the 'man' you keep addressing her as, thought DS Irvine.

'Anyway, Johnny Heart had made it known that he'd like a man-ager, and we met, and got on great in those days. Well Mr Heart was easy to get on great with. He was a bit of... well, he liked to smoke a lot of grass, and he liked to have fun.'

'Where was Johnny Heart from?'

'A man without a soul doesn't come from anywhere, man,' came the reply, leading DS Irvine to believe that Mr Heart had been kind enough to share his cannabis with Mr Carter-Houston.

'I hope I'm not out of order here but why...' DS Irvine realised, once he had started his question, that it was going to be difficult to complete without appearing to insult Carter-Houston. 'Why would an up and coming pop group pick, an um, inexperienced manager?'

'Oh that, man...' it seemed Carter-Houston didn't discriminate. 'He was a novice as well. He was selling records, or his group Radio Cars were, but he hadn't a clue why, and if I'm honest, man, I'd say I had the right accent and the right vibe and...' Carter-Houston smiled a smile that distorted his face the way a clay beauty-mask cracks when its owner grows restless and grins. 'He thought I was really cool 'cause I took him to all those posh parties.'

'Oh,' was all Irvine could say in acknowledgement.

'So how did you get on with Peter O'Browne back then?' WPC Coles inquired as Irvine recovered.

'Well, fine, really. Oh, he was suspicious of me. Up to the point I came along he had direct dealing with the group, man. He was a sharp cat, man – he ruled the roost. He'd say jump and four heads would hit his ceiling in unisonic reply. But the main problem was that they, Camden Town Records, were just starting out and they were cutting their teeth with Radio Cars.'

'Just like yourself?' Irvine suggested not maliciously, merely establishing the facts.

'Sure, cool man. Yea that's hip, I know where you're coming from, but that was different in a way. I was coming from a different angle, man, and I wasn't getting in the group's way. He was, man. Grab the moment, that's what it's all about, and he was doing it, man. They were selling records so it was time to move on, man, to grab another moment. We had to move to a major label. I – the group, needed to become players. We were ready to move up a step or two.

'Come on, it was a joke, man. Camden Town Records was forever running out of stock or the stock would be fine but there would be no sleeves. They were always behind the demand.'

'So what happened?' WPC Anne Coles pressed. This was all very interesting, but DI Kennedy was going to be looking for facts. He loved facts; he loved compiling all the information and spreading it all over his noticeboard and then wandering around his room staring at it until something hit him.

'Well, it's simple man. When Peter found out that we were look-ing – well, actually that I was talking to a major – he blew a gasket. Very, very uncool.'

Irvine did a Nigel Mansell, allowing his bushy dark eyebrows to exclaim, 'I don't blame him!'

'I pointed out – much to my later cost – that the group didn't have a written deal with Camden Town Records. Nothing had been signed, they had merely discussed some kind of arrangement. I also pointed out that the band were free to do as they wished and that they wished, under my guidance, to sign to Butterfly Records. Butterfly Records had offered a great deal, man, a fucking real cool deal which secured Johnny Heart's and Radio Cars' future.

'Well, Mr Peter Bloody O'Browne effed and blinded at me. He told me I'd never work again. He'd make sure everything I did would fail. I thought it was idiotic, ludicrous. Here I was sitting on a great deal with a band riding high in the charts. So I told him he was Mickey Mouse and to grow up.

'There was no reasoning with him. I think I might have called Camden Town Records another amateur paddy outfit. He and one of his henchmen threw me out of the building. Man, it was so uncool, so embarrassing, the manager of a hip chart act being treated that way. I couldn't believe it.' Talking about it was obviously getting him worked up all over again, nearly twenty years later. He took a yellow pen from the cup on his desk and doodled on his scribble pad.

'Was that the end of your dealings with Peter O'Browne?' WPC Coles asked. Apples for the teacher, facts for Kennedy.

'Nah, man, that was just the start. They owed the band about £30,000 in royalties and when we asked for the bread they wrote to us saying that if there was no written agreement between Radio Cars and Camden Town Records, then equally there was no arrangement under which Camden Town records could owe Radio Cars money.'

'We threatened to take them to court but our lawyer advised us not to. He figured that if we managed to win our case, there would be a very good chance Peter in turn could successfully take action against us to prevent us leaving Camden Town records.'

'So you and the band were never paid a penny for that first album?' DS Irvine inquired, convincing in his new role as the doubting Thomas.

'Correct! Fucking correct man! Can you believe it?' Jason shouted, beseeching both officers in turn. 'And you know what was the saddest thing of all?' He appeared to want one of them to reply, but when neither did he answered his own question: 'It was their biggest disc. Oh yeah, man, Johnny Heart made a few bob, as in a lot of bob, on the publishing.

'Hate to say it, but his songs became boring too. Butterfly Records dropped them after the first record,' DS Irvine noticed that the royal 'we' of the group in their successful days had now become 'them'.

'I got them a deal with PCA Records. But to be honest, man, I have to admit they would sign anybody. The group made two albums with PCA and, man, in this biz it's like, when you're hot you're hot, and when you're not, you have to climb into a fridge just to warm up.

'So PCA dropped the band – which is probably the biggest insult you could have – and then the band fired me. Man, such ungrateful mothers some of these musos are.' Carter-Houston threatened to brush his fingers through his blue-black hair and would have done so were he not frightened the majority of it would have come out in his hand. 'Look, with ninety-five acts out of a hundred, they have a big album and after that it's downhill. Few consistently top the charts. It's such a hard thing to do. Really it's just getting the big album and then dealing with the aftermath. Anyway, Radio Cars made one final album, a live one, and that was it,' Jason Carter-Houston concluded glumly, evidently thoroughly disgruntled that he'd been made to relive such a disastrous period of his life.

'And now?' posed the fact-finder.

'And now, well man, it's cool. A bit of wheeling and dealing, a bit of ducking and diving. I've got this band – cool band, man – they're called, Two Humps and a Tail, and their thing, man, is doing all of Camel's material live. Yeah man, a Camel tribute band. They are going to be bigger than The Bootleg Beatles.' Jason was pitching to the wrong people. When he saw that maybe Coles and Irvine were not going to rush out to the next Two Humps and a Tail gig he added, 'No, really, man it's cool. You know Camel were really very, very big in Austria and Finland and so I'll get lots of work for them over there, I just need to get them an agent.

'The secret of success in this biz is just to stick with something, and eventually it will become big, and hip. You know, like some day your ship will come in, man, it's cool.'

'When was the last time you saw Peter O'Browne?' Some questions just had to be asked and WPC Anne Coles asked that one.

'Well, man, actually, I was in his building – let me see.' Jason Carter-Houston flipped through the pages of his desk diary. 'Yes, three weeks ago I was in talking to his A&R man. That's a talent scout: all record companies have them. They're easy to spot: they all have tea towels where their ears should be,' Jason laughed, but this well worn joke missed the two members of Camden CID by about a million miles.

'I've got this other act, called Brian. Don't you think that's brilliant, man? A one-word name just like Dylan. Brian. He's great, a prophet for the E generation. And "Also", a new Brit Pop band from Oldham. Not quite Manchester, I know, but then Richmond, the home of the Stones, wasn't quite London, either.

'So I was in the building playing some tapes and I saw Peter as I was leaving. I don't think he saw me though, and if he did he might not have recognised me. I've changed quite a lot since the early days.'

'You mean after all that had gone on, you were still prepared to work with his company again?' WPC Coles asked in disbelief.

'Look, maan,' Jason looked around his office. 'You take what you can get for your artists. And I was right; Ted liked the cassette.

'So did you get a contract for Brian or for Also?' DS Irvine felt impelled to ask.

'Nah, man. They wouldn't even make an offer in the end. But Ted told me he liked the tape and that if it were up to him he'd sign both my acts. He felt both were on the cutting edge of music, maybe just too ahead of their time for Camden Town Records. These guys, they never use the word No. They don't know how. That way they can never be wrong. "Yeah," they'll all say, "I was really into so-and-so but I couldn't do a deal because..." And then they'll list one of their hundred standard reasons. That way when the groups become successful with someone else, they can always say, "Yeah, I was into that one. I saw that one. I tried to do a deal." It's like the thing about success being a bastard and failure an orphan. You know.'

'I think you mean, success had many fathers, failure is an orphan,' the WPC corrected.

'Yeah, man. That's it. That's a cool one, isn't it?'

'And finally,' DS Irvine began, rising from his chair a split second before the WPC did the same. 'What were you doing last night between six o'clock and midnight?'

Jason Carter-Houston just sat there staring at them. He looked at each of them in turn, slowly, as though he hadn't understood the question. It was asked again, this time by WPC Coles.

'Well,' he said eventually. 'I was here 'til about seven, then I walked over to Union Chapel to see Penguin Cafe Orchestra. Afterwards we, my partner and I, we went to dinner. I think we got home about twenty-to-one. They're a cool group, Penguin Cafe Orchestra. Have you ever seen them? Don't think they've got any singles, though.'

By now, Jason, having failed to decide which one of them to address, was looking directly at a space midway between them.

A few minutes later WPC Coles and DS Irvine were in the car weaving their way through the busy afternoon traffic. The DS was the first to speak and then as much to himself as to WPC Coles: 'I wonder who his partner is? When people these days describe their mate as a partner it usually means that they are a member of the same sex.'

'Oh, man! Surely not always. It's cool,' she joked, adding, 'I would say partner is also used, and perhaps more often by either partner in a heterosexual relationship, to show the equality of both.'

'So he's either gay or politically correct?' Irvine suggested bluntly. To him a wife was a wife, and a girlfriend was a girlfriend. 'We'll find out when we check his alibi.'

'I was wondering more about the name of his partner,' WPC Coles conjectured without taking her eyes from the road.

'Oh yeah?' Irvine replied, backsliding into his strong Scottish brogue.

'Well, I was thinking – assuming of course we are talking female – were his partner to be called Miss Thatcher-Devon and they married, does that mean they would be called Mr and Mrs Carter-Houston-Thatcher-Devon?'

'No,' came the dry reply. 'Just Mr and Mrs Richard Head for short!'

WPC Coles stopped their laughter with, 'He's a bit of a John Major, though, isn't he?'

'What? He hasn't got grey hair?'

'No,' Anne Coles agreed. 'But I bet he tucks his shirts into his underpants though.'

'Aye,' said Irvine. 'When the shirt reaches that far, that is.'

Chapter Thirty-One

Then sends out for the doctor who pulls down the shade
— Bob Dylan

'So, what can you tell me, good doctor?' Kennedy smiled as he poured tea into two large, white bone china cups.

'Well, old chap, quite a bit, and devilishly interesting – or, at least, I think it is,' began Dr Leonard Taylor. He was dressed in the way you expect an old fashioned English country doctor to dress. Tweed suit, green checked waistcoat, green dicky-bow and a huge smile which made it all work.

'Good. I could do with a bit of good news on this one.' Yet Kennedy felt that his current dark mood probably had more to do with the storm clouds gathering around ann rea's shoulders, than the murder case. He had left her feeling... well, feeling like maybe he shouldn't have left her. They could have comforted each other if they had hung on together for just another five minutes in her car. But ann rea had to return to the *Camden News Journal* for an appointment and Kennedy had promised to make Dr Taylor one of his special cups of tea in return for an 'in person' review of the autopsy report.

Of course life is full of compromises, but Kennedy didn't feel that he should be making them at that (or indeed any) point in his relationship with ann rea.

'Peter O'Browne was strangled.'

'Yes,' came Kennedy's impatient reply, which did not hide the fact that Dr Taylor's opening comment was about as big a surprise as traffic jams on the M25.

'Let me qualify that. All the rope marks, and in particular the inverted V on the side of his neck, indicate that the deceased was hanged. But he didn't have a broken neck, which would lead me to believe that he didn't receive any sort of sudden jolt, as would be usual with hanging. For instance, in the days when people were executed by hanging, with the trapdoor and all that, it was the weight of the body, the sudden fall, that snapped and broke the neck. One can only deduce that Peter O'Browne was hoisted up from the floor; or something similar.'

'Hmmm.' Kennedy thought for a few seconds. 'Would this mean that two or more people were involved in the murder? It would take a considerable amount of strength to lift up a dead weight with a rope.'

'It would be hard work, yes, but I dare say one man could do it.'

'But not a woman?'

'Oh,' the doctor chuckled as he took another sip of tea. 'I wouldn't have thought so. It would be much too heavy, unless of course we're talking about one of those Russian javelin throwers.' Both Kennedy and the doctor laughed. Then Leonard Taylor opened his hands away from his body. 'Of course I am talking about a normal circumstance. But there is a possibility that a woman trying to kill someone could find hidden superhuman strength. All that increased activity in the adrenal glands.'

The doctor took another sip from his cup; it was magnificent tea. One of those rare cups of tea which are so refreshing and enjoyable, you want to drink it quickly to enjoy the tea fully, but at the same time you want to drink slowly, so as to prolong the experience.

The doctor set off on another tack. 'His hands had been tied together in front of him.'

'In front of him? How do you know that?' Kennedy searched around his cluttered desk for a pen to commit his thoughts and the doctor's information to paper. Taylor produced one from his breast pocket and handed it to Kennedy. He was a famous compulsive supplier. He always had all sorts of useful items about his person – pens, pencils, erasers, paper clips, pins, elastic bands, blotting paper, calendar, multi-blade Swiss army knife, even a plastic spoon. Kennedy could remember one scene of crime he'd attended with the doctor. They'd found, easily enough, tea-making facilities but had trouble when it came to cups. Leonard Taylor had miraculously produced two polystyrene cups from an inside pocket. On this occasion a pen was sufficient and the doctor passed it over the desk and answered Kennedy's question.

'When someone ties your hands behind your back – ' the doctor rose to his feet to demonstrate the point, though he had trouble joining his hands behind his burly frame – 'the most natural thing to do is to tie them in an X shape. This means that at least one of the inside wrists will have a rope burn. However, when your hands are tied in front of you, the most obvious way is to tie them inside wrists together, which will leave no rope burn on either inside wrist.'

'A lemon entry, my dear Watson. A lemon entry!' Kennedy cheered.

Leonard Taylor sat down again and returned his attention to the report. 'His legs were also bound together at the ankles.' There were no observations this time from the DI so he continued. 'Mr O'Browne's last meal was nothing other than a large helping of French fried potatoes. I would probably say that, taking into consideration body temperature and how cold the Mayfair Mews Studio was, he probably would have died at 9.30pm at the earliest and as late as 10.30pm, at the outside.'

'It doesn't make sense, all this tying up and then hanging and then untying and laying out the body. It's like some kind of statement isn't it?' Kennedy suggested.

'Yes it is,' agreed Taylor. 'The other thing, the final thing in fact: if you had been wondering how Peter O'Browne was overpowered the answer is chloroform. I found traces of chloroform in his blood.'

Chapter Thirty-Two

You move much better when you know
When you know
Why you are happy
— Mary Margaret O'Hara

Two things of varying significance happened at the end of that Thursday afternoon, approximately twenty-one hours after the death by strangulation of Mr Peter O'Browne. And as so often is the case, both things were happening simultaneously.

WPC Anne Coles had an unexpected visit from the golden-voiced DS Sandy Johnson of the Fraud Squad, New Scotland Yard. And Mr Paddy George, Peter O'Browne's original partner in the record shop, received an equally unexpected visit from the police in the person of Detective Inspector Christy Kennedy of Camden CID.

The WPC was quite taken with the owner of the attractive voice. So often in the past, a wonderful telephone voice would turn out to belong to either a wimp or a person of over-ample proportions. Neither of these types appealed to WPC Anne Coles; no, she went more for the Christy Kennedy type. She wasn't really sure what the Kennedy type was (which probably made him more attractive), except that her DI was always clean-shaven, well-dressed, slim, seemingly deep, but still amusing and courteous. But what were his faults? Everyone had faults. WPC Coles would have liked to have got to know those of DI Kennedy, but she was too sensible and too ambitious to get involved with her boss.

She had been summoned to the reception by the desk sergeant, the ever jolly Timothy Flynn. Here DS Sandy Johnson confidently stepped up and introduced himself. 'I chased down those couple of names as I promised and well, you know I just had to see the owner of such a vibrant voice.'

God, you don't believe in beating about the bush, do you? thought Anne Coles. DS Johnson saw only that she blushed slightly as she replied: 'Good to meet you, too. Thanks for delivering the names in person. Come on through and I'll treat you to a cup of station treacle – sorry, I mean coffee.

'I suppose one good turn deserves another.'

At this point in their embryonic relationship, if indeed a relationship was to be born, they shared a faultlessness. It was too early for them to be aware of each other's flaws. At that stage it was all looks and glances and words, all of which merely hinted, probably erroneously, at a personality known only through two short conversations. In 99 per cent of relationships – even the ones which last forever – it's all down-hill all the way from there, albeit with a couple of pleasant detours along the way.

'I see what you mean,' offered Johnson, tentatively sipping the coffee. He smiled at WPC Coles, who merely stared at him. Eventually, in the absence of any further comment, she had to say, her eyebrows raised, 'Well?'

'Well?'

'Well, you've brought some information for me, I believe.' Anne laughed a very non-WPC laugh.

'Oh, shit, sorry. Of course,' DS Johnston stammered, realising that his behaviour was only two notches – maybe even one – above that of a village idiot. 'I've brought you the names, of the two team leaders. I think you'll find that the team members sometimes cross over from project to project.

'The main team is run by a chap called Dave Anderson – known as Normal to his mates,' Johnson went on, belatedly warming to his theme. 'Don't ask my why. Probably had a brother called Mad Max. He works out of the Hyde Park area of Leeds. The second chap, Hugh Guttridge, is based in Birmingham. Here are their addresses and telephone numbers.' He passed WPC Coles a piece of paper.

No, sorry, their fingers did not touch – not even the lightest of brushes. But the WPC did offer this poor, drowning man, a bit of a lifeline. 'Thanks. Thanks a lot. Particularly for delivering it to me in person. I suppose it means I owe you a drink?'

'That would be great, just great.'

'Well, I'll give you a ring some time,' she replied, folding the piece of paper in two and then in two again.

DS Sandy Johnson looked like he'd found a five-pound note but lost a tenner. Go for broke, son, he told himself, It's now or never. 'Well, what about now? After all, I'm on your patch, and there's no time like the present. What time do you get off duty?'

He must have been mad to be so pushy, he thought to himself, but something inside was driving him. Women like WPC Anne Coles are seldom unattached. There was a danger, a real danger, that the next time they met she would have connected with someone else. Sandy Johnson did not want this to become another case of What If…

The WPC checked her wristwatch, white dots and arms on a black background, for longer than she needed, giving herself time to make a decision. Was this a situation where she should be impulsive or sensible?

'Well, in fact I get off in ten minutes. And I suppose, after all your trouble, it would be inhospitable of me – well for that matter of Camden CID – not to entertain you.'

DS Johnson was holding his breath.

'There's a pub nearby, called the Edinboro,' Anne went on. 'Shall we meet there in, say...' Again she stared at her watch as if it were making her decisions for her. '...say, twenty minutes? I've a few things to do.' She unfolded the note again and rechecked the details. The paper, New Scotland Yard standard issue, was fresh and crisp and made a sound like pigeon wings flapping as she unfolded and then refolded it.

'I know it well. I'll see you there in twenty minutes,' Johnson replied. His relief was palpable. They shook hands awkwardly.

WPC Coles had completed a memo containing the details of Dave 'Normal' Anderson and Hugh Guttridge and placed it carefully on DI Kennedy's desk before she freshened herself up for the eagerly anticipated drink. She wasn't to know it at the time, but the drink was to lead to dinner later the same evening at her favourite Italian Restaurant, Vegia Zenia in Princess Street, a few streets away from North Bridge House, and, even later the same evening a good old-fashioned snog (but no more!).

*

As Anne Coles and Sandy Johnson were about to start the first of their two drinks ('You've never seen a bird fly on one wing,' claimed DS Johnson), DI Kennedy was conducting an interview with Paddy George in the latter's home at the posher end of Arlington Street.

If Mr George were the old oak he was said to resemble, he would have had sixty-three concentric circles on his inner trunk, bent and battered by the wind and the rain. He was a gentle man, probably a gentleman as well. He still had a few things on the boil, but generally he had sold off most of his business interests and now seemed intent on spending his quieter years in the more appealing company of his wife.

Paddy George had already heard through the grapevine about the death of Peter O'Browne. Camden's bush telegraph is second to none: local news travels through the numerous shops on Parkway quicker than Damon Hill could dump the 'shoemaker' from the track at Silverstone. He had thought that perhaps the murder element of the story was perhaps a bit on the imaginative side – after all, murders only happen on books, on television and in the movies.

'He was great in the early days, you know,' Paddy was reminiscing to Kennedy. 'He was totally, I mean totally, into the music. He lived only for that. He'd have a copy of everything, absolutely everything, which came in.

'And he wasn't like some of the collectors, who would add the albums unplayed to their collections. Peter would devour them until he knew the songs inside out. Then he would badger his customers into buying his favourites. He'd play them non-stop in the shop. I'm sure he personally sold five hundred copies of "Astral Weeks". I think that was his favourite album of all time. I remember him going on and on about how it was a new language, a breakthrough album, and that no one would ever better it.

'Peter was great to have in a shop – the records would just walk off the shelves. That's why I suggested we open the record shop together. I didn't think it would be long before he decided to do it by himself in any case, so I thought, Why not jump the gun and help him set one up? That way I wasn't losing a great shop manager, I was gaining a shop.'

'Weren't you upset that you didn't have a share of the record company?'

'Good heavens, no. Not at all. He came to me with the idea and asked me to put up £500 to start the record company off. I said no, for two reasons. First, I believe in doing what you know, and doing it well. I knew about selling records. I knew sweet FA about making them or about dealing with the people who write and record them.

'Secondly I reasoned that if he didn't have the £500 he couldn't set up the record company. If he couldn't set up his record company then our shop would do better and I hoped at the time that perhaps we would set up a few more shops, maybe even a chain.

'The next thing I heard was that his mate Martyn Farrelly, the song-writer, had given him the five hundred lids and Camden Town Records was born. The rest is history, as I'm sure you know, Inspector.' Kennedy thought that Paddy George had an excellent story-telling voice. Age had removed the need to rush his words. He was happy with life and what it had given him and his wife.

'Peter became famously successful,' the story continued. 'But the more successful he became, the less happy he was. And, judging by the last few times I spoke to him, music had ceased to be a joy.'

'Have you any idea who might have wanted to kill him?' Kennedy inquired as he languished in a comfortable armchair by the front window of George's sitting room. He had noticed that older people were happy to neglect the fashionable in food, furniture and clothes in favour of comfort.

'God, now there's a question. I wouldn't have a clue. The business he's in now… sorry, I mean was in, is so cut-throat. It could have been anyone. That's not a big help, I know. But I've been thinking about that same question since the rumours started,' Paddy replied sadly.

'Did you still see him, socialise with him?'

'No, not a lot. I think the last time I saw him was about a year ago. He and the girlfriend he had then – what was her name. Doris? No, Diane, yes that's it, Diane – came over here for dinner with me and the missus. It was the happiest I'd seen him in years. She was a great girl, very down to earth. We took to her immediately. She was just right for Peter, not in the least impressed with the pop crap. We supposed she loved him for the man he was.'

'And that's the last time you saw him?'

'Yes, we move in different circles these days.'

And that was about the extent of the information Kennedy extracted from Paddy George. He had tried to find out more about Diane, but neither Paddy nor his wife could remember her last name. They thought that she might have been a school-teacher but they weren't sure.

So ended the day during which Peter O'Browne's body had been found. Kennedy was regretting that the day had passed without his managing to uncover more. He felt that on a murder case, the first day was vital. What you did (or didn't do) could lead to success or failure in solving the case.

Back at his office Kennedy looked at the memo from WPC Coles. She's good, he thought. She has the makings of a good detective. She was thoughtful, resourceful, efficient, imaginative and, probably most important, didn't seem to mind a bit of hard work.

Before going home to shower and shave before joining ann rea and Leslie Russell for dinner, he updated his noticeboard.

Chapter Thirty-Three

I am out undoing
All the good I've done

– John Prine

Later that Thursday evening, Leslie Russell, ann rea and DI Christy Kennedy were sitting in the Engineer, a former pub converted into a restaurant/wine bar, situated about a hundred yards along Princess Street from Vegia Zenia, on the corner of Gloucester Road.

Russell had dressed down from his solicitor's uniform and was now casually attired: red polo-neck pullover, grey slacks and, to shield him from the cold and damp, a navy blue duffel coat, which he hung to the left of the entrance. He had recently showered – the rain couldn't have been so successful under the hood of his duffel coat. Kennedy, also feeling the need for a change, wore a white collarless shirt and his favourite black and green patterned waist coat. ann rea was stunning. Devilishly beautiful. Kennedy wasn't sure if it was his imagination, or the subtle lighting in the restaurant, but she looked like she was glowing. She dressed very simply but effectively in a loose fitting white blouse, short black skirt and black tights. Her favourite jacket, three quarter length black leather hung close to Russell's over garment and Kennedy's black crombie.

It was highly unusual for a detective inspector to dine with a witness, but Russell had suggested it. His logic made sense: he had important meetings all afternoon and he was sure that Kennedy and his team had enough to do to fill the afternoon without him. They would all have to eat at some point, so why not combine the two?

This comfy approach was all very well if one (Kennedy) assumed that one's dinner partner (Russell) had nothing to do with the murder. Kennedy did not have enough information or proof to make such an assumption, but his instinct told him Russell was in the clear and he was willing to give a little information in the hope of receiving a lot more in return.

ann rea observed that Leslie Russell was obviously used to talking, to talking all the time. He kept up his side of the dialogue as he stabbed aimlessly in the salad bowl with his fork, never losing eye contact, not even for a second.

'So, what do you imagine all that faffing about over the trip to the TE Lawrence territory was?' he offered as a few more lettuce leaves fell victim to indiscriminate proddings of the fork.

'Pardon?' replied Kennedy confused by the shift in gear from pleasantries to business without the gentle acceleration through second and third.

'Dorset. The trip to Dorset. Was that a wild goose chase, or what?'

'It's all a bit spooky, as if the murderer is leaving clues, but his clues don't add up to anything,' said ann rea.

'Well, there are two assumptions in your last sentence, ann rea, that I'm not sure we can afford to make.' Kennedy smiled directly at her to ensure that his remark was not taken as a rebuff.

'Two?'

'Well, the first one would have to be that we can't be sure the slayer is, in fact, male,' Russell offered.

ann rea and Kennedy spoke simultaneously. 'Okay, agreed,' from ann rea and, 'Correct!' from the detective.

'But the second?' He returned his fork to the empty salad bowl, clasping both hands into a fist which he placed under his chin, distributing the weight of his head through the triangle created by his elbows, on to the table.

'We can't really assume that the clues don't mean anything until we have the complete picture.' Kennedy was struggling to keep up with his dinner partners on the eating front. His potato and leak soup was hot, and furthermore, it was pretty hard to speak with a mouthful of soup. 'Even if they are red herrings, not part of our main picture, they will still give some information on the murderer, which, might even turn out to be the means we use to convict him or her, or even them.' He finally emptied his soup bowl, which was more like soup bucket, with three full spoon trips to his mouth.

'How likely is it that this murder would have been committed by either a she or a them?' ann rea inquired. She was surprised she had not considered either of these options before. But then, she was not a police officer.

'Well, let's look at this.' Kennedy outlined his hypothesis. 'Let us assume, for the purposes of this discussion, that last Friday night, just as he was about to leave his office, Peter O'Browne was telephoned, in fact, by the murderer. If we go with this theory then we have to automatically rule out Mary Jones, as she was leaving the building with Peter as the call came through.' Kennedy refilled their wine glasses.

'Unless. Unless of course you go for the Them option, old chap. In which case Mary's accomplice could have made the call,' Russell interrupted, happy to have his wine glass recharged, and, relishing the opportunity to join in the policeman's "let's suppose" scenario.

'But then why would Mary have contacted me with her fears for Peter?' asked ann rea, who stopped filling her wine glass in mid flow to offer her flaw in Russell's scenario. 'She could easily just have stayed quiet until his body was found.'

'Well, contacting you and, or, the police would have been exactly what she would have been expected to do,' replied Kennedy, taking a sip of his wine and nodding to the waitress to bring them another bottle. The trouble, he felt, with great red wine was that it flowed down the gullet a little too easily. By this time, the Engineer was filling up with people, and making himself heard above the noise was proving thirsty work. Leslie Russell had a habit of checking every new patron, his eyes resting for a few seconds longer on the female contingent.

'Anyway, you were saying old chap?' Russell prompted as he smiled a smile that said 'I'm glad someone ordered a second bottle of wine, because I don't want to have to refuse the last glass in the bottle just to be polite'.

'So, say the murderer telephoned Peter O'Browne. O'Browne must have known who it was, because he went willingly to meet him – or her – at Mayfair Mews studio. He must have considered this meeting important enough to blow out the appointment to view a new group with Mary Jones.

'The murderer is waiting for O'Browne to arrive. He overpowers him with the help of chloroform which could take anything up to sixty seconds to take effect. Perhaps that rules out a woman, perhaps not. The element of surprise might have worked in the assassin's favour.

'By the time O'Browne regains consciousness, he is bound hand and foot, and gagged, consequently in the power of the murderer. The killer takes O'Browne's credit cards and first thing on Saturday morning takes a train from Waterloo to Wareham, using the aforementioned cards to pay for the ticket. He, or she (ish), takes a train to Corfe Castle, has lunch and disappears. Then he presumably returns to London, and goes directly to O'Browne's house on England's Lane to plant an incendiary device which torches the house on Sunday evening.

'We have to imagine that he or she had to return to Mayfair Mews. Again, this is an assumption based on the fact that O'Browne somehow had access to a toilet. His clothes were not soiled and it seems he was also fed and watered. So our murderer must have visited the studio several times before his final return on Wednesday evening sometime before nine-thirty. The killer threw a rope over a roof beam, tied the other end around O'Browne's neck and pulled until he was dangling in the air.'

'I'm not sure I'm fit for the main course,' ann rea groaned. Kennedy felt just the opposite. A mushroom and pastry dish like the one he'd ordered had recently been delivered to the next table and the blend of rich aromas from the mushroom sauce and freshly baked pastry was making Kennedy's mouth water. For now he satisfied himself with another mouthful of wine.

'The slayer then either tied the free end of the rope to something or held it while Peter O'Browne struggled for air and eventually strangled. This would have taken a few minutes, perhaps even quite a few, and a lot of guts. When the evil deed was completed O'Browne was lowered to the floor and his body prepared for discovery.'

'How was that?'

'I'm sorry, but we have to keep that information secret for the time being,' Kennedy replied gently. 'But I can tell you that some kind of statement was undoubtedly being made.

'Finally, the murderer tidied up the place, packed away his bits and pieces and left Mayfair Mews Studio probably no later than ten-thirty.' The end of Kennedy's summary coincided neatly with the arrival of the main course.

ann rea was happy she had ordered the ravioli and not the lamb, as recommended by their waitress. All three of them were silent for a while, though lots of ambient noise was provided by the pepper mills, salt shakers, knives and forks, and added to by the surrounding hubbub.

Kennedy felt it was time to move away from the murder scene so vividly planted in the mind of everyone at the table. He had to find a tangent to travel upon. There were several possible tangents, and each would eventually traverse.

His starting question was, 'So, how long had you known Peter O'Browne?'

Chapter Thirty-Four

It doesn't pay to drive too fast
All it does is make your life last shorter
– Gilbert O'Sullivan

'Must be over twenty years now,' Russell replied without hesitation, his bass-baritone crackle voice ensuring that his part of the conversation would not carry to the neighbouring tables. 'He came to me the first time he fell into trouble. It was that turn of his called Radio Cars.

'They were selling records, lots of them, and their manager wanted to take them to another record company. It wasn't even a request: as far as this chap Jason Carter-Houston was concerned he was off, with "his boys" in tow, the lure of a big commission cheque being too strong to resist.

'Peter's shop partner, Paddy George, had used my father's services for years and he brought Peter around to our offices. Father brought me into the meeting with Peter and Paddy. I think he reckoned that Peter and I spoke the same language, so he suggested that we went off and sorted out Peter's problems, leaving the grown-ups to their own problem; namely, a love of fifteen-year-old malt whisky.

'As it turned out, there was not a lot I could do for him at that stage. Basically, he didn't have any sort of written agreement with Radio Cars. And so they left, went off to enjoy a career rich only in obscurity with a label I forget the name of.'

'Butterfly Records?' ann rea suggested.

'Absolutely correct.' Russell nodded his head in a northeast to southwest direction. 'But Peter had the last laugh. Let me tell you a little story, I do this in the strictest of confidence, of course. When they came back to him some time later seeking royalty payment, Peter said, "What royalties? Remember, we don't have a contract, and if there is no contract how can there be any agreement to pay royalties?"' Russell afforded himself a laugh, a laugh loud enough to draw the attention of some of their fellow diners. 'I didn't feel at the time that Peter was 100 per cent legal in his argument, but it was some kind of poetic justice.'

'How did he come to start up the record company in the first place, it seems such a weird ambition?' ann rea quizzed.

'I suppose to Peter it was a natural progression from the record shop, which had been a natural progression from managing the group. He was always helping new bands who dropped by the shop. He started falling for the American sounds of Jackson Browne,

Leonard Cohen, Crosby, Stills, Nash and Young (together and separately), Joni Mitchell and some of the new West Coast soft rock groups who were springing up practically weekly at that point.

'Peter started writing to some of these groups whose records you could only purchase on import. He was eager for news on their careers and future releases, and the UK music rags, as ever, were about a year behind the time. One such group, Half Moon Bay Express asked Peter to put out their new album in Britain. It wasn't that they thought he was great or anything, they just couldn't get anyone else interested, but they did like and trust Peter. He was flattered but, because he liked them so much, he was scared of being the cause of "bad vibes". He was still pretty hurt that he had lost his oldest friend due to the business side of the music.

'Around this time, he had a call out of the blue from his friend, Martyn Farrelly, and after a very drunken evening Martyn gave Peter £500 for his new venture. Peter opened a new account at his local Lloyds branch in the name of Camden Town Records. He was now the sole owner of a record company. He decided that rather than manufacture his records, he would begin by importing American copies of the Half Moon Bay Express album.

'They agreed to his request and sent two hundred "cut-out" copies. "Cut-out" is where albums have had the top left hand corner of the sleeve cut-off to signify a "freebie" or promotional copy. That way they avoid having to pay both import and export duty. American album sleeves were generally produced with thicker card than used on the UK releases. The one inch triangle missing from one corner made the release quite mysterious for the UK collectors, and, to add further to the intrigue, Americans shrink-wrapped their releases.

'Peter sold fifty of these in the Camden Records shop and he distributed the remaining one hundred and fifty around like-minded record stores in London. To Peter, this was like when he went around on the underground on his original trip to London to try and find gigs for "the boys". This time he was going around with boxes of records to try and sell recorded music.'

'He sold out his entire stock of two-hundred copies over the following two weekends and his next shipment of five-hundred copies from Half Moon Bay arrived a week later. Being out of stock actually helped increase demand on the bush telegraph: then and still the most effective form of record promotion.

'The five-hundred copies, all at a special price of £4.50 (to customers, £3.75 to the shops) all went within a week. This time he used his little green book of Blues by Five gigs and record stores and he sold to mates in Manchester, Birmingham, Bristol, Brighton, Bath, Edinburgh and Newcastle. Soon all the stores were on to him for more copies of Half Moon Bay Express and he had another shipment sent over from America: this time a thousand copies, and a month later a further thousand copies. Peter was paying the band less than a pound per copy. He was making serious profit.

'His network of shops were all becoming very friendly with him – there's nothing like success to encourage success. They soon began to inquire about any other similar records he could get his hands on. Peter took a thousand copies of each of Half Moon Bay Express' first two records and started to quiz Adam Francis, the band's bass player and Peter's contact in the group. Peter promised Adam if he looked after the American side of things, purchasing and shipping the record then he (Peter) would look after Adam.

'So Adam came up with Ozark Mountain Daredevils, Pure Prairie League and also found out that Van Morrison's new album "Moondance" was going to be released in America six weeks before it would hit the UK shops. Van's previous album, "Astral Weeks" had become the bedsitter/hippie classic of the early Seventies. Peter predicted that the demand for the follow-up, "Moondance" would be phenomenal. He ordered 5,000 copies.

'As Van's records were released on Warner Bros, Adam Francis was forced, due to lack of contacts, to pay nearly two pounds per record. Peter knew how committed Van's fans were and priced the albums at £4.95 each. The entire 5,000 copies sold out over the first weekend including an incredible 680 copies through Camden Records. This time Peter had taken two adverts, one in *Melody Maker* and another in a new London magazine, *Time Out*.

'At the end of that weekend, Peter set down, worked out his sums and sent a cheque for £500 to Martyn Farrelly, who returned it immediately claiming the initial cheque had been a present, not a loan.'

'Was Farrelly not annoyed about not being an official part of Camden Town Records? After all, without his money there would not have been a company,' Kennedy asked, though conscious he might have upset Russell's flow.

The solicitor thought carefully for a few minutes. 'No I don't think so,' he said slowly and then speeded back up into his story. 'Now that Peter knew the system and how to work it, he needed a challenge. He had been thinking for some time about the possibility of putting out a proper Camden Town Records release, instead of just distributing someone else's.

'There was a young R&B band called Radio Cars, who he'd been to see a few times and was quite impressed by. What they lacked in musical ability they made up for with visual excitement. Their lead singer, Andy, was quite wild on stage. Peter invited Radio Cars to the office for a meeting. Camden Town Records had the floor above the Regent Bookshop on Parkway and his record label was run from the back storage room. He made an agreement with them to release an EP.

'Radio Cars had already been to a four-track demo studio and had recorded six of their best live numbers – no frills no production – just as close a representation of their live sound as they could get. One of the songs was a cover of an early Them classic, "Mystic Eyes".

'They didn't draw up a formal agreement, that wasn't Peter's style. He just put his thoughts down on a scrap of paper, saying how he saw them working together, how many copies of the EP he would press, the unit cost for pressing them, how much the sleeves would cost, how much the band would receive for each copy sold– no percentages, no deductions. Twenty-pence for every copy sold and he'd sell them to the band for a pound each. They all agreed and added their names at the end of the scrap of paper.

'He pressed up a thousand copies initially. The thousand were devoured immediately. Peter now became adventurous and pressed up an additional 5,000; they sold out immediately. Another 5,000 and they were gone as quick as he could press the records and print the sleeves. The back of Camden Records looked like a bomb site, sleeves, records, flyers everywhere.

'It wasn't that the music was great or polished or professional or slick, in fact it was none of these things. But Radio Cars and a lot of similar bands were selling underground around England as a reaction against the pomp rock and the likes of Rod Stewart and Elton John, who were more interested in talking about blondes and money (respectively) than in making good music.

'The small bands, who had been squeezed out by record companies too busy ass-licking the likes of Rod, Elton and ELP, were taking matters into their own hands, making their own music and getting it out. This movement, and it was more than just punk, was starting to take over the asylum, with the help of independent-minded people like Peter O'Browne.

'Anyway, Peter decided that he needed help and enlisted another friend from Trinity College, Tom Best. Tom was another vinyl junkie, who originally hailed from Belfast, and had an eye, and ear, for the obscure. Peter quickly introduced Tom to the Camden Town Records set-up and network of friends who sold their records,' Russell enthused.

'Ah, so Tom Best wasn't involved in the record shop, just the record company?' Kennedy had thought Tom had started working for Peter at the time of the shop.

'Yes, just the record company. Tom Best had no job description, he just did anything and everything that needed doing. He was ambitious and saw the potential of their blossoming cottage industry. Tom Best began to cultivate a relationship with the press, seeing this as being an economical and quick way of drawing attention to Camden Town Records' releases.

'Radio Cars were now venturing out of London for gigs and were selling out each and every club they played in. They also sold a copy of their EP to every second person in attendance. Eventually Peter's network demanded a Radio Cars album, so Peter brought the boys back in (this time to an even more packed office) to go through the figures, jot them down on a scrap of paper and give the boys a copy of same. Peter (Camden Town Records) would put up the money Radio Cars needed to record the album and buy the band some new amps, guitars and drum kit, which he would take back from the initial sales.

'He worked out, so that the group could see, that including the printing of sleeves and pressing of records, they would need to sell in the region of 10,000 copies. On every record they sold over 10,000 copies he would pay them a pound per record. Camden Town Records pressed 15,000 copies of their (and Radio Cars') first album release, "After Russia, What next?", given the serial number, NW1. Radio Cars were at last the album band they had dreamed of becoming.

'The 15,000 copies took exactly two and a half days to sell and the album entered the charts at number 37. They suffered in this position slightly due to the fact that not all of Peter's network were chart return shops. But the band didn't worry too much: "After Russia, What next?" was in the national album charts, a dream come true. More importantly, the girls were now paying attention to their Camden Sound and cool stage suits, which was really a Beatles collarless jacket rip-off.

'The following week, the record dropped to 49 in the charts due mainly to the album being unavailable. Peter pressed another 15,000 copies and shipped them to the shops in time for the album to jump back up to 32 in the next chart. Then the album plotted its way further up the charts, 28 to 25 to 21, dropped to 22 (oops), then back up until it leaped into the top ten and all hell broke loose as every shop in the country placed orders for Radio Cars' "After Russia, What next?"

'Unfortunately for Peter, these new shops, outside his network, wanted to deal differently. The network shops paid Peter as they reordered. The new shops, spoilt by the majors, wanted twenty-eight days credit and discounts and the freedom to return what they didn't sell. 'Peter either had to go along with it, which meant fronting the money himself, or, stick to his network, and watch the group fall down the charts. The album had by now sold 58,000 copies and normally everyone would have been delighted. But the group and their newly appointed manager, Mr Jason Carter-Houston, were hungry for more chart success.

'Peter O'Browne decided to stick to his network shops, feeling the new shops could cripple him if they took advantage of their returns facility. Some of the new stores accepted Camden Town Records' cash up-front policy but most didn't, so the following week the album dropped to 18 and then moved further down to 26 then 31 and finally out of the top 50 altogether.

'Following the falling out with Radio Cars, Peter concentrated on American releases and persuaded Half Moon Bay Express and their American record label, Picture Records, that the band's new album – a live, in-concert set called "Alive and Dreamin'" should officially be on Camden Town Records for Europe. This would avoid all of their import/export problems, which were growing as customs paid more attention to shipments. The album sold a respectable 32,000 copies and would have done better if the band had toured.

'Around 1978 Peter sensed another buzz around London's pubs and clubs and signed a new band called EP. They were his first new signing since Radio Cars, who had since disbanded due to lack of interest from Butterfly Records. Actually the name EP was Peter's idea, as the band were called Erect Penis when Peter found them,' said Russell somewhat quietly.

'In quick succession, he signed three more punk bands in the wake of the success of The Clash, Buzzcocks and Sex Pistols. The other three were Rags, from Islington, a very aggressive band, always fighting with either each other or the audience or one of the support bands. Twat, a Newcastle band of three girls with a boy drummer, who had sent a tape to one of Peter's network shops which had passed it on to Peter, and the jewel in Peter's punk crown, Wire Crates. Peter felt that they had a very talented guitarist and songwriter, David Cummings, who was using the punk movement to launch his own music. The punk movement exploded and Peter was selling about 10,000 albums a week across the four new bands. This time I had made sure that all the bands were signed on water-tight contracts. Peter had also increased his network and was using an independent distributor, Fox, to cover the rest of the country. Fox took 36p per record.

'Twat's first single, "I Just Wanna be Shagged' entered the singles chart in its first week at 18, but the BBC refused to mention them, or play the record and wouldn't allow them on *Top of The Pops*. The more the media and industry ignored the single, the more it sold and within two weeks it was number two. Camden Town Records were to be denied their first number one single the following week when The Pistols entered at number one. The single sold a staggering 186,000 copies and took the group's debut album, "Twat: We All Need One' to over 100,000 copies, giving the band and Camden Town Records their first gold album.

'Every band in the land now wanted to sign to Camden Town Records who, along with Stiff and Chiswick, were *the* punk labels.

'Wire Crates' album sold the least of Peter's new bands with a still respectable 26,000, but Peter felt silently confident about them. He sent a copy of their album, "The Lonely Road" to his friends at Picture

Records in America. Picture Records loved the album and released it as soon as they could get it out. Camden Town Records had their first official release (via Picture Records) in the US of A.

'1979 was a great year for Camden Town Records. Wire Crates had sold 1.3 million copies in the US alone and soon the European sales would take the final figure over a staggering 2 million copies.

'Peter was now selling, across his eight UK signings an average of 35,000 albums per week. They had increased the staff to eight and Peter decided the time was ripe to move to a permanent home. So he bought the garage on the corner of Gloucester Avenue and Parkway and built a trendy blue building just opposite your station,' Russell nodded to Kennedy.

'It turned out to be trendy quite by accident. As the site was close to the railway bridge they could not put in deep foundations. So they built a permanent temporary-type structure with light cladding,' ann rea stated, revealing her knowledge of Camden history.

'By the mid-Eighties, Wire Crates had sold a total of twenty million across their five albums.' Russell recited his own little bit of Camden history. 'The Camden Records shop had peaked, thanks in part to the new supermarket style of record shops. Peter still had a soft spot for it and still kept it on as a going concern; it always broke even, at the very least.

Grabaphone, one of the major record companies, decided to bolster their weak A&R department. They made Peter an offer for Camden Town Records. At first he refused to listen but after fifteen months of haggling they eventually made him an offer he couldn't refuse. Grabaphone would pay Peter O'Browne £6 million for 51 per cent of Camden Town Records. Peter would have been happier to sell 49 per cent of his company for £4m but Grabaphone pressurised Peter for the extra, and most important, 2%.

'And you have been his solicitor all this time?' Kennedy asked.

'Yes.'

'Did he have any financial difficulties at the time of his death?' A police question from a policeman.

'Good Lord, no. None whatsoever. He was what the eastenders call "sweet", very sweet in fact. The Grabaphone buy-out gave him all the money he would need for the rest of his life, and then some.'

'What about girlfriends?' a newspaper question from a newspaper person.

'Well, he was like lots of us men.' Russell's narrative slowed down, as he began to pick his words more carefully. ann rea felt that if she hadn't been there, perhaps his answer might have been more *Nudge, nudge; wink, wink*. 'Men like us who make ourselves a slave to success, working all the hours that God sends at the expense of our personal lives.

'Occasionally he would meet someone, fall head-over-heels in love with her and have a whirlwind romance. Then he would claim that "familiarity tarnishes beauty" and he would start to neglect them as he busied himself once more in his work. And as often happens with such men, the women grew bored sitting around waiting and clear off, or they become boring, so you clear off.'

'Are you speaking from experience?' ann rea raised a false smile to sweeten her question.

'Absolutely, I'm afraid to say. You keep telling yourself that it's just because you haven't met the right person. But, I fear, that even if you were to meet the right person, you'd commit the same sin. Take Diana Alexander for instance...' Kennedy's ears pricked up. 'Peter was convinced she was it, the right person. And you know what, I sincerely think that she could have been – she was a truly delightful girl. But once the novelty of the romance wore off, he started to neglect her for his work.

'The second he did, Diana was off like a light. No hanging around. I think he lived to regret losing her. He often told me he thought that if he couldn't make it work with someone like Diana he couldn't make it work with anyone. I think he gave up all thought of serious relationships after that.

'I don't know about women,' Russell continued, looking at ann rea as he took a break from his food, placing his knife and fork on the plate and his clasped hands in front of him, elbows on the table. 'But I think the older that single men become, the harder it gets to be part of a successful relationship. You start to enjoy your space, your own company, and you become selfish. But worse than that, you don't feel it's wrong to be selfish.'

'I would agree with that,' said ann rea. 'I think it is the same for a woman, maybe even harder. We have a different set of rituals we love which are no less important to us, nor do we behave any less selfishly.'

'I suppose that makes me the romantic,' Kennedy cut in. 'I believe that it doesn't matter when you meet the person you are going to fall in love with, because love waits. When you meet her you fall in love, and that's it, all the rest falls into place. You forget all the rules you have built up to protect yourself from getting hurt. I don't think you see abandoning selfishness as a sacrifice with someone you love; you only protect your space around people you don't love.'

'You could be right,' Russell agreed.

'What, that he is a romantic? Of course he is!' ann rea smiled brushing the nape of Kennedy's neck with her thumb and index finger.

'No, no, actually about falling in love. I suppose if you are, it gives hope to someone such as myself.

ann rea wondered, from the little she knew of Leslie Russell – he looked okay, was good company, courteous, incredibly well groomed – how he could have reached that stage of his life without meeting someone special. Another on the never-shortening list of eligible bachelors. But then Kennedy, until he and ann rea had met, had been in exactly the same situation, so maybe he was right after all. ann rea certainly hoped so, because that would mean that she and Kennedy had a chance.

'Do you know anything at all about this chart hyping and blackmailing?' Kennedy asked, happy to move back towards safer ground.

'Well, on the record, Kennedy, speaking as Peter's solicitor, I've got to tell you I knew absolutely nothing about it. But as his friend, I did hear about it; and speaking as his friend I'll tell you anything that might help your investigation.'

'Why did he get involved in hyping in the first place?'

'Because they practically all do it. Because it's possible to do it. And, at the point when Peter was involved, he was doing a deal to sell off part of his record company. He wanted as high a chart profile as possible. And besides, it works, it sells records, albeit indirectly. It's a good investment. You pay someone fifteen grand to "market" your record and as a result you can sell hundreds of thousands of records, even millions of records, if you get it right.'

'But hyping is illegal,' ann rea reminded him.

'Absolutely! I agree with you, but if you are competing in a business where it is seen not so much as illegal but more as standard practice, you are either going to have join in to survive, or steer clear of it and see your competitors steam ahead.

'I told him, I said: "Peter, if you stop it and you persuade all the rest of them to stop it, you are all going to be playing on a level pitch again and none of you will need to do it." It was as simple as that. All he had to do was get everyone together and unilaterally agree to stop hyping. They would all save money and no one would risk going to jail.'

'Logical, logical. And what did he say to that?' ann rea inquired.

'He told me that apparently they had tried a couple of times to do just that but what had happened was that one of the companies would have an important release one week, a release they just absolutely had to get into the charts. So they would renege on the deal, and the following week the others would notice the chart action, and say, "Well, if they are going to do it, then so are we," and you are back to where you started.'

'But the record companies cannot guarantee that everyone will like the record and buy it,' said ann rea. 'Surely there must be some role for the music to play in this corrupt process.'

'The sad fact is that mostly it doesn't matter. I imagine, on a guess, that 90 per cent of the population buy what is successfully marketed to them. If people are told something is good, and this fact is hammered home at them enough – on TV, in the press, on the radio, with posters – then this great nation of consumers will be happy to buy whatever it is.'

'I just can't believe that. No one is going to buy something they don't like. Sorry, no way!' ann rea was getting quite heated. She hated to think that something that she cared about as much as music could be dealt with as a commodity.

Russell smiled a warm, forgiving smile excited by ann rea's passion, 'Look, I'm sorry, I'm really sorry but it's true. I'll give you an example if you will permit me to. Each year there will be two or three mega albums that sell at least a million copies in this country alone. They are known as coffee table albums and the record companies kill to get them.'

'Do you have proof of that, sir?' Kennedy joked, pulling out his official notebook, pencil at the ready.

'What? Oh yes, "kill", very good, detective inspector.' They all laughed and had some more wine.

'Yes, coffee table albums, and that is exactly what they are, albums that are fashionable to leave lying on your coffee table with the latest Hansel photo book. Most are not played a lot, and when they are, it's usually as background music for dinner parties and that kind of thing. These are albums by people like Brian Adams, Tina Turner, Simply Red, Phil Collins, Enya, Dire Straits. I think the names speak for themselves – they're got about as much to do with cutting edge as putty. But they are presented and promoted as albums you have got to have, and people do subscribe to this American marketing ploy: If you associate yourselves with hip and cool things, then you are hip and cool.'

'Well, interesting. I'm not sure I agree with you on Dire Straits, though, I still love their first record, still play it. But more to the point, how did Peter find the hypers in the first place?' asked Kennedy. ann rea was so disgusted by this stage that she had stopped eating her food and was sitting back in her chair quietly fuming.

'Don't forget that Peter got to see the other side of it when he ran his record shop. He would already have met several of them and I think it was a Camden chap who put Peter in touch with Hughie Guttridge, the man behind one of the nationwide teams.'

'Do you know who the Camden chap is?' ann rea asked. Kennedy imagined his name and likeness splashed all over the front page of the *Camden News Journal* as ann rea sought revenge on the music wreckers with a major exposé.

'As a matter of a fact I do. He's a chap called Barney Noble, a bit of a wheeler-dealer. He dabbles in everything. He's been busted for drugs a couple of times, which is how I know of him. One of the partners in my firm represents him. I can get you his address – off the record of course.'

'Thanks a million, that would be helpful.' Kennedy was beginning to feel this unconventional interview was justified. 'Do you think there is a chance this chap could be tied up in the blackmail?'

'What? Do you think Peter was murdered as a result of the blackmail going wrong?'

'It's too early to rule out any possibilities.'

'Oh. Well, in that case, I was at my parents' house in Oxford for the weekend. I left straight from the office and arrived there in time for tea at seven o'clock. You can check it out,' Russell smiled. He made this statement not as someone trying to defend himself, but someone who wished to head off at the pass any danger of his being considered as suspect.

He took his wallet from his back trouser pocket and opened it to reveal a small note-pad on the left hand side. He wrote down his father's name and address, briskly tore the page from the pad, handed it to Kennedy, refolded his wallet and replaced it in his pocket, all in as much time as it would take one of the hypers to buy a single.

Kennedy thanked Russell for the info and placed the folded page in the middle of his notebook.

'Did Peter ever talk to you about the blackmailing?' ann rea inquired, suspecting that she knew the answer.

'Why yes, of course. And he paid up – against my advice, I might add. I felt that he might be leaving himself open to further blackmailing. 'Russell returned to his plate to finish the last morsels of his meal. ann rea had noticed that he ate part of his meat, then part of his potatoes, then part of the vegetables, never mixing mouthfuls the way she did.

'How much was it?' Kennedy inquired.

'Not big league. I think it was a couple of grand. Again, Peter thought it was money well spent. At that point he was well advanced with the Grabaphone deal and adverse publicity could have scared them off.'

'Even though they were probably doing exactly the same thing as Peter by hyping their own records,' ann rea stated in disgust.

'Undoubtedly, and to a much greater degree than Peter was. But it's the old double standards, thing isn't it?'

The second bottle of wine had bitten the dust and nobody volunteered to order another. Kennedy was not disappointed. Both he and ann rea were merry enough to enjoy some ADA (after dinner activity) and more alcohol may have cooled the spirits.

Instead ann rea and Russell ordered coffee, and Kennedy (surprise, surprise) ordered tea, over which he inquired about Martyn

Farrelly, Tom Best and Carter-Houston, and Russell inquired about the bill. Leslie Russell received the bill, (despite protests from ann rea and Kennedy) Kennedy did not receive any additional information on his current list of suspects. But he had two more leads: Barney Noble and Diana Alexander.

Chapter Thirty-Five

I could have been a sign post
I could have been a clock
— Nick Drake

The following day (Friday) moved fast, very fast, towards an unsatisfactory conclusion.

It started for Kennedy with an 8am visit to the scene of the crime. Kennedy was not exactly sure what he was looking for. Well, in a way he did know what he was looking for: he was looking for clues. But what clues in particular, he had no idea. He just wanted to walk around the scene, as he often did on a murder investigation, and soak up his surroundings

This usually helped to him to work out how the murder hadn't happened, rather than how it had. The SoC was taped off and a police constable, a rookie called Tony Essex, was guarding the front door of the studio. Kennedy found it easy to remember his name because he shared it with two members of the string quartet featured on the most covered song of all time: Paul McCartney's 'Yesterday'.

The PC unlocked the studio door and showed Kennedy inside, turning on the lights to expel the darkness from the window-free room. Kennedy paced the distance from the door to the chalk marks that sketched out the spot where Peter O'Browne's body had lain. Five generous steps were sufficient to cover the distance.

The beam from which Peter had been hanged was a further three paces into the building. They had been able to locate the exact beam from the rope hairs found on it. More had been discovered on the floor.

The damp patch, less visible than it had been the previous morning, was about midway between the hanging point and the internal door in the corner of the studio. Kennedy passed through this door and into the cramped domestic quarters.

Visits to the kitchen, bedroom, bathroom, toilet, and lounge produced nothing inspirational. Once again, he noted the contrast between the murder room, cleaned and tidied by the murderer, and the home of Marianne MacIntyre.

The main difference might have been the obvious premeditation of the O'Browne killing, but the net result was exactly the same: the loss of a human life. Society dictated, and paid Kennedy to ensure, that such loss of life did not go unpunished.

To Kennedy, this work, his work, was a pleasure. The murders always upset him, upset him immensely in fact, but the detection and in successful cases, the subsequent capture of the perpetrator, were the main reasons for his existence. The punishment of the criminal sometimes left him cold.

There were always mitigating circumstances. The offender's father had beaten him; his mother didn't love him; he was abused; he was bullied at school, someone stole his lollipop. There was always some excuse, and some clever lawyer would appeal for leniency based on society's debt, not to the victim, but to the destroyer. Kennedy was of the opinion, which he mostly kept to himself, that bad was bad and we all, no matter what our pasts hold, control the absolute power to make the decision to do wrong or right. If we decide to do wrong, then we must be prepared to accept the consequences. After all, mitigating circumstances are of no comfort to the victims or to their families.

Such thoughts filled Kennedy's head that Friday morning as he walked around the studio and domestic quarters, the fingers of his right hand flexing repeatedly.

As he left the building he said, half to himself, half to PC Essex, 'Anyone who is going to be that tidy and methodical in committing a murder is going to have a watertight alibi,' and then as an after-thought added, 'Aren't they?'

'Yes, I suppose so, sir,' the PC replied tentatively. 'Or maybe they think that they are so clever, they think they will never need an alibi as they are never going to be caught.'

As he left the mews and stepped into Regents Park Road, under Fitzroy Flowers at No 77, Kennedy noticed to his right an unlit neon sign above a fish and chip shop. *Regent*, it proclaimed. Kennedy used this chip shop himself from time to time – it was famed for its mushy peas.

The Regent's staff would undoubtedly have a hard time remembering someone buying one portion of chips two nights previous. But it might be worth a punt. He made a mental note to have it checked when it was open.

Chapter Thirty-Six

My hair's still curly and my eyes are blue
Why don't you love me like you used to do?
— Hank Williams

'Hello, it's me.' A funny way to introduce yourself, Kennedy thought, even as he uttered the words. He'd received a message, concise as usual, to ring ann rea.

'Hi, Kennedy.' Kennedy was forever searching her voice for a hint of what was coming. If the truth be known, what he was expecting was, 'Look, Kennedy, this is not really working out and I think we need to take a break/get married/split up.' Delete as appropriate. It was funny that in the cold light of day or morning you could take little comfort from last night's passion.

'Listen, Kennedy, I feel bad about telling you this.'

God I was right – here it comes, Kennedy thought as his heart pretended it was Tyson to the Bruno of his chest. 'Yeah?' he said as casually as he could.

'Well, I was talking to Mary Jones this morning,' ann rea began gingerly.

What on earth has Mary Jones got to do with you packing me in? Kennedy thought in confusion, barely managing another, 'Yeah?'

'Well she told me. Oh God well, Kennedy it's like this – she told me in confidence, and I don't know. I told her that I would have to tell you in case it affects the case, but she wasn't happy about it.'

So the Big E was not on offer for that Friday, at least not in the morning. Tyson stopped thrashing Bruno and he was fluent again. 'ann rea, what is it, exactly, that you are trying to tell me?'

'Oh, I wish I wasn't… wasn't your friend, then I'd be happy to let you find it out for yourself. But shit, you'll find out anyway.'

'ann rea!'

'Peter O'Browne was having an affair with Colette Farrelly!'

'What!'

'Yes, I know. I thought the same thing. She and Martyn seemed so happy, so much a couple.'

'How long had this been going on?'

'Quite a few years, apparently. But it was quite weird really.'

'I like weird, tell me more.'

'Kennedy!'

'Sorry.' He wasn't really, and both of them knew so and enjoyed the moment before Kennedy prompted, 'So, what was weird?'

'It seems that it wasn't really a normal relationship.'

'Well it wouldn't be, would it? She already had one of those with her husband.'

'Kennedy I can't believe you're being so frivolous at a time like this,' ann rea replied. If she had known what Kennedy, had been expecting her to say, his frivolity would have been very understandable. 'If you've settled down, I'll continue. It seems it was more of a fraternal relationship; she cared for him, she liked him. In fact it was Colette who fixed him up with his last girlfriend, the teacher Diana Alexander.

'Allegedly, occasionally, it seems they did have sex, but Mary reckons it was no big thing to either of them; they enjoyed it, but neither was hung up about it. Not love, just lust.'

'Hmmm,' Kennedy murmured taking all this in, writing Colette's name on his note pad, coincidentally under Diana Alexander's, and drawing ever-growing concentric rectangles around it. 'How did they manage to keep it a secret?'

'Mary didn't think anyone knew about it, apart from her – that's why she was so insistent I didn't tell you. But now with Peter's death, well, she has started to wonder whether Martyn might have known. Martyn is so in love with Colette that Mary was worried that he may have found out about it and, well… killed Peter. And I remembered that you told me he claimed to have been alone in the music room that night.'

'Yes,' Kennedy replied. 'But lack of an alibi does not necessarily equate to proof of guilt.'

'But if first of all he doesn't have an alibi, and then it appears he might also have had a motive, doesn't that add up to something?'

'It certainly doesn't prove anything, but it might nudge me in a certain direction of thought. Do you think there may be anything else floating around out there that Mary isn't telling us about?'

'No. She assured me that was all. Mary liked Colette. She says she really cared for Peter. Apparently Colette often rang Mary just to check how Peter was doing.'

Someone knocked on DI Christy Kennedy's door.

'Look, ann rea, thanks a million for this – I have to go, I'm late for a meeting. Will I see you later?'

'Ah, I don't know, Kennedy. I'm miles behind here. Maybe I'll just work late and go straight home tonight. I've got to go. We'll talk later.'

He wondered whether she was really behind with her work or whether she was just cooling down and trying to gradually back off.

Before then, Kennedy had rarely thought about the possibility of them splitting up, but here he was for the second time that morning having such thoughts. This worried Kennedy.

Chapter Thirty-Seven

All these people that you mention
Yes, I know them, they're quite lame
I had to rearrange their faces
— Dylan

WPC Anne Coles was the owner of the hand that had been knocking upon Kennedy's door. When Kennedy had finished on the phone and called her into the office, he could tell immediately that she was excited. Well, he was a detective.

'We've found him, sir,' she gushed and before he could inquire as to whom she had found, she gushed more. 'We've found Barney Noble, the London connection for Hughie Guttridge's Brum hyping team.'

The WPC told Kennedy that her new Fraud Squad contact (omitting exactly what good friends they had become), DS Sandy Johnson, had just called her with this thrilling piece of information.

WPC Coles also forgot to tell DI Kennedy that in the same call her New Scotland Yard friend had invited her out on another date (their first real date, since they had kind of fallen into the unofficial one). The WPC had willingly accepted the invitation; they were going to see Elvis Costello and the Attractions at the re-opening of the legendary Roundhouse, Chalk Farm, the following night, followed by, 'Well, we'll see how we feel afterwards, dinner, drinks, or something.' Should the DI have used his immense powers of ascertainment he would have detected an extra inch to the WPC's step that morning.

'Shall we go and see Barney Noble now, sir?' she offered hopefully.

'Yes. No time like the present.' And indeed, in less time than it takes to melt some Cherry Garcia in a microwave, they were in one of the pool cars, a dark blue Ford Granada, and on their way to the Railway Arches at Cheyne Road near King's Cross Station.

The WPC and DI were greeted by a hand-painted sign, green on a black background, bearing the legend, *Erection and Demolition Promotions*. The wooden doors, reflecting the shape of the arch, were painted dark blue. When open they would have admitted one of the famous red London Routemaster buses which frequently (perhaps infrequently would be more appropriate) passed no more than six feet away. A normal sized door had been cut out of the larger left-hand one.

Kennedy knocked several times on the smaller door but doubted anyone would hear him. A loud bass thud from within was shifting wind in his direction. He tried the handle. It turned and the door opened to his push, allowing the natural light from the street to spill into the arch and mix with that from rows of yellow bulbs.

At the far end of the arch a person was seemingly packing cases. When he noticed the two strangers introduced by the first rays of daylight, he seemed like a rabbit caught in the glare of a car's headlights. Unlike such a rabbit however, he was not trapped in the beam of light. He calculated, probably from the electronic static of WPC Coles' walkie-talkie, that they were fuzz. The only way out of the arch was past them. To distract them he turned up the mega bass portable cassette player to an ear piercing volume which rattled the speakers with a sound that was a cross between Deep Purple and five thousand eggs frying.

Before Kennedy had a chance to ask him whether he was Barney Noble, he was struck by a large cardboard box, lobbed through the air at him. It was thrown with such lack of effort that Kennedy assumed it was empty. Not so. The box contained the video player crudely drawn on the side and it hit Kennedy full on the chest, toppling him over.

Kennedy tested his limbs to ensure that he was okay and tried to rise as his assailant came charging directly at him. Kennedy's attempted movement created a sharp pain which cut right across his chest and made a speedy journey up through his shoulders, neck, ears and centred on a point in his forehead.

Out of the corner of his eye, Kennedy saw Anne Coles moving towards his attacker. The man had obviously been expecting this because he flung her to one side, just as one might swish a fly with the back of one's hand. As the WPC fell backwards, she managed to stick her foot between the assailant's legs and tripped him up.

Kennedy stumbled to his feet and made his way across to the man, who was back on his feet again within seconds and squared up to Kennedy. The detective's heart was beating faster than Ringo could do paradiddles, each beat feeling as though someone was plucking at his ribs through the skin.

Kennedy hadn't a clue, not the slightest of clues, what to do. Unarmed combat (nor even armed combat, for that matter) was not really his thing, but he deduced that if the geezer was so anxious to get away from him there must be some equally good reason why it would be in Kennedy's best interest to detain him. So he swung his fist hopefully at the gaping mouth. But with one slick movement, the fist was knocked aside by an agile left forearm, while a right fist came crunching into his gut. Fuck this for a game of soldiers, Kennedy thought as the thug made gestures to indicate that not only was he enjoying himself, but that he knew exactly what to do next.

Our Detective Inspector was not enjoying the skirmish and didn't know what to do next, but out of the corner of his eye, as he hunkered on the ground, he noticed a piece of spare Dexion shelving. In the absence of any better plan, he grabbed the giant Meccano section, rose to his feet, placed his other hand to this makeshift weapon and with all the energy he could muster, swung it backhand style in the direction of his opponent.

As the metal hit its target, the wrist which had so ably defected Kennedy's previous attempted blow, he heard a crack. You would have thought, judging by the look of absolute shock and horror on the villain's face, that he'd suddenly found himself in a dentist's chair.

Kennedy used this shock to his advantage. Before the injured man had a chance to do anything other than grip his damaged wrist with his good hand, Kennedy took aim and this time delivered a similar double back-handed whack to the good wrist. It was but good only for a millisecond longer.

The sheer panic and agony on the stranger's face gave him the air of someone who had a major toilet problem. He couldn't think of which hand to hold as he hopped from foot to foot.

WPC Anne Coles smiled admiringly. 'Wow. Where did you learn that?'

Kennedy tried to utter a blasé, 'Oh it was nothing' *à la* Bond, but if he had a Bond in mind it would have been more of a Brooke Bond. He was sweating profusely, and not just from his forehead. He felt that his entire body was covered by a film of sweat and wondered whether he should be sending for brown trousers.

'Are you okay?' was all he could manage.

'I'm fine,' smiled Anne as she brushed herself down.

The defeated opponent was still doing his Native American war dance. Kennedy nudged him in the chest toppling him over and effectively immobilising him as he was unable to use his hands to help himself up from the floor. All he was fit to do was swear. This he did continuously and repeatedly.

'Now that we have your attention sir, can we assume you are Barney Noble?' Kennedy said sarcastically.

'Fuck you!'

'Strange name,' the WPC quipped.

'Fuck you too!'

'Oh they're not that bad, sir. Though Bono may be slightly misguided, I grant you,' Kennedy replied.

'What?'

Kennedy did not bother to respond. He felt as though someone was hitting him repeatedly in the chest with an iron bar. His head was throbbing so much he wondered whether someone had cut through his teeth with a hacksaw. WPC Coles noticed that he was in pain as he furrowed his forehead.

'Are you okay?' and as an afterthought, 'Sir?'

'He fucking won't be next time we meet. Fucking asshole,' came a muffled voice from the ground beneath and between them.

Kennedy up-ended the video box which had been thrown at him and gingerly sat on it. He motioned the WPC to a nearby wooden chair. 'When we find out your name, we can radio to the station for help,' Kennedy told the thwarted heap on the floor. The detective reasoned that pretty soon the body of the injured man, no longer needing the adrenaline of combat, would return to normal, and when it did, he would start to feel two very sharp and extreme lightning strikes in both arms.

'You can't do that! You've broken both my fucking arms,' the man screamed.

'Self defence,' Kennedy maintained smugly.

'I've got fucking rights, and…'

'We need to know your name before they apply.' This was not strictly true, but Kennedy was still severely winded and was relishing the breather. Particularly when his foe was in such obvious discomfort on the floor.

Eventually a mumbled, 'Barney Noble' was heard from the contorted body.

'Okay,' said Kennedy now taking no joy in the proceeding, his own injuries catching up with him. 'WPC Coles, charge him and read him his rights.'

Barney swore some more, 'Fuck you! Fuck you, asshole. Charge me with what?'

'Attacking police officers in the course of their duty, with intent to cause GBH.'

'I didn't know who you were. You could have come to do me harm. I was protecting myself. I had to! It's self-defence,' Noble shouted defiantly.

Kennedy sighed, knowing that some smart-arsed red-bracered solicitor might well get him off such a charge. Such was life in the '90s. 'Let's just check what we have here, WPC, before we radio in!'

At this, Noble, who felt, correctly that he was being taken advantage of, flew into a renewed rage and started kicking out. The Doc Martin on his left foot missed the WPC's head by about six inches as she swerved as gracefully as Prince Haseem warming up.

Kennedy crossed the room, retrieved the iron bar, returned to Mr Barney Noble and threatened, 'Now, here's the thing, any more of that – even the slightest hint of that – and I deal with both your ankles in exactly the same way I dealt with your wrists!'

Kennedy and Anne Coles moved to the darker corner of the arch, passing box after box of CDs and music cassettes. When they were out of earshot Kennedy asked the WPC to ring for an ambulance. There was no point in hanging around much longer. There didn't seem to be much there apart from the CDs and cassettes and they could have the boys go through those properly.

And the sooner Mr Barney Noble received medical attention, the sooner Kennedy could start his questioning.

Chapter Thirty-Eight

I know all your fears,
I know all your tears
– Christie Hennessy

'I believe, Mrs Farrelly, that you – er – had a relationship with Peter O'Browne.' Kennedy shifted uncomfortably in Colette Farrelly's kitchen chair. This interview was going to be difficulty and Kennedy knew that to get anywhere, he was going to need to act with the utmost sensitivity.

Her house, as before, smelt of freshly cooked food. This time the smell was richer, because this time Kennedy had been invited down to the kitchen living area in the basement. The Farrellys had knocked through all the walls in the basement to create one big open family area. It was obviously the hub of the house, the walls littered with both formal family photographs and more carefree snapshots, children's drawings, first paintings, Martyn's album sleeves, community group flyers. The longer he sat there absorbing the homely concoction of smells, sights and sounds – Radio Four, car wheels passing on the outside tarmac like a fast-flowing river, and the clicking of the oven timer and large wall clock – the less he thought it possible that this apparently contented earth mother could have had an affair with Peter O'Browne.

Colette did not reply immediately, nor did she show surprise. Instead she turned to the cupboards behind him and produced a packet of Walkers Chocolate Chip Shortbread (a particular favourite of Kennedy's). She did not place the biscuits on a plate but put the pack in front of him, thus inviting Kennedy to help himself. He preferred it this way. Neither he nor his host would be embarrassed by the number he took, indeed, neither would be aware of the exact number except that maybe Kennedy would probably know that he had taken one more than he should have done. ann rea had brought this habit to his attention on more than one occasion declaring that he should be heavier than his ten and a half stone from all the goodies he ate, and claiming that she would bulge out immediately should she indulge herself like he did. He wondered why he should be thinking of ann rea at such a moment. Perhaps it was the smell of food and suggestion, or accusation, of infidelity. He felt it necessary to repeat his question.

'I asked if you had a relationship with Peter O'Browne.'

'No, you didn't, Detective Inspector,' Colette Farrelly replied. 'You said, "I believe, Mrs Farrelly, that you had a relationship with

Peter O'Browne." That was a statement, not a question. I assumed that as I hadn't contradicted you, you would know that your statement was correct.'

Well, we certainly went around the houses with that one, Kennedy thought, but eventually it got us there.

'Do you think you could tell me about it?' he inquired.

Kennedy was so calm and quiet that Colette couldn't believe that he really was a policeman. He seemed more like an old friend who'd come round for a cup of tea and a chat. And this was something she wanted to chat about; something she *needed* to talk through. She sighed.

'Well, we are... sorry, were friends, and it was different, I suppose. Oh, shit. Where do I start?' Colette paused as she took off her apron, to reveal an ankle length Laura Ashley style dress, slightly-waisted, just a hint. She turned off the radio, poured herself a cup of tea and came and sat at the table with Kennedy.

They fell silent for a while. Kennedy let the silence be. Bit by bit, as their ears grew accustomed to the absence of the radio, the daytime sounds came back: the clicking of the two clocks, the occasional car on the road above them, Kennedy removing another cookie from the packet, both of them sipping their tea.

Kennedy smiled at Colette. He found it easy to smile at her – she was a passionate woman. He had never thought that about her before this moment, but now he was sure of it. Her shoulder-length straight blonde hair, her sharp-featured face with only hints of make-up, dark thick eyebrows and her smell of cleanness and femininity made him wonder why he had not seen this in her on his last visit. Perhaps he had looked upon her only as someone's wife, not as someone else's mistress too. Now there was another dimension to her. He of all people should have known that things are not always what they seem.

Colette broke their silence. 'Well, I suppose I liked him. I always liked Peter. He's an easy man to like. He was a man it was easy for women to like. He didn't feel the need to come on to everything in a skirt. So I found myself talking to him more and more. It was like he gradually became a part of my life. You feel safe talking to him about things, even some things you wouldn't talk to your husband about.

'Then he and Martyn fell out. I mean it was stupid. I think Martyn got the wrong end of the stick and made a mountain out of a molehill. I think that he was hurt that Peter didn't want to work with him any more and so he created, in his mind, a reason for being angry with Peter and used that anger to make himself feel better about the split.

'I let some time pass – you have to remember that I couldn't talk to Peter then either. Martyn expects me to be loyal in all things, even when he's wrong. Then I started to suggest to Martyn that just maybe he'd been wrong about Peter. I pointed out that he had done his absolute best for Martyn, and at that time it had been hard to get any deal, let alone a good deal, for a new act.

'Anyway, eventually Martyn came round. I think it was easier for him then because he was successful in his own right and that meant he could deal with Peter as an equal. So they had their famous dinner where they both got quite drunk and ended up back here, and we all were mates again.' Colette stopped talking and poured Kennedy another cup of tea.

She thought his tea-drinking was quite comical. Detectives on TV all seemed to be hard-hitting, hard-drinking types: even Morse, with his unusual love for Wagner, liked the odd pint, or five, of real ale. But here was this gentle man with an Irish sounding name who had an absolute passion for a good old cup of tea. And here she was talking to him about something she had never discussed with anyone in the world before.

'And then,' Colette sighed, 'one day – it was a Friday, I think; yes it was a Friday – I bumped into Peter on Parkway in Camden. Martyn was at home minding Naimee and Sean and I was meant to be having a girls afternoon with my friend Diana Alexander. She was taking the afternoon off school and we were going to go to the Sanctuary in Covent Garden and beautify ourselves for hours. You know, the works.'

'Actually, I don't know,' offered Kennedy with a smile.

Colette laughed. 'Oh girlie things: waxing, facials, massage, manicuring, body massage, hair, make up, recreating ourselves totally.'

'I get the picture,' said Kennedy wondering why on earth a woman so naturally beautiful as Colette needed to do that. It showed, he thought, just how little he knew about this mysterious half of the human race.

'Anyway,' Colette continued, noticing that Kennedy had drained the remains of his second cup of tea, and rising to make a second pot as she talked. 'Diana's afternoon off was cancelled – two teachers phoned in sick and she had to cover for one of them. I was feeling a little down so I decided to continue with the Sanctuary plan on my own and then go home early and have dinner with Martyn.

'The treatment did the trick, and as they say in the adverts, I came out a new woman. I stopped off to pick up a few bits and pieces in Parkway and bumped into Peter. He seemed a bit taken aback at how I looked, as if he was looking at me for the first time.

'We stood there on Parkway chatting and laughing for about ten minutes and he suggested that we went down to Cafe Delancey for a cup of coffee instead of standing on the street. I was in no hurry to get home, Martyn wasn't expecting me, so I agreed.

'I still felt delicious from my Sanctuary visit and it's rare for me to be free, with no one depending on me.' Her voice dropped to a conspiratorial whisper. 'It's like you've escaped. From whom, and to where, you never really figure out, but believe me, the feeling is bliss.

'Before we knew it, an hour had passed, we'd moved from coffee to wine, and you know the inhibitions disappear with wine.

'I got the feeling that he was flirting with me. He kept saying how beautiful I was.

'Yeah, that's always a bit of a giveaway, isn't it?' Kennedy suggested playfully.

Colette smiled, more, Kennedy thought, from the scenes she was reliving than at his joke.

'Yes. Peter was saying how beautiful he thought I was, and that I was glowing. Probably a combination of the Sanctuary glow and the three glasses of wine. I was having a rare old time. After demolishing the wine we left the cafe and walked back to the top of Parkway.

'We were saying our goodbyes at the corner of Delancey Street and Parkway, across from Camden Town Records. I think I said something like how much I had enjoyed our chat and was sorry that it was over, and he said he had enjoyed it as well, so if I was not in a rush to go home why didn't we go over to his office, listen to some of his new acts and have another bottle? So we did. It seemed harmless. He was great company, and I think we were both enjoying ourselves because we both felt that there were no sexual undertones. Obviously we were wrong, but they had never been there before.

'Then the conversation took a more intimate turn with the new atmosphere – we were on our own then, not in a safe, crowded cafe. I started to let my frustrations come out. I told him that I was slightly disappointed in Martyn. That shocked him. He claimed that he had always considered Martyn and me to be the perfect married couple and that he was slightly envious of us.

'The wine kept flowing and so did the conversation. I told him that although I loved Martyn dearly, and he still loved me, he was no longer interested in me sexually and had even stopped pretending that he was. I remember telling Peter that I had not expected to grow old happily with my mate, with him lacking interest in me in that way. I told him everything about my relationship with Martyn. That on the rare occasions we did have sex, Martyn was not really interested in my pleasure, and sometimes not even in his own.

'He would fake it and that perplexed me. But then I realised that he was only doing it because he felt he had to carry out his duty to me. He didn't know how bad that made me feel: so unattractive that my own husband needed to fake an orgasm with me.

'Obviously, it was a dangerous subject for us to be discussing. Peter tried to console me. He put his arm around me and told me not to be ridiculous, that of course I was attractive, an extremely attractive and beautiful woman.

'I said, "You're only saying that because I'm upset." He denied it, and went on about how beautiful and sensual I was. Then I stopped him and said, 'Okay, prove it!'

'You should have seen the look of shock on his face. I'd crossed an invisible line which had existed between us for years. He said, 'What! What on earth do you mean?' By this stage I was feeling wicked, totally abandoned. I told him he knew exactly what I meant.

'I didn't have to ask twice. Within seconds we were all over each other. It appeared that both of us had been equally frustrated.' Colette paused as she returned to the table with the fresh pot of tea. Preparing the tea had enabled Colette to avoid eye contact with Kennedy during this part of the story.

'Well!' Kennedy said whistling through his teeth as Colette poured him a third cup. 'Thank you for being so candid with me.'

'To be honest, part of me cannot believe I'm sitting here, sipping tea and calmly telling you all of this. Telling a policeman all this, a policeman I hardly know. I've never told anyone about it before. Telling you, I seem to have made it real. Does that sound weird?'

'No, not at all, quite logical, to me, anyway. Did you, um, did you and Peter...?'

'Do it again?' she interjected, to cut short Kennedy's embarrassment.

He nodded.

'Well, Detective Inspector, that is not so easy to answer. Look, this may sound strange, but we didn't actually do it on that first evening.'

'But I thought...'

'Yes. That's the weird bit. We did everything but make love. That was our rule – Peter's rule, really. We could do everything and anything to each other but not, well, you know, full penetration. I thought in a way it was as if I, or we, were stopping just short of betraying Martyn. Peter had other ideas about excitement. He had this big thing about anticipation being better than participation.

'And I must admit we had several glorious months of anticipation. I'd never known anything so exciting in my life, we'd literally rush into each other's arms and tear the clothes from each other's bodies. More married couples should try it.' She was blushing but unashamed.

Kennedy was lost for words. He had a few scenes running through his mind but no word to fill his mouth.

'We met occasionally. I mean, what can I tell you, except that it was great, absolutely great. We were not in love, but we had great sex, we were good friends and neither of us was looking for more out of the relationship other than what we were getting. I became a happier person because I didn't feel that that part of my life was redundant. I liked Peter, and I cared for him. I wanted to see him happy. I even fixed him up with my girlfriend Diana Alexander, who was my best mate. I thought that they would be great together. It turned out that he wasn't prepared to put enough into the relationship to make it work, so she broke it off.'

Colette smiled again at her memories. 'I was thinking of the time Diana and Peter came round for dinner and we'd all had a lot of wine. Peter and I left Diana and Martyn in the living room watching TV while we came down here to the basement to wash the dishes. We couldn't keep our hands off each other, even in my own house: Martyn's and mine. It was the one time, the only time we made love proper.

'For me it was all so decadent, so thrilling, so anticipated, that for me it was the best, absolutely the best sex I've ever had in my life.

'Around that time Martyn was saying that I'd changed and he was being turned on by me again. I guess, because of Peter, I was feeling desirable again, so I was acting desirable and therefore being desirable.'

'There's sense in that,' Kennedy agreed. 'Did Martyn ever have any idea about this?'

'No. Absolutely not. If he had found out – if he finds out – he'd be destroyed. We are just starting to get on so well again.' Colette brushed back her hair, capturing it behind her ears. 'He won't have to know, will he?' she asked anxiously.

'Well, you know, that could be pretty difficult. I'll be honest with you: we can't rule Martyn out of our list of suspects.'

'What?'

'Well, look at it from the outside. They were mates. They fell out. Martyn felt he was cheated.'

'But they made it up!' she pleaded.

'Yes, but what if Martyn was just biding his time until a chance arose for him to get his own back? Vengeance is a very powerful and destructive force. Now we find out that Martyn's wife was sleeping with the murder victim. You've got to see all this must move Martyn up a few places on our suspect list. You've told me yourself that he would be devastated if he found out about your affair. What if he did find out?'

'But how could he have done? You are the only person who knows. Peter would never have breathed a word about it!' Colette cried.

'Mrs Farrelly, I came to you and told you that I believed you were having a relationship with Peter O'Browne. How do you think I knew this?'

'Not Marty?' she asked beseechingly.

'No, of course not. Mary. Mary Jones.'

'But Peter wouldn't have told Mary.'

'But Mary was Peter's PA. He wouldn't necessarily need to have told her. She could have worked it out, guessed for herself. Maybe from your phone calls to ask how Peter was doing; maybe someone saw you together and told her, maybe she knew he phoned you, maybe she noticed how his manner changed when you were around. Any one of a million things which you know women can pick up. So perhaps Martyn found out. After all, he would be more tuned into your wavelength than most.'

'No. I'd have known. Believe me, I can tell you that there is not the slightest possibility that he knew.'

Colette put her head in her hands, hair falling around her knees.

'Oh God. If he is a suspect, does that mean that you are going to question him? And if you question him, are you going to throw, "and your wife was cheating with Peter behind your back," at him? Oh my God, how awful,' she sobbed.

'Listen Colette, people are only exempt from suspicion if they have a cast-iron unbreakable alibi, if they are not physically capable of committing the murder or if they have no interest in the case whatsoever. Otherwise everyone involved is a suspect. Even you are on our list of suspects. The only reason to have a list is so we can remove names from it. Eventually by a process of elimination and deduction, most names will come off, leaving – hopefully – just one; that of the perpetrator of the crime.'

Kennedy paused, and added in a gentler voice, 'I would strongly advise you that it may be in your best interest, and easiest for you both, if you told Martyn about Peter yourself. I'm not saying that we would tell Martyn as a matter of course but it may come up, and if it does it would be far better if Martyn had already heard it from you.'

'But it's been over for ages. It was a mutual thing. Martyn was paying me attention again and, if I'm honest, I think with Peter, you know, after we eventually did it, the novelty wore off for him.' She thought for a while, wondering whether the fact that the relationship had been over would make telling Martyn any easier. She doubted it.

'Thanks, Inspector. I know you didn't need to tell me what you know. I know it ruins the surprise element with Martyn,' said Colette. She was quiet for a moment. 'But I suppose if I tell Martyn the truth – if he has the full picture at last – then we, or at least I, can start to grieve for Peter.'

'There was just one other thing I wanted to ask you, Mrs Farrelly,' said Kennedy. 'What happened to Diana Alexander when she and Peter parted? Is she still in the area?'

'Oh God! I had forgotten all about Diana,' replied Colette in distress. 'She'll be devastated. I must ring her.'

'Perhaps you'd like us to go and see her?' Kennedy offered helpfully.

Colette looked up in surprise. 'Oh no, Inspector – not unless you fancy a holiday. She's living in a little village just outside Milan with a jewellery designer. She finally met someone who knew how to make a commitment. He's a little possessive, but they are happily married and she's teaching English. I haven't seen her in over a year.'

As Kennedy left Colette to ponder the mountain she had to climb, he was consoled by the fact that his list of suspects was at least one name shorter.

Chapter Thirty-Nine

Honey you're my one and only
So pay me what you owe me
— Laurie Anderson

At that point in the day Kennedy had decided that he was having a bad day, and not the good day Americans wished the world and his brother. Even his aches were having aches and whenever he sat down, a dreaded stiffness set in. Waking up each morning was going to be joint-creaking agony for a few days. On top of that – if you could get on top of that – his conversation with Colette Farrelly had created another kind of discomfort. The first one wore away within minutes, but now he was conscious, over-conscious, of his relationship with ann rea.

He tried to think whether he had ever been anything less than honest about his feelings, both emotional and physical, for her. He could not recall a time when he had even considered faking it – he'd always been enjoying himself too much. Yet previous girlfriends had often complained that he never really expressed his feelings properly. Too many had claimed that they never really knew where they stood with him, for there not to be at least a hint of truth in the accusation.

Should he change? Could he change? Did he love ann rea enough to change for her? But surely that wasn't the point. He wouldn't want her to change, in any way. So the converse must be true. If ann rea loved him, she must also love all the baggage. If you change just to please your lover, perhaps you'll become someone your lover will no longer find attractive. Nevertheless he did not for one moment suppose this meant you should go around with the blinkered attitude, 'This is me and if you don't like the package, eff off.'

He hoped that his physical condition would not ruin the weekend he and ann rea had planned. Both were committed to their respective offices on Saturday morning but the rest of the time they just wanted to slum it, walking around Primrose Hill, Regent's Park and Camden Town. Camden Town Market on a Sunday morning was a total buzz, the streets packed way past overflowing with locals (not a lot), tourists (hundreds of thousands) and traders (enough).

Kennedy wondered whether Peter O'Browne had ever joined in the Sunday morning mayhem around Camden Lock. Perhaps they had passed within feet (even inches) of each other one such Sunday, as they went about their leisure pursuits.

The local offices were spewing out their respective work-forces as Kennedy returned to North Bridge House. By now he had a few additions for his noticeboard and so, via DS James Irvine, he summoned the team to his office for a general update on the case. He was then due to brief Superintendent Thomas Castle before the Super travelled north for a weekend conference in York.

Kennedy did not envy the Super his weekend. Kennedy felt that there were those who did and those who talked about doing, and although the Super was a paid-up member of the latter group, he was always prepared to give Kennedy a free rein (not to mention lots of support) in his endeavours to do.

'Okay,' Kennedy began, inviting his team to help themselves to tea. 'Let's see where we are up to with this one. WPC Coles, will you bring everyone up to date with our adventures with Barney What's-his-name?'

'Noble, sir.'

'The very same.' Kennedy took his seat behind his desk.

The WPC recalled their adventure with Mr Less-Than-Noble. Kennedy wasn't paying much attention. His shirt had lost its crispness, so he undid the buttons on the cuffs and rolled the cuffs up to his elbow. He also loosened his tie and opened the top button. He arranged papers around his desk and made up some new signs for his noticeboard. When the WPC reached the part of her narrative that dealt with what had been found after he had left, his ears pricked up.

'As well as thousands of CDs and cassettes, we found a vast quantity of cocaine, pure coke, some of it still packed in music cassette boxes – sealed in plastic bags, of course.'

'Now we know why Mr Noble was so anxious to get away from us,' Kennedy offered, feeling the sharp, painful reminders of his encounter with the villain across his chest.

'Yes. But that's not all, sir. We found explosives and packaging similar to that used in the device which caused the fire in Peter O'Browne's house.'

This was a breakthrough. 'When is Mr Noble due back from the hospital?'

'I believe they're bringing him,' the WPC checked her watch, 'in about fifteen minutes, sir.'

'Which means he'll be here in half an hour. Okay. Irvine, you and I will question him here,' Kennedy announced. The look in the eyes of DS James Irvine told him that the fun-loving nurse Rose Butler was going to have to start her fun without him tonight. Of this she was more than capable, so Kennedy resolved to try not to keep the DS away too late. Unfortunately, the twenty-four hour "clock" starts running the moment the suspect enters the station, during which time the police have to decide if they are going to charge or release their suspect: on this occasion the 'armless Barney Noble.

'So, what about our other suspects?' Kennedy said as he rose (slowly and painfully) from his chair and wandered over to the notice-board.

'Martyn Farrelly has certainly moved up a few positions,' Kennedy began.

'If this was the Sunday night pop charts, he'd probably be happier about it,' remarked DS Irvine dryly.

'As I was saying, he must move up the list with the news that his wife had been sleeping with the deceased. He now has two motives. One, he feels that Peter shafted him earlier in his career; and two, now he finds out that this same person has stolen his wife, or at least her affections.

'Moving right along, new entry, straight in at number four, Barney Noble. I think we'll have to wait 'til after our chat with him for an update. Tom Best. Yes… Have we uncovered anything else about him?'

No one spoke.

'Look, I know we've not been on this long, but you know me, I like to cover as much ground as possible in the initial forty-eight hours. Is there anyone else we should be thinking about? Maybe someone we don't even know yet?' Kennedy asked.

Again, no one spoke.

'WPC Coles, before you go off for the evening, could you please have another chat with Mary Jones? Try to get her to give you any-thing: office gossip, rumours, anything. She produced the Colette and Peter story, so maybe there is more there. She must know all the dark corners in this man's room. We need to go there, wherever it may be, and have a look.'

'Okay, sir.'

'Anything from the SoC people, DS Irvine?'

'Sorry, sir, not at the moment. They took away a pile of rubbish – you know, the pile that was in the back of the studio – papers, leaves, carbons, cardboard boxes, bits of wood, nails, soap. Just rubbish, lots of it. They are not sure how long it had been there, but they are going to go through it all with the proverbial fine-tooth comb. They'll give us a shout the minute they come up with anything.'

'Okay. But don't forget to keep nudging them,' Kennedy urged. 'What about door to door? Anything turn up? What about the chip-pie?'

'No, sir, no one seemed to notice anything out of the ordinary,' PC Allaway volunteered. 'It's a vibey village kind of atmosphere and no one can remember anything unusual this week.' He should know because it had been his feet which had pounded the streets and it had been he who had asked the questions.

'Then do me a favour. Take WPC West with you and do it again tonight. Perhaps there will be a different group of people on the hill for the weekend. Perhaps they'll remember something extra. It's only two days now since a man was taken from their midst and hanged by the neck until he died. Hanged by the neck 'til he died.' Kennedy allowed the words to hang in the air as much for himself as for his audience. 'I wonder if that's it. I wonder if someone felt they were officially punishing Peter O'Browne for some wrong?' Kennedy offered.

WPC Coles was the first to reply. 'Well, that might account for the way the corpse was laid out, sir.'

'But then why not leave him hanging for all to see?' this time the question was posed by DS Irvine.

'Well,' Kennedy began slowly. 'I suppose if Peter had been left hanging, there is a chance it could have been interpreted as a suicide. This way, the executioner left us in no doubt that Peter O'Browne had been hanged by somebody else.'

Kennedy did not feel that he was going to make much, if any, progress with that line of thought at that moment, but he wrote 'execution' in large letters on a sheet of paper and pinned it to his notice-board. As he did so, he glanced at another name on his board. 'What about Johnny Heart? Should he be in the frame?'

'Nah, sir I don't think so,' said Irvine. 'From what I can gather he spent all his money on women, booze and drugs.' After a short pause he added, 'The rest he wasted. Seriously, though,' he said above the laughter of his colleagues. 'From what I've been told, he's a total waster and would not have been capable, physically, or mentally, of carrying out such a crime, any major crime, come to that.'

'Okay, sergeant. Look if we finish with Barney Noble early enough you can go and see the delightful Staff Nurse Butler and I'll see if I can have another chat with Tom Best. That is, unless you would like to do a swap?' Kennedy smiled.

'No, sir, that's fine, perfectly fine. I can live with that deal – I'll do the same for you some day, sir.'

'Yes, I'll bet. Okay let's get on with it,' Kennedy announced and they broke off into a few groups ready to get off into the night, and overtime.

Chapter Forty

I met the fools that a young fool meets
– Jackson Browne

Barney Noble looked like the cat in the cat and mouse (and dog) cartoon where the cat always comes off worst. But no matter how pathetic the cat looks following one of its scraps with the dog, all battered and bruised and bandaged, you could never feel sorry for it. Barney Noble was every bit as pathetic as our cat, with both arms and wrists bandaged. He rested both elbows on the table, arms pointing upwards. He was obviously still in some pain but he still had that 'fuck you' smirk painted on his face. He was wearing an outrageous suit, a yellow number with black lines, which had clearly left a few Ford Cortina seats uncovered. His hair was shaved down to the skin of his head. However the hair outline betrayed the fact he probably had done so to hide his imminent baldness.

DS James Irvine opened the proceedings. Perhaps it was the lure of Staff Nurse Rose Butler which was putting an inch – at least – to his step, by announcing, for the benefit of the tape-recorder, the time, place and names of those present (Noble had refused a solicitor): 'So, you've a few things to tell us, then, Mr Noble.'

'I'll tell you shit. I'm in agony. That animal. I'm going to sue you. I'm going to take so much money from the police force. You can't go around behaving like…'

'I think you are forgetting who attacked whom,' Kennedy cut in icily, making it clear that he had neither the time nor the patience to go around the houses again on this particular point.

'Fucking right, I did. I was protecting myself.'

'Okay, let's change the record. Here's the thing. We are here to question you. Now in about half an hour…' Kennedy checked his watch. 'Sorry, make that twenty-six minutes, I go off for the weekend. If I don't make satisfactory progress in this interview with you in the next…' he looked at his watch again, '…the next twenty-five and-a-half minutes, I'll have to leave the balance of the questions 'til Monday morning.'

'You can't do that. You've got to charge me!' Noble announced smart-arse fashion.

'Fine, absolutely no problem. Then we'll charge you with GBH, with obstructing police officers in the execution of their duty. For that you'll get, with your form, about eighteen months. Not to mention possession of drugs, explosives, la-de-da-de-da. So if that's what you want we can leave it like that and dump you in the cells for the weekend. Then on Monday morning we'll start with the really serious stuff, like the murder of Mr Peter O'Browne. We can do it that way or...' Kennedy paused. '...or we can talk.'

'It's up to you,' DS Irvine added. 'Entirely up to you.'

Noble sat in indignant silence.

Kennedy tried a different approach. 'Why were you blackmailing Peter O'Browne?'

'Why fucking not?' Noble spat out in a snigger. 'He's no fucking better than me, is he?'

This time Kennedy retained an air of silence.

Unprompted, Barney continued, 'Well, I mean to say, you know what he was up to. And it wasn't exactly fucking legal, was it? Come on, you know what I mean.' He started to lean back in his chair but as his elbows lost the support of the table his arms reminded him he was carrying broken bones. He winced. 'Was what he was doing legal? I don't fucking think so! He should have to pay for it or something. But that's the thing isn't it?' he exploded, expecting Kennedy and DS Irvine to read his mind. 'If I do something illegal and break the law it's a big thing, and I have to do time, fair e-fucking-nuff. But if the suits bend the law, they're allowed to hide behind their lawyers and money and get away with it.'

'So,' DS Irvine interrupted. 'You took money from Peter O'Browne to hype his records illegally, and you used that information to extort money from him?'

'So what?'

'Really, a fine little firm you've got there, Barney. Nice work if you can get it,' Kennedy laughed.

'Yeah, but if you two fuckers think you can pin this murder on me, let me tell you, there's no way. Not my scene, man. You're not going to hang that one on me.'

'Look we are getting ahead of ourselves here. Can we stop jumping around so much and go back to the beginning?' Kennedy sighed.

'Okay. Look I work for a team. And we have squads of buyers who go around the country buying targeted singles to, shall we say, encourage them up the charts,' Barney began expansively.

'Does everyone, record companies I mean, do this?' DS Irvine inquired.

'Oh, you'd be surprised how many of them are at it. But they are all idiots fucking baboons. Even I can see that the more they do it the less effect the hyping has. In fact the only effect it has is to put more money into our pockets. Anyway, I heard that Mr Showbiz, Camden Town was trying to put a deal together to sell part of his company to a major. He's going to want to keep the deal sweet, isn't he? He's not going to want any scandals spoiling his pitch. So, I figured he'd be okay for a hit, a few grand now and again.

'It was a bit of justice, wasn't it? I mean, the guy is so fucking stingy he wouldn't give you the fucking steam from his tea, so I hit him where it hurts: in his pocket.' Barney Noble obviously took pride in his way of dishing out justice to the 'suits'.

'But this was all ages ago, literally ages ago. I'm having a hard time working out why you'd want to firebomb him all this time later,' Kennedy responded.

'Well, I just wanted to teach the fucker a lesson. You know, a real lesson. He wouldn't play ball, he made one measly payment then refused to pay any more. I thought I was on to a bit of a winner. I didn't know whether to go for one payment of ten grand or several small ones, say a couple of grand at a time. I made the wrong decision. The first payment, two and a half grand, he stumped up immediately, cash, all tenners, direct from Lloyds of Camden Town. But then he got cocky and wouldn't come across with any more.

'Asshole. I couldn't believe it. But I'm a patient man. So I wait for a time when it wouldn't be connected back to me. I also wanted to destroy the two notes I sent to him. I didn't think he'd keep them in his office. So fuck, I was getting my own back and covering my tracks in one hit. But then the asshole has to go and get stiffed at the same time as I'm torching his fucking house. Can you believe that?

'Then all hell breaks lose! I don't mind doing time for the drugs and blackmail and shit, but I'm not going to go down for his murder. No fucking way.'

'Yeah, yeah. How about Wednesday night? What were you doing between 7pm and midnight?' DS Irvine inquired, checking his watch.

'Ha, fucking easy that one, isn't it, I was with my fucking mates, wasn't I?'

'And where would that have been?' Irvine leaned forward on his folded arms as he spoke.

'We were all at the Dublin Castle, weren't we? They'll all swear to it!' Barney Noble added defiantly.

Irvine changed tack, 'So, what other singles did you work on?'

Noble reeled off a list as long as your arm which had both Kennedy and Irvine alternating, 'Wow, you're winding us up. That was hyped? I can't believe that. I bought a copy of it myself!'

Kennedy and DS Irvine left the desk sergeant, Timothy Flynn, to deal with the paperwork. As they parted on the steps of North Bridge House, DS Irvine said, 'I think our friend Mr Barney Noble practices safe sex.'

'What?' said Kennedy buttoning up his overcoat and wondering what his DS was on about.

'Yeah. I think his problem is he's been practising too much by himself.' A roar of Scottish laughter rolled down Parkway.

Chapter Forty-One

If songs were lines
In a conversation
The situation
Would be fine

– Nick Drake

'Oh God, it's the police again!' was the greeting afforded to Detective Inspector Christy Kennedy when he showed his ID to Tom Best.

'You'd better come in,' Best continued. 'But I hope you're not going to take long. I'm due to pick up my girlfriend for dinner in forty minutes.'

'Oh I'm sure it won't take that long,' Kennedy replied as he unbuttoned his coat.

'And I do have several American calls I need to make before I can go,' Best said politely as he closed the door behind the Detective Inspector.

Kennedy paused in the hallway, allowing Best to lead him up the stairs above the record shop into the office. It appeared that all of Best's staff had followed the old *Ready Steady Go* motto, 'The weekend starts here,' and had left Tom Best as the lone remaining soul of the fast dying week.

'I spoke to two of your colleagues yesterday, Detective Inspector,' Best began as he offered Kennedy a seat, a comfortable armchair to the left of his desk. Kennedy felt more like a guest on the 'Letterman' show than someone about to conduct an interview in a murder inquiry.

WPC Anne Coles had picked up a bad vibe from Tom Best and had said as much to Kennedy. Her DI, however, did not feel any such vibe. Perhaps it was just because it was the end of a long week, or perhaps it was Kennedy's rank, but to Kennedy, Tom Best was quite a pleasant and courteous fellow.

'Have there been any further developments since?' he asked, playing with six silver balls suspended on a frame on his desk.

'Several, in fact,' Kennedy assured him. 'I'm not at all certain how they will eventually fit into the overall picture. That takes time.'

Kennedy's aches were now exacerbated by tiredness. He tried to settle into a comfortable spot and remain there. Any new position brought new pain. God only knew how he was going to get up from the armchair. He thought that if Tom Best didn't very shortly offer him a cup of tea he might be forced to remove the 'good fellow' badge he had mentally pinned on the man's Ry Cooder sweatshirt.

As if reading his mind, Best said, 'Fancy a cup of coffee?'

'Ah,' Kennedy answered looking around the office in search of some Tetley Tea Folk. 'I wouldn't say no to a cup of tea.'

'Sure, of course,' Best replied as he jumped up and skied on his stockinged feet across the stripped and varnished pine floor to the back of his inner office.

'Milk and sugar?' he hollered from somewhere outside.

'Yes and two please,' Kennedy called.

'I wanted to ask you some more questions about your relationship with Peter O'Browne.' Kennedy paused to blow across the rim of his teacup. He took a sip of tea and, finding it still too hot for pleasant consumption, he continued. 'I know WPC Coles and DS Irvine have already asked you some questions. I just need to see if there is anything they might have missed, or, equally, that you might remember a second time around.'

Best lit a cigarette. If Anne Coles had been present she'd have been amazed he'd lasted this long without one. 'We were mates. Well, I suppose we were never really mates. I think Peter considered it pretty much a boss/employee relationship.'

'And you?' Kennedy prodded.

'I think that if it had been spelt out differently, I would have dealt with things differently. There were just the two of us, doing everything, and I do mean everything, ourselves. And we'd work every day, including Sunday, 'til ten o'clock. If someone had told me then that at some time down the line a major record company would pay six mil' for the wee company we had started, then...' Best nodded his head and formed the letter Y with his lips before saying, '...Yes, I would have sat down with him, forced him to do a deal with me and write it down on paper.

'But I didn't, and I suppose I should have, and therefore I'm as much to blame as he was. But I really thought we were mates, in it together and the love of the music and the artists we were working with would see us through. Wrong!'

'Why do you think it was that he didn't give you half, or even a quarter?'

'Hell, ten per cent would have been more realistic than a hundred G! Even bleeding agents get ten per cent.'

'So, why? Why do you think he didn't give you the six hundred thousand pounds?'

'As I say, I think the bottom line was that he saw our relationship differently from how I saw it. And you know the thing I really couldn't understand was that it didn't really make any difference to O'Browne.'

'What do you mean?'

'Well look at it. If you're doing okay in your life financially and then someone comes along and drops six mil' in your lap, surely you don't mean to tell me that 5.4 mil' won't create the same effect? But maybe it was just damage control. Maybe he was thinking, What's the least I'm going to have to pay to make this problem go away?

'Perhaps that was my problem. Maybe I just rolled over too easy. If I had pushed, maybe he would have paid me six hundred Gs. Hell, at a stretch I might even have got him up to the magic million. He was a great negotiator, we all knew that. Maybe he felt he had to negotiate to keep his hand in. Or maybe the big bread just made him greedy.

'I felt that the big pay day had come as a result of our joint efforts and that we all, including the artists who helped us get up there, deserved a bit of a "luck penny".'

'Like Martyn Farrelly?' Kennedy suggested.

'Yeah, exactly. Like Marty Farrelly.'

'Did you know that Martyn lent Peter five hundred pounds to start the label off in the first place?' Kennedy asked, happy that his tea was now cool enough to drink.

'Yeah. Yeah I did. You see there it is again. Don't you think that should have been remembered when the big fucking kite flew in through O'Browne's window? Come on, wouldn't you have given Marty Farrelly some money, like even a cheque for fifty G. Is O'Browne going to miss fifty lousy G out of six mil'. And Marty certainly would have found a use for it.'

'But Martyn Farrelly did refuse Peter's offer to return the original £500, didn't he?'

'Of course he did, come on. He had been insulted. You don't give him back his original money. It wasn't a loan, it was a gift. The right thing was not to return the gift but to give him a bigger gift by way of thanks, even a piece, doesn't matter how small, of the company.

'That would have made Marty feel good. It was the right thing to do. Hell, it might even have made O'Browne feel good. He'd been around the Irish ballrooms – with Marty, in fact – enough to know you always give back a luck penny. Didn't matter how big the showband was, or how many thousand dancers were crammed into the ballroom, the showband manager always had a sweet handshake for the ballroom manager at the end of the night.' Tom Best sighed and rolled himself a cigarette.

'Do you think Farrelly was still annoyed at Peter O'Browne?' Kennedy shook his head to refuse the offer of a DIY cigarette.

'What? Do you mean do I think that Marty was pissed off enough at O'Browne to top him?'

Kennedy nodded again, this time affirmatively.

'I don't know. I don't really know him that well, and who knows what we all think in the privacy of our own minds?'

'What about girlfriends?'

'What about them? We can't live with them and we can't live without them,' Best smiled knowingly.

Kennedy couldn't agree with that premise but did not contradict him. 'I meant what about Peter and his girlfriends?'

'Oh, I see. He wasn't really a ladies' man, he wasn't totally comfortable around them. He wasn't gay or anything like that, but you know I think that deep down every Irishman has a fear of women, sexually speaking. Oh, I know, a few beers, or a bottle of wine and they, we, can all do the biz and get by. But O'Browne never really seemed comfortable on the pull or chatting them up. He seemed much more comfortable talking to and dealing with other people's girlfriends or wives where there was never a need for him to have to chat them up. So he was more relaxed and natural and so got on a treat.'

'Was there ever anyone serious?'

'You know the funny thing is, there wasn't. There was usually a current girlfriend, but you were never surprised when you heard that she'd joined the ever-growing list of exes.'

'The people you dealt with in the early days. Do you think there was anyone who would have wanted to see him dead?'

'Ah, now, that's a leading question if ever I heard one,' Tom Best replied rolling up a third cigarette.

Kennedy smiled and tried unsuccessfully to banish the thought of how Tom's lungs would probably bear a striking resemblance to the packed ashtray on the desk.

'Let me see…' Tom Best continued expansively taking a large drag on, the soon to be not so new, cigarette. 'We had our trouble with Jason Carter-Houston, the manager of Radio Cars, and we had trouble with Radio Cars' lead singer, Johnny Heart. That was extremely unpleasant at the time and they bombed shortly after they left us, so I imagine there could be a major gripe there. But who knows if it would be enough to kill somebody.

'I mean, that's a real heavy thing to do, isn't it? Well of course it is. That was a stupid thing to say. Okay, at some point in our lives we all say, "Oh, I could kill them for what they did or didn't do," but how many of us could actually sit down in the cold light of day and plan to end someone's life, and then, actually carry out the execution?

'Crimes of passion are a different thing really, aren't they? Where some poor unfortunate is so possessed by love, or lust, and on being rejected lashes out to protect their emotions and claims a life. But the other – to execute someone. I mean, you've obviously met some of these people. What are they really like, are they any different to you or I, Detective Inspector?'

'Now there is a leading question.' Kennedy moved in his chair to ease a growing ache. 'I don't think that there is a single kind of person capable of committing murder. I think that for part of the time, these people lead normal, ordinary lives. That is if you believe there is such a thing as a normal, ordinary life. Maybe they are just like you or me. Then something happens which makes them feel aggrieved, vengeful, spiteful or angry towards someone and they are, well, they are bad. It's the simplest word I can use to describe them. They are bad, or they allow the bad which is in us all to take over. They are bad enough to calmly plan a killing. Because they are prepared to act without conscience they are very dangerous. Is there anyone else you and Peter crossed swords with?' he persisted.

'The only other person from the early days was Paddy George, O'Browne's original partner in the shop. But he's a great man in a world of few great men, and I believe they were mates up until Peter was killed.

'I think his solicitor, Leslie Russell, would probably be more of help in this area than I could ever be. As you know, I've been out of O'Browne's circle for some years now, and I wouldn't have a clue who he'd had a run-in with recently. But I'm sure you've chatted with Leslie. He knows where all the skeletons are buried. And,' Tom Best smirked, 'being a solicitor, I'm sure he even helped to bury some of them.'

'Are we talking in general here, Mr Best, or specifically?'

'Oh, in general, of course,' Best replied, glancing at the Mickey Mouse watch on his arm.

'Well, that will do for now. I'll leave you to an enjoyable evening.' Kennedy winced as he rose painfully from the (too) easy-chair. 'We'll chat again next week.'

Chapter Forty-Two

It was one of those occasions
Where believe you me
I would rather have been held ransom at the point of a gun
– Gilbert O'Sullivan

Kennedy woke up on Saturday morning unable to move. Well, he could move, but the slightest attempt to do so resulted in the most excruciating pain in his chest.

When he asked ann rea if she thought it could be his heart, she replied, smiling and unsympathetic, 'Oh, come on, Kennedy, wise up. You were in the wars yesterday. It's probably only a cracked rib.'

ann rea rolled astride and gently prodded his chest. Usually such an action would have had a predictable effect on Kennedy, but on that particular Saturday sex was as far from his mind as was children's welfare from Attila the Hun's.

About four inches up from his navel and three inches to the left, ann rea located the hub of the pain in the middle of the yellow and purple bruises.

'Weird place for a heart Kennedy, but I've always wondered about the location of yours.'

Kennedy yelped as she continued prodding.

'You know, there is not a lot to you. You're all skin and bones. You need fattening up a bit.'

Food, any food, was something else that was far from his mind at that moment. He'd like to have mobilised his body. He had a lot planned for that Saturday. He was glad he was off-duty. Kennedy would have hated to have had to call in sick. He was jealous of his 100 per cent record. He didn't know why such a record was important to him, it just was.

Kennedy had planned to drop into the office at some point during the morning. He wanted to review the case in the cold light of day. (Actually, it felt as if it was going to be mild on that day but, in the mild light of day doesn't quite have the same ring somehow).

ann rea hopped out of bed and walked across the polished wooden floor. A sight, not for sore eyes, the T-shirt she wore to bed was just about decent.

'Back in a sec.'

Kennedy lay there feeling sorry for himself. There he was with a beautiful semi-nude woman in his bedroom, and what was more, she had just spent seven and a half hours in bed with him and he hadn't engaged in any horizontal dancing. If you had told Kennedy this when he met ann rea for the first time, he would have arrested you for being a stranger to the truth.

ann rea returned to the bedroom with a bandage. 'Okay Kennedy. Who's going to tie who up?'

He managed a chuckle, nothing more.

She feigned dejection. 'In that case I'm going to have to do the tying. Sit up, then!'

Kennedy tried but the pain prevented him from rising but a fraction of an inch from the bed. ann rea gently rolled him to the side, amid a torrent of groans. When he was balanced right on the edge of the bed she moved his legs over and, using them as a lever, supported and lifted his upper torso into a sitting position.

The manoeuvre had been so painful that Kennedy broke out in a sweat.

'Make an aeroplane!' ann rea ordered.

'What on earth are you on about? I admire your sense of the surreal but I suggest you stop smoking crack.'

'Make an aeroplane,' she repeated through her laughter, lifting her arms to demonstrate. He feebly followed her example, allowing her to bind him tightly with the bandage. She wound it around his lower chest several times, kissing him gently on the neck, cheek, head and shoulders each time she circled, and fixed it tight with a safety pin. Then she moved behind Kennedy and started to massage his shoulders. He was as tight as a drum. ann rea made him drop his head as she worked her fingers, first gently, then firmly, deep into his neck, shoulders and upper back.

Kennedy was surprised how much relief from the pain the tightly, bound bandage brought. As ann rea moved closely about him, he started to become intoxicated with her fresh sensual natural scent and gradually he began to think that maybe, you know, Attila the Hun was quite fond of his direct family.

· Twelve minutes and forty-three seconds later, ann rea was the first to break their post passion calm. 'God, the lengths you'll go to, to attract a bit of attention,' she whispered, delicately stroking his cheek. 'You didn't need to go and get your self beaten up just to…'

'Yeah, yeah, yeah.'

'Oh, it speaks as well.'

Kennedy was sweating once more, but it was no longer the cold sweat of pain. He was lying on his back with one arm around ann rea's neck, his hand caressing her hair, and the other protecting his side as she lay snugly against him. He thought, not for the first time, how absurd bodies would look if you froze them in their lying position and stood them upright. No doubt Damien Hirst would get around to such an exhibit at some point.

'Tom Best reckons that…'

'Oh we are feeling better then. Our mind is back on the case, I see,' ann rea laughed into his shoulder. She was happy to lie with Kennedy in a mild daze, but such tranquillity had passed. 'Reckons what?'

'He reckons that Peter O'Browne never really had a serious girl-friend, just an ever growing list of future exes.'

'Some people are like that, Kennedy. The even sadder thing is that some of them marry their future ex-wives.'

Kennedy decided not to stir up ann rea's inherent fears about marrying badly. He let his mind drift through the characters in Peter O'Browne's life and death.

It was ann rea who broke the silence. 'Are things starting to fall into place yet?'

'That's the strange thing. Not at all. Yes, we're gathering lots of evidence, but we have yet to find some cement to tie it all together. So, all the parts are floating around and I keep trying to imagine different ways the pieces will fit together.

'But I'm always left with one spare piece, and the entire puzzle crumbles around me. I've often thought that solving a case is a bit like going on a mystery car journey. You have to be prepared to take a few wrong turns, but remember where you have been and what you have seen so that you can successfully retrace your steps and try another road.'

'So, what are your problems?'

'Well, the main one, I suppose, is that I haven't worked out how Peter O'Browne was murdered.'

'I thought that was obvious.'

'Yes, but how was he hanged? How was the body manoeuvred into position? Peter O'Browne was ten-stone-thirteen. That is a considerable weight for one person to move around.'

'Perhaps there were two of them,' ann rea offered as she followed the wall to ceiling border around the cream-painted bedroom.

'Perhaps, but personally, I doubt it. With two people there is more chance of being found out, and I think this was all too carefully planned to risk betrayal by an accomplice.'

'Okay, okay. How about – if – okay, how about if the accomplice has also been murdered?' ann rea suggested, concentrating now not on the ceiling line, but on the hairs on Kennedy's chest, pulling at them gently.

'Interesting, *Verly* interesting. But again highly unlikely.'

'Why?' ann rea drew the word out into three syllables.

'This is the real world, not a PD James novel. Besides, if the chances of getting away with one murder are pretty slim, the chances of getting away with two are practically zero. And anyway, there's no body.'

'What about what's his name and his wife who murdered all those people, including some of their own children, and buried them in the basement of the house?'

'The West family. Yes, but that's my point: they didn't get away with it. If one person commits a murder, he or she can keep it to themselves, but more than one and pretty soon everyone knows about it. Okay, it was ages before they were caught, but I get the feeling this is different. From the appearance of this corpse, whoever did it was on a mission, a mission of vengeance, and he or she planned it down to the smallest detail.

'If you overpower someone with chloroform you do have control over their body, but you still have to move the body around. Was Peter O'Browne dragged into the centre of the room, assuming he was overpowered at the door, and a rope placed around his neck?

'Did the murderer then throw the end of the rope around the roof rafter and did he then hoist the comatose O'Browne from the ground? Did he then secure the other end of a rope to something, a door handle perhaps, and watch the life drain from the body as it twitched around.'

'Ugh, Kennedy. Pl-ea-se, not before breakfast,' ann rea declared discontinuing the hair extending exercise. 'You are forgetting he was kept captive for a few days. Why was that?'

'I don't know. Alibi, maybe. Perhaps the first attempt at murder failed. Maybe the murderer wanted to put Peter O'Browne through a few days of misery before finally killing him. No, I think instead of trying to solve the case and then find the murderer I should try and first find the murderer and then let him—'

'Or her,' ann rea reminded him.

'Or her,' Kennedy corrected, 'tell us how the murder was carried out.'

'Are murderers usually so co-operative?' ann rea inquired innocently.

'Sometimes. They can be a pretty vain lot. And I feel that this one will be quite proud of his work. Yeah, he'll want to boast about it quite a bit,' Kennedy surmised.

'Okay, Detective, who could it have been?'

'Well, let's see,' he replied holding out his left hand. 'Martyn Farrelly.' He withdrew his index finger.

'Motive?'

'Two, maybe even three. First Peter lands him in a bad publishing deal. Then he uses Martyn's money to start up what becomes a very successful record company. And, three, Martyn could have found out about Peter and Colette sleeping together. Enough of a reason on its own.'

'Alibi?' ann rea rose from the bed and searched for her underclothes.

'Allegedly Martyn was in his music room. However, by his own admission, no one, not even his wife, saw him around the key time. So, in theory he could have slipped out, done the evil deed, and returned unseen to the seclusion of the music room.'

'Hang on a second, Kennedy. If you assume Peter O'Browne received a telephone call from the murderer on the Friday, just as he was about to leave his office, and you further assume that the murderer, in his telephone call, summoned Peter to a meet at Mayfair Mews Studio,' ann rea paused to try to get her own brain around the concept she was about to propose.

'Yes?' Kennedy said distracted by the vision performing the dress tease.

'Well,' the performer continued. 'Then surely you should also be checking his alibi for Friday evening, say seven to nine as well?'

'Good point, very good point,' Kennedy answered, making a mental note to do that very thing.

'Okay! Next suspect?' ann rea inquired as she moved across the room and plumped herself into Kennedy's very comfortable reading chair in the right hand corner, a window to one side and a packed book case to the other. She flicked through Kennedy's current reading matter – 'Writing Home' by Alan Bennett – without paying attention to the contents. It must be a very funny book because she had heard Kennedy laughing out loud as he was reading it.

'Tom Best.' Kennedy raised his hand again so that he could retract a second finger.

'Motive?'

'Simple. He feels aggrieved that although he help Peter set up the successful record company he did not share in the spoils.'

'I thought that it was Best who made the decision not to continue after the sell-out, when perhaps he could have made some money.'

'Not exactly. I think by that point the deal had been done and Best had accepted that he was not going to get anything, let alone the percentage he felt he was entitled to. I would guess that if Peter had offered him a fair share of the money and a major role in the new set-up with a high salary, he would have been happy with his thirty pieces of silver. I think he may have invented his principles as a way to vent his anger at Peter publicly. And, I must admit, after hearing the story a few times I'm not sure that he was not justified in his grievance.'

'The truth is that they probably needed each other. Best hasn't exactly been successful since the split. His office is hardly a hive of activity.'

'Alibi?' ann rea listed as she kept up the pace.

'He was giving a dinner party. He was with five people during the entire evening. They've all been checked out. Kennedy sat up in bed, grateful for the comfort the tight bandages were now affording him.

'What about last Friday at seven?'

'I'll check that. But it won't make any difference, because the bottom line is that he has a strong alibi for the time Peter O'Browne was actually murdered.'

'Make sure you do, check Kennedy. I don't want any sloppy police work on this,' ann rea teased. 'Okay, next?'

Jason Carter-Houston was finger number three.

'Motive?' ann rea pumped.

'Okay. He thinks he was stiffed big time by Peter O'Browne. The group he managed were on the brink of success and he was assured a bright financial future, but the deal went sour and band and manager fell out with Peter. His career has followed the direction of a cow's tail. The more successful Peter was, the more annoyed Carter-Houston would have become.'

'Alibi?'

'Night of murder, he's at a concert by the Splendid Cafe Orchestra.'

'Penguin Cafe Orchestra,' ann rea corrected.

'I'm sure they're splendid. Anyway he's at the concert with his partner on the night of the murder – but – I'll check last Friday,' he smiled.

'Next?'

'Barney Noble.'

'Motive?'

'Blackmail. Or a blackmail that went wrong. He would have less of a conscience than most of our suspects, although if it were him, I'm not sure he would have gone to the trouble of such an elaborate plan. He's more of a knife or a gun in a dark alley and dump the body in Camden Lock type of chap, but, who knows? One thing's for sure,' Kennedy offered rubbing his ribs, 'he's certainly not the friendly type, nor is he exactly intelligent. He'd think "Home thoughts from abroad" was Madonna's new tour book.'

'Alibi?'

'Night of the murder he was drinking with his mates, who'll all swear to it, on a pint of Guinness. Again, Friday night last, I'll check.

'Next?' ann rea inquired noticing Kennedy had only his thumb left.

'I suppose this,' Kennedy replied staring at his thumb, 'has to be the wild card, the Joker. It could be anyone inside, or outside, our frame.'

'For instance?'

'Lets see, Colette Farrelly? Dumped, jealous and…'

'No! I can't see that, Kennedy. Next?'

'Mary Jones?'

'Why on earth Mary?' ann rea was genuinely shocked.

'Because we don't know, ann rea. We don't know what goes on

between two people. We know only what we are told, what we are intended to think. But it wouldn't be the first time a PA and her boss have had an affair. Maybe they split up, maybe he was seeing someone else, maybe she was still in love with him; maybe she couldn't bear it and maybe...'

'Maybe pigs might fly, Kennedy. I think you're quite a bit off the track there.'

'ann rea, you just would not believe the number of murders that are committed by exes and shunned lovers.'

'She would have told me that she was having an affair with Peter. Or I'd have guessed. I've known her a while, Kennedy.'

'Did you know her well enough to know that she is having an affair with Leslie Russell?'

'No! Mary and Leslie? No...that's not true.'

Kennedy said nothing. He just grinned at ann rea.

'Kennedy, no. She couldn't. He's... How did you find that out? Mary and Leslie? Are you sure?' Now ann rea was smiling, her disbelief having made way for amazement.

Kennedy continued only to smile.

'God, I've known her all this time and I'd never guessed. And you've only known her a couple of days. How on earth did you find out?'

At last Kennedy broke his smile and spoke, 'Actually I didn't. I don't know if they are.'

'Kennedy!'

He laughed. 'You see. Within a few seconds you went from knowing I was totally wrong and saying "Impossible" to "Well, perhaps, how did you find out?" and in the end I know you felt that it was true. Anything can be true. People do the strangest things.

'Why? I don't know, maybe because they are lonely, because their true love doesn't want to know, because they felt they are never going to meet Ms or Mr Right, so they'll go with anybody. Because they are sexually frustrated. Necessity dictates what we do, not principles or emotions.'

'You don't believe that, Kennedy, I know you don't. Look how long you were alone before we met. And you're... you're... well you don't exactly look like the back end of a double-decker bus!' ann rea said as she rose from the chair and joined Kennedy on the bed, stroking his hair.

They sat in silence for a while until Kennedy said, 'Oh. It suited my argument. But you know what I mean, ann rea, we just do not know what goes on between two people or even what goes on between a person and themselves. Don't rule anything out. We can't afford to.'

'Okay.'

'And besides, to me it seems natural that Mary and Leslie would have had a scene. To me, they seem made for each other.'

ann rea mulled over this prospect for some seconds.

'Possibly,' she agreed. 'Any other wild cards, Kennedy?'

'Well now that we are talking about Leslie Russell, his name must be in there somewhere.'

She raised her eyebrows.

'Anything is possible, remember? They could have been doing a deal together. The deal could have gone wrong.'

'For heaven's sake, Leslie was Peter's lawyer for years.'

'Yeah, and what about Sting and his accountant? They had been together for years and he helped himself to millions of Sting's money. The more money there is around, the more likely it is that something will be going on. Then there are Johnny Heart, Paddy George. Someone out of the frame.'

'God you've got more suspects than cat's eyes on the M25. Still, I know who definitely didn't do it?'

'Who?' Kennedy urged.

'OJ Simpson.'

'Just as well. If he did, we'd never prove it.'

Chapter Forty-Three

Oh my, oh my, oh my, my, my, my
– Otis Redding

On Monday morning the case went pear-shaped.
The day started off well for Kennedy. Forensic had been
through the rubbish found in Mayfair Mews Studio and had
discovered two interesting pieces of information.

The lone pages of the previous Monday's edition of the *Evening
Standard* found beneath the cardboard at the top right hand end of the
studio, were found to contain traces of fish – haddock, to be precise –
and chips. Now at least it was certain what Peter O'Browne's last supper was, and maybe it had been purchased at the Regent Chippie.

The other clue was slightly more baffling. Forensic had also discovered the remains of a shop receipt. Just the top left hand corner,
which featured what looked like a ram's head in black print, and the
letters 'R' and 'A' and the figures 300849.

The boys and girls from Forensic liked to play the old Watson and
Holmes routine sometimes, just to prove that they were not merely
backroom boys and girls. So, by the process of elimination, deduction
and the use of Yellow Pages, they discovered that the full name of the
shop was RAMS – Rope and Marine Services Ltd (estd 1948) – situated
at 31 Yorkshire Road, London E14. The shop, according to the Yellow
Pages advert, specialised in lifting gear. They hired, they sold, they
manufactured, they repaired, they even tested, and on top of all that
they stocked steel wire rope, fibre rope, kuplex chain, chain blocks, tir-
for winches, pull-lifts, shackles, etc.

This information was proudly presented for the attention of
Detective Inspector Christy Kennedy. At that stage in the case,
Kennedy was very happy to receive any scraps thrown his way.

However, as the Inspector was bumming a lift with WPC Anne
Coles in the direction of the aforementioned RAMS, the case was
breaking (as they say in the papers) wide open a few miles across town
at the home of Mr Martyn Farrelly.

At precisely 10.28 that Monday morning, Martyn Farrelly, in the
comfort of his family home, confessed to the murder of Mr Peter
O'Browne.

Chapter Forty-Four

In ceremonies of the Horsemen
Even the Pawn must hold a grudge
                                    – Dylan

When Kennedy and WPC Anne Coles received this startling piece of information via the car radio, Kennedy asked the WPC to do a Hughie Green at the next opportunity and head back to North Bridge House.

Kennedy felt a bit empty. The case hadn't really been solved. But then again, the case had been concluded in the manner he and ann rea had discussed on Saturday morning: first find the murderer and let him (or her) explain how they had dispatched the evil deed.

Kennedy was disappointed and a little sad to discover that Martyn Farrelly, whom he quite liked, had been responsible for the murder. He had expected someone more devious and underhand. Obviously the pressure must have been boiling up inside Farrelly for some time before it finally exploded with such a force that it led to the ultimate sin: the unlawful killing of a human.

Soon all would be revealed. Kennedy had instructed DS Irvine not to start questioning Martyn Farrelly until he returned to the station. It took him exactly eleven minutes to get there, and now he was sitting across the table from a distraught Martyn Farrelly and his poorly-dressed solicitor, with DS Irvine to his right and Constable Tony Essex standing opposite them, behind Farrelly, guarding the door.

'Okay, it's Monday morning, 10.48,' Kennedy began for the benefit of the tape recorder. 'And present for this interview are Mr Martyn Farrelly, his solicitor, Mr Geoff Marsh, DS James Irvine, Constable Tony Essex, and myself, Detective Inspector Christy Kennedy. Mr Farrelly has been read his rights and has admitted, under caution, that he did wilfully murder Mr Peter O'Browne on or about Wednesday 18th October, last.

'Let's start at the beginning,' Kennedy carried on, turning his attention to Farrelly.

Farrelly stared right through Kennedy. His eyes betraying no sign of recognition.

'Tell us what happened,' DS Irvine prompted.

Silence, not golden but grey, clambered about every corner of the room.

'Look is there any chance we can get this interview started before I need a shave?' Kennedy suggested.

'There's nothing to start with, nothing to tell. I did him, the effing bastard I did him, and that's it, that's the end of it. What do I need to sign?' Farrelly's cold words clearly alarmed his solicitor, whose wise words of caution were falling on deaf ears.

'Well,' Kennedy said expansively, 'it's not quite as simple as that.'

'It might not be simple to you, mate, but to me it's exactly that simple. The effing bastard got exactly what he deserved, and I'm certainly not going to waste any more words or energy on him!' Farrelly's voice held a sense of finality which convinced Kennedy that further attempts at gathering information at that point would prove about as useful as a Phillishave to Gerry Adams.

Kennedy leaned back in his chair and clasped his fingers behind his head to afford himself an even steeper recline. He appeared to be deep in thought. Were his thoughts about the complexities of this case? No, they were about how badly the interview room was in need of a coat of paint.

At least it had been possible for someone to work up quite a professional shine on the chessboard-style Marley tiled floor. But the paint was peeling from the walls in some areas, and several futile retouching jobs gave the room its unique three shades of uneven cream, another South Bank art piece.

'This interview is terminated at 11.02,' Kennedy announced to the room in general and the tape recorder in particular. He hesitated, and did not press the 'stop' button. Instead he said to the solicitor, 'I think, Mr Marsh, you had better advise your client that there is a procedure here to be followed and he had better follow it…'

'Or what? Or you'll do what? 'Farrelly interrupted, spitting out the words and covering the table with a certain amount of liquid, none of which reached either DS Irvine or DI Kennedy. 'I've just admitted to murdering someone, so what additional punishment can you dish out that will make a ha'pence of difference to a man who is going to get life in prison?' His tone turned to mocking laughter.

DS Irvine thought, 'Oh God, here we go, if this was a film and I had it out on video, I'd fast forward this section.'

Kennedy declined to answer Farrelly, choosing instead to address Geoff Marsh, a friendly, family kind of solicitor who was clearly way out of his depth on this one.

'As I have said, I think you and your client should have a break to discuss the situation further. I'll order some tea.' Kennedy popped the 'Stop' button, moved his chair back, rose to his feet and left the room.

A few minutes later, Kennedy and Irvine were dunking Walkers Shortbread in tea in his office. Kennedy wanted to use the break not only to give Marsh a chance to talk to his client but also to find out from DS Irvine exactly how the confession had come about.

Apparently when the Police had arrived at the Farrelly household, called by Mr Farrelly, there had been quite an atmosphere. Colette had chosen the quietness of a family day, Sunday, to confess her affair to her husband. Twenty hours later, on the Monday morning, Farrelly was still fuming.

DS Irvine had put his highly agitated state down to the fact that he was trying to come to terms with having taken someone's life. The interview snowballed out of control like a runaway train.

'There was no one more shocked than me, guv, when Farrelly said, "Yeah it was me, I did the bastard." Actually his wife seemed more stunned. She screamed, "Oh no, no Martyn, please don't do this!".'

At that point Farrelly had requested the WPC to remove 'that tramp' from the room.

'Did he tell you how he did it?' Kennedy inquired.

'No, he didn't. I read him his rights, arrested him and brought him straight to the station. Sergeant Flynn processed him, sir, and, as per your instructions, he's been in the cell ever since. His brief was allowed access to him immediately he turned up.

'All done by the book, sir. I didn't want to fu... I mean mess up your case on the paperwork side.'

'No, of course not. Good. Was he as agitated at home as he was in the interview room?'

'About the same.'

At that precise moment Superintendent Thomas Castle burst into Kennedy's office. 'I say, damned good work, Kennedy, tying up the O'Browne murder so quickly. Absolutely. Excellent, you've made it all look so easy and yes, Irvine, good on you, too. I believe you were the arresting officer. Congratulations. Yes, well done.'

'Well, um, team work, sir,' was all Irvine could think of saying.

'Yes, it's looking good, but we haven't concluded our investigation,' Kennedy said.

'Haven't concluded the bloody investigation. Don't be so bloody modest, Kennedy. You've got someone in the cells who I believe confessed to the murder. I'd say that's a pretty damned successful conclusion to the investigation! Sterling work, Kennedy, great stuff. This is going to look great on your record, on both your records, in fact. Especially with the Marianne Faithfull-lookalike case being solved so quick as well.'

'We were very lucky there, sir. Very lucky. We nearly had the proverbial smoking gun on that one, sir. But here...' Kennedy attempted to hoist up the question mark, but before the top curve had broken surface, the Super interrupted him.

'Ah, Irvine. Do me a favour would you? The DI and I need to have a chat, a private chat.' He ushered DS Irvine to the door, congratulating him yet again, opened the door, showed him out and closed the door after him. He returned to Kennedy.

'Now look here, Kennedy, do I detect a note of doubt?'

Kennedy thought, I get the feeling you used to be a detective, but said nothing, merely nodded positive. The perkiness drained from the Super's face.

'The truth is I just don't know,' Kennedy explained. 'We've just started to interrogate him and he wouldn't talk about it.'

'What on earth do you need to talk to him about? Look, don't be upset just because he doesn't want to become your best mate. He's admitted it, that's all you need. Just tidy up the details, Kennedy. Don't complicate matters. Murder is complicated enough, but not all murderers have the PhDs Ruth Rendell and PD James would have us believe.'

'Yes, I know.'

'Don't give me the "Yes I know, but I disagree with you" routine. I don't need it, and what's more, I don't want it, Kennedy. Just let it rest.'

'But there are too many loose ends, sir.'

'Well just bloody well tie them up. Look, I'm telling you to conclude your interview with this Farrelly chap by lunch time. I want to give a press conference in the early afternoon. And I want to announce that we have charged somebody and that he's off the streets. People will thank us for that, Kennedy. They don't thank us for wasting money and time.

'This O'Browne, he was well known – hell, even my wife knew of him. This is a high-profile case and we're going to look good, my man.' The Superintendent rose from the chair opposite Kennedy and made to leave the room. 'Tidy it up by lunch time, Kennedy, and prepare yourself for some praise. And for God's sake learn to take it!'

Chapter Forty-Five

And love alone
Won't be your saviour
— Paul Buchanan

Kennedy was left seething in his office. He could feel the blood pounding past his temples and feel his forehead reddening as a result. My man, do this; my man, do that!

All they were really interested in at the end of the day was the press conference and the pat on the back from above. How high did you have to go before there was no one left to do the back patting. Unless, of course, the great big Super in the sky had three hands, the third of which was used only in instances of self-congratulation.

By and large Kennedy found Superintendent Castle okay to work for. He usually let Kennedy get on with it. Now Kennedy thought the method in his madness was that he believed this was the most efficient way to do things. Secure the results. Recently the super had become preoccupied with results, facts and figures. 'No, I can't give you more manpower to solve your case. Just solve it quicker.'

Maybe the Super was up for promotion and Kennedy would now have to play the fiddle to a different tune. Kennedy certainly knew a lot worse than Castle. And maybe, Kennedy was too fond of searching for the complicated angles on a case.

Perhaps it was simply that Kennedy did not want the murderer to be Farrelly. All that family happiness had evaporated, and whatever the outcome of all this, it was gone forever.

Kennedy purposefully finished his tea and Walkers Shortbread and reconvened the interview with the original cast exactly forty-one minutes after the false start.

This time Martyn Farrelly seemed calmer, easier to talk to. Either acceptance of the reality of the situation, or his solicitor's advice, had loosened his tongue.

He told those present that on the Friday night, while his wife thought he was hard at work in the studio, he had slipped out and gone over to Primrose Hill, where he knew Peter O'Browne would be working on his new studio project, Mayfair Mews Studio.

He hadn't gone over to the studio with the precise intention of murdering O'Browne. This was either the truth as he saw it, or what the brief had advised. He might receive a lighter sentence if they were able to prove the murder had not been premeditated.

Farrelly claimed Peter had taunted him about the affair with Colette, and that Peter had hinted that Colette had preferred him to

Farrelly because he was successful in everything he did. Farrelly confessed that he had lost his temper and attacked Peter, strangling him, and when Peter passed out he decided that he would finish him off and try to make it look like suicide.

He found a rope and tied one end around Peter's neck. The other he threw over the rafter, hoisting Peter into the air and watched him die. 'That's it,' Farrelly concluded.

'That's it?' Kennedy asked incredulously. 'You've nothing else to tell us?'

'No.'

'Nothing?'

'No. Look, I've told you. I've told you how, why and where. What else do you need?'

'I need to be satisfied that you are telling the truth.'

Geoff Marsh's eyebrows and Farrelly's mouth both said, 'What?'

'And,' Kennedy continued, prepared to stand no more nonsense from either Farrelly or Superintendent Castle. 'Quite frankly I'm not!'

'Not what?'

'Not satisfied that you are telling the truth. I would have been more convinced if you had blamed Jack Duckworth. He seems to get blamed for everything else, so why not this?'

DS James Irvine hadn't batted an eyelid so far. He agreed with Kennedy 100 per cent and wanted to observe Farrelly's every body movement searching for just one tell-tale sign betraying the story. The line about the 'Coronation Street' character had nearly thrown him, but now he saw what he'd been hoping for. Farrelly reached up with his right hand and pressed his open palm hard on his forehead. Then he started to move his hand, slowly, up and down, all the time pressing his forehead, trying to relieve his growing headache.

'So, let's go through this again,' Kennedy announced, sensing that the advantage was on his side of the table.

'Look, are you a masochist or what? Do you need to beat a confession out of me before you'll believe me? Is that how it goes?'

'Here's the thing, I'll tell you how it goes. I'll admit it to you in front of your solicitor. I'm convinced, absolutely convinced, that you did not murder Peter O'Browne. You haven't a clue what you are talking about.'

The laying out was still significant to Kennedy, and he felt that the murderer, would be proud of this and, several other features of the killing. Kennedy knew that it was virtually, if not entirely, impossible for a single person to raise the dead weight of an eleven stone body by pulling on a rope. He was pretty sure that this could have been achieved only with the assistance of some kind of mechanical power, a small engine, or an elaborate pulley system. Doctor Taylor's report had suggested no evidence of damage to the victim's neck caused by someone's hands as well as the rope, and Farrelly hadn't mentioned the chloroform.

'Having said that,' Kennedy carried on, 'we have to assume that at some point you are going to be allowed to return to your family. However, can I just say this, such a return is going to be greatly delayed if we have to charge you with obstructing the police. That is quite a serious charge in itself.'

Martyn Farrelly at last began to regain some contact with reality. 'Okay. Look, I'm sorry. Colette, told me about, you know – that she was unfaithful to me with Peter and I just snapped. I really wished I could have murdered the bastard. I suppose I just felt I was getting some kind of stupid revenge on her.'

'A way of getting even,' DS Irvine chipped in.

Kennedy moved across to Farrelly's side of the table and sat on the corner, very close to him, with his hands clasped in front of him. He spoke so quietly that both DS Irvine and Geoff Marsh had trouble hearing him.

'Martyn, I know you are feeling bad about this. But can I just tell you that I know your wife is feeling worse? I know you think it's stupid, but it's absolutely true. So look, help her through it; make it at least a bit easier for her, and I think that way you just might make it a little easier for yourself. I've seen what you two have. Don't throw it away. Not for this. Please.' He stood up. 'Mr Marsh would you please take your client away and get him out of my sight before we lock him up for something, anything, nothing. Just get him out of here.' Kennedy hit the Stop button on the tape recorder.

He and the DS made their way to Castle's office, one suspect lighter on the case.

'You know, sir, what if he's very, very clever and has totally out-foxed us?'

'How do you mean, Jimmy?'

'Supposing he really did kill Peter O'Browne, but knew that if he didn't give us the correct details we'd think that he couldn't have done it?'

'Bit of a risk, isn't it, Jimmy?' Kennedy thought for some seconds as they walked along the corridor.

'And I suppose the Super would accuse us of getting too compli-cated if we were to go and present him with a theory like that.' Kennedy smiled. 'And with the mood he's going to be in when he hears he hasn't got his press-bloody-conference… well, I'm not sure, Jimmy, that I would want to chance that theory, but please feel free to run it by the Super the next time you meet.'

They had reached the door of Superintendent Castle's office. Kennedy took a deep breath and knocked as DS Irvine quietly scarpered.

Chapter Forty-Six

But now you're here
Brighten my Northern Sky
— Nick Drake

'Okay, that's fine. Keep me posted,' was the only reply Kennedy received from the Super to his appraisal of recent developments in the Peter O'Browne case.

No breath of fire, no wrath of God, just a sprinter who had dreamed of beating Linford Christie to the tape. Thank goodness Castle realised it was exactly that: a dream. He seemed happy to return immediately to reality.

Kennedy's reality, on the other hand, was somewhat different. Whereas the Super had someone, muggins, on whom to rely on to go out and find another suspect, Kennedy had no such luxury. He was the man on the sharp end of the stick. And at that point he was a man with few clues and even fewer suspects.

He returned to his office, up-dated his noticeboard, sat down on his desk and rested his feet on the chair, a move which would have gained him a clip on the ear from his mother thirty years earlier. He placed his elbows on his knees and leaned his chin in the safety of his hands, drumming his fingers on his cheeks.

He felt he needed to talk to Leslie Russell, Carter-Houston, Tom Best and Mary Jones in no particular (but certainly not that) order. He also needed to chase down the details on the torn RAMS receipt. But, apart from that, he had zero, to go on. The trail was dangerously close to growing cold, as cold as a Henry Moore statue. He rang ann rea. She was busy on the phone, which annoyed him. He didn't know why ann rea being busy should annoy him.

He felt aimless. He desperately wanted to find some way of getting on with the case, into the case. Sometimes you had to concentrate on the obvious, and concentrate on it intensely. He remembered the words his first Detective Inspector, a Welshman Eamon Thomas, would keep uttering to anyone who would listen. 'In playing cards, and solving cases, the secret is not to be dealt a good hand, but to be dealt a bad hand and play it well.'

How was he to play this atrocious hand?

Perhaps he should return to the motive. Why would anyone be prepared to risk spending the rest of their life in jail in order to kill. No matter how much you hated someone and wanted to throw a brick through their window, smash up their house, shag their missus, stick a cork up their dog's arse to stop it soiling the pavements, accidentally scratch the side of their car, whatever, it was still a giant step away from murdering someone.

It's a big word, murder. It's an easy word to say, but it represents the biggest and most terrible act a man and woman can perpetrate on another human being.

When he was growing-up, adults would speak in hushed tones whenever they used the word. His entire village would stop to discuss the taking of a life which had happened down in the city, Belfast, or even as far away as London. Had TV, the movies and the electronic media, with their ever increasing appetite for the macabre, cheapened life to such a degree that victims had become dispensable and murderers the celebrities?

Kennedy wondered whether there had been an audience for the hanging of Peter O'Browne. Had the killer stood or sat in attendance as the life had drained in spurts from the weary limbs? Or had Peter's executioner been happier to wait outside the doors of Mayfair Mews Studio as the limbs concluded their involuntary jerks? Could the reason for the pennies on the eyes be to stop the murderer from being stared at from the other side of life.

Where had the murderer found the old pennies? Did he have them in a private collection? Was he a collector? Did he collect other things as well? If so, what other things?

At that junction in the train of Kennedy's thought he became aware of a ringing. The more he let his previous thoughts drift off to their astral circuit, the louder the ringing became until he realised that it was his telephone. He picked up the receiver to hear ann rea's voice in the earpiece.

'Hi, Kennedy. What's up?'

'Oh, I was just looking for inspiration.'

'I'm flattered, although not sure I should be if you were hoping I'd set you off on the trail of a murderer.'

'Yeah. I know what you mean. This is all so frustrating. There is no light at the end of the tunnel. In fact, at this exact moment, I'd be happy just to find the entrance to the tunnel.'

'Well, I've had a bit of excitement today!'

'Yeah?'

'Yeah. You'll never guess who asked me out.'

'kd lang?'

'That's not even funny, Kennedy. Besides, she's a bit heavy on the bass drum for me. No, actually it was your friend and mine, Mr Leslie Russell.'

'Leslie Russell! But he knows that you and I are dating, an item, or whatever.'

'"Or whatever?" Very romantic, Kennedy. No, he said that he realised of course that you and I were together, but he'd love just to have lunch, or dinner, or whatever and get to know me better. Nothing heavy. He said it just might be nice socially.'

Kennedy said nothing. In the mood he was in he wouldn't have been surprised (well maybe just a little, more like a lot actually) if ann rea had told him that she'd agreed to meet Russell.

'Aren't you even curious about what I said to him?'

'Worried would be a better word, actually.'

'Oh, Kennedy you are hopeless. Too honest for your own good. Well I'll tell you, since you haven't asked. I told him that it would be inappropriate. I told him that you and I were at the beginning of a long relationship. A relationship which I wanted to last forever. I told him that dating other men just might get in the way of that dream coming true.'

Kennedy was too flabbergasted to speak.

'Kennedy?'

'You said that? You meant that? I mean, wow. Shit, you've never even said that to me. I suppose,' he went on, trying to get back into his stride, 'that it's par for the course. Lawyers hear everything first.'

'Thanks. Well, I'm glad to hear you've perked up a bit. Anyway, it wasn't really a surprise that Leslie invited me out. Mary told me that it would happen sooner or later. It's not that he's a ladies' man or anything, he just likes new girls.'

'Did Mary tell you whether she's had a scene with Leslie?'

'No, I mean, no, she didn't say. I can't believe you. Here I am declaring my undying love for you, and ten seconds later your mind is tripping back on to the case. You see that is one of my biggest fears, getting taken for granted. I just didn't think it would happen this quickly,' ann rea laughed. As Kennedy heard her laughter down the telephone line, he imagined how her eyes would look. When ann rea's eyes were smiling, she could rule the world.

Good news tends to create good moods. Kennedy's mood had definitely moved up quite a few gears into good. Although it would be unfair, not to say inaccurate, to say that his previous mood had been bad. Solemn would be a better word.

'Well, Kennedy, you may have time for tittle-tattle, but I haven't. Some of us have work to do. See you tonight?'

'And that's a fact.'

And with that ann rea was gone, leaving Kennedy with an earful of electronic crackle.

Chapter Forty-Seven

I wish I was a fisherman
Tumbling on the seas
Far away from dry land
And its bitter memories

– Mike Scott

'Why do we take it as read that we should be able to find the murderer?' Kennedy and DS Irvine were travelling down Parkway by car, in the general direction of Islington with the eventual hope of reaching Yorkshire Road, E 14, the location of RAMS shop.

'I mean, it's pretty big-headed of us to assume that. What we're effectively saying, Jimmy, is that we are a lot smarter than the villain,' Kennedy persisted. DS Irvine had assumed the DI's question to be rhetorical, so he hadn't replied, conserving his brain power to negotiate the car around the pedestrians crossing the road, against their own red light on the corner of Parkway and Camden High Street.

It was quite a drive to the east end, and DS Irvine hoped Kennedy would listen to one of his loves (Radio Four) and not engage him in conversation. DS Irvine found it difficult to drive and talk at the same time – especially with DI Kennedy. General banter was fine, but Kennedy's conversations were usually a lot more thought provoking. Often he would voice his thoughts on a case, whether they made enough sense to be worth voicing, or not.

Sometimes this was quite amusing and DS Irvine would have a hard time keeping his laughter undercover. Kennedy would castigate himself: 'Oh don't be such an idiot, Kennedy!' Or reason with himself. 'You don't really think that old son, do you?' followed by, 'No, I didn't think you did. Back to the drawing board.' When the penny finally dropped, as it invariably did, 'Idiot, idiot. If it had been a dog it would have bitten you!'

Today was going to be one of those days. Radio Four remained entombed behind the on/off switch as Kennedy rattled out his ideas: 'Now, take this O'Browne matter. At some point in his life he did something, probably unconsciously, and this thing, whatever it was, caused our murderer to make a decision to end O'Browne's life. O'Browne crossed a line.

'I wonder if he was aware he was doing it. I wonder, if someone had said to him, "Look, you do that, and you are going to lose your life as a result of it," what he would have said. "Bugger off and don't be stupid," or something similar? Or would he, given the choice, have apologised and said, "You're perfectly right. How could I ever have considered doing that?" and backtracked and lived to tell the tale.

'It's a funny old show really, when a solution to a problem is to take another's life. Why should that be a possibility? Why should it be a solution? How come, we, the so-called intelligent species, behave in such a manner? Like the animals we consider ourselves superior to. Even they generally kill only of necessity, for food!'

DS James Irvine thought, God, he's definitely off on one, I'll leave him to it.

'Well, I don't know and that's for sure, but I can tell you that in my mind that's the major flaw in the perfect beast, the human. Someone fucked up big time with the initial programming of the super beast. Super beast? I don't think so!' Kennedy lectured.

'Of course, sir,' offered DS Irvine. 'If they had done their programming properly, you and I would be out of a job, wouldn't we?'

'No, not really. The job would not have existed in the first place, would it?'

'Mmmm,' conceded Irvine.

'What would you have done if you weren't doing this, Jimmy?' Kennedy noticed a wry smile float on to the Detective Sergeant's face.

'No, Jimmy, I don't think spending more time in the sack with the able Staff Nurse Rose Butler would count as a job.'

'No, probably not, sir, but it is damned good fun.' Irvine thought about it. 'A farmer, I think. I would have liked to have been a farmer. What about you, guv?'

'A carpenter,' Kennedy replied without a moment's hesitation. 'Ah, here we are.' They pulled into a gift of a parking space directly in front of RAMS. Kennedy read the sign above the shop window, *RAMS – Rope and Marine Services Ltd. Established 1948.* The shop would have been one year old when Kennedy was born.

The ram's head used above the shop was identical to the one the Forensic Department – bless their cotton socks – had turned up on the corner of the torn receipt.

As Kennedy walked into the shop and saw the pulleys and ropes he thought of the hangman's noose. 'Well, our killer is either a wimp or a woman!' he said quietly to DS Irvine.

'Isn't that a bit sexist, sir?'

'What I meant was that the hang-person used a pulley system to hoist Peter O'Browne off the ground,' Kennedy replied still in a quiet voice.

The smell of the ropes and wood varnish from boat fittings filled the DI's nostrils as ropes and pulleys and pulleys and ropes and tackle and hoists and wooden accessories engaged his eyes. Some of them were wood, hand-carved or machine-turned, hard to say these days. Others were in highly polished brass. Posters, old and new, filled the little empty space on the walls, describing in great detail, with the help of bikini clad nubiles, the uses of the various wares.

Kennedy purchased a small, compact eight-way pulley system with nylon rope, 'Strong enough to hoist a car engine!' the sales assistant assured him. Kennedy inquired if any similar purchases had been made over the last few weeks. He was, he advised the friendly shop assistant, thinking of someone non-trade, someone definitely not a boat person.

'Well, I could check the stock files for sales but we get so many people though here in a day, let alone two weeks, it would be hard to put a face to the purchase. They don't all look like boat people when they come in here, anyway. Some of them come in their lunch hour to pick up bits and pieces for their weekend tubs.'

The shop manager went round the rest of the staff, repeating Kennedy's question. But without a photograph it was like looking for a needle in a haystack, worse in fact, in such a packed shop.

Chapter Forty-Eight

I – I feel – feel like I am- in a burning building And I gotta go
– Laurie Anderson

'Let's go back to Mayfair Mews Studio, Jimmy,' Kennedy sighed as he painfully replaced himself in the car.

'Do you think you are on to something?'

'Oh, I don't know, I was never great at physics, but I think I do remember a little.

'The more pulleys you have in a system, the lighter the load becomes. But, the greater the distance you have to pull the effort-end of the rope. With this system, our pristine eight pulleys,' Kennedy replied as he removed his purchase from the RAMS bag: two sets of four pulleys in a block with hooks at opposite ends, 'the body will appear to weigh one quarter of its actual weight and you would have to pull the effort-end eight feet to raise the body one foot off the ground.'

DS Irvine tried to remember the sketches he too had completed in his blue exercise books all those years ago. He could remember how neat and tidy he was whenever the books were crisp and new, and how his neatness evaporated with the newness of the book. He thought this probably said a lot about him, though he wasn't exactly sure what.

'Do you think, then,' he said, 'that if, as you suspect, the murderer used a pulley system, his or her lack of strength was a significant factor?'

'It's a definite possibility.'

'Well, that probably rules out Tom Best, and moves Carter-Houston further up the list. He's a bit of a wimp.'

Kennedy offered, 'It must also promote Colette Farrelly to our list, wouldn't you say?'

Later, when Kennedy repeated this thought to ann rea after she had joined them at Mayfair Mews Studio, she disagreed violently.

'Not possible, Kennedy. Not even in your wildest dreams.'

'And why not?'

'Well, just look at her – a loving mother like her is not going to commit such a crime and risk leaving her children motherless when she's sent to prison.'

'But you're assuming she thought she was going to be caught. It is my experience that murderers – though I grant you, I am talking about murderers who plan and not those who kill accidentally or commit crimes of passion – it is my experience that they never believe they are going to get caught. That's part of the buzz, avoiding detection. The planning, down to the last little detail is a very exciting part of the process.'

'But why would she want to kill him? She liked him, she was obviously very fond of him, even though I don't think we could say she loved him. Hell, she even fixed him up with a girlfriend, so she couldn't have been jealous. And she convinced Martyn to contact Peter again following their falling out. I just can't see why she would want Peter dead.'

'Other people's relationships are never quite what they seem. And DS Irvine here will tell you that not all murderers are schizos with piercing heartless eyes, dishevelled hair and dog's breath, who chew off cats' heads just for fun. Sometimes they are normal, loving, family people. Sometimes something in their lives just snaps and they'll carry out the evil deed and manage to keep it separate from the rest of their lives, leaving no obvious clues in their daily existence. But there will be something lurking just under the surface, and if you can dig deep enough to uncover it, you'll expose the whole ugly can of worms.'

DS Irvine was saying nothing. He was keeping well out of it. He liked ann rea, she was good for Kennedy. They were good for each other. Neither letting their partner get away with shit.

He could never imagine ann rea and Kennedy in a scene, with ann rea at home, getting the supper, slippers and pipe ready for Kennedy. She was a fiery lass and a bit of a cracker. Of course this was something he would never voice to Kennedy, but DS Irvine thought that ann rea had a body to die for. In fact, some nights when he'd had a few whiskies and he and Staff Nurse Rose Butler were playing doctors and nurses he found himself thinking about ann rea. But that was another story. He was even scared to think about it, let alone talk about it.

Kennedy tied a rope around the rafter in the studio roof and attached the pulley system to it. He stretched the pulley to its full extent, bringing the lower end to about six inches above his head. To the lower end he fixed another piece of rope which he secured under his arms, a procedure he'd seen used in helicopter rescues. The DI then invited ann rea to pull on the effort-end rope, with him as the load. ann rea complied with his request with great frivolity.

'Ah, Kennedy, now I have you exactly where I want you.'

Kennedy was rising slowly into the air, an inch at time, as ann rea pulled in her end of the rope, eight inches at a time. Quite soon he was dangling and rotating in the air about a foot above the concrete floor.

Suddenly the penny dropped with ann rea. 'You mean bastards. You just brought me here to see if a mere woman could lift a solid man off the ground.'

An impish smile stole across her face as she extended her end of the rope to the far wall and tied it around a wooden beam used to support the workbench. 'Detective Sergeant James Irvine and myself are going to go and have a leisurely cup of cappuccino,' she announced as her accomplice checked the the rope was fastened securely. She took DS Irvine by the arm and led him in the direction of the door.

'ann rea, ann rea! ann rea, come on, let me down!' Kennedy pleaded catching a fit of the giggles.

'Or what Kennedy? What will you do if I don't let you down?'

'I'll... I'll spell your name in capitals from now on, that's what I'll do!'

ann rea and Irvine both laughed loudly. 'That's below the belt. But all right, if you're going to play dirty, I'd better let you down.' She shrugged her shoulders in mock surrender.

'Okay, one last thing.' Kennedy said through his giggles as he was lowered gently to the floor. He disengaged himself, detached the pulley and threw the rope over the rafter, again fixed himself to one end. The other he offered to ann rea, asking her to try lifting him from the ground again.

She couldn't.

DS Irvine had a go. After a lot of huffing and puffing and the galvanising of a good deal of macho Scottish pride, he finally managed to raise Kennedy from the ground.

'So it was either a woman or a weed,' conceded ann rea. 'Now, do I get my cappuccino – which I hope is on Camden CID?'

'Of course. You have been a great help to my research,' Kennedy smiled as he picked up the rope and pulleys and the three of them went to Cafe 79, as famous for its great cup of tea as it was for cappuccino and cakes.

Kennedy was glad to sit down. He probably shouldn't have subjected himself to all that strain with his bruised ribs.

'What about Mary Jones?' Kennedy inquired, as he wiped a dab of cream from the corner of his mouth and washed the remains of a delicious cake down with a mouthful of tea.

'What about Mary Jones?' ann rea replied. 'You are not starting to think it could have been Mary, are you?'

'Look, don't string me up again, but we've got to give everyone another look, this time giving a bit more attention to the females.'

'You'll enjoy that, Kennedy, won't you?'

'She's not really my type.'

'Really? What is your type?' ann rea inquired playfully as DS Irvine went off to pay the bill.

'Oh, you know, the unavailable type.'

'You don't know the half of it,' she joked. 'The sad thing is you're probably not kidding.'

'Yeah. But come on though, ann rea – what about Mary? Any more thoughts?'

'Well,' ann rea began, deep in thought. 'I suppose, if I'm honest, I've always thought that Mary had a bit of a thing about Peter – unrequited, unfulfilled I suppose, but as you keep telling me you just never know.

'Quite frankly though, I should have thought even Mary would be a more likely candidate than Colette Farrelly.'

Chapter Forty-Nine

She said she's stick around
'Til the bandages came off
— Tom Waits

The following day, Tuesday, brought confirmation that Kennedy had indeed cracked a rib in his skirmish with Barney Noble. This fact would still have remained undiscovered had it not been for ann rea, who thought Kennedy's continuous wincing was indicative of something more serious than Kennedy's diagnosis: 'Oh, I just pulled something.'

Kennedy had an aversion to doctors and hospitals. How could you not be suspicious of a profession whose emblem was a serpent on a stick? Dentists were not too far behind, if they were behind at all. He hated taking medication of any kind. He worked on the principle that to be doing you some good, a drug had to be inflicting harm on another part of the body. Add to that the fact he detested being under the influence of anything unnatural.

Instead Kennedy maintained to himself that if you ignored an ailment it would eventually go away. ann rea was more of the if-it's-slightly-wrong-fix-it-before-it-breaks school. She felt guilty now about having kept him suspended on the rope in Mayfair Mews Studios. But it had been funny at the time and Kennedy had probably laughed the loudest.

The doctor at the local Primrose Hill Clinic bound him tight and he returned to the waiting room to greet ann rea with, 'It couldn't have been Mary Jones.'

'What?'

'It couldn't have been Mary Jones,' Kennedy repeated more quietly to avoid the stares of the patients in the waiting room. When Kennedy and ann rea were out in the street he elucidated. 'Mary Jones was with Peter O'Browne when he was leaving Camden Town Records on Friday night. She was with him, and the receptionist at Camden Town Records confirmed this when he took the call inviting him, we assume, to Mayfair Mews studio. So obviously, the caller wasn't Mary.

'Then she went on to The Forum in Kentish Town and was in company for the remainder of the evening. So that rules her out.'

Back at North Bridge House, Kennedy leant back in his chair and stretched his arms behind his head. He sighed. Of course he had to accept that he was making progress. They had solved the England's Lane fire mystery and uncovered the chart-hyping teams; they had cleared Martyn Farrelly, but not his wife Colette. They had established, they thought, how Peter O'Browne had been murdered.

But, and it was indeed a big but, not only had they failed to identify the killer, they appeared to be no closer to doing so. The trail was getting so cold you could practically chill your beer on it. That was, of course, if you could find the trail in the first place.

As Kennedy saw it, he had one remaining suspect, Colette Farrelly. In spite of ann rea's violent opposition to the theory, Kennedy felt that it had distinct possibilities. Colette had certainly had the opportunity – her husband had been locked away in the music room, giving her the freedom to come and go as she pleased – and she had the motive, or rather a string of motives. Was she a jealous, spurned lover or the avenger of her husband's treatment at the hands of Peter O'Browne? It couldn't be both. Or could it?

Kennedy didn't think so. His other problem was that he couldn't make either motive stand up on its own. It was only when you put the two together that you had some substance. Individually, the motives seemed to be as useful as Radio Four's Shipping Forecast was to Londoners. He thought he might just be putting two and two together and getting five.

H turned his chair to face his noticeboard and sought inspiration. He needed a break. Genius was ten per cent inspiration and 90 per cent perspiration, so he decided to spend the rest of the day talking again to all the main characters in the case. It was a bit like a TV series the way each case threw up its own cast of characters.

What Kennedy wanted to know was, had the star entered the ensemble yet, or was that great director in the sky saving him – or her – for a very dramatic last scene.

Chapter Fifty

When trouble gets too close to home
My anger turns to fear
— Christy Moore

As they drove to their next meeting, WPC Coles used the opportunity to quiz Kennedy about the possibility of moving over to the detective side. He was encouraging her to apply to become a WDC, Woman Detective Constable, and in the meantime – limbo land – she would be an accredited Detective Constable.

'I hear you've been checking out my alibi again,' was the greeting Kennedy and WPC Anne Coles received on being shown into Tom Best's office in Camden Town.

'Well I'm sure you would not wish us to be anything but thorough, sir.'

'Yes, yes, I'm impressed. I gather that both Brian and Sally and Ted and John have been re-interviewed to see was there anything they'd forgotten,' Tom smiled, as always giving away the 'Y' of his first word with silent mouth movement.

'Yes, well on a murder case such as this, we have to check and recheck every eventuality,' Kennedy explained in an official tone.

'Of course. What did you expect them to come up with? "Yes, actually we've just remembered, haven't we dear?"' Tom grinned sarcastically, his voice rising an octave or two, as he mimicked his camp friends. '"That during dessert Tom excused himself and disappeared for forty minutes to murder that bastard O'Browne.'"

'No,' Kennedy smiled. 'Not exactly, sir. But as I say, you'd be surprised what people remember about certain situations a few days later.

'Anyway, here we are again, to see if you yourself have recalled anything new that might be relevant to the case?'

'Listen, as I have told you already, I wasn't exactly sorry that someone one topped him. In my book he had it coming, what goes around comes around, and all that. I have to tell you that, since we last spoke, Peter O'Browne has been the furthest thing from my mind. I've been much more preoccupied with a single we have breaking at the minute by a new singer called Laurel McHardy.'

'I've heard of him,' offered the WPC.

'Good. Great in fact,' Tom Best smiled at the WPC as they all stood around in his office. 'If the bobby on the beat has heard of him, I must be doing my job properly.

'Anyway, he's just charted and I'm afraid that's been taking up an awful lot of my time. So I haven't really had that much time to dwell on your case.'

'Oh, well. I've just got a couple of questions for you, Mr Best, and then I'll leave you to bask in the light of your star,' Kennedy replied, annoyed at Best's dismissive air with the WPC. 'Had you and Peter O'Browne ever committed any details of your working to paper?'

'No, of course not, If we had there would have been no need for all the trouble. I trusted him. We were mates when we were starting out, as I've told you before.'

'Yes, I know that. But it's usual, when two people are starting a business, friends or not, for them to write something down, or even just to discuss how they are to work together. I mean, if the WPC here and myself were to form a pop group, we'd have a discussion about how best to set it up.

'Now I imagine the WPC, because of her looks, would be the front person,' Kennedy carried on, enjoying exercising his imagination. WPC Coles felt herself blushing. 'So, she'd probably have a lot more work to do. If that were the case, I'm sure it would be fair for her to receive a share of the money commensurate with that role. But equally if, say, we used some of my money to get the project started, then perhaps I would want a larger share to pay off my investment.

'Did you use any of your money to set up Camden Town Records?'

'You know I didn't!'

'And you didn't agree a deal in advance?'

'No. Peter always said we'd work it out and he would look after me.' Best was fast becoming ratty and was trying hard not to show it.

'Tell me, did he pay you regular wages?'

'Why yes, of course he did.'

'Good wages?' Kennedy prodded further.

'Yes, I suppose they were.'

'Can you see what's been bothering me? If two people are partners, I mean real partners, then one doesn't pay the other wages. It affects the balance of power, you see.'

'Look, Detective Inspector, I really don't see where this is going. As I've said, I'm very busy, very busy; so, if…'

'I'm not quite finished yet, sir,' Kennedy cut in as he extended one of the silver balls on Best's desk toy and let it go. It smashed into the remaining five, repelling the lone one at the opposite end of the set, which in turn swung back into the troupe and sent the original ball back towards Kennedy's waiting fingers. 'You see, what I'm trying to suggest sir, is that Peter O'Browne looked after you very well. I believe you received a very handsome pay-off when the Grabaphone deal was finalised?'

'Only because I fought for it and, even then, only thanks to the intervention of Leslie Russell who wanted to avoid resorting to the courts.' Tom Best reached for his tobacco and skins on the desk to develop a roll-up.

'Now, there again, I would take a different view. Perhaps they were taking pity on you.'

'Pity? Pity? I'll give you pity. I built that fucking company. I was the reason, the sole reason, that fucking asshole got his six fucking million pounds. Without me Camden Town Records would have been worth nothing. He was a flake. I did all the fucking work, he did all the fucking up. The guy was a walking nightmare.' Best rose from his chair, the veins bulging in his neck. His normal pale complexion was rising to match the colour of his hair. Now that he found himself on his feet, he made an excuse of crossing to the other side of the room to fetch the lens-cloth to clean his glasses.

'Yeah, it was a pity, a pity that I was always saving his ass. He'd go out to a gig, meet a beautiful girl, give her a line, you know, "I think you could make a great record." Girls always fall for that; always. You'd be surprised even today how much of that still goes on and the more powerful the record company person is, the more it goes on.

'Peter would take them home, do the biz and kick them out with an "Oh, speak to Tom Best about fixing up some time in the studio." And I'd have to be the bad guy, the one who says, "No, sorry, that's not going to work, we're going to need demos first," and then just keep delaying until eventually the girl gives up. Or, if she was really great in the sack and he wanted a return bout or two, I'd have to put them in the studio and pretend we were doing something and keep up the facade until he got bored and ditched her.

'Pity me, did they? Peter was the pathetic one. He did that once too often.'

'Well, he didn't exactly do badly since you parted company.' Kennedy looked pointedly round Best's office. There was no comparison with Peter's set up.

'If you've got money, it's fucking easy. You can buy everything you want, even success. You can even buy your fucking records into the charts. Surely even you must know that by now. But I don't see what this has got to do with anything. Peter is dead, and all that's over. What difference does it make if we had a written deal or not.' Best sighed and took a large drag, such a large drag that the WPC couldn't help wondering whether perhaps he was wishing his brain was being massaged by another plant.

'Well, as I say, we have to follow up every angle,' said Kennedy calmly. 'We never know what is going to show up. Could you please tell me what you were doing the Friday before last? From say, six o'clock until midnight.'

'That's easy,' Best began without batting an eyelid. He took another large drag before answering. 'I was here, by myself, working late. I was finishing off the marketing plans for the Laurel McHardy single. I find it the best time of the day to do things like that. The phones are dead and you can give it your full attention.'

'No one else here with you?'

'I only wish I could find staff who would work that late,' Best smiled, the lack of colour returning to his face.

'My final question is, did you on or about last Wednesday murder Peter O'Browne?' Kennedy did not change his measured tone, or raise the level of his voice. WPC Anne Coles was totally gobsmacked by the question and she imagined Best must have been thunderstruck. But if he was, he wasn't showing it.

Instead he forced a laugh. 'But I was having dinner with Brian and Sally and Ted and John, as you know perfectly well. You've asked them about it enough.'

'I was just checking.' Kennedy made to depart the tea-less interview. 'We'll find our own way out.'

Chapter Fifty-One

But kids don't know
They can only guess
How hard it is
To wish you happiness

– John Prine

Detective Inspector Christy Kennedy was happy to report that at his next interview, with Colette Farrelly, the tea flowed more abundantly. She answered his questions freely and obviously had nothing to hide. It helped that she had a watertight alibi for the Friday evening, she had one of her mates over for, 'a little dinner, a bit of gossip and a lot of wine.' Deep inside, Kennedy knew that Colette could not have murdered Peter. He just needed to prove it. The scenario that was building slowly in his mind, piece by piece, was already pulling him in a different, but more difficult direction.

'How are you and Martyn getting on?' Kennedy asked, shifting away from interview mode having heard all he needed to hear.

'Oh, I think we're going to get through it. I think – I hope – the worst is over. There'll be a few scars which will take time to heal, if they ever will heal entirely. But I suppose the main thing is, in spite of all the pain, we want to stay together. Splitting up is not an option either of us want to consider.

'You know,' she laughed. 'We were married for better or for worse. Well, this is definitely the worst. It can only get better from now on. It's a bit like that Beatle song, oh what's it called? The one where Paul sings, "It's getting better all the time," and John chips in with, "It can't get much worse!"'

Kennedy and WPC Coles rose to leave. Offering thanks for his tea, Kennedy declared, 'I don't think we'll be bothering you any more, Mrs Farrelly.'

'Bothering us? After what you did for Martyn, it's no bother, believe me. Come back and see us some time and bring your girlfriend along, the one you told me about from the *Camden News Journal*. Come to tea. Yes, come to tea and I'll make sure we're well stocked up on your favourite shortbread, Walkers isn't it?'

Kennedy smiled. It was his job to be objective, but he couldn't help being happy that neither Colette nor Martyn were involved in the murder of Peter O'Browne. That was the good news. The bad news was that he didn't know how to proceed with the case.

The ideas taking shape in his brain were improbable, to put it mildly. By the process of elimination and deduction, he was down to one suspect. He was ambivalent about this. If his hunch was correct, he was on the home straight.

If not, he would be back at the beginning again, or rather, even further back than the beginning. The first time round he had been given several avenues to investigate. But should his number one and only suspect, the suspect with a perfect alibi, prove to be innocent, then Kennedy had nothing other than a big mighty zero on which to hang his case.

If that happened, it would take more than a couple of gold discs for Superintendent Thomas Castle's wife to appease him.

Chapter Fifty-Two

I need the noises of Destruction
When there's nothing new
Oh nothing new
The sound of breaking glass
— Nick Lowe

That evening Detective Inspector Christy Kennedy took his girl-friend out on a hot date. He took ann rea to the scene of the crime. Wandering around the Mayfair Mews Studio, Kennedy's fingers flexed furiously.

'I can see why you are so successful with girls,' said ann rea.

'What?'

'You take them to all the exciting places.'

Kennedy just grunted.

'There's that smell again!'

'Listen, Kennedy, I told you about being rude on dates. I have to tell you that not all girls are going to be as forgiving as me. But that's only because they don't know what's for afters dearest.'

'ann rea!'

'What, Kennedy? That sounded very nearly like capitals to me, and you promised.'

'That smell. I know what it is. It's putty. I knew what it was, but it didn't surface into my consciousness because I didn't register it as being important. But it's putty, most definitely putty.'

'Okay. I concede that one – it's putty. Take the full ten points. But what year is it?'

'This year – a vintage year for putty.'

With that Kennedy went on a wander round the studio and found exactly what he was looking for in the annex. Just to the left, near the entrance to the domestic quarters, a single pane of glass in a six-pane window had recently been replaced.

Although the putty had been fixed for about a week, it was still soft to the touch of Kennedy's fingers.

'Great, so they know how to replace windows, Kennedy. Big deal.'

'Actually, it is a big deal!'

ann rea came to look.

'Because there was no apparent forced entry we assumed that whoever was waiting for Peter O'Browne that Friday had his own keys.

'That's exactly what the killer wanted us to think. Another smoke screen, just like that whole Corpse Castle trip.'

Kennedy took a page from the *Evening Standard* stuffed in his pocket. He used one of the sports pages – the main story was about Formula One driver Eddie Irvine leaving Jordan to join Ferrari, another step forward in a future world champion's career. Kennedy placed the page over the window pane and traced the perimeter with his pen. Then he closed up the studio and led ann rea by the hand to the hardware store, RJ Welsh, directly across the street at Regents Park Road.

'They're closed, Kennedy,' ann rea proclaimed. 'And don't forget you promised me an Italian. If we don't hurry up, Vegia Zenia will be full up.'

'No, it's okay, the owner lives on the premises.' His mind was speeding ahead as he rang the door bell.

'Hello, sorry to disturb you at night,' Kennedy began as he flashed his ID card to a smiling elderly lady, someone's favourite grandmother. 'I'm Detective Inspector Christy Kennedy from Camden CID.'

The woman smiled one of her Bet Lynch 'What can I do for you, chuck?' smiles. Kennedy heard the strains of the theme music to *Coronation Street* flowing down the stairwell. He knew he needed to be quick. 'I wonder if you remember someone recently buying a pane of glass this size?' he asked holding up the marked page of the *Standard*.

The woman opened up the door wider and revealed herself as a shorter fuller version of Bet Lynch. She thought for a moment. 'Aye, come to think of it, love, I do actually. About a week ago, it was.'

'Do you remember anything, about the person who purchased it?' Kennedy asked. He would have crossed his fingers if they (his fingers) were not so busy in their own flexing activity.

'Yes, love, funnily enough, I do. I'll tell you why. He came late – just as we were closing. It would have been a Thursday, yes two Thursdays ago. I know it was a Thursday because it wasn't a *Coronation Street* night.

'Anyway, I told him to come back the following morning and I'd have it cut and waiting for him. But he refused to leave. He said it was urgent and he needed it immediately, something about his mother and how she would only be able to get a good night's sleep if she knew the window had been repaired. Well, love, I couldn't really refuse after that could I. So I closed up the shop front and took him through to the back and he waited while I cut it. Now let me see, it came to four pounds and thirty five pence and he gave me a fiver and by the time I'd managed to get his change he'd gone. Let himself out. I heard him walk over the mat. It triggers the bell, you see.'

'Do you remember what he looked like?'

'Aye now let me see, not much to him, wire frame glasses and copper-coloured hair.'

A few minutes later Kennedy and ann rea were walking hand in hand down Sharples (as in Ena) Hall Street, through Chalcot Square and down Chalcot Road towards Princess Street, the home of Vega Zenia.

'But it can't be Tom Best!' ann rea declared as they turned the corner of Princess Street. 'He has a perfect alibi.'

'Yes. Perhaps it's too perfect,' was all that Kennedy would say on the subject. 'I don't know about you, but I'm so hungry I could eat a tree.'

'Is that meant to be the vegetarian's equivalent of eat a horse, Kennedy?'

'No, it means I'm hungry enough to eat *tree* horses.'

They both laughed the laughter of a couple in love and in search of Pasta.

Chapter Fifty-Three

Give me a broom
And I'll sweep
My way to Heaven

– Terre Roche

It's funny how you can sit around looking at your noticeboard containing your case notes and clues, searching deep and hard, and nothing presents itself. And then...

Well, Kennedy supposed 'funny' might not be the right word. He lay back in his steaming bath, trying hard to think of the apt one: coincidental, frustrating, amusing, aggravating? He also thought of a saying DS Irvine liked to repeat at times such as this: 'People who wear glasses look closer, because they have to.'

His bath was as hot as Kennedy could bear it. The hotter it was the more relief it gave his aching limbs. It was extremely satisfying to just lie back and completely immerse himself in the healing water. Soon the only bit of him breaking the surface of the water were his nose and eyes.

Having his ears underwater made all the subterranean noises louder. He could hear the water dripping through the overflow. The more he submerged himself, the more water gushed down the metal tunnel. As he listened to these strange marine sounds, Kennedy's mind's eye replayed the scene at Mayfair Mews Studio as it appeared on his first visit.

He could smell the putty again and see the rafters. He visualised a pulley system like the one he'd bought, attached to the rafters. He could see the body of Peter O'Browne rotating with the twists in the rope, from the other end of the pulley.

How could Tom Best have been in two places at the same time? His alibi was foolproof. This was not as common as might be imagined: often an innocent suspect would be frustrated by the fact that his potential alibi let them down by thirty minutes either way.

In the natural course of living, you rarely feel you are going to need to account for your movements minute by minute. However, were you to know in advance that your innocence was going to be called into question, then you would make sure that your every move before and after the vital time could be backed up by as many witnesses as possible.

Unless you were psychic, the only reason you'd know in advance was that you were the murderer.

Obviously this was an over-simplification, Kennedy continued to himself over the soundtrack of water dripping through the bath overflow. The heat was so soothing to his aches and pains, he felt he could stay in the half-suspended state forever, lost in his thoughts. He was back at Mayfair Mews Studio and he was now concentrating on the floor. Suddenly the damp patch on the floor came into view like a scene in a film. The more he focused on it, the louder the sound of the water escaping through the overflow became.

'SHIT!' he shouted, sitting bolt upright in the bath. As he did so, he lost his grip and slid back under the water.

Spluttering and splashing, he pulled himself up, gasping for air. He shouted to ann rea in the bedroom two floors above, who didn't hear him: 'I've sussed it, I've sussed it. He is one hell of a clever bastard!'

He hauled himself out of the bath and ran dripping up to the bedroom, shouting to ann rea.

When she saw Kennedy, wet to the bone and dripping water everywhere, she burst out laughing. He caught sight of himself in the mirror and joined the laughter. Kennedy jumped on the bed and shook himself violently like a wet dog, spraying water all over ann rea.

'Okay, you've got my attention, Mr Isaac Newton; what have you discovered? With all this fuss it had better be nothing short of the secret of eternal youth.'

Kennedy looked at her naked body, now soaking wet, and thought perhaps he had discovered that too.

Chapter Fifty-Four

If I was the Lone Ranger
Hiding behind a mask
Wouldn't be any danger
To the questions I ask
          – Grant Lee Phillips

'But how did he manage to do it, Kennedy?' was all the Super could say when he was briefed early the next morning by Kennedy.

'All in good time, sir. I still have a wee bit of research to do yet, but I am convinced that Best's our man,' Kennedy replied confidently.

He loved this stage of the case; the part where he had just found his way through the woods. There were still bits and pieces to tie up of course, but when he sussed it, or cracked it as they said in police circles, then he could really relax and enjoy one hundred percent the art of police work.

'Are you going to bring him in and charge him?' the Super quizzed, happy in the knowledge that having left Kennedy to get on with the case he hadn't been let down.

He had eventually come to the conclusion the more he left Kennedy to get on with it, the more efficiently the cases were solved. It was just that sometimes the damn police politics (PP as Kennedy called them) tended to confuse the wood and the trees.

'No, I don't think so, sir. I still have a few leads left to follow up. I think it will take a considerable amount of time to crack our friend Best. Perhaps the full limit of time.' He was well aware that from the minute he arrested Tom Best, he would have only 24 hours before he needed to charge him.

If at that point, he wasn't in a position to bring charges he could apply to the Super for an extension of another twelve hours. After that there were only two options available to him. Either he could go to the court and apply for a second extension, this time for a further 48 hours, or else he would have to let Tom Best go. The Courts usually only granted the extension when the suspect was believed to be involved in terrorist activities. So, as they said down Camden Market way, after the initial 36 hours you had to be ready to shit or get off the pot.

'I don't think Tom Best has any fears of being found out, sir. I rattled him the other day but I think he feels he's committed the perfect crime. I don't think that he'll be going anywhere.' As he was not being offered any tea he rose from his chair to leave the Super's office.

'Good. Keep me posted.'

*

Kennedy returned to his office and offered tea to his first visitor, WPC Anne Coles.

'You interviewed the two couples who had dinner with Best on the night of the murder, what were their names...?'

Kennedy searched through his notes but before he could find the names the WPC volunteered, 'Yes, Brian and Sally Baxter and the gay couple, Ted and John.'

'Apart from confirming that they were at Tom Best's house, did they say anything else?' Kennedy pieced his first question together as he was speaking, aware that it might be a bit vague.

Anne Coles checked her notes this time. 'Let's see. They did. It was a regular thing. They'd all been friends for years and every fortnight, apart from Christmas and Summer holidays, they met up, using a sort of rota system.

'Actually Ted – of Ted and John – it's funny how some people who are parts of a couple are always identified as half of that couple...'

Kennedy wondered if he and ann rea were always thought of a part of a couple. If so, was it 'ann rea and Christy' or 'Christy and ann rea'? or was it 'Kennedy and ann rea' or 'ann rea and Kennedy'? Instead of posing the above question to the WPC he merely replied, 'Yes, isn't it.'

WPC Anne Coles continued. 'Well, anyway, Ted said that the last dinner party was supposed to be at their place. They live in Hampstead. But Best asked if it would be possible to do a swap. He claimed it was something to do with Mavis, Best's girlfriend, being very busy the following fortnight when it was meant to be their turn. Ted agreed as it made no difference to them – Ted and John, that is, sir.'

'Anything else?'

'No. Well...'

'Come on, anything. Don't worry about how insignificant it appears to be. I don't even know what I'm looking for, but there must be something else.'

'Well, both Ted and the Baxters commented on how much fun it was. They said Best had been on particularly good form, and they all got, "seriously rat faced", sir.' She quoted the 'seriously rat faced' from her notes.

'Good.' Kennedy nodded. 'Good. That helps.'

'So you think that it is Tom Best, sir?'

'Oh yes. I'm convinced of it. But he must be a bit of a magician.'

'But, sir, how could he have possibly been with the Baxters and Ted and John...'

'Not to mention Mavis,' Kennedy reminded her.

'Yes,' WPC Coles smiled. 'And Mavis. But how could he possibly have been with all five of them and at the same time carried out the murder? The forensic report ties in the time of death right in the middle of the dinner party.'

'More like the last supper.' Kennedy afforded himself a smile.

'So,' WPC Coles continued. 'Even if the forensic report is out by an hour or so either way, even two hours either way. Tom Best is still covered.'

'Yes he is. Isn't he a clever bastard? Perhaps he a bit too well covered if you ask me,' Kennedy replied and took a long swig of tea. 'When you finish your tea, let's go and find DS James Irvine and do a bit more shopping,' He nodded in the direction of the RAMS carrier bag beside his desk. 'We'll return to the scene of the crime and see if we can throw a little more light on this, this perfect crime.'

'I suppose the perfect crime deserves a lot of light, doesn't it, sir?'

Chapter Fifty-Five

I'm so lonesome
I could cry

— Hank Williams

Kennedy sometimes found that it was useless to just sit around and think. They were the times when the mind simply refuses to take information on board. No matter what the boffins think, the human brain is not like a computer. How many computers can become stimulated by being fed a problem other than the one currently being worked on?

Now, just as all this information was circulating in various holding patterns above Kennedy's head, and about to attempt a symphonic landing, Castle had an urgent errand he needed Kennedy to run. Forget the fact that Kennedy is a Detective Inspector; forget the fact that he feels he is just about to solve a murder case. Police work is police work, and at that exact moment Castle was more interested in prevention than he was in detection. Kennedy's solution would have to wait.

An ex-colleague of both the Super and Kennedy was in – and causing – trouble.

Detective Inspector Alan Hoyle had been 'retired' prematurely three years previously due to a drink problem. Sadly DI Hoyle turned to drink not due to the pressure of work, nor because a loved one left him. No, he turned to drink simply because he was, and, always would be, an alcoholic. Castle and Kennedy had tried hard to support Hoyle, sometimes going right to the edge, but never crossing the line. But for help to be effective it first has to be asked for.

DI Hoyle, according to a complaint Castle had received, had chosen that particular week to try to extort two bottles of whisky from the off-licence on Parkway using an out-of-date warrant card. Kennedy did not like such chores but, when the off-licence owner had deposited DI Hoyle on his posterior upon the Parkway the previous day, the ex-copper had threatened to return with a gun. The Super felt the former DI was just a step away from being gunned down while attempting armed robbery.

The Super wanted Kennedy to make the visit because Hoyle and Kennedy knew each other. Kennedy had never been one to be matey with his colleagues, although he always respected the keener detectives. He was the type of policeman who was proud to be part of the force, but who lived a separate life.

DI Hoyle lived in a tip not far, mentally and physically, from

Arlington Road. The drunk was buzzing drunk when Kennedy arrived. Obviously not long out of bed and fresh on the sauce. He greeted Kennedy like a long-lost brother but became very annoyed when Kennedy refused a drink.

'Look Hoyle, what's all this carry-on about robbing an off-licence?' Kennedy asked, irritated and unable to find anywhere clean enough, or safe enough, to sit.

'Oh you mean the tight-assed bitch? I just offered to do her a favour,' the drunk winked knowingly to Kennedy.

'Listen, that's not what I heard, Alan. Something about flashing a warrant card.'

At the mention of the Christian name the Alan in question became all matey and swung his arm around Kennedy using the other to try and open a can of lager. 'Here, son,' he offered. 'Have some of this.'

Hoyle had the strength of a drunk and Kennedy felt his face and the can moving towards each other at an alarming speed. Hoyle's drunken aim had the can en route to Kennedy's nose, not mouth. 'Ah for God's sake, Hoyle,' Kennedy complained as he swung his arm up hitting the can and sending it flying through the room, landing and spilling on and over the dishevelled bed in the corner of the room.

Hoyle went stumbling after the can and tried, in vain, to prevent the spilling. The bed stains already in place had new friends arriving. After his exertions, Hoyle lay crying and cussing in a heap on the bed. Kennedy picked up what looked and smelt like Hoyle's current, if not only jacket, searched through the pockets and found the offending warrant card. 'I'm taking this. Hoyle, you more than anyone, should know it's an offence to impersonate a Policeman!'

'Then how come you're getting away with it, DI, high and bloody mighty, Kennedy?' Hoyle's crying had turned to tears of laughter which streamed down his cheeks. He nearly pissed himself laughing at his own joke. When he'd regained his senses he continued. 'Fucking team. You all have to be part of a bloody team. I don't want to be part of a team. I want to be a lone, but I don't want to be alone.' Hoyle's drunken mind then went to work dissecting the wisdom of his words.

'Listen, Alan, the graveyards are packed with drunks, so you're not going to be short of company if you keep this up.'

'Oh yeah, but do you realise that the only thing that's guaranteed is…'

Kennedy filled in the expected 'you're going to die' in his mind but said nought as Hoyle slurred, 'You're going to be dead a lot longer than your are alive.' The drunk smiled once again, proud of his words of drunken wisdom.

'Look Alan, you've really got to get a grip,' Kennedy started pleading. He knew this was a total waste of time but he felt that he had to give Hoyle at least one fair shot. 'You've got to get help. 'But you've got to ask for it; you've got to feel you need it, before the help will do any good. There has to be more to life than this,' Kennedy carried on as his eyes circled the room.

'Oh what's the point, what's the bloody point. It all means shit. It's all a waste of time, the whole thing,' Hoyle spluttered. 'Look at you, out risking your life tracking down murderers and thugs and then some fucking do-gooder will either get them off on a technicality or some other fucking do-gooder will get the sentence reduced just because our fucking criminal has learnt to read books, or paint fucking pictures or... It's all a waste of time... You and your bloody team. I don't want to be part of your team, I don't want to be part of a bloody AA team, I want to be a-lone.' Hoyle had peaked and was fast running out of steam, his last words disappearing into an inaudible murmur. 'But I don't want to be lonely.'

Kennedy felt it was time to leave but, before he could do so, he had one bit of unfinished business to attend to. 'Where's the gun Hoyle?'

'What bloody gun?'

'The one you were threatening to return to the off-licence with.'

'Oh that. I was lying! I just wanted to scare the tight-assed bitch. Probably gave her her first wet knickers of the year! Haaagghhh!'

'Come on Hoyle, drunks can't keep secrets, you know that. She was making you mad and you were thinking, "If only she knew, if only she knew I could blow her away!" Come on man, where is it? Where is the gun?'

'You mean this?' Hoyle smirked, pulling a revolver from under the mattress. 'You're not so high and bloody mighty now, are you Mr Kennedy? Once again an Irish Bastard is looking down the barrel of an Englishman's gun!'

Kennedy thought of ann rea, his mother, his father, Peter O'Browne, his lottery tickets, Reg Holdsworth, Tom Best. The look in Hoyle's eyes. That look led Kennedy to believe that Hoyle was going to pull the trigger and he was going to die.

Then he started to calculate, 'Well if I just stand here like a lemon, he's going to get a good shot in and possibly kill me. But, if I charge at him, or distract him in some way he may hit me in the shoulder, or leg, or arm and I'll just be wounded. Wounded but alive. But then what if I'm confined to a wheelchair for the rest of my life. What if I couldn't make love with ann rea? If only I'd something in my hands I'd throw it at him.'

Hoyle was still sitting on the bed close to the beer stains and all Kennedy could think of doing was to say something, to say something stupid. 'God, Hoyle, you've fucking pissed yourself!' Kennedy yelled staring at Hoyle's crotch.

'What?' Hoyle's eyes glimpsed the damp patch.

The split second distraction was all that Kennedy needed to rush across and kick with all his might at Hoyle's gun hand, forcing the pistol barrel upwards. The shock caused Hoyle to pull the trigger involuntary and a round was fired off into the ceiling.

The noise and smell filled Kennedy's eyes, ears and nose as he overpowered former Detective Inspector Alan Hoyle. This was not a hard task as the drunk had gone completely limp in surrender and this time it sounded like he really was pissing himself.

Kennedy radioed for a back-up car, returned to the station and reported the incident to Superintendent Thomas Castle.

'Kennedy, we tried. At least now he'll be forced to take professional help.'

'He's pretty far gone, sir.' Kennedy replied. 'He just doesn't care anymore. He's going to need a lot of help, a hell of a lot.'

Chapter Fifty-Six

Could you find me
Would you kiss my eyes
Lay me down

— Van Morrison

There's nothing like staring down the barrel of a revolver (or any firearm for that matter) to give a person a clear head. Usually such sharpness of vision occurs only on early walks on Primrose Hill. The Sunday morning walks are the best. To be on top of the hill while the city sleeps, with no one to be seen or heard, save for a few souls on their way to work.

Sky blue, as blue as the deepest water. Kennedy's thoughts returned to water and to Tom Best and he thought he saw the penny dropping. The pulley, the water, the hanging, how it all now fitted together. He decided to take a walk on Primrose Hill before returning to North Bridge House.

Unfortunately, due to dogs, fog, and noisy kids, Kennedy couldn't recreate the sharp scene his mind's eye had provided for him. He felt as if he were in suspension, someone with a story to tell but either not yet ready to tell it, or else not sure who to tell it to; a long distance runner with the tape in sight, but who hadn't managed to cross the finishing line. So, Kennedy went on a detour. He walked to the bottom of the hill, crossed Primrose Hill Road and went into the old fashioned red phone box just outside The Queens pub at the foot of St George's Terrace. As he was entering the phone box a maroon saloon, a Jaguar XJ2, caught his attention. The image triggered something in his memory but he didn't know what was familiar about it. He checked the number plate: 248RPA. He thought he should recognise it, but he didn't.

Kennedy dialled ann rea's number.

'Hello, Features.'

'Hi, ann rea.'

'Kennedy. How are you? I tried to get you at the station but they said you were out and about. Where are you?'

'Outside the Queens.'

'Are you okay?'

'Yeah I'm fine,' Kennedy lied as he recalled he had nearly been need of brown trousers about half an hour earlier.

The BT line crackle filled the silence between them.

'Have you worked out how Best was at a dinner party and murdering Peter at the same time?'

'I think so. I'll tell you later. Listen I just wanted to say…' more crackle. Kennedy thought that perhaps BT should provide a button to summon the crackle and sell it off to customers in need of something to fill embarrassing silences.

'Kennedy?'

'Yeah, sorry. Look, I just wanted to tell you…'

'Christy?' ann rea pleaded softly. She rarely used his Christian name and on the special occasions she did Kennedy loved the way she barely whispered it.

'I needed to tell you how much I love you.'

The line melted into total silence as the crackling ebbed.

'God, don't do that. I thought for one moment there you were going to tell me it was all over between us.'

'I don't want this ever to be over, ann rea. I hope that doesn't sound naïve, or scare you. We shouldn't be talking about this on the phone, but I just needed to hear your voice. And then I had this tremendous desire…'

'Kennedy,' ann rea cut in. 'The *Camden News Journal* does not permit obscene phone calls.'

'I had this desire to tell you that I love you. We've both been treading water for a time now and I sensed in you a hesitation to commit. Then I thought perhaps you were getting the same vibe from me and I thought if I didn't tell you, you'd never know. And that would have been sad. Very sad.'

ann rea sensed something had happened. Kennedy was not telling her the full story. She also knew that he would not tell her what it was until he was ready. He had some funny ways. She knew how much it had taken him to tell her that he loved her, and she wasn't going to cheapen it with an I-love-you-too. Particularly when she couldn't stand the bass player. Kennedy however was a different matter altogether because she loved him more deeply than she ever had, or ever would, love anyone in her life.

'Kennedy, I'd like to see you tonight.'

'Oh?' Kennedy was surprised. It was supposed to be their night off from each other. 'Fine. I'll be late though.'

'That's okay, Kennedy.' He could hear the smile in her voice. 'I want to be with you tonight, it doesn't matter what time.'

'I'll see you later.'

'Kennedy?'

'Yes?'

'We're going to be okay, you and I. We're going to be okay.'

Chapter Fifty-Seven

I've much to say, I've more to tell
The words will soon be spilling from my tongue
— Mike Scott

Kennedy now felt clear enough in his mind to return to North Bridge House. He went straight to his office and brewed up, pausing only to instruct DS James Irvine to pick up Tom Best, reminding him to do everything by the book. It was a difficult enough case to prove as it was, without some clever-arsed lawyer applying the rules and getting his client freed on a technicality.

Twenty minutes later, DS Irvine stuck his head round the door. 'Tom Best is here, Guv. He's in the interview room.'

'How was he on the way down?'

'Pretty nonchalant, sir. He seemed more interested in discussing how bad the English football team are.'

Kennedy smiled. Best had been on safe ground with Irvine on that point. 'So what's new?'

They both laughed a nationalistic laugh. Personally, Kennedy couldn't care less about football. Though he did always remember the golden rule, 'Never criticise your hairdresser's football team.' Kennedy stood up, collected his jacket from the back of his chair and accompanied the DS to the interview room.

DS James Irvine sat down opposite Tom Best on one of the four hard chairs round the rectangular stripped pine table. WPC Anne Coles moved another to one end of the table, so that like a net umpire at Wimbledon, she could see them both. Again, Constable Essex stood guard by the door.

Kennedy did not sit down. Instead he wandered around the room, slowly, hands deep in pockets. He strolled behind Tom Best and nodded over his head to DS Irvine to switch on the tape recorder that lay on the table by the wall, and start the interview officially. DS James Irvine announced the names of those present and further stated for the record that Tom Best had refused his right to have a solicitor present. Then there was silence. Kennedy ambled around the room, ever so slowly, looking absently out of the window.

Two minutes of silence is a long time.

Tom Best just smiled, feeling that a number was being done on him. He fervently hoped that his smile was proclaiming, 'I know what you bastards are trying to do, and it's not working.'

'Tom Best,' Kennedy said eventually in his quiet, gentle voice. 'We are here to charge you with the murder of Peter O'Browne.' He parked himself just to the left of WPC Coles, leaning against the wall, hands still in pockets, his eyes burning into Best, who in turn stared at James Irvine, his face fixed in a smirk that said, What the fuck is he on about?

For another three minutes, the only audible sounds were the noise of the clock and, from the other side of the door, a Police Station busy about it's day.

Eventually Best broke the silence. 'A-n-d?'

'And what?' smiled Kennedy.

'Well aren't you meant to say, "On such and such a day you blah blah blah blah?" And then I say, "But on that date and at that time I couldn't possibly have murdered Peter O'Browne because I was having dinner with my girlfriend and four friends?" And then you let me go. It's as simple as that. I'm not wasting money on a solicitor. Do you realise how much they charge these days?'

'It only happens like that on TV,' Kennedy laughed. 'Out here in the real world we just gather the evidence, charge you, and give our evidence to the prosecutor. Then it's up to our man, your expensive lawyer, twelve men and women, and a geezer with a major hair problem to sort it out. You go off to the cells and we go off to try and solve some more crimes.'

'What do you mean, I go off to the cells? I wasn't there. I have an alibi,' Best asserted.

'And an "I didn't do it" would have been nice,' DS Irvine added, not sure of exactly where the DI was going with this one, other than trying to rattle Best's cage.

'But, if I wasn't there, and I have an alibi, how could I possibly have committed this crime? What about wrongful arrest? Does that only happen on TV as well?'

Best looked to WPC Anne Coles. Her face was immobile, she was looking at DS James Irvine. Best turned around 180 degrees in his seat and looked to the PC by the door. Essex was staring straight ahead, out of the window.

'Jesus, this is a new one,' remarked Best. 'I thought it would be rubber pipe, good guy, bad guy, sorry, bad *gal*.' He looked at WPC Coles again. 'But just a, "We think you did it, so off you go to the cells." You must admit, it's a bit novel.'

'Take him out and have the desk sergeant process him. If he still refuses a solicitor, get the desk sergeant to appoint one for him. Now we've got him, we don't want him getting off on a technicality.'

'Getting off what on a fucking technicality,' exploded Best. 'Can't you bastards get it into your fucking heads that I have an unbreakable alibi? Remember that word? Hello, is anyone sensible listening. I have an alibi!' Best leaned over towards the tape recorder and shouted at it, 'I, Tom Best, have an alibi for the night Peter O'Browne was murdered. I was having a dinner party with five individuals –

let's count them: one, two, three, four, five. That's Brian and Sally Baxter, Ted Lester, John O'Sullivan and my girlfriend, Mavis Moore. 'They all confirm that I was with them at the time of the murder. But Detective Inspector Kennedy will not listen. It's as plain as the fact that The Beatles were better than the Stones. But he's still charging me!'

Best's tirade ended on such a high-pitched note that the word banshee sprang to mind.

'Actually,' this time the quiet voice of reason was that of the WPC. 'The microphone for the tape recorder is suspended above your head.'

Best looked up above his head and then at the WPC, who added, 'It is put there, sir, so that it can pick up everything that happens in this room.'

The DS, again taking a cue from Kennedy, pushed back his chair, stood up and started to put on his tweed jacket.

'Just listen to me!' pleaded Best. 'You're making a mistake. I don't want to go to the cells. For heaven's sake, I didn't do anything. Will someone listen to me? I'll say it in English. I couldn't have murdered Peter O'Browne. I was somewhere else at the time. Why are you doing this?'

'Okay, DS Irvine, sit down again. Just for the record, let's recap for Mr Best how he, while dining with Brian and Sally Baxter and Ted and John O'Sullivan and Maggie, hanged Peter O'Browne until he died from strangulation.'

The WPC thought, 'This is going to be interesting.'

Chapter Fifty-Eight

'Well here's a boy if ever there was
Who's going to do big things'
That's what they all say and that's how the trouble begins
— Elvis Costello

'Picture a scene...' Kennedy resumed his walk round the room. He took off his black jacket and hung it over the back of the spare seat next to DS Irvine. He was wearing grey trousers, grey shirt, black woollen waistcoat, grey tie and black shoes. He looked good because he felt comfortable in his clothes. ann rea's attempts to nudge his dress sense in a more ostentatious direction were slowly succeeding. The fingers of his right hand were flexing busily.

'It's Friday evening and the offices are closing. You know, because of your connections at Camden Town Records, that Peter O'Browne is about to leave his own office with his assistant, Mary Jones. You ring him and tell him you've got to see him urgently.

'Perhaps, to stress just how important it is that he comes, you drop into the conversation a few of the rumours you've been hearing that he is hyping records. Perhaps he thinks it must be important because it's an unusual request from you. In any event, he agrees to your suggestion to meet outside Mayfair Mews Studio, the studio Peter has just bought. It's private and it's not too far away.

'He doesn't see you when he arrives at the studio – thanks to the window you are already inside, so he lets himself in with his own keys to wait for you inside. But you are already there. You overpower him with chloroform. When he's unconscious, you secure him in a seated position, binding his legs individually to the legs of a chair and his hands down the sides.'

Best unclasped his hands and moved one up to scratch his chin. He took out his roll-up gear and prepared himself a cigarette. He tried to speak but Kennedy held up his hand to silence him.

'You'll have your turn. Please bear with me, as this is all rather complicated. Smoking is not permitted in here. Now where was I? Yes. You keep him captive for a few days, either to fit in with the timing of your plan or, perhaps, because you want to give yourself a bit of leeway in case he didn't turn up on the Friday night.

'You even feed him on fish and chips, or perhaps just chips and unbind him to the extent he is able to use the lavatory with his hands tied in front of him, so at least you weren't totally inhumane. In the meantime you take his credit cards and have a high old time laying a false trail to Dorset. I suppose you hoped that no one would check the description of the man using the card, or maybe you did disguise yourself as Peter O'Browne? We'll have to check on that.

'Anyway, let's move on and concentrate on the night of the murder, Wednesday. The night of your great alibi.'

DS Irvine and WPC Coles both leaned forward a fraction in their chairs fascinated by what was coming next. Neither could tell how much of this Kennedy actually knew and how much he was guessing, but both were successful at suppressing their curiosity in front of the suspect.

'On Wednesday night, you rush home from the office and stop off at the Mayfair Mews Studio. In the intervening five days you have arranged everything you need to carry out the murder. You place Mr O'Browne, tied to his chair, on one of the platforms in the studio – I believe they are called drum-risers because they are sometimes used to elevate the drummer and his ego up in the vision of the audience, rather than leave him stuck out of sight behind the band.

'You place the rear legs of the chair at the very edge of the drum-riser. You have probably offered Mr O'Browne, now elevated some thirty inches in the air, some sort of explanation – that you are holding him for a ransom, perhaps? Anyway, you can fill in some of the grey areas for me at the end of the story. I don't want to lose the thread.

'You put a noose round his neck and you secure the rope onto an eight pulley compact block and tackle system which you attach to the iron rafters supporting the roof of the studio. The pulley is not directly overhead but about three feet away from the edge of the riser so that the angle of the rope from Peter's neck to the roof is about thirty degrees.

'Still with me? Good. Thus the body, or more specifically the neck, forms the load end of the pulley system. The effort-end of the rope, which raises the load, in this case Peter O'Browne, is attached to an empty bucket.

'Now you nip into the studio annexe and up into the bathroom on the first floor. You have already made some adjustments to this bathroom to save time on Wednesday night. You had disconnected the overflow pipe on the bath, a point borne out by recent scratches around the clamp. To the overflow you attach your own water hose, which you have run through the annexe into the studio at rafter height and over to the bucket attached to the effort-end of the rope. Next you fix the hose to the inside of the bucket.

'Now all you have to do is turn on the water tap on the bath at a slow drip. This was a very difficult part of the operation to carry out as I discovered during my own experiments. If you set the drip too slow, the water will eventually stop running altogether. If the flow is too fast everything will happen too quickly to match your alibi.

'I estimated that, with a pretty slow drip, the bath would have taken about three and a half hours to fill to overflow. Then the water would run slowly down the hose and drip into the waiting bucket.

'The magic of the pulley system is that a little effort can raise a large weight. In this instance a full bucket of water was more than adequate to lift the body weight of Peter O'Browne.

'It would probably have taken another thirty minutes for the bucket to fill and activate the pulley system. At this time, while you were entertaining friends at your famous-alibi dinner party, the rope would have been tightening around Mr O'Browne's neck. Eventually the rope would have pulled Peter and chair to the limit of balance at the edge of the drum riser. The next step is obvious.

'Peter and chair would have overbalanced both swinging backwards away from the platform.

'Within about ten minutes, Peter O'Browne would have been strangled by his own weight. The following morning you returned early to Mayfair Mews Studio on your way to the office to cut Peter down and tidy up your handiwork.

'You had, in your mind, committed the perfect murder!'

No one spoke. Kennedy scrutinised Best for a reaction while WPC Coles, DS Irvine and Constable Essex all pictured the horrific scene.

'Sounds like a clever bit of fiction to me, Inspector. Now if only I had thought of that,' Best laughed sarcastically. 'If only I were that clever. But you'd be laughed out of court if you tried to convict me using that story. Where's your proof? And even if your ridiculous theory is true, any one of your list of suspects – and knowing O'Browne I imagine it's a long list of suspects – could have a cast iron alibi and still have murdered the bastard.'

Chapter Fifty-Nine

If you haven't got a penny
A ha'penny will do
If you haven't got a ha'penny
Then God bless you

— Anon

'Sorry, there's more. Did you think that was all?' Kennedy smiled.

WPC Coles thought, More? This is nearer movie land, Hollyweird, than Camden Town. She ought to have known better than to expect anything simple from DI Christy Kennedy. James Irvine had told her that she would not believe some of the theories their DI came up with, especially during his in-car monologues. He had also felt it worth pointing out that sometimes Kennedy's theories were wrong. Yes, sometimes they were very wrong. But they were certainly never boring.

'Now, Mr Best,' Kennedy continued. 'Let's go through the evidence which ties you into this intriguing murder.

'First, you wanted to make it appear that the murderer was someone who had access to the studio, so you broke in by smashing one of the panes of glass in the annex window. To cover this up you replaced the glass with a new pane purchased from RJ Welsh. The owner, Mrs Welsh, will pick you from a line up. You did clean all your finger prints from the glass, but you left a few in the putty!'

'Secondly, you purchased a compact block and tackle pulley system from RAMS in E14. You thought you had destroyed the receipt, but you left just enough of it behind in the rubbish for us to identify the source. I'm sure the shop assistant will remember your face. He definitely remembered the sale.'

'Thirdly, you changed the order of your fortnightly dinner party to accommodate your alibi. I believe last week was originally meant to be held at Ted and John's. Obviously time would not have permitted that.'

DS James Irvine thought to himself in his best Sean Connery accent, You're pushing it a bit on point three old chap. I'm not sure that would stand up in a court of law. However points one and two will do the business for you.

Kennedy continued, 'I have to hand it to you, it's a clever crime, as clever a one as I have seen. Even to the point of laying out the body like a corpse with tu'penny bits on the eyes.'

'Old pennies' corrected Tom Best, apparently involuntarily. Then when he understood the enormity of what he had just said he seemed to decide that there was nothing for it but to continue, eight eyes keenly focused on him. 'Actually, it wasn't two penny bits on the eyes, it was one old penny on each. They did that in the old days, to stop the eyes from staring at you, you know.

Kennedy inwardly breathed a major sigh of relief. Until that precise moment, he hadn't been convinced that he had enough hard evidence to convict Tom Best. But he had counted on the murderer being very proud of his work. Once found out and caught, Kennedy hoped that the killer would be only too happy to boast of his perfect crime.

And boast Best did. He sang like the proverbial bird. All his utterances were made under caution and recorded on tape.

'DS Irvine, take him down and have Sergeant Flynn do the business,' said Kennedy, once the last sentence of the confession had been laid down on to the tape.

'You know, he really deserved to die,' spluttered Best as Irvine tapped him on the shoulder. 'He was living a lie. He was just another bread-head posing as someone who loved music.'

'If that is a crime punishable by death, old son, then, from what little I know of the music business there will be more than a few people running for cover,' Kennedy retorted as Best was led from the room, taking the first incarcerated steps of the rest of his life.

Kennedy returned to his office in a pensive mood. As he removed the O'Browne case cards and notes for his noticeboard he ran over the case again.

Best hadn't ever seemed like a killer. Perhaps one of the reasons he had planned such an elaborate murder was because he didn't have the guts to do it physically, with his bare hands. Best had sought his revenge on someone he felt had cheated him. The issue was not whether or not Peter O'Browne had cheated Best out of a piece of Camden Town Records. What was important was that Best believed that O'Browne had. That was Best's reality. He had waited, perhaps letting the hate fester away, planned and eventually executed the person responsible for his situation. In Best's reality there was no choice in the matter.

Chapter Sixty

In the fragments of the songs
Carried down the wind from some radio
– Jackson Browne

The problem with police work, Kennedy felt, was that even when you were successful, it was impossible to take any real satisfaction from it. So he had detected Tom Best as the murderer of Peter O'Browne, but what pleasure could Kennedy take out of the loss of a life? Kennedy's predominant feeling, as usual after such a case, was one of emptiness. But things were different now he had ann rea in his life. He found it much easier to leave a case behind him, to allow himself the simple luxury of being happy in her company.

Thanks to Best's co-operation, Kennedy was going to be home much earlier than expected. So, although it was wet and windy, he decided to walk home over Primrose Hill. The twenty-two windows on the front of North Bridge House were all lit as he departed. It was a splendid sight, banishing the darkness on Parkway and warming the wintry night.

ann rea was waiting for Kennedy at his house. She was playing Jackson Browne's, 'I'm Alive', one of Kennedy's current favourite CDs. The music filled his comfortable, well-lit house from top to bottom. ann rea was baking bread. The smell of rising yeast, the sound of wondrous soulful music, the natural warmth, all made him feel at home as he took off his overcoat. He realised that in the many years he had lived in London, this was his first time he had really thought of his house as home. Up until that point he had probably considered home to be his parent's house in Portrush, Northern Ireland. But at that moment, with the sound of music playing, the smell of bread, and the sight of ann rea smiling, this was most definitely their home.

He thought about trying to put his feelings into words and found himself tuning into Jackson Browne, whose joyous voice was filling every room. Jackson's words were about a love lost rather than a love found, but Kennedy supposed you first had to find it before you could lose it.

He and ann rea were both so filled with emotion, reacting to some strong chord pulling their souls together, that neither spoke, scared of breaking a spell.

They caressed each other, gently at first, but then more passionately as a different kind of hunger took over.

'If you need holding
Call my name and I'll be there.'

The voice from the speakers gently cried out as all thoughts disappeared from Kennedy's mind. His head was filled with magic sounds and his heart with love; love for ann rea and love for himself. He felt good about himself.

'Like a river flow
Rolling 'til it ends in the sea
Our pleasure grows
Rolling 'til it ends in you and me'

And then he was lost, there was no music, no smells, no heat, no cold, no light.

Kennedy couldn't pinpoint the exact moment when they all dissolved. He wasn't sure if they had all faded together, or gradually, one by one, but they had all definitely disappeared. Now he was just being and being was enough.

'I like the part of that song, you know the beginning of the last one.'

'What?' Kennedy murmured hoarsely, still floating.

'You know,' coaxed ann rea. 'The bit that goes...' and she started to sing, to sing in a gentle whisper,

'All good things got to come to an end
The thrills have to fade'

Then she raised her voice and smiled slightly:

'Before they come 'round again.'

Kennedy returned her smile and more...

And finally...

Although the characters are all figments of my imagination, I have taken the liberty of (fondly) including several actual locations in the Camden Town/Primrose Hill area, when describing DI Christy Kennedy's patch. For instance, North Bridge House, the home of Camden Town CID in *I Love The Sound of Breaking Glass* and the oldest building in the area, is actually a school, and I located the fictitious Camden Town Records in the unique blue Design Building at the top of Parkway.

Mayfair Mews Studio is a disused recording studio, and places such as The Regent (Fish and Chip Shop), RJ Welsh (Hardware), Regent Bookshop, Fitzroy's, Vegia Zenia, the Edinboro, the Engineer and the Queens are all actual, and well-loved locations. And yes, RAMS is a genuine shop in E14.

Two people were tireless with their energy and hard work in helping get clearance on the use of song lyrics: Christina Czarnik and Kenny MacPherson, thank you both.

And many thanks too to Gerry Rafferty/Heathside Music; Warlock Music Ltd & Rykomusic for Nick Drake; Christy Moore/Newbury Music; Nick Lowe/Plangent Visions Music Ltd & Chrysalis Music & Rock Music Co Ltd; Elvis Costello/Plangent Visions Music Ltd; Ray Davies/Davray Music Ltd & Carlin Music Ltd & Kassner Music; John Prine/Bug Music Ltd; Jackson Browne/Wixen Music Publishing Inc; Mark Knopfler/Rondor Music; Paul Brady/Rondor Music; The Roches/DeShufflin Inc; Terre Roche/DeShufflin Inc;, Mary Margaret O'Hara/BMG Music; Paul Simon/Paul Simon Music; Christie Hennessy/ Redemption Songs; Tom Waits/WCM; Grant Lee Philips/Chrysalis Music; Laurie Anderson/Difficult Music; Clifford T Ward/Chrysalis Music; Gilbert O'Sullivan/Grand Upright Music Ltd; Andersson & Ulveaus/Polar Music; Bob Dylan/Special Rider Music & Sony Music; Mike Scott/Dizzy Heights Music & Chrysalis Music & Blue Mountain Music & Polygram Music; Acuff Rose for Hank Williams; Van Morrison/WCM; Peter Gabriel/Hit and Run Music. and Paul Buchanan/ WCM.

And finally, all the water experiments were carried out at Maccroft Workshops. Thanks to Ian Ferguson and sorry for the broken rafter!

Cheers,
Paul Charles.
Camden Town, April 1997.